Rose O'Paradise

Grace Miller White

Rose O'Paradise

The present edition is a reproduction of previous publication of this classic work. Minor typographical errors may have been corrected without note, however, for an authentic reading experience the spelling, punctuation, and capitalization have been retained from the original text.

ISBN: 978-1-64799-250-7

CHAPTER I

FATHER AND DAUGHTER

On a hill, reared back from a northern lake, stood a weather-beaten farmhouse, creaking in a heavy winter blizzard. It was an old-fashioned, many-pillared structure. The earmarks of hard winters and the fierce suns of summer were upon it. From the main road it was scarcely discernible, settled, as it was, behind a row of pine trees, which in the night wind beat and tossed mournfully.

In the front room, which faced the porch, sat a man,—a tall, thin man, with straight, long jaws, and heavy overhanging brows. With moody eyes he was staring into the grate fire, a fearful expression upon his face.

He straightened his shoulders, got up, and paced the floor back and forth, stopping now and then to listen expectantly. Then again he seated himself to wait. Several times, passionately insistent, he shook his head, and it was as if the refusal were being made to an invisible presence. Suddenly he lifted his face as the sound of a weird, wild wail was borne to him, mingling with the elf-like moaning of the wind. He leaned forward slightly, listening intently. From somewhere above him pleading notes from a violin were making the night even more mournful. A change came over the thin face.

"My God!" he exclaimed aloud. "Who's playing like that?"

He crossed the room and jerked the bell-rope roughly. In a few moments the head of a middle-aged colored woman appeared at the door.

"Did you tell my daughter I wanted to see her?" questioned the man.

"No, sah, I didn't. When you got here she wasn't in. Then she slid to the garret afore I saw 'er. Now she's got to finish her fiddlin' afore I tell 'er you're here. I never bother Miss Jinnie when she's fiddlin', sah." The old woman bowed obsequiously, as if pleading pardon.

The man made a threatening gesture.

"Go immediately and send her to me," said he.

For perhaps twenty minutes he sat there, his ears straining to catch, through the whistling wind, the sounds of that wild, unearthly tune,—a tune different from any he had ever heard. Then at length it stopped, and he sank back into his chair.

He turned expectantly toward the door. Footsteps, bounding with life, with strength, were bearing down upon him. Suddenly a girl's face,—a rosy, lovely face,—with rapturous eyes, was turned up to his. At the sight of her stern father, the girl stopped, bringing her feet together at the heels, and bowed. Then they two,—Thomas Singleton the second and Virginia, his daughter,—looked at each other squarely.

"Ah, come in!" said the man. "I want to talk with you. I believe you're called Virginia."

1

·"Yes, sir; Jinnie, for short, sir," answered the girl, with a slight inclination of her head.

Awkwardly, and with almost an embarrassed manner, she walked in front of the grate to the chair pointed out to her. The man glanced sharply at the strongly-knit young figure, vibrant with that vital thing called "life." He sighed and dropped back limply. There followed a lengthy silence, until at last Thomas Singleton shifted his feet and spoke slowly, with a grim setting of his teeth.

"I have much to say to you. Sit back farther in your chair and don't stare at me so."

His tones were fretful, like those of a man sick of living, yet trying to live. He dropped his chin into the palm of his hand and lapsed into a meditative gloom.

Virginia leaned back, but only in this did she obey, for her eyes were still centered on the man in silent attention. She had little awe of him within her buoyant young soul, but much curiosity lay under the level, penetrating glance she bent upon her father. Here was a man who, according to all the human laws of which Virginia had ever heard, belonged to her, and to her alone. There were no other children and no mother. Yet so little did she know of him that she wouldn't have recognized him had she met him in the road. Singleton's uneasy glance, seeking the yellow, licking flames in the grate, crossed hers.

"I told you not to stare at me so, child!" he repeated.

This time the violet eyes wavered just for an instant, then fastened their gaze once more upon the speaker.

"I don't remember how you look," she stammered, "and I'd like to know. I can't tell if I don't look, can I?"

Her grave words, and possibly the steady, piercing gaze, brought a twitch to the father's lips. Surely his child had spoken the truth. He himself had almost forgotten he had a girl; that she was the only living creature who had a call upon the slender thread of his life. Had he lived differently, the girl in front of him would have been watching him for some other reason than curiosity.

"That's why I'm looking at you, sir," she explained. "If anyone on the hills'd say, 'How's your father looking, Jinnie?' if I hadn't looked at you sharp, sir, how'd I know?"

She sighed as her eyes roved the length of the man once more. The ashes in the grate were no grayer than his face.

"You're awful thin and white," she observed.

"I'm sick," replied Singleton in excuse.

"Oh, I'm sorry!" answered Virginia.

"You're quite grown up now," remarked the man presently, with a meditative air.

"Oh, yes, sir!" she agreed. "I'm a woman now. I'm fifteen years old."

"I see! Well, well, you are quite grown up! I heard you playing just now. Where did you ever learn such music?"

2

Jinnie placed her hand on her heart. "I got it out of here, sir," she replied simply.

Involuntarily Singleton straightened his rounded shoulders, and a smile touched the corners of his mouth. Even his own desperate condition for the moment was erased from his mind in the pride he felt in his daughter. Then over him swept a great regret. He had missed more than he had gained in his travels abroad, in not living with and for the little creature before him.

Her eyes were filled with contemplation; then the lovely face, in its exquisite purity, saddened for a moment.

"Matty isn't going to take me across her knee never any more," she vouchsafed, a smile breaking like a ray of sunshine.

The blouse slipped away from her slender throat, and she made a picture, vivid and beautiful. The fatherhood within Thomas Singleton bounded in appreciation as he contemplated his daughter for a short space, measuring accurately the worth within her. He caught the wonderful appeal in the violet eyes, and wished to live. God, how he wanted to live! He would! He would! It meant gathering his supremest strength, to be put forth in efforts of mere existing. Something out of an unknown somewhere, brought to him through the stormy, wonderful music he had heard, made the longing to live so vehement that it hurt. Then the horror of Virginia's words drifted through his tortured brain.

"What?" he ejaculated.

"Now I'm fifteen," explained the girl, "I get a woman's beating with a strap, you see. A while ago I got one that near killed me, but I never cried a tear. Matty was almost scared to death; she thought I was dead. Matty can lick hard, Matty can."

Virginia sighed in recollection.

"You don't mean to say the nigger whipped you?"

The girl shook her curly head.

"Whipped me! No! Matty don't whip; she just licks with all her muscle.... Matty's muscle's as strong as a tree limb."

Mr. Singleton bowed his head. It had never occurred to him in all those absent years that the child was being abused. How simply she had told her tale of suffering!

"But I'm fifteen now," she repeated gladly, "so I stand up, spread my feet like this"—she rose and suited the action to the words—"and Matty lays her on damn hard, too."

He covered his mouth with one thin hand, choked down a cough, and endeavored to change the subject.

"And school? Have you been to school?"

"Oh, yes!" assured the girl, sitting down again. "I went to school back in the hills. There were only five boys and me. There wasn't any girls. I wish there had been."

"You like girls, I imagine, then," said her father.

"Oh, yes, sir! Yes, indeed, sir! I often walk five miles to play a while

3

with one. None of the mothers around Mottville Corners'll let their girls be with me. You see, this house has a bad name."

A deep crimson dyed the man's ashen skin. He made as if to speak, but Jinnie went on.

"Over in the Willow Creek settlement the kids are awful bad, but I get along with 'em fine, because I love 'em right out of being hellish."

She was gazing straight into her father's face in all sincerity, with no trace of embarrassment.

"You know Mrs. Barker, the housekeeper you left me with?" she demanded a little later. "Well, she died when I was ten. Matty stayed, thinking every day you'd come home. I suppose maybe I did grow up sort of cussed, and I suppose everybody thinks I'm bad because I've only a nigger to live with, and no mother, not—not even you."

Singleton partly smothered an oath which lengthened itself into a groan, looked long at the slim young figure, then at the piquant face.

"Just lately I've been wanting some one of my own to love," she pursued. "I only had Milly and her cats. Then the letter come saying you'd be here—and I'm very glad."

The smile lighting her face and playing with the dimples in her cheeks made Thomas Singleton feel as if Heaven's breath had touched him.

"Do you care at all for me?" he asked gloomily.

There had come over him a desire that this winsome girl,—winsome in spite of her crudity,—would say she did. Wonder, love, sympathy, were alive in her eyes. Jinnie nodded her head.

"Oh, yes, sir!" she murmured. "Of course I love you! I couldn't tell you how much.... I love—why, I even love Mose. Mose's Matty's man. He stole and ate up all our chickens—but I love him just the same. I felt sorry about his killing the hens, because I loved them too."

"I see," sighed the father.

"Now there's Molly—I call her Molly the Merry——"

"Who's Molly the Merry?" interrupted Singleton.

"Old Merriweather's daughter. She's prettier than the summer roses, and they're pretty, believe me. Her smiles're warmer'n the sun."

"Ah, yes! I remember the Merriweathers. Is the old man still alive?"

"Well, yes, but he's as good as dead, though. Ain't walked in three years. And Matty's man, Mose, told Matty, and Matty told me, he's meaner'n forty damn devils."

"So you swear, too?" asked the father, breathing deeply.

Virginia opened wide and wider two sparkling blue eyes.

"Swear, sir?" she protested. "I didn't swear."

"Pardon me," replied Singleton, laconically. "I thought I heard you say 'damn' several times."

Virginia's smile showed two rows of white teeth.

"Oh, so you did!" she laughed, rising. "But 'damn' isn't swearing. You ought to hear me really swear sometimes. Shall I show you how I—I can swear?"

Singleton shook his head.

4

"I'd rather you wouldn't!... Sit down again, please."

The man at intervals turned a pair of burning bright eyes upon her. They weren't unlike her own eyes, only their expression puzzled Virginia.

She could not understand the rapid changes in her father. He wasn't the man she had mentally known all these years. But then, all she had had by which to visualize him was an old torn picture, turned face to the wall in the garret. He didn't look at all like the painting—he was thinner, older, and instead of the tender expression on the handsome, boyish face, time had placed one of bitterness, anxiety, and dread. He sat, crouched forward, stirring the grate fire, seemingly lost in thought. Virginia remained quiet until he was ready to speak.

"I'm going to die soon,—very soon."

It was only natural that Virginia should show how his statement shocked her. She grew deathly white, and an expression of misery knit the lovely young face.

"How soon?" she shivered, drawing back.

"Perhaps to-night—perhaps not for weeks, but I must tell you something before then."

"All right," agreed Virginia, "all right.... I'm here."

"I haven't been a good father to you," the man began after a pause, "and I'm not sure I could do better if I should stay on here with you. So I might as well go now as any time! Your mother would've done differently if she'd lived. You look some like her."

"I'm sorry I don't remember her," remarked Virginia apologetically.

"She went away when you were too little even to know her. Then I left you, too, though I don't suppose anyone but her could have made you happy."

"Oh, I've been happy!" Jinnie asserted. "Old Aunt Matty and the cats're all I need around, and I always have my fiddle. I found it in the garret."

It was easy to believe that she was telling the truth, for to all appearances she looked happy and healthy. However, Mr. Singleton's eyes darkened and saddened under the words. Nothing, perhaps, had ever touched him so deeply.

"It's no life for a girl of fifteen years to live with cats and niggers," he muttered.

One less firmly faithful to conscience would have acquiesced in this truthful statement; not so Virginia.

"Matty's a good nigger!" she insisted, passionately. "She'd do anything she could for me!"

Seemingly the man was not impressed by this, for his strong jaws were set and unyielding upon the unlighted cigar clenched between his teeth.

"I might as well tell you to-night as to-morrow," he concluded, dropping the cigar on the table. "Your mother left you her money and property when she died."

"I know it, sir, and it's a lot, too! Matty told me about it one

5

night along with 'er ghost stories, sir.... Ever heard Matty's ghost stories, sir?"

"No, but I didn't bring you here to talk about Matty. And tell me, what makes you say 'sir' to me all the time?"

His impatient tone, his sharp, rasping voice, didn't change Virginia's respectful attitude. She only bent her head a trifle and replied:

"Anybody must always say 'sir' to another body when she's kind of half afraid of him, sir."

She was composed for a moment, then went on:

"It isn't every day your father comes home, sir, and I've waited a long, long time. I'd be a hell of a kid if I couldn't muster up a 'sir' for you."

Singleton glanced sidewise at his young daughter, bending his brows together in a frown.

"You're a queer sort of a girl, but I suppose it's to be expected when you've only lived with niggers.... Now will you remember something if I tell it to you?"

"Yes, sir," breathed Virginia, drawing back a little from his strong emotion.

"Well, this! Don't ever say 'sir' to any human being living! Don't ever! Do you understand me? What I mean is, when you say 'sir,' it's as if you were—as if you were a servant or afraid—you make yourself menial. Can you remember, child?"

"Yes, sir,—yes, I'll remember.... I think I'll remember."

"If you're going to accomplish anything in the world, don't be afraid of any one."

A dozen explanations, like so many birds, fluttered through Virginia's mind. Before her rose her world of yesterday, and a sudden apology leapt to her lips. She turned on her father a wondering, sober glance.

"I've never said 'sir' or 'ma'am' before in all my life—never!" she remarked.

"So you're afraid of me?"

"A little," she sighed.

"Ah, don't be, child! I'm your father. Will you keep that in mind?"

"I'll try to; I will, sure."

Mr. Singleton shifted uneasily, as if in pain.

"This money is coming to you when you're eighteen years old," explained Mr. Singleton. "My dying will throw you into an ocean of difficulties. I guess the only service I've ever done you has been to keep your Uncle Jordan from you."

"Matty told me about him, too," she offered. "He's a damn bad duffer, isn't he, mister?"

"Yes, and I'm going to ask you not to call me 'mister,' either. Look here!... I'm your father! Can't anything get that into your head?"

"I keep forgetting it," answered the girl sadly. "And you're so big and thin and different from any man I know. You look as weak as a—as a cat."

She stretched forth her two strong legs, but sank back.

6

"Yes, your Uncle Jordan is bad," proceeded Singleton, presently, "bad enough to want to get us both out of the way, and he wouldn't find much of an obstacle in you."

A clammy chill clutched at Virginia's heart like tightening fingers. The import of his words burned deep within her. She got to her feet—but reseated herself at once at a wave of her father's hand. The thought of death always had a sobering effect upon her—it filled her with longing, yet dread. The beautiful young mother, whose picture hung in the best room, and whose eyes followed her in every direction, was dead. Matty had told her many times just how her mother had gone, and how often the gentle spirit had returned to hover over the beloved young daughter. Now the memory of it was enhanced by the roar of the wind and the dismal moaning of the tall pines. Virginia firmly believed that her mother, among other unearthly visitants, walked in the night when the blizzard kept up its incessant beating. She also believed that the sound through the pines—that roaring, ever-changing, unhuman sound—was not of the wind's making. It was voices,—spirit voices,—voices of the dead, of those who had gone down into the small cemetery beyond the road.

Only the day before Matty had told her how, one night, a tall, wandering white thing had walked in silence across the fields to Jonathan Woggles' house. In the story, Jonathan's grandpa was about to pass away. The glittering spirit stalked around and around the house, waiting for the old man's soul. She was about to relate the tale when her father repeated:

"Your uncle is bad enough to want us out of the way."

The shuddering chill again possessed her. She was torn between horror and eagerness—horror of what might be and eagerness to escape it.

"But he can't get us out, can he?" she questioned.

"Yes, I'm afraid he can and will! Your Uncle Jordan is your mother's stepbrother, no direct relation to you, but the only one left to look after you in the world but me. If you've any desire to live, you must leave here after I've gone, and that's all there is to it!"

Virginia then understood, for the first time, something of the danger menacing her. Her heart beat and pounded like an engine ploughing up hill. From sheer human desire of self-preservation, she partly rose from the chair, with the idea of immediate departure.

"I could go with Matty, couldn't I?" she suggested.

Mr. Singleton made a negative gesture with his head, flinging himself down again.

"Matty? Matty, the nigger? No, of course not. Matty is nothing to anyone who hasn't money, and you'll have none to pay her, or anyone else, after I'm gone. You must eat and live for three long years. Do you understand that?... Sit back in your chair and don't fidget," he concluded.

The girl obeyed, and a silence fell between them. The thought of the wonderful white presence of which Matty had told her faded from her mind. Her heart lay stone-like below her tightening throat, for her former world and all the dear familiar things it held were to be dashed from her, as a rose jar is broken on a marble floor, by a single decision of the thin,

7

tall father whom yesterday she had not known. She understood that if her uncle succeeded in his wicked plans, she, too, would join that small number of people, dead and buried, under the pines. Her father's words brought the cemetery, with its broken cross and headstones, its low toolhouse, and the restless night spirits, closer than Matty, with her vivid, ghastly tales, had ever done. In the past, Matty had stood between her and her fears; in the future, there would be only a stranger, her uncle, the man her father had just warned her against. At length Mr. Singleton coughed painfully, and spoke with evident effort.

"The doctor told me not long ago I might die at any moment. That's what made me escape—I mean, what drove me home."

He rose and walked nervously up and down the room.

"The doctor made me think of you. I can't live long."

"It's awful bad," answered the girl, sighing. "I wouldn't know where to go if there wasn't any Matty—or—you."

Her voice lowered on the last word, and she continued: "I wish I had my mother. Matty says mothers kiss their girls and make over 'em like Milly Ann does with her kittens—do they? Some of 'em?"

The father glanced curiously into the small, earnest, uplifted face.

"I couldn't help being your girl," pursued Virginia. "I'd have had another father if I could, one who'd 've loved me. Matty says even fathers like their kids sometimes—a little." She paused a minute, a wan, sweet smile passing over her lips. "But I've got Milly Ann and her kittens, and they're soft and warm and wriggley."

What a strange child was this daughter of his! She spoke of cats as if they were babies; of loving as if it were universal. Each moment, in her presence, he realized more and more what he had missed in thus neglecting her. But he had hurried to Mottville from foreign lands to perform one duty, at least,—to save her, if possible. So he returned to his vital subject.

"Your Uncle Jordan's coming, perhaps this week. He's found out I'm here! That's why you must go away."

"Shall I—just go?" queried Virginia. "I don't know of any special place—do you?" and she shivered again as the wind, in a fierce gust, blew out from the slumbering fire a wreath of smoke that encircled the room and hung grey-blue about the ceiling.

"I only know one man," reflected Mr. Singleton, presently, "and you'll have to find him yourself—after I've gone, of course; but if Jordan Morse should come, you'd have to go quickly."

"I'd go faster'n anything," decided the girl, throwing up her head.

"Your mother's father used to have a family in his tenement house on this place, and they were all very fond of her when she was a girl. One of the sons moved to Bellaire. He's the only one left, and would help you, I know."

"Mebbe if you'd talk to my uncle——" Virginia cut in.

An emphatic negative gesture frightened her.

"You don't know him," said Singleton, biting his lips. "He's nearer

8

being a devil than any other human being." It was a feeling of bitterness, of the deadly wrong done him, that forced him to sarcasm. "The great—the good Jordan Morse—bah!" he sneered. "If he's 'good,' so are fiends from perdition."

He sent the last words out between his teeth as if he loathed the idea expressed in them. If they brought a sombre red to the girl's cheeks, it was not because she did not have sympathy with him.

Sudden leaping flames of passion yellowed the man's eyes, and he staggered up.

"May God damn the best in him! May all he loves wither and blight! May black Heaven break his heart——"

Jinnie sprang forward and clutched him fiercely by the arm. "Don't! Don't!" she implored. "That's awful, awful!"

Singleton sank back, brushing his foaming lips with the back of his hand.

"Well," he muttered, "he followed me abroad and did for me over there!"

"Did for you?" Virginia repeated after him, parrot-like, gazing at him in a puzzled way as she sat down again.

"Yes, me! If I'd had any sense, I might have known his game. In the state of his finances he'd no business to come over at all. But I didn't know until he got there how evil he was. Oh, God! I wish I had—but I didn't, and now my only work left is to send you somewhere——Oh, why didn't I know?"

The deep sadness, the longing in his voice brought Virginia to her feet once more. She wanted to do something for the thin, sick man because she loved him—just that! Years of neglect had failed to kill in the young heart the cherished affection for her absent parent, and in some subtle way he now appealed to the mother within her, as all sick men do to all heart-women.

"I'd like to help you if I could, father," she said.

The man, with a quick, spasmodic action, drew her to him. Never had he seen such a pair of eyes! They reminded him of Italian skies under which he had dreamed brave dreams—dreamed dreams which would ever be dreams. The end of them now was the grave.

"Little girl! My little girl!" he murmured, caressing her shoulders. Then he caught himself sharply, crushing the sentiment from his voice.

"Hide yourself; change your name; do anything to keep from your uncle. When you're old enough to handle your own affairs, you can come out of your hiding-place—do you understand me?"

"I think I do," she said, tears gathering under her lids.

"I don't know of any one I could trust in this county. Jordan Morse would get 'em all under his spell. That would be the last of you. For your mother's sake——" His lips quivered, but he went on with a masterful effort to choke down a sob,—"I may honestly say, for your own sake, I want you to live and do well."

There was some strain in his passionate voice that stirred terrific

9

emotion in the girl, awakening new, tumultuous impulses. It gave her a mad desire to do something, something for her father, something for herself. At that moment she loved him very much indeed and was ready to go to any length to help him. He had told her she must leave. Perhaps——

Virginia glanced through the window into the darkness. Through the falling snow she could see a giant pine throw out appealing arms. They were like beckoning, sentient beings to the girl, who loved nature with all the passionate strength of her young being. Yet to-night they filled her with new wonder,—an awe she had never felt before. Despite her onrushing thoughts, she tried to calm her mind, to say with eager emphasis:

"Shall I run to-night—now?"

"No, not to-night; don't leave me yet. Sit down in the chair again; stay until I tell you."

"All right," murmured Virginia, walking away.

The father watched the fire a few minutes.

"I'll give you a letter to Grandoken, Lafe Grandoken," he said presently, looking up. "For your mother's sake he'll take you, and some day you can repay him. You see it's this way: Your mother trusted your uncle more than she did me, or she'd never have given you into his care in case of my death. Well, he's got me, and he'll get you."

With no thought of disobedience, Virginia slipped from the chair to her feet.

"He won't get me if I run now, will he?" she questioned breathlessly; "not if I go to—what'd you say his name was?"

She was all excitement, ready to do whatever she was bidden. Slowly, as she stood there, the tremendous suspense left her.

"Why couldn't we both go, you and me?" she entreated eagerly. "Let's both go to-night. I'll take care of you. I'll see you don't get wet."

Her glance met and held his for a few seconds. The vibrant voice thrilled and stirred the father as if he had been dead and suddenly slipped back to life again. A brave smile, tenderly sweet, broke over Virginia's lips.

"Come," she said, holding out her hands. "Come, I'll get my fiddle and we'll go."

He was struck by the vehemence of her appeal. He allowed himself to listen for a moment—to overbalance all his preconceived plans, but just then his past life, Jordan Morse, his own near approaching end, sank into his mind, and the fire in his eyes went out. There was finality in the shake of his shoulders.

"No, no," he murmured, sinking back. "It's too late for me. I couldn't earn money enough to feed a pup. I'm all to pieces—no more good to anyone. No, you'll have to go alone."

"I'm sorry." The girl caught her breath in disappointment. She was crying softly and made no effort to wipe away her tears.

The silent restraint was broken only by the ticking of the shadowy clock on the mantel and Virginia's broken sobs. She stifled them back as her father spoke comfortingly.

10

"Well, well, there, don't cry! If your mother'd lived, we'd all 've been better."

"I wish she had," gasped the girl, making a dash at her eyes. "I wish she'd stayed so I'd 've had her to love. Perhaps I'd 've had you, too, then."

"There's no telling," answered Singleton, drawing up to his desk and beginning to write.

Virginia watched the pen move over the white page for a space, her mind filled with mixed emotions. Then she turned her eyes from her father to the grate as a whirl of ashes and smoke came out.

Matty's story came back to her mind, and she glanced toward the window, but back to the fire quickly. The blizzard seemed to rage in sympathy with her own riotous thoughts. As another gust of wind rattled the casements and shook down showers of soot from the chimney, Virginia turned back to the writer.

"It's the ghosts of my mother's folks that make that noise," she confided gently.

"Keep quiet!" ordered Singleton, frowning.

After the letters were finished and sealed, Mr. Singleton spoke. "There! I've done the best I can for you under the circumstances. Now on this,"—he held up a piece of paper—"I've written just how you're to reach Grandoken's in Bellaire. These letters you're to give to him. This one let him open and read." Mr. Singleton tapped a letter he held up. "In this one, I've written what your uncle did to me. Give it to Grandoken, telling him I said to let it remain sealed unless Jordan Morse claims you. If you reach eighteen safely, burn the letter."

He paused and took out a pocketbook.

"Money is scarce these days, but take this and it'll get you to Grandoken's. It's all I have, anyway. Now go along to bed."

He handed the envelopes to her, and his hand came in contact with hers. The very touch of it, the warmth and life surging through her, gave a keener edge to his misery.

Virginia took the letters and money. She walked slowly to the door. At the threshold she halted, turning to her father.

"May I take the cats with me?" she called back to him.

She started to explain, but he cut her words off with a fierce ejaculation.

"Hell, yes!" he snapped. "Damn the cats! Get out!"

Once in the hall, Virginia stood and looked back upon the closed door.

"I guess he don't need me to teach him swear words," she told herself in a whisper.

Then she went down to the kitchen, where Matty sat dreaming over a wood fire.

CHAPTER II

A WHITE PRESENCE

"Does yer pa want me?" grunted Matty, lifting a tousled black head.

Virginia made a gesture of negation.

"No, he told me to get the hell out," she answered. "So I got! He's awful sick! I guess mebbe he'll die!"

Matty nodded meaningly.

"Some folks might better 'a' stayed to hum for the past ten years than be runnin' wild over the country like mad," she observed.

Virginia reached behind the stove and drew Milly Ann from her bed.

"Father"—Jinnie enjoyed using the word and spoke it lingeringly— "says he wishes he'd stayed here now. You know, my Uncle Jordan, Matty——" She hesitated to confide in the negro woman what her father had told her. So she contented herself with:

"He's coming here soon."

Matty rolled her eyes toward the girl.

"I'se sorry for that, honey bunch." Then, without explaining her words, asked: "Want me to finish about Jonathan Woggles' grandpa dyin'?"

But Virginia's mind was traveling in another channel.

"Where's Bellaire, Matty?" she demanded.

"Off south," replied the woman, "right bearin' south."

"By train?"

"Yes, the same's walkin' or flyin'," confirmed Matty. "Jest the same."

"Then you can finish the story now, Matty," said Virginia presently.

Matty settled back in her chair, closed her eyes, and began to hum.

"How far'd I tell last night?" she queried, blinking.

"Just to where the white thing was waiting for Grandpa Woggles' spirit," explained Virginia.

"Oh, yas. Well, round and round that house the white shadder swep', keepin' time to the howlin' of other spirits in the pine trees——"

"But there aren't any pine trees at Woggles'," objected Virginia.

"Well, they'd be pines if they wasn't oaks," assured Matty. "Oaks or pines, the spirits live in 'em jest the same."

"I 'spose so," agreed Virginia. "Go on!"

"An' round and round he went, meltin' the snow with his hot feet," mused Matty, sniffing the air. "And in the house Betty Woggles set beside the old man, holdin' his hand, askin' him to promise he wouldn't die.... Hum! As if a human bein' could keep from the stalkin' whiteness beckonin' from the graveyard. 'Tain't in human power."

"Can't anybody keep death away, Matty?" inquired Virginia, an expression of awe clouding her eyes.

She was thinking of the man upstairs whom she but twice had called "father."

"Nope, not after the warnin' comes to him. Now Grandad Woggles had that warnin' as much as three days afore the angel clim' the fence and flopped about his house. But don't keep breakin' in on me, little missy, 'cause I cain't finish if ye do, and I'se jest reachin' the thrillin' part."

"Oh, then hurry," urged Jinnie.

"Well, as I was sayin', Betty set by the ole man, starin' into his yeller face; 'twas as yeller as Milly Ann's back, his face was."

"Some yeller," murmured Virginia, fondling Milly Ann.

"Sure! Everybody dyin' gets yeller," informed Matty.

Virginia thought again of the sick man upstairs. His face was white, not yellow, and her heart bounded with great hope. He might live yet a little while. Yes, he surely would! Matty was an authority when she told of the dead and dying, of the spirits which filled the pine trees, and it seldom occurred to Virginia to doubt the black woman's knowledge. She wanted her father to live! Life seemed so dizzily upset with no Matty, with no Milly Ann, and no—father, somewhere in the world. Matty's next words, spoken in a sepulchral whisper, bore down on her with emphasis.

"Then what do ye think, honey bunch?"

"I don't know!" Virginia leaned forward expectantly.

"Jest as Betty was hangin' fast onto her grandpa's spirit, another ghost, some spots of black on him, come right longside the white one, wavin' his hands's if he was goin' to fly."

Virginia sat up very straight. Two spirits on the scene of Grandpa Woggles' passing made the story more interesting, more thrilling. Her sparkling eyes gave a new impetus to the colored woman's wagging tongue.

"The white spirit, he sez, 'What you hangin' round here fer?'"

Matty rolled her eyes upward. "This he sez to the black one, mind you!"

Virginia nodded comprehendingly, keeping her eyes glued on the shining dark face in front of her. She always dreaded, during the exciting parts of Matty's nightly stories, to see, by chance, the garden, with its trees and the white, silent graveyard beyond. And, although she had no fear of tangible things, she seldom looked out of doors when Matty crooned over her ghost stories.

Just then a bell pealed through the house.

Matty rose heavily.

"It's yer pa," she grumbled. "I'll finish when I git back."

Through the door the woman hobbled, while Virginia bent over Milly Ann, stroking her softly with a new expression of gravity on the young face. Many a day, in fancy, she had dreamed of her father's homecoming. He was very different than her dreams. Still she hoped the doctor might have made a mistake about his dying. A smile came to the corners of her mouth, touched the dimples in her cheek, but did not wipe the tragedy from her eyes. She was planning how tenderly she would care for him, how cheerful he'd be when she played her fiddle for him.

She heard Matty groping up the stairs—heard her pass down the hall and open the door. Then suddenly she caught the sound of hurried steps and the woman coming down again. Matty had crawled up, but was almost falling down in her frantic haste to reach the kitchen. Something unusual had happened. Virginia shoved Milly Ann to the floor and stood up. Matty's appearance, with chattering teeth and bulging eyes, brought Jinnie forward a few steps.

"He's daid! Yer pa's daid!" shivered Matty. "And the house is full of spirits. They're standin' grinnin' in the corners. I'm goin' hum now, little missy. I'm goin' to my ole man. You'd better come along fer to-night."

Jinnie heard the moaning call of the pine trees as the winter's voice swept through them,—the familiar sound she loved, yet at which she trembled. Confused thoughts rolled through her mind; her father's fear for her; his desire that she should seek another home. She could not stay in Mottville Corners; she could not go with Matty. No, of course not! Yet her throat filled with longing sobs, for the old colored woman had been with her many years.

By this time Matty had tied on her scarf, opened the door, and as Virginia saw her disappear, she sank limply to the floor. Milly Ann rubbed her yellow back against her young mistress's dress. Virginia caught her in her arms and drew her close.

"Kitty, kitty," she sobbed, "I've got to go! He said I could take you and your babies, and I will, I will! I won't leave you here with the spirits."

She rose unsteadily to her feet and went to the cupboard, where she found a large pail. Into this she folded a roller towel. She then lifted the kittens from the box behind the stove and placed them in the pail, first pressing her lips lovingly to each warm, wriggley little body. Milly Ann cuddled contentedly with her offspring as the girl covered them up.

Jinnie had suddenly grown older, for a responsibility rested upon her which no one else could assume.

To go forth into the blizzard meant she must wrap up warmly. This she did. Then she wrapped a small brown fiddle in her jacket, took the pail and went to the door. There she stood, considering a moment, with her hand on the knob. With no further hesitancy she placed the kittens and fiddle gently on the floor, and went to the stairs. The thought of the spirits made her shiver. She saw long shadows making lines here and there, and had no doubt but that these were the ghosts Matty had seen. She closed her eyes tightly and began to ascend the stairs, feeling her way along the wall. At the top she opened reluctant lids. The library door stood ajar as Matty had left it, and the room appeared quite the same as it had a few moments before, save for the long figure of a man lying full length before the grate. That eternal period, that awful stop which puts a check on human lives, had settled once and for all the earthly concerns of her father. The space between her and the body seemed peopled with spectral beings, which moved to and fro in the dimly lit room. Her father lay on his back, the flames from the fire making weird red and yellow twisting streaks on his white, upturned face.

The taut muscles grew limp in the girl's body as she staggered forward and stood contemplating the wide-open, staring eyes. Then with a long sigh breathed between quivering lips, she dropped beside the lifeless man. The deadly forces eddying around her were not of her own making. With the going of this person, who was her father by nature, everything else had gone too. All her life's hopes had been dissolved in the crucible of death. She lay, with her hands to her mouth, pressing back the great sobs that came from the depths of her heart. She reached out and tentatively touched her father's cheek; without fear she moved his head a little to what she hoped would be a more comfortable position.

"You told me to go," she whispered brokenly, "and I'm going now. You never liked me much, but I guess one of my kisses won't hurt you."

Saying this, Jinnie pressed her lips twice to those of her dead father, and got to her feet quickly. She dared not leave the lamp burning, so within a short distance of the table she drew a long breath and blew toward the smoking light. The flame flared thrice like a torch, then spat out, leaving the shivering girl to feel her way around the room. To the sensitive young soul the dark was almost maddening. She only wanted to get back to Milly Ann, and she closed the door with no thought for what might become of the man inside. He was dead! A greater danger menaced her. He had warned her and she would heed. As she stumbled down the stairs, her memories came too swiftly to be precise and in order, and the weird moans of the night wind drifted intermittently through the wild maze of her thoughts. She would say good-bye to Molly the Merry, for Molly was the only person in all the country round who had ever spoken a kindly word to her. Their acquaintance had been slight, because Molly lived quite a distance away and the woman had never been to see her, but then of course no one in the neighborhood approved of the house of Singleton.

Later by five minutes, Virginia left the dark farmhouse, carrying her fiddle and the pail of cats, and the blizzard swallowed her up.

CHAPTER III

JINNIE'S FAREWELL TO MOLLY THE MERRY

Virginia turned into the Merriweather gate, went up the small path to the kitchen, and rapped on the door. There was no response, so she turned the handle and stepped into the room. It was warm and comfortable. A teakettle, singing on the back of the stove, threw out little jets of steam. Jinnie placed the pail on the floor and seated herself in a low chair with her fiddle on her lap. Molly would be back in a minute, she was

15

sure. Just as she was wondering where the woman could be, she heard the sound of voices from the inner room. A swift sensation of coming evil swept over her, and without taking thought of consequences, she slipped under the kitchen table, drawing the pail after her. The long fringe from the red cloth hung down about her in small, even tassels. The dining room door opened and she tried to stifle her swiftly coming breaths. Virginia could see a pair of legs, man's legs, and they weren't country legs either. Following them were the light frillings of a woman's skirts.

"It's warmer here," said Miss Merriweather's voice.

Molly and the man took chairs. From her position Virginia could not see his face.

"Your father's ill," he said in a voice rich and deep.

"Yes," replied Molly. "He's been near death for a long time. We've had to give him the greatest care. That's why I haven't told him anything."

The man bent over until Jinnie could see the point of his chin.

"I see," said he.... "Well, Molly, are you glad to have me back?"

Molly's face came plainly within Jinnie's view. At his question the woman went paler. Then the man leaned over and tried to take one of her hands. But she drew it away again and locked her fingers together in her lap.

"Aren't you glad to see me back again?" he repeated.

Molly's startled eyes came upward to his face.

"I don't know—I can't tell—I'm so surprised and——"

"And glad," laughed the stranger in a deep, mesmeric voice. "Glad to have your husband back once more, eh?"

Virginia's start was followed quickly by an imploration from Molly.

"Hush, hush, please don't speak of it!"

"I certainly shall speak of it; I certainly shall. I came here for no other reason than that. And who would speak of it if I didn't?"

Molly shivered. There was something about the man's low, modulated tones that repelled Virginia. She tried in vain to see his face. She was sure that nowhere in the hills was there such a man.

"You've been gone so long I thought you'd forgotten or—or were dead," breathed Molly, covering her face with her hands.

"Not forgotten, but I wasn't able to get back."

"You could have written me."

The man shrugged himself impatiently.

"But I didn't. Don't rake up old things; please don't. Molly, look at me."

Molly uncovered a pair of unwilling eyes and centered them upon his face.

"What makes you act so? Are you afraid?"

"I did not expect you back, that's all."

"That's not it! Tell me what's on your mind.... Tell me."

Molly's white lids fell, her fingers clenched and unclenched.

"I didn't—I couldn't write," she whispered, "about the baby."

"Baby!" The word burst out like a bomb. The man stood up. "Baby!" he repeated. "You mean my—our baby?"

Molly swallowed and nodded.

"A little boy," she said, in a low voice.

"Where is he?" demanded the man.

"Please, please don't ask me, I beg of you. I want to forget——"

"But you can't forget you're married, that you've been the mother of a child and—and—that I'm its father."

Molly's tears began to flow. Virginia had never seen a woman cry before in all her young life. It was a most distressing sight. Something within her leaped up and thundered at her brain. It ordered her to venture out and aid the pretty woman if she could. Jinnie was not an eavesdropper! She did not wish to hear any more. But fear kept her crouched in her awkward position.

"I just want to forget if I can," Molly sobbed. "I don't know where the baby is. That's why I want to forget. I can't find him."

"Can't find him? What do you mean by 'can't find him'?"

Molly faced about squarely, suddenly.

"I've asked you not to talk about it. I've been terribly unhappy and so miserable.... It's only lately I've begun to be at all reconciled."

"Nevertheless, I will hear," snapped the man angrily. "I will hear! Begin back from the letter you wrote me."

"Asking you to help me?" questioned the girl.

"Yes, asking me to help you, if you want to be blunt. Molly, it won't make you any happier to hatch up old scores. I tell you I've come to make amends—to take you—if you will——"

"And I repeat, I can't go with you!"

"We'll leave that discussion until later. Begin back where I told you to."

Molly's face was very white, and her lids drooped wearily. Virginia wanted so much to help her! She made a little uneasy movement under the table, but Molly's tragic voice was speaking again.

"My father'd kill me if he knew about it, so I never told him or any one."

"Including me," cut in the man sarcastically.

"You didn't care," said Molly with asperity.

"How do you know I didn't care? Did you tell me? Did you? Did I know?"

Molly shook her head.

"Then I insist upon knowing now, this moment!"

"My father would have killed me——"

"Well!" His voice rushed in upon her hesitancy.

"When I couldn't stay home any longer, I went away to visit a cousin of my mother's. At least, my father thought I'd gone there. I only stayed with Bertha a little while and father never knew the truth of it."

"And then after that?"

"I didn't know what to do with my baby. I was afraid people'd say I wasn't married, and then father——"

"Go on from the time you left your cousin's."

Molly thought a minute and proceeded.

"I looked in all the papers to find someone who wanted a baby——"

"So you gave him away? Well, that's easy to overcome. You couldn't give my baby away, you know."

"No, no, indeed! I didn't give him away.... I boarded him out and saved money to pay for him. I even took summer boarders. The woman who had him——"

Molly's long wait prompted the man once more.

"Well?" he said again. "The woman what?"

"The woman began to love the baby very much, and she wasn't very poor, and didn't need the money. Lots of times I went with it to her, and she wouldn't take it."

A thought connected with her story made Molly bury her face in her hands. The man touched her.

"Go on," he said slowly. "Go on. And then?"

"Then once when I went to her she said she was going to take the baby on a little visit to some relatives and would write me as soon as she got back."

"Yes," encouraged the low voice.

"She never wrote or came back. I couldn't find where she'd gone, and father was terribly ill, and I've hoped and hoped——"

"How long since you last saw him?"

Molly considered a moment.

"A long time," she sighed.

"How many years?"

"One!"

"Then he was almost seven years with the woman?"

"Yes," breathed Molly, and they lapsed into silence.

The man meditated a space and Jinnie heard a low, nervous cough come from his lips.

"Molly," he said presently, "I'm going to have a lot of money soon. It won't be long, and then we'll find him and begin life all over."

"Oh, I'd love to find him," moaned Molly, "but I couldn't begin over with you. It's all hateful and horrible now."

The man leaned over and touched her, not too tenderly. When Molly's face was turned to him, he tilted her chin up.

"You care for someone else?" he said abruptly.

The droop of the girl's head was his answer. He stood up suddenly.

"That's it! That's it! What's his name?"

A shake of her head was all the answer Molly gave him.

"I asked you his name. Get up! Stand up!"

As if to force her to do his will, he took hold of her shoulders sharply and drew her upward.

"What's his name?"

18

"It doesn't matter."

"What's his name?"

Virginia did not catch Molly's whisper.

A disbelieving grunt fell from the stranger's lips.

"I remember him as a boy. Weren't they one summer at the Mottville Hotel? He's years younger than you."

Molly gathered courage.

"He doesn't know how old I am," she responded, "and his mother loves me, too. They were with me three summers." Then, remembering the man's statement, she added, "Ages don't count nowadays. And I will be happy."

"You'll get happiness with me, not with him," said an angry voice. "Has he ever told you he loved you?"

"No, no, indeed not. But he was here to-day! His mother's ill and wanted me to come as her companion, but I couldn't leave father right now."

"Does he know you love him?"

An emphatic negative ejaculation from Molly brought a sigh of relief from the man.

"Forget him!" said he. "Now I'm going. I shall come back to-night, and remember this. I'll leave no stone unturned to find that boy. I've always longed for one, and I'll move Heaven and earth to find him."

Virginia saw him whirl about, open the door, and stride out.

Molly Merriweather stood for a few minutes in silence, trembling.

"I didn't dare to tell him the baby was blind," she whispered, too low for Jinnie to hear.

Then she slowly glided away, leaving the girl under the table, with her pail full of cats, and the fiddle. Presently Virginia crawled out cautiously, the pail on her arm, and hugging her fiddle, she opened the door swiftly, and disappeared down the road, running under the tall trees.

CHAPTER IV

JINNIE TRAVELS

Virginia took the direction leading to the station. Many a time she had watched the trains rush by on their way to New York, but never in those multitudinous yesterdays had it entered her mind that someday she would go over that same way, to be gone possibly forever. The wind was blowing at such a terrific rate that Jinnie could scarcely walk. There was no fear in her heart, only deep solemnity and a sense of awe at the

19

magnificence of a storm. She had left the farmhouse so suddenly that the loneliness of parting had not then been forced upon her as it was now; the realization was settling slowly upon the clouded young mind.

She was a mere puppet in the hands of an inexorable fate, which had shown her little mercy or benevolence.

Out of sight of the Merriweather homestead, she kept to the path along the highway, now and then shifting the pail from one hand to the other, and clasping the beloved fiddle to her breast. Once she looked down to find Milly Ann peeping above the rim of the pail. Jinnie could see the glint of her greenish eyes. She stopped and, with a tenderly spoken admonition, covered her more closely with the roller towel. When the lighted station-house glimmered through the falling snow, Jinnie sighed with relief.

"I couldn't 've carried you and the fiddle much farther, Milly Ann," she murmured.

At that moment a tall figure, herculean in size, loomed out of the night and advanced hastily. The man's head was bent forward against the storm. Virginia caught a glimpse of his face as he passed in the streak of light thrown out from the station.

He sprang to the platform and disappeared in the doorway. Jinnie saw him plainly when she, too, entered, and her eyes followed him as he went out.

She had never seen him before. Like the man in the Merriweather kitchen, he bore the stamp of the city upon him.

Virginia bought her ticket as her father had directed, and while the pail was still on the floor, she bent to examine Milly Ann and the kittens. The latter were asleep, but the mother-cat lazily opened her eyes to greet, with a purr, the soft touch of Jinnie's fingers. The girl waited inside the room until the shriek of the engine's whistle told her of its approach; then, with the fiddle and the pail, she walked to the platform.

The long, snakelike train was edging the hill, its headlight bearing down the track in one straight, glittering line.

For the first time in her life, Jinnie felt really afraid. In other days, with beating heart, she had hugged close to the roadside as the monster slipped either into the station and stopped, or rushed around the curve. Tonight she was going aboard, over into a strange land among strange people.

She tilted the pail lovingly and hugged a little more tightly the fiddle in her arm. Whatever happened, she had Milly, her little family, and the comforting music. Jinnie could never be quite alone with these. As the train slowed up, the conductor jumped down.

It seemed to Virginia like a dream as she walked toward the steps at the end of the car. As she was about to lift her foot to climb up, she heard a voice say:

"Let me help you, child. Here, I'll take the pail."

Virginia looked upward into the face of a man,—the same face she had seen in the station a few moments before,—and around the handsome mouth was a smile of reassuring kindliness.

She surrendered the pail with a burning blush, and felt, with a strange new thrill, a firm hand upon her arm. The next thing she knew she was in a seat, with the pail on the floor and the fiddle lying beside her.

She gazed around wonderingly. There was no one in sight but the tall man who, across the aisle, was arranging his overcoat on the back of the seat. Jinnie looked at him with interest—he had been so kind to her— and noted his thick, blond hair, which had been cropped close to a massive head. She admired him, too. Suddenly he looked up, and the girl felt a clutch at her heart. Just why that happened she could not tell. Again came the charming smile, the parted lips showing a set of dazzling white teeth.

Jinnie smiled back, responsively. The man came over.

"May I sit beside you?" he asked.

Jinnie moved the fiddle invitingly and huddled herself into the corner. When the man started to move the pail, Jinnie stayed him.

"Oh, don't, please," she protested. "It's only Milly and——"

"Milly and what?" quizzically came the question.

"Her kitties—see?"

She drew aside the towel and exposed the sleeping family.

A broad smile lit up the man's face.

"Oh, cats! I see! Where're you taking them?"

"To Bellaire."

"Ah, Bellaire; that's where I'm going. We'll have a nice ride together, almost two hours."

"I'm glad." Jinnie leaned back, sighing contentedly.

In those few minutes she had grown to have great faith in this stranger, the third of the puzzling trio that had come into her life that night. First her father, then the man with Molly the Merry, and now this brilliant new friend, who quite took away her breath as she peeped up at him. His smile seemed to be ever ready. It warmed her and made her glow with friendliness. She liked, too, the deep tones in his voice and the sight of his strong hands as they gestured during his speeches.

"Where are you going in Bellaire?" he questioned.

Virginia cogitated for a moment. She couldn't tell the story her father had told her, yet she must answer his kindly question.

At length, "The cats and I are going to live with my uncle," said she.

"He lives in Bellaire?"

"Yes, but I've never seen him. I'll find him, though, when I get there."

It didn't occur to the man to ask the name of her relatives, and Jinnie was glad he did not.

"Perhaps I shall see you some time in the city," he responded to her statement. Jinnie hoped so; oh, how she hoped she might see him again!

"Mebbe," was all she said.

"You see I live there with my mother," continued the man. "Our home is called Kinglaire. My name is King."

Virginia lifted her head with a queer little start.

"I've read about your people," she said. "I've got a book in our garret that tells all about Kings."

"That's very nice," answered Mr. King. "I won't have to explain anything about us, then."

"No, I know," said Jinnie in satisfaction.

At least she thought she knew. Hadn't she read over and over, when seated in the garret, the story of the old and new kings, how they sat on their thrones, and ruled their people sometimes with a rod of iron? Jinnie brought to mind some of the vivid pictures, and shyly lifted a pair of violet eyes to scan the face above her. Surely this King was handsomer than any in the book. She tried to imagine him on his throne, and wondered if he were always smiling as now.

"You're quite different from your relations," she observed presently.

Theodore King laughed aloud. The sound startled the girl into a straighter posture. It rang out so merrily that she laughed too after making up her mind that he was not ridiculing her.

"Really you are!" she exclaimed. "I mean it. You know the picture of the King with a red suit on,—he doesn't look like you. His nose went sort of down over his mouth—I mean, well, yours don't."

She stumbled through the last few words, intuitively realizing that she had been too personal.

"You like to read, I gather," stated Mr. King.

"Yes, but I like to fiddle better," said Jinnie.

"Oh, you play, do you?"

Jinnie's eyes fell upon the instrument standing in the corner of the opposite seat, wrapped in an old jacket. She nodded.

"I play some. I love my fiddle almost as much as I do Milly Ann and her kitties."

"Won't you play for me?" asked Mr. King, gravely putting forth his hand.

Jinnie paused a moment. Then without further hesitancy she took up the violin and unfastened it.

"I'll be glad to fiddle for a king," she said naïvely.

She did not speak as she turned and twisted the small white keys.

Outside the storm was still roaring over the hills, sweeping the lake into monstrous waves. The shriek of the wind mingled with the snap of the taut strings under the agile fingers of the hill girl. Then Jinnie began to play. Never in all his life had Theodore King seen a picture such as the girl before him made. The wondrous beauty of her, the marvelous fingers traveling over the strings, together with the moaning of the night wind, made an impression upon him he would never forget. Sometimes as her fingers sped on, her eyes were penetrating; sometimes they darkened almost to melancholy. When the last wailing note had finally died away, Jinnie dropped the instrument to her side.

"It's lonely on nights like this when the ghosts howl about," she observed. "They love the fiddle, ghosts do."

22

Theodore King came back to himself at the girl's words. He drew a long breath.

"Child," he ejaculated, "whoever taught you to play like that?"

"Why, I taught myself," answered Jinnie.

"Please play again," entreated Mr. King, and once more he sat enthralled with the wonder of the girl's melodies. The last few soulful notes Mr. King likened to a sudden prayer, sent out with a sobbing breath.

"It's wonderful," he murmured slowly. "What is the piece you've just played?"

"It hasn't any name yet," replied the girl. "You see I only know pieces that're in my head."

Then all the misery of the past few hours swept over her, and Jinnie began to cry. A burden of doubt had clouded the usually clear young mind. What if the man to whom she was going would not let her and the cats live with him? He might turn them away.

Mr. King spoke softly to her.

"Don't cry," said he. "You won't be lonely when you get to your uncle's."

But she met his smiling glance with a feeling of constraint. He did not know the cause of her tears; she could not tell him. If she only knew,— if she only had one little inkling of the reception she would receive at the painter's home. However, she did cheer up a little when Mr. King, in evident desire to be of some service, began to tell her of the city to which she was going.

In a short time he saw the dark head nodding, and he drew Jinnie down against his arm, whispering:

"Sleep a while, child; I'll wake you up at Bellaire."

CHAPTER V

LIKE UNTO LIKE ATTRACTED

Jinnie Singleton watched Theodore King leave the train at the little private station situated on his own estate. As she drew nearer the city depot, her heart beat with uncertainty, for that day would decide her fate, her future; she would know by night whether or not she possessed a friend in the world.

For some hours she sat in the station on one of the hard benches, waiting for daylight, at which time she and Milly Ann would steal forth into the city to find Lafe Grandoken, her mother's friend.

23

A reluctant, stormy dawn was pushing its way from the horizon as she picked up the pail and fiddle and stepped out into the falling snow.

Stopping a moment, she asked the station master about the Grandokens, but as he had only that week arrived in Bellaire, he politely, with admiration in his eyes, told her he could not give her any information. But on the railroad tracks Virginia saw a man standing with his hands thrust deep into his pockets.

"What'd you want of Lafe Grandoken?" asked the fellow in reply to her question.

"I've come to see him," answered Jinnie evasively.

"He's a cobbler and lives down with the shortwood gatherers there on Paradise Road. Littlest shack of the bunch! He ain't far from my folks. My name's Maudlin Bates."

He went very near her.

"Now I've told you, you c'n gimme a kiss," said he.

"I'll give you a bat," flung back Jinnie, walking away.

Some distance off she stood looking down the tracks, her blue eyes noting the row of huts strung along the road and extending toward the hills. At the back of them was a marshland, dense with trees and underbrush.

"My father told me Mr. Grandoken was a painter of houses!" Jinnie ruminated: "But that damn duffer back there says he's changed his work to cobbling. I'll go and see! I hope it won't be long before I'm as warm as can be. Wonder if he'll be glad to see me!"

"It's the smallest house among 'em," she cogitated further, walking very fast. "Well! There ain't any of 'em very big."

She traveled on through heavy snow, glancing at every hut until, coming to a standstill, she read aloud:

"Lafe Grandoken, Cobbler of Folks' and Children's Shoes and Boots."

Jinnie turned and, going down a short flight of steps, hesitated a moment before she knocked timidly on the front door. During the moment of waiting she glanced over what she hoped was to be her future home. It was so small in comparison with the huge, lonely farmhouse she had left the night before that her heart grew warm in anticipation. Then in answer to a man's voice, calling "Come in!" she lifted the latch and opened the door.

The room was small and cheerless, although a fire was struggling for life in a miniature stove. In one corner was a table strewn with papers. Back from the window which faced the tracks was a man, a kit of cobbler's tools, in the disarray of daily use, on the bench beside him. He halted, with his hammer in the air, at the sight of the newcomer.

"Come in and shut the door," said he, and the girl did as she was bidden. "Cold, ain't it?"

"Yes," replied Jinnie, placing the pail and fiddle on the floor.

The girl looked the man over with her steady blue eyes. Then her heart gave one great bound. The grey face had lighted with a sweet, sad smile; the faded eyes, under the bushy brows, twinkled welcome. A sense of wonderful security and friendship rushed over her.

"Well, what's your business? Got some shoes to mend?" asked the man. "Better sit down."

Jinnie took a chair in silence, a passionate wish suffusing her being that this small home might be hers. She was so lonely, so homesick. The little room seemed radiant with the smile of the cobbler. She only felt the wonderful content that flowed from the man on the bench to herself; she wanted to stay with him; never before had she been face to face with a desire so great.

"I've come to live with you," she gulped, at length.

The cobbler gave a quick whack at the little shoe he held in the vise.

"I'm Jinnie Singleton, kid of Thomas Singleton, the second," the girl explained, almost mechanically, "and I haven't any home, so I've come to you."

During this statement the cobbler's hammer rattled to the floor, and he sat eyeing the speaker speechlessly. Then he slowly lifted his arms and held them forth.

"Come here! Lass, come here!" he said huskily. "I'd come to you, but I can't."

In her mental state it took Jinnie a few seconds to gather the import of the cobbler's words. Then she sprang up and went forward with parted, smiling lips, tears trembling thick on her dark lashes. When Jinnie felt a pair of warm, welcoming arms about her strong young shoulders, she shivered in sudden joy. The sensation was delightful, and while a thin hand patted her back, she choked down a hard sob. However, she pressed backward and looked down into Lafe Grandoken's eyes.

"I thought I'd never cry again as long as I lived," she whispered, "but—but I guess it's your loving me that's done it."

It came like a small confession—as a relief to the overburdened little soul.

"I guess I've rode a hundred miles to get here," she went on, half sobbing, "and you're awful glad to see me, ain't you?"

It didn't need Lafe's, "You bet your boots," to satisfy Jinnie. The warmth of his arms, the shining, misty eyes, set her to shivering convulsively and shaking with happiness.

"Set here on the bench," invited the cobbler, softly, "an' tell me about your pa an' ma."

"They're both dead," said Jinnie, sitting down, but she still kept her hand on the cobbler's arm as if she were afraid he would vanish from her sight.

The man made a dash at his eyes with his free hand.

"Both dead!" he repeated with effort, "an' you're their girl!"

"Yes, and I've come to live with you, if you'll let me."

She drew forth the letters written the night before.

"Here's two letters," she ended, handing them over, and sinking down again into the chair.

25

She sat very quietly as the cobbler stumbled through the finely written sheets.

"Mottville Corners, N. Y.
"Dear Mr. Grandoken," whispered Lafe.
"My girl will bring you this, and, in excuse for sending her, I will briefly state: I'm very near the grave, and she's in great danger. I want to tell you that her Uncle Jordan Morse has conquered me and will her, if she's not looked after. For her mother's sake, I ask you to take her if you can. She will repay you when she's of age, but until then, after I'm gone, she can't get any money unless through her uncle, and that would be too dangerous. When I say that my child's life isn't worth this paper if she is given over to Morse, you'll see the necessity of helping her. I don't know another soul I could trust as I am trusting you. The other letter Virginia will explain. Keep it to use against Morse if you need to.

"I can't tell you whether my girl is good or not, but I hope so. I've woefully neglected her, but now I wish I had a chance to live the past few years over. She'll tell you all she knows, which isn't much. What you do for her will be greatly appreciated by me, and would be by her mother, too, if she could understand her daughter's danger. "Gratefully yours,
"THOMAS G. SINGLETON"

The cobbler put down the paper, and the rattling of it made Jinnie raise her head.

"Come over here again," said the shoemaker, kindly. "Now tell me all about it."

"Didn't the letter tell you?"

"Some of it, yes. But tell me about yourself."

Lafe Grandoken listened as the girl recounted her past life with Matty, and when at the finish she remarked,

"I had to bring Milly Ann——"

Grandoken by a look interrupted her explanation.

"Milly Ann?" he repeated.

Then came the story of the mother-cat and her babies. Jinnie lifted the towel, and the almost smothered kittens scrambled over the top of the pail. Milly Ann stretched her cramped legs, then proceeded vigorously to wash the faces of her numerous children.

"She wouldn't 've had a place to live if I hadn't brought her," explained Jinnie, looking at the kittens. "I guess they won't eat much, because Milly Ann catches all kinds of live things. I don't like 'er to do that, but I heard she was born that way and can't help it."

"I guess she'll find enough to eat around here," he said softly.

"I brought my fiddle, too," Jinnie went on lovingly. "I couldn't live without it any more'n I could without Milly Ann."

The cobbler nodded.

"You play?" he questioned.

26

"A little," replied the girl.

Mr. Grandoken eyed the instrument on the floor beside the pail.

"You oughter have a box to put it in," he suggested. "It might get wet."

Virginia acquiesced by bowing her head.

"I know it," she assented, "but I carried it in that old wrap.... Did Father tell you about my uncle?"

"Yes," replied the cobbler.

"And that he was made to die for something my uncle did?"

"Yes, an' that he might harm you.... I knew your mother well, lass, when she was young like you."

An expression of sadness pursed Jinnie's pretty mouth.

"I don't remember her, you see," she murmured sadly. "I wish I had her now."

And she heard the cobbler murmur, "What must your uncle be to want to hurt a little, sweet girl like you?"

They did not speak again for a few moments.

"Go call Peg," the cobbler then said.

At a loss, Virginia glanced about.

"Peg's my woman—my wife," explained Lafe. "Go through that door there. Just call Peg an' she'll come."

In answer to the summons a woman appeared, with hands on hips and arms akimbo. Her almost colorless hair, streaked a little with grey, was drawn back from a sallow, thin face out of which gleamed a pair of light blue eyes. Jinnie in one quick glance noted how tall and angular she was. The cobbler looked from his wife to her.

"You've heard me speak about Singleton, who married Miss Virginia Burton in Mottville, Peggy, ain't you?" he asked.

"Yes," answered the woman.

"His kid's come to live with us. She calls herself Jinnie." He threw his eyes with a kindly smile to the girl, standing hesitant, longing for recognition from the tall, gaunt woman. "I guess she'd better go to the other room and warm her hands, eh?"

Mrs. Grandoken, dark-faced, with drooping lips, ordered the girl into the kitchen.

Alone with his wife, Lafe read Singleton's letter aloud.

"I've heard as much of her yarn as I can get," he said, glancing up. "I just wanted to tell you she was here."

"We ain't got a cent to bless ourselves with," grumbled Mrs. Grandoken, "an' times is so hard I can't get more work than what I'm doin'."

A patient, resigned look crossed the cobbler's pain-worn face.

"That's so, Peg, that's so," he agreed heartily. "But there's always to-morrow, an' after that another to-morrow. With every new day there's always a chance. We've got a chance, an' so's the girl."

The woman dropped into a chair, noticing the cobbler's smile, which was born to give her hope.

27

"There ain't much chance for a bit of a brat like her," she snarled crossly, and the man answered this statement with eagerness, because the rising inflection in his wife's voice made it a question.

"Yes, there is, Peg," he insisted; "yes, there is! Didn't you say there was hope for me when my legs went bad—that I had a chance for a livin'? Now didn't you, Peggy? An' ain't I got the nattiest little shop this side of way up town?"

Peg paused a moment. Then, "That you have, Lafe; you sure have," came slowly.

"An' didn't I make full sixty cents yesterday?"

"You did, Lafe; you sure did."

"An' sixty cents is better'n nothin', ain't it, Peg?"

Mrs. Grandoken arose hastily.

"Course 'tis, Lafe! But don't brag 'cause you made sixty cents. You might a lost your hands same's your feet. 'Tain't no credit to you you didn't. Here, let me wrap you up better! You'll freeze all that's left of your legs, if you don't."

"Them legs ain't much good," sighed the cobbler. "They might as well be off; mightn't they, Peg?"

Peggy wrapped a worn blanket tightly about her husband.

"You oughter be ashamed," she growled darkly. "Ain't you every day sayin' there's always to-morrow?"

This time her voice was toned with finality, and she turned and went out.

CHAPTER VI

PEG'S BARK

Virginia and Lafe Grandoken sat for some time with nothing but the tick-tack of the hammer to break the silence.

"It bein' the first time you've visited us, kid," broke in the man, pausing, "you can't be knowin' just what's made us live this way."

Virginia made a negative gesture and smiled, settling herself hopefully for a story, but Lafe brought a frightened expression quickly to her face by his low, even voice, and the ominous meaning of his words.

"Me an' Peg's awful poor," said he.

"Then mebbe I'd better not stay, Mr. Lafe," faltered Jinnie.

The cobbler threaded his fingers through his hair.

"The shanty's awful small," he interjected, thoughtfully.

28

"I think it's awful nice, though," offered the girl. Some thought closed her blue eyes, but they flashed open instantly.

"Cobbler," she faltered, "is Mrs. Peggy mad when she grits her teeth and wags her head?"

As if by its own volition the cobbler's hammer stayed itself in the air.

"No," he smiled, "just when she acts the worst is when she's likely to do her best ... I've knowed Peggy this many a year."

"She was a wee little bit cross to me," commented the girl.

"Was she? I didn't hear anything she said."

"I'll tell you, then, Mr. Lafe," said Virginia. "When I was standing by the fire warming my hands, she come bustling out and looked awful mad. She said something about folks keeping their girls to home."

"Well, what after that?" asked the cobbler, as Jinnie hesitated.

"She said she could see me eating my head off, and as long as I had to hide from my uncle, I wouldn't be able to earn my salt."

"Well, that's right," affirmed the cobbler, wagging his head. "You got to keep low for a while. Your Uncle Morse knows a lot of folks in this town."

"But they don't know me," said Virginia.

"That's good," remarked Lafe.

As he said this, Peg opened the door roughly and ordered them in to breakfast.

Virginia sat beside the cobbler at the meager meal. On the table were three bowls of hot mush. As the fragrant odor rose to her nostrils, waves of joy crept slowly through the young body.

"Peggy 'lowed you'd be hungry, kid," said the cobbler, pushing a bowl in front of her.

Mrs. Grandoken interrupted her husband with a growl.

"If I've any mem'ry, you 'lowed it yourself, Lafe Grandoken," she muttered.

A smile deepened on the cobbler's face and a slight flush rose to his forehead.

"I 'lowed it, too, Peggy dear," he said.

"Eat your mush," snapped the woman, "an', Lafe, don't 'Peggy dear' me. I hate it; see?"

Virginia refused to believe the startling words. She would have adored being called "dear." In Lafe's voice, great love rang out; in the woman's, she scarcely knew what. She glanced from one to the other as the cobbler lifted his head. He was always thanking some one in some unknown place for the priceless gift of his woman.

"I'll 'Peggy dear' you whenever I feel like it, wife," he said gravely, "for God knows you're awful dear to me, Peg."

Mrs. Grandoken ignored his speech, but when she returned from the stove, her voice was a little more gentle.

"You can both stuff your innards with hot mush. You can't starve on that.... Here, kid, sit a little nearer!"

So Virginia Singleton, the lame cobbler, and Peggy began their first meal, facing a new day, which to Lafe was yesterday's to-morrow.

A little later Virginia followed the wheel chair into the cobbler's shop. Peggy grumblingly left them to return to her duties in the kitchen.

"Terrible cold day this," Lafe observed, picking up a shoe. "The wind's blowin' forty miles the hour."

Virginia's next remark was quite irrelevant to the wind.

"I'm hoping Mrs. Peggy'll get the money she was talking about."

"Did she tell you she needed some?"

Virginia nodded, and when she spoke again, her tongue was parched and dry.

"She said she had to have money to-night. I hope she gets it; if she doesn't I can't stay and live with you."

"I hope she gets it, too," sighed the cobbler.

Of a sudden a thought seemed to strike him. The girl noticed it and looked a question.

"Peggy's bark's worser'n her bite," Lafe explained in answer. "She's like a lot of them little pups that do a lot of barkin' but wouldn't set their teeth in a biscuit."

"Does that mean," Jinnie asked eagerly, "if she don't get the two dollars to-night, Mrs. Peggy might let me stay?"

"That's just what it means," replied Lafe, making loud whacks on the sole of a shoe. "You'll stay, all right."

The depth of Virginia's gratitude just then could only be estimated by one who had passed through the same fires of deep uncertainty, and in the ardor of it she flung her arms around the cobbler's neck and kissed him.

When Lafe, with useless legs, had been brought home to his wife, she had stoically taken up the burden that had been his. At her husband's suggestion that he should cobble, Mrs. Grandoken had fitted up the little shop, telling him grimly that every hand in the world should do its share. And that was how Lafe Grandoken, laborer and optimist, began his life's great work—of cobbling a ray of comfort to every soul entering the shack. Sometimes he would insist that the sun shone brighter than the day before; then again that the clouds had a cooling effect. But if in the world outside Lafe found no comfort, he always spoke of to-morrow with a ring of hope in his voice.

Hope for another day was all Lafe had save Peggy, and to him these two—hope and the woman—were Heaven's choicest gifts. Now Peggy didn't realize all these things, because the world, with its trials and vicissitudes, gave her a different aspect of life, and she was not in even her ordinary good humor this day as she prepared the midday meal. Her mind was busy with thoughts of the new burden which the morning had brought.

Generally Lafe consulted her about any problem that presented itself before him, but, that day, he had taken a young stranger into their home, and Mrs. Grandoken had used all kinds of arguments to persuade him to send the girl away. Peggy didn't want another mouth to feed. She didn't care for anyone in the world but Lafe anyway.

When the dinner was on the table, she grimly brought her husband's wheel chair to the kitchen. Virginia, by the cobbler's invitation, followed.

"Any money paid in to-day?" asked Peggy gruffly, drawing the cobbler to his place at the table.

"No," he said, smiling up at her, "but there'll be a lot to-morrow.... Is there some bread for——for Jinnie, too?"

Peggy replied by sticking her fork into a biscuit and pushing it off on Virginia's plate with her finger.

Virginia acknowledged it with a shy upward glance. Peg's stolid face and quick, insistent movements filled her with vague discomfort. If the woman had tempered her harsh, "Take it, kid," with a smile, the little girl's heart might have ached less.

Lafe nodded to her when his wife left the room for a moment.

"That biscuit's Peg's bite," said he, "so she'll bark a lot the rest of the day, but don't you mind."

CHAPTER VII

JUST A JEW

When the cobbler was at work again, Virginia, after picking up a few nails and tacks scattered on the floor, sat down.

"Would you like to hear something about me and Peggy, lassie?" he inquired, "an' will you take my word for things?"

Jinnie nodded trustfully. She had already grown to love the cobbler, and her affection grew stronger as she stated:

"There isn't anything you'd tell me, cobbler, I wouldn't believe!"

With slow importance Lafe put down his hammer.

"I'm a Israelite," he announced.

"What's that?" asked the girl, immediately interested.

The cobbler looked over his spectacles and smiled.

"A Jew, just a plain Jew."

"I don't know what a Jew is either," confessed Jinnie.

Lafe groped for words to explain his meaning.

"A Jew," he ventured presently, "is one of God's——chosen——folks. I mean one of them chose by Him to believe."

"Believe what?"

"All that God said would be," explained Lafe, reverently.

"And you believe it, cobbler?"

"Sure, kid; sure."

31

The shoemaker saw a question mirrored in the depths of the violet eyes.

"And thinking that way makes you happy, eh, Mr. Lafe? Does it make you smile the way you do at girls without homes?"

As she put this question sincerely to him, Jinnie reminded the cobbler of a beautiful flower lifting its proud head to the sun. In his experience with young people, he had never seen a girl like this one.

"It makes me happier'n anything!" he replied, cheerfully. "The wonderful part is I wouldn't know about it if I hadn't lost my legs. I'll tell you about it, lass."

Jinnie settled back contentedly.

"A long time ago," began Mr. Grandoken, "God led a bunch of Jews out of a town where a king was torturin' 'em——"

The listener's eyes darkened in sympathy.

"They was made to do a lot of things that hurt 'em; their babies and women, too."

Jinnie leaned forward and covered the horny hand with her slender fingers.

"Have you ever had any babies, Lafe?" she ventured.

A perceptible shadow crossed the man's face.

"Yes," said he hesitatingly. "Me and Peggy had a boy—a little fellow with curly hair—a Jew baby. Peggy always let me call him a Jew baby, though he was part Irish."

"Oh!" gasped Jinnie, radiantly.

"I was a big fellow then, kid, with fine, strong legs, an' nights, when I'd come home, I'd carry the little chap about."

The cobbler's eyes glistened with the memory, but shadowed almost instantly.

"But one day——" he hesitated.

The pause brought an exclamation from the girl.

"And one day—what?" she demanded.

"He died; that's all," and Lafe gazed unseeingly at the snow-covered tracks.

"And you buried him?" asked Virginia, softly.

"Yes, an' the fault was mostly mine, Jinnie. I ain't had no way to make it up to Peggy, but there's lots of to-morrows."

"You'll make her happy then?" ejaculated the girl.

"Yes," said Lafe, "an' I might a done it then, but I wouldn't listen to the voices."

A look of bewildered surprise crossed the girl's face. Were they spirit voices, the voices in the pines, of which Lafe was speaking? She'd ask him.

"God's voices out of Heaven," said he, in answer to her query. "They come every night, but I wouldn't listen, till one day my boy was took. Then I heard another voice, demandin' me to tell folks what was what about God. But I was afraid an' a—coward."

The cobbler lapsed into serious thought, while Virginia moved a small nail back and forth on the floor with the toe of her shoe. She wouldn't cry again, but something in the low, sad voice made her throat ache. After the man had been quiet for a long time, she pressed him with:

"After that, Lafe, what then?"

"After that," repeated the cobbler, straightening his shoulders, "after that my legs went bad an' then—an' then——"

Virginia, very pale, went to the cobbler, and laid her head against his shoulder.

"An' then, child," he breathed huskily, "I believed, an' I know, as well as I'm livin', God sent his Christ for everybody; that in the lovin' father"—Lafe raised his eyes—"there's no line drawed 'tween Jews an' Gentiles. They're all alike to Him. Only some're goin' one road an' some another to get to Him, that's all."

These were quite new ideas to Virginia. In all her young life no one had ever conversed with her of such things. True, from her hill home on clear Sunday mornings she could hear the church bells ding-dong their hoarse welcome to the farmers, but she had never been inside the church doors. Now she regretted the lost opportunity. She wished to grasp the cobbler's meaning. Noting her tense expression, Grandoken continued:

"It was only a misunderstandin' 'tween a few Jews when they nailed the Christ to the cross. Why, a lot of Israelites back there believed in 'im. I'm one of them believin' Jews, Jinnie."

"I wish I was a Jew, cobbler," sighed Jinnie. "I'd think the same as you then, wouldn't I?"

"Oh, you don't have to be a Jew to believe," returned Lafe. "It's as easy to do as 'tis to roll off'n a log."

This lame man filled her young heart with a deep longing to help him and to have him help her.

"You're going to teach me all about it, ain't you, Lafe?" she entreated presently.

"Sure! Sure! You see, it's this way: Common, everyday folks—them with narrer minds—ain't much use for my kind of Jews. I'm livin' here in a mess of 'em. Most of 'em's shortwood gatherers. When I found out about the man on the cross, I told it right out loud to 'em all. ... You're one of 'em. You're a Gentile, Jinnie."

"I'm sorry," said the girl sadly.

"Oh, you needn't be. Peg's one, too, but she's got God's mark on her soul as big as any of them women belongin' to Abraham, Isaac and Jacob——I ain't sure but it's a mite bigger."

The speaker worked a while, bringing the nails from his lips in rapid, even succession. Peg was the one bright spot that shone out of his wonderful yesterdays. She was the one link that fastened him securely to a useful to-morrow.

Virginia counted the nails mechanically as they were driven into the leather, and as the last one disappeared, she said:

"Are you always happy, Lafe, when you're smiling? Why, you smile—when—even when—" she stammered, caught her breath, and finished, "even when Mrs. Peggy barks."

33

An amused laugh came from the cobbler's lips.

"That's 'cause I know her, lass," said he. "Why, when I first found out about the good God takin' charge of Jews an' Gentiles alike, I told it to Peg, an', my, how she did hop up an' down, right in the middle of the floor. She said I was meddlin' into things that had took men of brains a million years to fix up.

"But I knew it as well as anything," he continued. "God's love is right in your heart, right there——" He bent over and gently touched the girl.

She looked up surprised.

"I heard He was setting on a great high throne up in Heaven," she whispered, glancing up, "and he scowled dead mad when folks were wicked."

Lafe smiled, shook his head, and picked up his hammer.

"No," said he. "No, no! He's right around me, an' He's right around you, an' everything a feller does or has comes from Him."

Virginia's thoughts went back to an episode of the country.

"Does He help a kid knock hell out of another kid when that kid is beating a littler kid?"

Her eyes were so earnest, so deep in question, that the cobbler lowered his head. Not for the world would he have smiled at Virginia's original question. He scarcely knew how to answer, but presently said:

"Well, I guess it's all right to help them who ain't as big as yourself, but it ain't the best thing in the world to gad any one."

"Oh, I never licked any of 'em," Jinnie assured him. "I just wanted to find out, that's all."

"What'd you do when other kids beat the littler ones?" demanded the cobbler.

"Just shoved 'em down on the ground and set on 'em, damn 'em!" answered Jinnie.

Lafe raised his eyes slowly.

"I was wonderin' if I dared give you a lesson, lass," he began in a low voice.

"I wish you would," replied Virginia, eagerly. "I'd love anything you'd tell me."

"Well, I was wonderin' if you knew it was wicked to swear?"

Like a shot came a pang through her breast. She had offended her friend.

"Wicked? Wicked?" she gasped. "You say it's wicked to swear, cobbler?"

Lafe nodded. "Sure, awful wicked," he affirmed.

Virginia took a long breath.

"I didn't know it," she murmured. "Father said it wasn't polite, but that's nothing. How is it wicked, cobbler?"

Lafe put two nails into position in the leather sole and drove them deep; then he laid down the hammer again.

"You remember my tellin' you this morning of the man with angels, white angels, hoverin' about the earth helpin' folks?"

34

"Yes," answered Virginia.

"Well, He said it was wicked."

An awe-stricken glance fell upon the speaker.

"Did He tell you so, Lafe?"

"Yes," said Lafe. "It ain't a question of politeness at all, but just bein' downright wicked. See, kid?"

"Yes, cobbler, I do now," Jinnie answered, hanging her head. "Nobody but Matty ever told me nothing before. I guess she didn't know much about angels, though."

"Well," continued Lafe, going back to his story, "God give his little boy Jesus to a mighty good man an' a fine woman—as fine as Peg—to bring up. An' Joseph trundled the little feller about just as I did my little Lafe, an' bye-an'-bye when the boy grew, He worked as his Father in Heaven wanted him to. The good God helped Joseph an' Mary to bring the Christ down face to face with us—Jews an' Gentiles alike."

"With you and me?" breathed Virginia, solemnly.

"With you an' me, child," repeated the cobbler in subdued tones.

Virginia walked to the window and drummed on the pane. Through mere force of habit the cobbler bent his head and caught the tacks between his teeth. He did it mechanically; he was thinking of the future. In the plan of events which Lafe had worked out for himself and Peg, there was but one helper, and each day some new demonstration came to make his faith the brighter. In the midst of his meditation, Jinnie returned to her seat.

"Cobbler, will you do something I ask you?"

"Sure," assented Lafe.

"Get busy trusting Peg'll get the two dollars to-night."

"I have long ago, child, an' she's goin' to get it, too. That's one blessin' about believin'. No one nor nobody can keep you from gettin' what's your own."

"Mrs. Peggy doesn't think that way," remarked Virginia, with keen memories of Mrs. Grandoken's snapping teeth.

"No, not yet, but I'm trustin' she will. You see how 'tis in this shop. Folks is poor around here. I trust 'em all, Jews and Gentiles alike, but Peg thinks I ought to have the money the minute the work's done. But I know no man can keep my money from me, so I soothe her down till she don't whine any more. That's how I know her bark's worser'n her bite. Didn't I tell you about the biscuit?"

"Yes," replied Virginia, "and I hope it'll only be bark about the money; what if she didn't get it?"

"She'll get it," assured Lafe, positively.

Just before bed time Lafe whispered in Jinnie's ear, "Peggy got the two! I told you she would. God's good, child, and we've all got Him in us alike."

And that night, as the air waxed colder and colder, Virginia Singleton, daughter of the rich, slept her tired sleep amid the fighters of the world.

CHAPTER VIII

"EVERY HAND SHALL DO ITS SHARE,"
QUOTH PEG

The fifth day of Jinnie's stay in the cobbler's home crept out of the cold night accompanied by the worst blizzard ever known along the lake. Many times, if it had not been for the protecting overhanging hills, the wood gatherers' huts would have been swept quite away. As it was, Jinnie felt the shack tremble and sway, and doubted its ability to withstand the onslaught.

After breakfast found Lafe and Jinnie conversing interestedly in the shop. The cobbler allowed several bright nails to fall into his palm before he answered the question which was worrying the girl.

"There ain't no use troublin' about it, child," commented he. "We can't starve."

"If I could only work," said Jinnie gloomily, "I bet Peg'd soon like me, because she wouldn't have to go out in the cold at all. But you think it'd be bad for me, eh, Lafe?"

"Well, you couldn't go around to the factories or stores very well," replied Lafe. "You see your uncle's tryin' to trace you. I showed you that this mornin' in the paper, didn't I, where he mourned over you as lost after findin' your father dead?"

Jinnie nodded.

"Yes, I read it," she said.

"An' he can't get your money for seven years. That makes him madder'n a hatter, of course."

"If he'd let me alone, I'd just as soon give him the money," Jinnie said mournfully.

Lafe shook his head.

"The law wouldn't let you, till you was of age. No, sir, you'd either have to die a natural death or—another kind, an' you're a pretty husky young kid to die natural."

"I don't want to die at all," shivered Jinnie.

Lafe encouraged her with a smile.

"If he finds you," pursued Lafe, "I'd have to give you up. I couldn't do anything else. We might pray 'bout it."

A wistful expression came over Jinnie's face.

"Is praying anything like wishing, cobbler?"

"Somethin' the same," replied Mr. Grandoken, "with this difference—wishin' is askin' somethin' out of somewhere of someone you don't know; prayin' is just talkin' to someone you're acquainted with! See?"

"Yes, I think I do," responded the girl. "Your way is mostly praying, isn't it, Lafe?"

"Prayin's more powerful than wishin', lass," said Lafe. "When I was first paralyzed, I done a lot of wishin'. I hadn't any acquaintance with anybody but Peggy. After that I took up with God, an' He's been awful good to me."

"He's been good to me, too, Lafe, bringing me here."

This seemed to be a discovery to Virginia, and for a few minutes her brain was alive with new hopes. Suddenly she drew her chair in front of Grandoken.

"Will to-morrow ever be to-day, cobbler?"

Lafe looked at the solemn-faced girl with smiling, kindly eyes.

"Sure, kid, sure," he asserted. "When you get done wishin' an' there ain't nothin' left in the world to want, then to-morrow's to-day."

Jinnie smiled dismally. "There'd never be a day, cobbler, that I couldn't think of something I'd like for you—and Peg."

Lafe meditated an instant before replying. Then:

"I've found out that we're always happier, kid, when we've got a to-morrow to look to," said he, "'cause when you're just satisfied, somethin's very apt to go smash. I was that way once."

He paused for some seconds.

"Jinnie," he murmured, "I haven't told you how I lost the use of my legs, have I?"

"No, Lafe."

"Well, as I was sayin', there didn't used to be any to-morrow for me. I always lived just for that one day. I had Peg an' the boy. I could work for 'm, an' that was enough. It's more'n lots of men get in this world."

His voice trailed into a whisper and ceased. He was living for the moment in the glory of his past usefulness. The rapt, wrinkled face shone as if it had been touched by angel fingers. Virginia watched him reverently.

"It's more'n two years ago, now," proceeded the cobbler presently, "an' I was workin' on one of them tall uptown buildin's. Jimmy Malligan worked right alongside of me. We was great chums, Jimmy an' me. One day the ropes broke on one of the scaffoldin's—at least, that's what folks said. When we was picked up, my legs wasn't worth the powder to blow 'em up—an' Jimmy was dead. ... But Peg says I'm just as good as ever."

Here Mr. Grandoken took out his pipe and struck a match. "But I ain't. 'Cause them times Peg didn't have to work. We always had fires enough, an' didn't live like this. But, as I was sayin', me an' Peg just kinder lived in to-day. Now, when I hope that mebbe I'll walk again, I'm always measurin' up to-morrow——Peg's the best woman in the world."

Jinnie shivered as a gust of wind rattled the window pane.

"She makes awful good hot mush," she commented.

"Anyhow," went on Lafe, "I was better off'n Jimmy, because he was stone dead. There wasn't any to-day or to-morrow for him, an' I've still got Peggy."

"And this shop," supplemented the girl, glancing around admiringly.

"Sure, this shop," assented Lafe. "I had clean plumb forgot this shop—I mean, for the minute—but I wouldn't a forgot it long."

He knocked the ashes out of his pipe and set to work.

Neither girl nor man spoke for a while, and it wasn't until Lafe heard Peg's voice growling at one of Milly's kittens that he ceased his tick-tack.

"You wouldn't like to join my club, lass, would you?" he ventured.

Jinnie looked up quickly.

"Of course I would," she said eagerly. "What kind of a club is it?"

The girl's faith in the cobbler was so great that if Lafe had commanded her to go into danger, she wouldn't have hesitated.

"Tell me what the club is, Lafe," she repeated.

"Sure," responded Lafe. "Come here an' shake hands! All you have to do to be a member of my club is to be 'Happy in Spite' an' believe everythin' happenin' is for the best."

A mystified expression filled the girl's earnest blue eyes.

"I'm awful happy," she sighed, "and I'm awful glad to come in your club, but I just don't understand what it means."

The cobbler paid no attention for some moments. He was looking out of the window, in a far-away mood, dreaming of an active past, when Jinnie accidentally knocked a hammer from the bench. Lafe Grandoken glanced in the girl's direction.

"I'm happy in spite—" he murmured. Then he stopped abruptly, and his hesitation made the girl repeat:

"Happy in spite?" with a rising inflection. "What does that mean, Lafe?"

Lafe began to work desperately.

"It means just this, kid. I've got a little club all my own, an' I've named it 'Happy in Spite.'" His eyes gathered a mist as he whispered, "Happy in spite of everything that ain't just what I want it to be. Happy in spite of not walkin'—happy in spite of Peg's workin'."

Virginia raised unsmiling, serious eyes to the speaker.

"I want to come in your club, too, Lafe," she said slowly. "I need to be happy in spite of lots of things, just like you, cobbler."

A long train steamed by. Jinnie went to the window, and looked out upon it. When the noise of the engine and the roar of the cars had ceased, she whirled around.

"Cobbler," she said in a low voice, "I've been thinking a lot since yesterday."

"Come on an' tell me about it, lassie," said Lafe.

She sat down, hitching her chair a bit nearer him, leaned her elbow on her knee, and buried a dimpled chin in the palm of her hand.

"Do you suppose, Lafe, if a girl believed in the angels, anybody could hurt her?"

"I know they couldn't, kid, an' it's as true's Heaven."

"Well, then, why can't I go out and work?"

Lafe paused and looked over his spectacles.

"Peggy says, 'Every hand should do its share'," he quoted.

Jinnie winced miserably. She picked up several nails from the floor. It was a pretext for an activity to cover her embarrassment.

38

The cobbler allowed her to busy herself a while in this way. Then he said:

"Sit in the chair an' wrap up in the blankets, Jinnie. I want to talk with you."

She did as she was bidden, sitting quietly until the man chose to speak.

"I guess you're beginnin' to believe," said he, at length, "an' if you do, a world full of uncles couldn't hurt you. Peg says as how you got to work if you stay, an' if you have the faith——"

Jinnie rose tremblingly.

"I know I'll be all right," she cried. "I just know you and me believing would keep me safe."

Her eagerness caused Lafe to draw the girl to him.

"Can you holler good an' loud?" he asked.

The girl shot him a curious glance.

"Sure I can."

"Can you walk on icy walks——"

"Oh, I'm as strong as anything," Jinnie cut in, glancing downward at herself.

"I know a lot of kids who earn money," said Lafe meditatively.

"What do they do?"

"Get wood out of the marsh behind the huts there. Some of 'em keeps families on it."

"Sell wood! And there's lots of it, Lafe?"

"Lots," replied Lafe.

Sell wood! The very words, new, wonderful, and full of action, rang through Jinnie's soul like sweet sounding bells. Waves of unknown sensations beat delightfully upon her girlish heart. If she brought in a little money every day, Peggy would be kinder. She could; she was sure she could. She was drawn from her whirling thoughts by the cobbler's voice.

"Could you do it, kid? People could think your name was Jinnie Grandoken."

Jinnie choked out a reply.

"And mebbe I could make ten cents a day."

"I think you could, Jinnie, an' here's Lafe right ready to help you."

Virginia Singleton felt quite faint. She sat down, her heart beating under her knit jacket twice as fast as a girl's heart ought to beat. Lafe had suddenly opened up a path to usefulness and glory which even in her youthful dreams had never appeared to her.

"Call Peggy," said Lafe.

Soon Peg stood before them, with a questioning face.

"The kid's goin' to work," announced Lafe, "We've got a way of keepin' her uncle off'n her trail."

Mrs. Grandoken looked from her husband to Virginia.

"I want to work like other folks," the girl burst forth, looking pleadingly at the shoemaker's wife.

Peggy wiped her arms violently upon her apron, and there flashed

39

across her face an inscrutable expression that Lafe had learned to read, but which frightened the newcomer.

Oh, how Jinnie wanted to do something to help them both! Now, at this moment, when there seemed a likelihood of being industriously useful, Jinnie loved them the more. She was going to work, and into her active little brain came the sound of pennies, and the glint of silver.

"I want to work, Peggy," she beseeched, "and I'll make a lot of money for you."

"Every hand ought to do its share," observed Peg, stolidly, glancing at the girl's slender fingers. They looked so small, so unused to hard work, that she turned away. An annoying, gripping sensation attacked her suddenly, but in another minute she faced the girl again.

"If you do it, miss, don't flounce round's if you owned the hull of Paradise Road, 'cause it'll be nothin' to your credit, whatever you do. You didn't make yourself."

At the door she turned and remarked, "You've got t'have a shoulder strap to hold the wood, an' you musn't carry too much to onct. It might hurt your back."

"I'll be careful," gulped Jinnie, "and mebbe I could help make the strap, eh, Lafe?"

An hour later Jinnie was running a long needle through a tough piece of leather. She was making the strap to peddle shortwood, and a happier girl never breathed.

Peg watched her without comment as Lafe fitted the strap about her shoulders. In fact, there was nothing for the woman to say, when the violet eyes were fixed questioningly upon her. Peggy thought of the hunger which would be bound to come if any hands were idle, so she muttered in excuse, "There's nothin' like gettin' used to a thing."

"It's a fine strap, isn't it, Lafe?" asked the girl, "It's almost as good as a cart."

"You can't use a cart in the underbrush," explained Lafe. "That's why the twig gatherers use straps."

"I see," murmured Jinnie.

When the cobbler and girl were once more alone together, they had a serious confab. They decided that every penny Jinnie brought in should go to enriching the house, and the girl's eyes glistened as she heard the shoemaker list over the things that would make them comfortable.

Most delightful thoughts came to endow the girl's mental world, which now reached from the cobbler's shop to the marsh, over a portion of the city, and back again. It was rosy-hued, bright, sparkling with the pennies and nickels she intended to earn. All her glory would come with the aid of that twig gatherer's leather strap. She looked down upon it with a proud toss of her head. Jinnie was recovering the independent spirit which had dominated her when she had wandered alone on the hills away to the north.

"I wouldn't wonder if I'd make fifteen cents some days," she remarked later at the supper table.

"If you make ten, you'll be doin' well, an' you and Lafe'll probably bust open with joy if you do," snapped Peg. "Oh, Lord, I'm gettin' sick to my stomick hearin' you folks brag. Go to bed now, kid, if you're to work to-morrow."

Jinnie fell asleep to dream that her hand was full of pennies, and her pockets running over with nickels. She was just stooping to pick up some money from the sidewalk when Peg's voice pierced her ear,

"Kid," said she, "it's mornin', an' your first workin' day. Now hurry your lazy bones an' get dressed."

CHAPTER IX

BY THE SWEAT OF HER BROW

Over the bridge into Paradise Road went the lithe, buoyant figure of a girl, a loose strap hanging from one straight shoulder. Jinnie was radiantly happy, for her first day had netted the family twenty cents, and if Paradise Road had been covered with eggs, she would not have broken many in her flight homeward. If she had been more used to Mrs. Grandoken, she would have understood the peculiar tightening at the corners of the woman's thin lips when she delivered the precious pittance. Virginia searched the other's face for the least sign of approbation. She wished Peg would kiss her, but, of course, she dared not suggest it. To have a little show of affection seemed to Jinnie just then the most desirable thing in the world, but the cobbler's wife merely muttered as she went away to the kitchen, and Virginia, sighing, sat down.

"Now suppose you tell me all about it, Jinnie," Lafe suggested smilingly; "just where you went an' how you earned all the money."

Fatigued almost beyond the point of rehearsing her experiences, Jinnie took Milly Ann on her lap and curled up in the chair.

"I guess I've walked fifteen miles," she began. "You know most folks don't want wood."

Lafe took one sidewise glance at the beautiful face. He remembered a picture he had once seen of an angel. Jinnie's face was like that picture.

"Well, first, Lafe," she recounted, "I gathered the wood in the marsh, then I went straight across the back field through the swamp. It's froze over harder'n hell——"

Lafe uttered a little, "Sh!" and Jinnie, with scarlet face, supplemented,

"I mean harder'n anything."

"Sure," replied Lafe, nodding.

"Mr. Bates and his kids were there, but he c'n carry a pile three times bigger'n I can!"

"Well, you're only a child. Sometimes Bates can't sell all he gets, though."

"I sold all mine," asserted Jinnie, brightening.

The cobbler recalled the history of Jinnie's lonely little life—of how during those first fifteen years no kindly soul had given her counsel, and now his heart glowed with thanksgiving as he realized that she was growing in faith and womanliness. He wanted Jinnie to give credit where credit was due, so he said,

"You sold your wood because you had a helpin' hand."

Jinnie was about to protest.

"I mean——" breathed Lafe.

"Oh, angels! Eh?" interrupted the girl. "Yes, I sold my last two cents' worth by saying what you told me—'He gives His angels charge over thee'— and, zip! a woman bought the last bundle and gave me a cent more'n I charged her."

"Good!" Lafe was highly pleased. "It'll work every time, an' to make a long story short, it works on boots an' shoes, too."

"Wood's awful heavy," Jinnie decided, irrelevantly.

"Sure," soothed Lafe again. He hesitated a minute, drew his hand across his eyes, and continued, "An', by the way, Jinnie——"

Jinnie's receptive face caused the cobbler to proceed:

"I wouldn't have nothin' to do with Bates' son Maudlin, if I was you.... He's a bad lot."

Jinnie's head drooped. She flushed to her hair.

"I saw him to-day," she replied. "He's got wicked eyes. I hate boys who wink!"

A look of desperation clouded the fair young face, and the cobbler, looking at the slender girlish figure, and thinking the while of Maudlin Bates, suddenly put out his hand.

"Come here, lassie," he said.

Another flame of color mounted to Jinnie's tousled hair. With hanging head, she pushed Milly Ann from her lap and walked to the cobbler's side.

"What did Maudlin say to you?" he demanded.

"He said he'd—he'd crack my twigs for me if—if I'd kiss him, and he pinched me when I wouldn't."

Anger and deep resentment displayed themselves on Lafe's pale face.

"Jinnie, lass," he breathed. "I c'n trust you, child. Can't I trust you? You wouldn't——"

Jinnie drew away from Lafe's embrace.

"I guess I'd rather be killed'n have Maudlin kiss me," she cried passionately.

Just then Peg came to the door.

42

"Run to the butcher's for a bit of chopped steak, Jinnie," she ordered, "an' make your head save your heels by bringin' in some bread."

Jinnie jumped up quickly.

"Please use some of my money to buy 'em, Peggy," she begged. "Oh, please do."

Peggy eyed her sternly.

"Kid," she warned. "I want to tell you something before you go any farther in life. You may be smart, but 'tain't no credit to you, 'cause you didn't make yourself. I'm tellin' you this for fear makin' so much money'll turn your head.... Here's your ten cents.... Now go along."

After Jinnie had gone, Mrs. Grandoken sat down opposite her husband.

"The girl looks awful tired," she offered, after a moment's silence.

"She's been earnin' her livin' by the sweat of her brow," replied Lafe, with a wan smile.

"Mebbe she'll get used to it," growled Peg. "Of course I don't like her, but I don't want her hurt. 'Twon't make her sick, will it?"

"No, she's as strong as a little ox. She's got enough strength in her body to work ten times harder, but Peg——" Here Lafe stopped and looked out to the hill beyond the tracks, "but, Peggy, perhaps we c'n find her somethin' else after a while, when there ain't so much fear of her uncle. To make a long story short, Peg, danger of him's the only thing that'll keep the kid luggin' wood."

"I was wonderin'," returned Peg, "if we couldn't get someone interested in 'er—the Kings, mebbe. They're a good sort, with lots of money, an' are more'n smart."

Lafe's eyes brightened visibly, but saddened again. He shook his head.

"We can't get the Kings 'cause I read in the paper last night they're gone away West, to be gone for a year or more.... It's a good idea, though. Someone'll turn up, sure."

"When they do, my man," Peg said quickly, "don't be takin' any credit to yourself, 'cause you hadn't ought to take credit for the plannin' your sharp brains do."

As he shook his head, smiling, she left him quickly and shut the door.

CHAPTER X

ON THE BROAD BOSOM OF THE "HAPPY IN SPITE"

Thus for one year Jinnie went forth in the morning to gather her shortwood, and to sell it in the afternoon.

Peg always gave her a biscuit to eat during her forenoon's work, and Jinnie, going from house to house later, was often presented with a "hunk of pie," as she afterwards told Lafe. If a housewife gave her an apple, she would take it home to the cobbler and his wife.

Late one afternoon, at the close of a bitter day, Jinnie had finished her work and was resting on the door sill of an empty house on an uptown corner.

She drew forth her money in girlish pride. Twenty-seven cents was what she'd earned,—two cents more than any day since she began working. This money meant much to Jinnie. She hadn't yet received a kiss from Mrs. Grandoken, but was expecting it daily. Perhaps when two cents more were dropped into her hand, Peggy might, just for the moment, forget herself and unwittingly express some little affection for her.

With this joyous anticipation the girl recounted her money, retained sufficient change for the dinner meat, and slipped the rest into her jacket pocket. She rose and had started in the direction of the market when a clamor near the bridge made her pause. A crowd of men and boys were running directly toward her. Above their wild shouts could be heard the orders of a policeman, and now and then the frightened cry of a small child.

At first Jinnie noticed only the people. Then her eyes lowered and she saw, racing toward her, a small, black, woolly dog. The animal, making a wild dash for his life, had in his anguish lost his mental balance, for he took no heed as to where he ran nor what he struck. A louder cry of derision rose up from many throats as the small beast scuttled between the legs of a farmer's horse, which gave him a moment's respite from his tormentors.

An instant later they were clamoring again for his unhappy little life. Suddenly he ran headlong into a tree, striking his shaggy head with terrific force. Then he curled up in a limp little heap, just as Jinnie reached him.

Before Maudlin Bates, the leader of the crowd, arrived, the girl had picked up the insensible dog and thrust him under her jacket.

"He's dead, I guess," she said, looking up into the boy's face, "I'll take him to the cobbler's shop and bury him.... He isn't any good when he's dead."

Maudlin Bates grinned from ear to ear, put his hands behind his back, and allowed his eyes to rove over the girl's straight young figure.

"Billy Maybee was tryin' to tie a tin can to his tail," he explained, stuttering, "and the cur snapped at him. We was goin' to hit his head against the wall."

"He's dead now," assured Jinnie once more. "It isn't any use to smash dead dogs."

This reasoning being unanswerable, Maudlin turned grumblingly away.

Jinnie's heart beat loudly with living hope. Perhaps the little dog wasn't dead. Oh, how she hoped he'd live! She stopped half way home, and pushed aside her jacket and peeped down at him. He was still quite limp, and the girl hurried on. She did not even wait to buy the meat nor the bread Peg had asked her to bring in.

As she hurried across the tracks, she saw Grandoken sitting in the window.

He saluted her with one hand, but as she was using both of hers to hold the dog, she only smiled in return, with a bright nod of her head.

Once in the shop, she looked about cautiously.

"I've got something, Lafe," she whispered, "something you'll like."

When she displayed the hurt dog, Lafe put out his hand.

"Is the little critter dead?" he asked solemnly.

"Oh, I hope not!" replied Jinnie, and excitedly explained the episode.

"Lafe took the foundling in his hands, turning the limp body over and over.

"Jinnie, go ask Peg to bring some hot water in a pan," he said. "We'll give the little feller a chanct to live."

Peg came in with a basin of water, stared at the wide-eyed girl and her smiling husband, then down upon the dog.

"Well, for Lord's sake, where'd you get that little beast?" she demanded. "'Tain't livin', is it? Might as well throw it in the garbage pail."

Nevertheless, she put down the basin as she spoke, and took the puppy from her husband. At variance with her statement that the dog might as well be thrown out, she laid him in the hot water, rubbing the bruised body from the top of its head to the small stubby tail. During this process Lafe had unfastened Jinnie's shortwood strap, and the girl, free, dropped upon the floor beside Peg.

Suddenly the submerged body of the pup began to move.

"He's alive, Peg!" cried Jinnie. "Look at his legs a kicking!... Oh, Lafe, he's trying to get out of the water!"

Peg turned sharply.

"If he ain't dead already," she grunted, "you'll kill him hollerin' like that. Anyway, 'tain't no credit to hisself if he lives. He didn't have nothin' to do with his bein' born, an' he won't have nothin' to do with his goin' on livin'. Shut up, now!... There, massy me, he's coming to."

Jinnie squatted upon her feet, while Lafe wheeled his chair a bit nearer. For some moments the trio watched the small dog, struggling to regain consciousness. Then Peggy took him from the water and wrapped him carefully in her apron.

"Lordy, he's openin' his eyes," she grinned, "an' you, girl, you go in there by the fire an' just hold him in your arms. Mebbe he'll come round all right. You can't put him out in the street till he's better."

For the larger part of an hour, Jinnie held the newcomer close to her thumping heart, and when a spasm of pain attacked the shaggy head resting on her arm, she wept in sympathetic agony. Could Peg be persuaded to allow the dog to stay? She would promise to earn an extra penny to buy food for this new friend. At this opportune moment Mrs. Grandoken arrived from the market.

"How's he comin' on?" she asked, standing over them.

"Fine!" replied Jinnie. "And, Peg, he wants to stay."

"Did he tell y' that?" demanded Peg, grimly.

"Well, he didn't say just those words," said the girl, "but, Peggy, if he could talk, he'd tell you how much he loved you——"

"Look a here, kid," broke in Mrs. Grandoken, "that dog ain't goin' to stay around this house, an' you might as well understand it from the beginnin'. I've enough to do with you an' Lafe an' those cats, without fillin' my house with sick pups. So get that notion right out of your noddle!... See?"

Jinnie bowed her head over the sick dog and made a respectful reply.

"I'll try to get the notion out," said she, "but, Peggy, oh, Peggy dear, I love the poor little thing so awful much that it'll be hard for me to throw him away. Will you send him off when he's better, and not ask me to do it?"

Jinnie cocked her pretty head inquiringly on one side, closed one eye, and looked at Peg from the other.

Peggy sniffed a ruse. She came forward, spread her feet a bit, rolling her hands nervously in her apron. She hated an everlasting show of feelings, but sometimes it was difficult for her to crush the emotions which had so often stirred in her breast since the girl came to live with them.

"I might as well tell you one thing right now, Jinnie Grandoken," she said. "You brought that pup into this house an' you'll take him out, or he won't get took; see?"

There was a certain tone in Peg's voice the girl had heard before.

"Then he won't get kicked out 't all, Peg," she said, with a petulant, youthful smile. "I just won't do it! Lafe can't, and if you don't——"

Mrs. Grandoken made a deep noise in her throat.

"You're a sassy brat," said she, "that's what you are! An' if Lafe don't just about beat the life out of you when I tell him about this, I will, with my own hand, right before his eyes. That's what——"

Jinnie interrupted her eagerly. "Lafe won't beat me," she answered, "but I'll let you make me black and blue, Peg, if I can keep the puppy. Matty used to beat me fine, and she was a good bit stronger'n you."

Peggy's eyes drew down at the corners, and her lip quivered.

"Keep him if you want to, imp of Satan, but some day——here, see if the beast'll eat this bit of meat."

Jinnie placed the shivering dog on the floor, and Peg put a piece of

46

meat under his nose. In her excitement, Jinnie rushed away to Lafe. Peg's mumble followed her even through the closed door.

"Cobbler, oh, dear good Lafe," cried the girl, "the dog's living! Peg says I can keep 'im, and I'm goin' to fiddle for him to-night. Do you think he'll forget all about his hurt if I do that, Lafe?"

At that moment, shamed that she had given in to the importunate Jinnie, Mrs. Grandoken opened the shop door, shoving the half wet dog inside.

"Here's your pup, kid," she growled, "an' y'd best keep him from under my feet if you don't want him stepped on."

The cobbler smiled his slow, sweet smile.

"Peg's heart's bigger'n this house," he murmured. "Bring him here, lassie."

The girl, dog in arms, stood at the cobbler's side.

"What're you goin' to name him?" asked Lafe, tenderly.

"I dunno, but he's awful happy, now he's going to stay with us."

"Call 'im 'Happy Pete'," said the cobbler, smiling, "an' we'll take 'im into our club; shall we, kid?"

So Happy Pete was gathered that day into the bosom of the "Happy in Spite."

CHAPTER XI

WHAT HAPPENED TO JINNIE

With a sigh Jinnie allowed Lafe to buckle the shortwood strap to her shoulder. Oh, how many days she had gone through a similar operation with a similar little sigh!

It was a trying ordeal, that of collecting and selling kindling wood, for the men of Paradise Road took the best of the shortwood to be found in the nearer swamp and marsh lands, and oftentimes it was nearly noon before the girl would begin her sale.

But the one real happiness of her days lay in dropping the pennies she earned into Peg's hand.

Now Peggy didn't believe in spoiling men or children, but one morning, as she tied a scarf about Jinnie's neck, she arranged the black curls with more than usual tenderness.

Pausing at the door and looking back at the woman, Jinnie suddenly threw up her head in determination.

"I love you, Peggy," she said, drawing in a long breath. "Give me a little kiss, will you?"

47

There! The cat was out of the bag. In another instant Jinnie would know her fate. How she dared to ask such a thing the girl could never afterwards tell.

If Peg kissed her, work would be easy. If she denied her——Peggy glanced at her, then away again, her eyes shifting uneasily.

But after once taking a stand, Jinnie held her ground. Her mouth was pursed up as if she was going to whistle. Would Peg refuse such a little request? Evidently Peggy would, for she scoffingly ordered.

"Go along with you, kid—go long, you flip little brat!"

"I'd like a kiss awful much," repeated Jinnie, still standing. Her voice was low-toned and pleading, her blue eyes questioningly on Peg's face.

Peg shook her head.

"I won't kiss you 'cause I hate you," she sniffed. "I've always hated you."

Jinnie's eyes filled with tears.

"I know it," she replied sadly, "I know it, but I'd like a kiss just the same because—because I do love you, Peg."

A bit of the same sentiment that had worried her for over a year now attacked Mrs. Grandoken. Her common sense told her to dash away to the kitchen, but a tugging in her breast kept her anchored to the spot. Suddenly, without a word, she snatched the girl close to her broad breast and pressed her lips on Jinnie's with resounding smacks.

"There! There! And there!" she cried, between the kisses. "An' if y' ever tell a soul I done it, I'll scrape every inch of skin off'n your flesh, an' mebbe I'll do something worse, I hate y' that bad."

In less seconds than it takes to tell it, Peg let Jinnie go, and the girl went out of the door with a smiling sigh.

"Kisses 're sweeter'n roses," she murmured, walking to the track. "I wish I'd get more of 'em."

She turned back as she heard Peg's voice calling her.

"You might toddle in an' bring home a bit of sausage," said the woman, indifferently, "an' five cents' worth of chopped steak."

Mrs. Grandoken watched Jinnie until she turned the corner. She felt a strangling sensation in her throat.

A little later she flung the kitchen utensils from place to place, and otherwise acted so ugly and out of temper that, had Lafe known the whole incident, he would have smiled knowingly at the far-off hill and held his peace.

Late in the afternoon Jinnie counted seventeen pennies, one dime and a nickel. It was a fortune for any girl to make, and what was better yet, buckled to her young shoulders in the shortwood strap was almost her next day's supply. As she replaced the money in her pocket and walked toward the market, she murmured gravely,

"Mebbe Peg's kisses helped me to get it, but—but I musn't forget Lafe's prayers."

Her smile was radiant and self-possessed. She was one of the world's

48

workers and loved Lafe and Peg and the world with her whole honest young heart.

"Thirty-two cents," she whispered. "That's a pile of money. I wish I could buy Lafe a posy. He does love 'em so, and he can't get out like Peg and me to see beautiful things."

She stopped before a window where brilliant blossoms were exhibited. Ever since she began to work, one of the desires of Jinnie's soul had been to purchase a flower. As she scrutinized the scarlet and white carnations, the deep red roses, and the twining green vines, she murmured.

"Peg loves Lafe even if she does bark at him. She won't mind if I buy him one. I'll make more money to-morrow."

She opened the door of the shop and drew her unwieldy burden carefully inside. A girl stood back of the counter.

"How much're your roses?" asked Jinnie, nodding toward the window and jingling the pennies in her pocket.

"The white ones're five cents a piece," said the clerk, "and the red ones're ten.... Do y' want one?"

"I'll take a white one," replied the purchaser.

"Shall I wrap it in paper?" asked the other.

"No, I'll carry it this way. I'd like to look at it going home."

The girl passed the rose to Jinnie.

"It smells nice, too," she commented.

"Yes," assented Jinnie, delightedly, taking a whiff.

Then she went on to the meat market to buy the small amount of meat required for the three of them.

One of the men grinned at her from the back of the store, calling, "Hello, kid!" and Maudlin Bates, swinging idly on a stool, shouted, "What's wanted now, Jinnie?" and still another man came forward with the question, "Where'd you get the flower, lass?"

"Bought it," replied Jinnie, leaning against the counter. "I got it next door for the cobbler. He's lame and can't get out."

The market man turned to wait upon her.

"Five cents' worth of chopped meat," ordered Jinnie, "and four sausages."

"Ain't you afraid you'll overload your stomachs over there at the cobbler's shop?" laughed one of the men. "I'll tell you what I'll do, Jinnie ... Do you see that ring of sausage hangin' on that hook?"

The girl nodded wonderingly, looking sidewise at Maudlin.

"Well, if you'll give us a dance, a good one, mind you, still keepin' the wood on your back, I'll buy you the hull string. It'll last a week the way you folks eat meat."

Jinnie's face reddened painfully, but the words appealed to her money-earning spirit, and with a curious sensation she glanced around. Could she dance, with the wondering, laughing, admiring gaze of the men upon her? And Maudlin, too! How she detested his lustful, doltish eyes!

She straightened her shoulders, considering. The wood was heavy,

49

and the strap, bound tightly about her chest and arms, made her terribly tired. But a whole string of sausage was a temptation she could not withstand. In her fertile imagination she could see Lafe nod his approbation, and Peggy joyously frying her earnings in the pan. She might even get three more kisses when no one was looking.

"I don't know what to dance," she said presently, studying the rose in her confusion.

"Oh, just anything," encouraged the man on the stool. "I'll whistle a tune."

"Hand her the sausage, butcher;" sniggered Maudlin, "then she'll be sure of it. The feel of it'll make her dance better."

The speaker grinned as the butcher took the string from the hook. Jinnie slipped the stem of the cobbler's rose between her white teeth, grasped the sausage in one hand and gripped the shortwood strap with the other. Then the man started a rollicking whistle, and Jinnie took a step or two.

Everyone in the place drew nearer. Here was a sight they never had seen—a lovely, shy-eyed, rosy, embarrassed girl, with a load of kindling wood on the strong young shoulders, turning and turning in the center of the market. In one hand she held a ring of sausage, and between her lips a white rose.

"If you'll give us a grand fine dance, lass," encouraged the butcher, "you c'n have the chopped meat, too."

The man's offer sifted through Jinnie's tired brain and stimulated her to quicker action. She turned again, shifting the weight more squarely on her shoulders, her feet keeping perfect time with the shrill, whistling tune.

"Faster! Faster!" taunted Maudlin. "Earn your meat, girl! Don't be a piker!"

Faster and faster whirled Jinnie, the heft of the shortwood carrying her about in great circles. Her cap had fallen from her head, loosing the glorious curls, and her breath whistled past the stem of Lafe's white flower like night wind past a taut wire.

Jinnie forgot everything but the delight of earning something for her loved ones—something that would bring a caress from Lafe. She was sure of Lafe, very sure!

As voices called "Faster!" and still "Faster!" Jinnie let go the shortwood strap to fling aside her curls. Just at that moment she whirled nearer Maudlin Bates, who thrust forth his great foot and tripped her. As she staggered, not one of those watching had sense enough to catch her as she fell. At that moment the door swung open and Peg Grandoken's face appeared. She looked questioningly at the market man.

"I thought I saw Jinnie come in," she hesitated——

Then realizing something was wrong, her eyes fell upon the stricken girl.

"She was just earnin' a little sausage by dancin'," the butcher excused.

50

Peggy stared and stared, stunned for the moment. The hangdog expression on Maudlin's face expressed his crime better than words would have done. Jinnie's little form was huddled against the counter, the shortwood scattered around her, and from her forehead blood was oozing. On the slender arm was the ring of sausage and between her set teeth was Lafe's pale rose. With her outraged soul shining in her eyes, Peggy gathered the unconscious girl in her two strong arms.

"I bet you done it, you damn Maudlin!" she gritted, and without another word, left the market.

Within a few minutes she had laid Jinnie on her bed, and was telling Lafe the pathetic story.

CHAPTER XII

WATCHING

There was absolute quiet in the home of the cobbler for over a week. The house hung heavy with gloom. Jinnie Grandoken was fighting a ghastlier monster than even old Matty had created for her amusement.

Of course Jinnie didn't realize this, but two patient watchers knew, and so did a little black dog. To say that Lafe suffered, as Peggy repeated over and over to him the story of Jinnie's loving act, would be words of small import, and through the night hours, when the cobbler relieved his wife at the sick girl's bed, shapes black and forbidding rose before him, menacing the child he'd vowed to protect.

Could it be that Maudlin Bates had anything to do with Jinnie's fall? Even so, he was powerless to shield her from the young wood gatherer. A more perplexing problem had never faced his paternal soul. After his little son had gone away, there had been no child to love until—and now as he looked at Jinnie, agony surged through him with the memory of that other agony—for she might go to little Lafe.

There came again the stabbing pain born with Peg's tale of the dance. The white rose lay withered in the cobbler's bosom where it had been since his girl had been carried to what the doctor said would in all probability be her deathbed. It was on nights like this that dead memories, with solemn mien, raced from their graves, haunting the lame man. Even Lafe's wonderful portion of faith had diminished during the past few days. He found himself praying mighty prayers that Jinnie would be spared, yet in mental bitterness visualizing her death. Oh, to keep yet a while within the confines of his life the child he loved!

"Let 'er stay, Lord dear, let my Rose o' Paradise stay," Lafe cried out into the shadowy night, time and time again.

Peggy came, as she often did, to wheel him away and order him to bed, but this evening Lafe told Peg he'd rather stay with Jinnie.

"She looks like death," he whispered unnerved.

"She is almost dead," replied the woman grimly.

The doctor entered with silent tread. Stealing to the bed, he put his hand on the girl's brow.

"She's better," he whispered, smilingly. "Look! Damp! Nothing could be a surer sign!"

"May the good God be praised!" moaned Lafe.

Jinnie stirred, lifted her heavy lids, and surveyed the room vacantly. Her glance passed over the medical man as if he were not within the range of her vision. She gazed at Lafe only, with but a faint glimmer of recognition, then on to Peg wavered the sunken blue eyes.

"Drink of water, Peggy dear," she whispered.

Mrs. Grandoken dropped the fluid into the open, parched mouth from a spoon; then she bent low to catch the stammering words:

"Did Lafe like the rose, Peggy, and did you get the ring of sausage?"

Peg glanced at the doctor, a question struggling to her lips, but she could not frame the words.

"Tell her 'yes'," said the man under his breath.

"Lafe just doted on the flower, honey," acknowledged Peggy, bending over the bed, "and I cooked all the sausage, an' we two et 'em. They was finer'n silk.... Now go to sleep; will you?"

"Sure," trembled Jinnie. "Put Happy Pete in my arms, dear."

Mrs. Grandoken looked once more at the doctor. He nodded his head slightly.

So with the dog clasped in her arms, Jinnie straightway fell asleep.

Then Peggy wheeled Lafe away to bed, and as she helped him from the chair, she said:

"I lied to her just now with my own mouth, Lafe. I told her we et them sausages. We couldn't eat 'em 'cause they was all mashed up an' covered with blood."

The cobbler's eyes searched the mottled face of the speaker.

"That kind of lies 're blessed by God in his Heaven, Peg," he breathed tenderly. "A lie lendin' a helpin' hand to a sick lass is better'n most truths."

Before going to bed Peg peeped in at Jinnie. The girl still lay with her arm over the sleeping Pete, her eyes roving round the room. She caught sight of the silent woman, and a troubled line formed between her brows.

"How're you going to get money to live, Peggy?" she wailed. "I'm just beginning to remember about the dance and getting hurt."

Peggy stood a moment at the foot of the bed.

"Lafe's got a whole pocket full o' money," she returned glibly.

"That's nice," sighed the girl in relief.

52

"Shut up now an' go to sleep! Lafe's got enough cash to last a month."

And as the white lids drooped over the violet eyes, Peg Grandoken's guardian angel registered another lie to her credit in the life-book of her Heavenly Father.

CHAPTER XIII

WHAT JINNIE FOUND ON THE HILL

The days rolled on and on, and the first warm impulses of spring brought Jinnie, pale and thin, back to Lafe's side.

She was growing so strong that days when the weather permitted, Peg put a wrap on her, telling her to breathe some color into her cheeks.

For a long time Jinnie was willing to remain quietly on the hut steps where she could see the cobbler whacking away on the torn footwear. She knew that if she looked long enough, he would glance up and smile the smile which always warmed the cockles of her loving heart.

As she grew better, and therefore restless, she walked with Happy Pete along the cinder path beside the tracks. Each day she went a little further than the day before, the spirit of adventure beginning to live again within her. The confines of her narrow world were no longer kept taut by the necessity of selling wood, and to-day it seemed to broaden to the far-away hill from whence the numberless fingers of shadow and sunshine beckoned to the sentimental girl.

She wandered through Paradise Road with the little dog as a companion, and finding her way to the board walk, strolled slowly along.

Wandering up above the city, she discovered a lonely spot snuggled in the hills, and gathering Happy Pete into her arms, she lay down. Over her head countless birds sang in the sunshine, and just below, in the hollow, were squirrels, chattering out their happy existence. Dreamily, through the leaves of the trees, Jinnie watched the white clouds float across the sky like flocks of sheep, and soon the peace of the surrounding world lulled her to rest.

When Happy Pete touched her with his slender tongue, Jinnie sat up, staring sleepily around. At a sound, she turned her head and caught sight of a little boy, whose tangled hair lay in yellow curls on his head.

The sight of tears and boyish distress made Jinnie start quickly toward him, but he seemed so timid and afraid she did not speak.

Suddenly, two slight, twig-scratched arms fluttered toward her, and still without a word Jinnie took the trembling hands into hers. Happy Pete crawled cautiously to the girl's side; then, realizing something unusual, he threw up his black-tipped nose and whined. At the faint howl, the boy's hands quivered violently in Jinnie's. He caught his breath painfully.

"Oh, who're you? Are you a boy or a girl?"

His eyes were touched with an indefinable expression. Jinnie flushed as she scanned for a moment her calico skirt and overhanging blouse. Then with a tragic expression she released her hands, and ran her fingers through her hair. With such long curls did she look like a boy?

"I'm a girl," she said. "Can't you see I'm a girl?"

"I'm blind," said the boy, "so—so I had to ask you."

Jinnie leaned forward and scrutinized him intently.

"You mean," she demanded brokenly, "that you can't see me, nor Happy Pete, nor the trees, nor the birds, nor the squirrels, skipping around?"

The boy bowed his head in assent, but brightened almost instantly.

"No, I can't see those things, but I've got lots of stars inside my head. They're as bright as anything, only sometimes my tears put 'em out."

Then, as if he feared he would lose his new friend, he felt for her hand once more.

Jinnie returned the clinging pressure. For the second time in her life her heart beat with that strange emotion—the protective instinct she had felt for her father. She knew at that moment she loved this little lad, with his wide-staring, unseeing eyes.

"I'm lost," said the boy, sighing deeply, "and I cried ever so long, but nobody would come, and my stars all went out."

"Tell me about your stars," she said eagerly. "Are they sky stars?"

"I dunno what sky stars are. My stars shine in my head lovely and I get warm. I'm cold all over and my heart hurts when they go out."

"Oh!" murmured Jinnie. "I wish they'd always shine."

"So do I." Then lifting an eager, sparkling face, he continued, "They're shinin' now, 'cause I found you."

"Where're your folks?" asked Jinnie, swallowing hard.

"I dunno. I lost 'em a long time ago, and went to live with Mag. She licked me every day, so—I just runned away—I've been here a awful long time."

Jinnie considered a moment before explaining an idea that had slipped into her mind as if it belonged there. She would take him home with her.

"You're going to Lafe's house," she announced presently. "Happy Pete and me and Peg live at Lafe Grandoken's home. Peggy makes bully soup."

"And I'm so hungry," sighed the boy. "Where's the dog I heard barking?"

He withdrew his hands, moving them outward, searching for something. The girl tried to push Pete forward, but the dog only snuggled closer to her.

"Petey, dear, I'm ashamed of you!" she chided lovingly. "Can't you see the little fellow's trying to feel you?"

Then Happy Pete, as if he also were ashamed, came within reach of the wavering hands, and crouched low, to be looked over with ten slender finger tips.

"He's awful beautiful!" exclaimed the boy. "His hair's softer'n silk, and his body's as warm as warm can be."

Jinnie contemplated Happy Pete's points of beauty. Never before had she thought him anything more than a homely, lovable dog, with squat little legs, and a pointed nose. In lightninglike comparison she brought to her mind the things she always considered beautiful—the spring violets, the summer roses, that belt of wonderful color skirting the afternoon horizon, and all the wonders of nature of which her romantic world consisted. The contrast between these and the shaking black dog, with his smudge of tangled hair hanging over his eyes, shocked Jinnie's artistic sense.

"If——if you say he's beautiful, then he is," she stammered almost inaudibly.

"Of course he is! What's your name?"

"Jinnie. Jinnie Grandoken... What's yours?"

"Blind Bobbie, or sometimes just Bobbie."

"Well, I'll call you Bobbie, if you want me to.... I like you awful well. I feel it right in here."

She pressed the boy's fingers to her side.

"Oh, that's your heart!" he exclaimed. "I got one too! Feel it jump!"

Jinnie's fingers pressed the spot indicated by the little boy.

"My goodness," she exclaimed, "it'll jump out of your mouth, won't it?"

"Nope! It always beats like that!"

"Where's your mother?" asked Jinnie after a space.

"I suppose she's dead, or Mag wouldn't a had me. I don't know very much, but I 'member how my mother's hands feel. They were soft and warm. She used to come to see me at the woman's house who died—the one who give me to Mag."

"She must have been a lovely mother," commented Jinnie.

"She were! Mag tried to find her 'cause she said she was rich, and when she couldn't, she beat me. I thought mebbe I'd find mother out in the street. That's why I run away."

Jinnie thought of her own dead father, and the child's halting tale brought back that one night of agony when Thomas Singleton died, alone and unloved, save for herself. She wanted to cry, but instead she murmured, "Happy in Spite," as Lafe had bidden her, and the melting mood vanished. The cobbler and his club were always wonderfully helpful to Jinnie.

"My mother told me onct," Bobbie went on, "she didn't have nothin' to live for. I was blind, you see, and wasn't any good—was I?"

The question, pathetically put, prompted Virginia to fling back a ready answer.

"You're good 'nough for me and Happy Pete," she asserted, "and Lafe'll let you be his little boy too."

The blind child gasped, and the girl continued assuringly, "Peg'll love you, too. She couldn't help it."

"Peg?" queried Bobbie.

"Oh, she's Lafe's wife. Happy Pete and me stay in her house."

The blind eyes flashed with sudden hope.

"Mebbe she'll love me a little! Will she?"

"I hope so. Anyway, Lafe will. He loves everybody, even dogs. He'll love you; sure he will!"

The boy shook his head doubtfully.

"Nobody but mothers are nice to blind kids. Well—well—'cept you. I'd like to go to Lafe's house, though, but mebbe the woman wouldn't want me."

Jinnie had her own ideas about this, but because the child's tears fell hot upon her hands, the mother within her grew to greater proportions. Three times she repeated softly, "Happy in Spite."

"Happy in Spite," she whispered again. Then she sat up with a brilliant smile.

"Of course I'm going to take you to Lafe's. Here at Lafe's my heart's awful busy loving everybody. Now I've got you I'm going to take care of you, 'cause I love you just like the rest. Stand up and let me wipe your nose."

"Let me see how you look, first," faltered the boy. "Where's your face?... I want to touch it!"

His little hands reached and found Jinnie's shoulders. Then slowly the fingers moved upwards, pressing here and there upon the girl's skin, as they traveled in rhythmic motion over her cheeks.

"Your hair's awful curly and long," said he. "What color is it?"

"Color? Well, it's black with purple running through it, I guess. People say so anyway!"

"Oh, yes, I know what black is. And your eyes're blue, ain't they?"

"Yes, blue," assented Jinnie. "I see 'em when I slick my hair in the kitchen glass ... I don't think they're much like yours."

Bobbie paid no heed to the allusion to himself.

"Your forehead's smooth, too," he mused. "Your eyes are big, and the lashes round 'em 're long. You're much prettier'n your dog, but then girls 're always pretty."

A flush of pleased vanity reddened Jinnie's skin to the tips of her ears, and she scrambled to her feet. Then she paused, a solemn expression shadowing her eyes.

"Bobbie," she spoke soberly, "now I found you, you belong to me, don't you?"

Bobbie thrust forth his hands.

"Yes, yes," he breathed.

"Then from now on, from this minute, I'm going to work for you."

Jinnie's thoughts were on the shortwood strap, but she didn't mention it. Oh, how she would work for money to give Peg with which to buy food! How happy she would be in the absolute ownership of the boy she had discovered in the hills! Tenderly she drew him to her. He seemed so pitifully helpless.

"How old 're you?" she demanded.

"Nine years old."

"You don't look over five," said Jinnie, surprised.

"That's because I'm always sick," explained the boy.

Jinnie threw up her head.

"Well, a girl sixteen ought to be able to help an awful little boy, oughtn't she?... Here, I'll put my arm round you, right like this."

But the boy made a backward step, so that Jinnie, thinking he was about to fall, caught him sharply by the arm.

"I'll walk if you'll lead me," Bobbie explained proudly.

Thus rebuffed, Jinnie turned the blind face toward the east, and together they made their way slowly to the plank walk.

CHAPTER XIV

"HE'S COME TO LIVE WITH US, PEGGY"

They trailed along in silence, the girl watching the birds as flock after flock disappeared in the north woods. Now and then, when Jinnie looked at the boy, she felt the pride which comes only with possession. She was going to work for him, to intercede with Peg, to allow the foundling to join that precious home circle where the cobbler and his wife reigned supreme.

As they reached the plank walk, the boy lagged back.

"I'm tired, girl," he panted. "I've walked till I'm just near dead."

He cried quietly as Jinnie led him into the shadow of a tree.

"Sit here with me," she invited. "Lay your head on my arm."

And this time he snuggled to her till the blind eyes and the pursed delicate mouth were hidden against her arm.

"I told you, Bobbie," Jinnie resumed presently, "I'd let you be Lafe's little boy, didn't I?"

"Yes, girl," replied the boy, sleepily.

"Now wasn't that awful good of me?"

"Awful good," was the dreamy answer. "My stars're glory bright now."

"And most likely Lafe'll help you see with your eyes, just like Happy

57

Pete and me!" Jinnie went on eagerly. "All the trees and hundreds of birds, some of 'em yellow and some of 'em red, an' some of 'em so little and cunning they could jump through the knothole in Peg's kitchen.... Don't you wish to see all that?"

The small face brightened and the unseeing eyes flashed upward.

"I'd find my mother, then," breathed Bobbie.

"And you'd see a big high tree, with a robin making his nest in it!... Have y' ever seen that?"

Jinnie was becoming almost aggressive, for, womanlike, with a point to make, each argument was driven home with more power.

"No," Bobbie admitted, and his voice held a certain tragic little note.

"And you've never seen the red running along the edge of the sky, just when the sun's going down?"

Again his answer was a simple negative.

"And hasn't anybody tried to show you a cow and her calf in the country, nipping the grass all day, in the yellow sunshine?"

Jinnie was waxing eloquent, and her words held high-sounding hope. The interest in the child's face invited her to go on.

"Now I've said I'd let my folks be yours, and didn't I find you, and have you got any one else? If you don't let me help you to Lafe's, how you going to see any of 'em?" She paused before delivering her best point, which was addressed quite indifferently to the sky. "And just think of that hot soup!"

This was enough. Bobbie struggled up, flushed and agitated.

"Put your arm around me, girl," which invitation Jinnie quickly accepted.

Then they two, so unlike, went slowly down the walk toward the tracks to Lafe Grandoken's home.

Jinnie's heart vied with a trip-hammer as they turned into Paradise Road. She did not fear the cobbler, but the thought of Peggy's harsh voice, her ruthless catechizing, worried her not a little. Nevertheless, she kept her arm about the boy, steadily drawing him on. When they came to the side door of the house, the girl turned the handle and walked in, leading her weary companion.

Resolutely she passed on to the kitchen, for she wanted the disagreeable part over first. She fumbled in hesitation with the knob of the door, and Peg, hearing her, opened it. At first, the woman saw only Jinnie, with Happy Pete by her side. Then her gaze fell upon the other child, whose blind, entreating eyes were turned upward in supplication.

"This is Bobbie," announced Jinnie, "and he's come to live with us, Peggy."

Poor Peggy stared, surprised to silence. She could find no words to fit the occasion.

"He hasn't any home!" Jinnie gasped for breath in her excitement. "Mag, a woman somewhere, beat him and he ran away and I found 'im. So he belongs to us now."

She was gaining assurance every moment. She hoped that Peggy was

58

silently acquiescing, for the woman hadn't uttered a word; she was merely looking from one to the other with her characteristically blank expression.

"I'm going to give him half of Lafe, too," confided Jinnie, nodding her head toward the waiting child.

Then Peggy burst forth in righteous indignation. She demanded to know how another mouth was to be fed, and clothes washed and mended; where the brat was to sleep, and what good he was anyway.

"Do you think, kid," she stormed at Jinnie, "you're so good yourself we're wantin' to take another one worser off'n you are? Don't believe it! He can't stay here!"

Jinnie held her ground bravely.

"Oh, I'll start right out and sell wood all day long, if you'll let him stay, Peg."

A tousled lock of yellow hair hung over Bobbie's eyes.

"Oh, Peggy, dear, Mrs. Good Peggy, let me stay!" he moaned, swaying. "I'm so tired, s'awful tired. I can't find my mother, nor no place, and my stars're all out!"

Sobbing plaintively, he sank to the floor, and there the childish heart laid bare its misery. Then Jinnie, too, became quite limp, and forgetting all about "Happy in Spite," she knelt alongside of her newly acquired friend, and the two despairing young voices rose to the woman standing over them. Jinnie thrust her arms around the little boy.

"Don't cry, my Bobbie," she sobbed. "I'll go back to the hills with you, because you need me. We'll live with the birds and squirrels, and I'll sell wood so we c'n eat."

When she raised her reproachful eyes to Peg, and finished with a swipe at her offending nose with her sleeve, she had never looked more beautiful, and Peggy glanced away, fearing she might weaken.

"Tell Lafe I love him, and I love you, too, Peggy. I'll come every day and see you both, and bring you some money."

If she had been ten years older or had spent months framing a speech to fit the need of this occasion, Jinnie could not have been more effective, for Peg's rage entirely ebbed at these words.

"Get up, you brats," she ordered grimly. "An' you listen to me, Jinnie Grandoken. Your Bobbie c'n stay, but if you ever, so long as you live, bring another maimed, lame or blind creature to this house, I'll kick it out in the street. Now both of you climb up to that table an' eat some hot soup."

Jinnie drew a long breath of happiness. She had cried a little, she was sorry for that. She had broken her resolve always to smile—to be "Happy in Spite."

"I'll never bring any one else in, Peg," she averred gratefully.

Then she remembered how sweeping was her promise and changed it a trifle.

"Of course if a kid was awful sick in the street and didn't have a home, I'd have to fetch it in, wouldn't I?"

Peggy flounced over to the table, speechless, followed by the two children.

CHAPTER XV

"WHO SAYS THE KID CAN'T STAY?"

Twenty minutes later Mrs. Grandoken entered the shop and sat down opposite her husband.

"Lafe," she began, clearing her throat.

The cobbler questioned her with a glance.

"That girl'll be the death of this hull shanty," she announced huskily. "I hate 'er more'n anything in the world."

Lafe placed a half-mended shoe beside him on the bench.

"What's ailin' 'er now, Peggy?"

"Oh, she ain't sick," interrupted Peg, with curling lip. "She never looked better'n she does this minute, settin' in there huddlin' that pup, but she's brought home another kid, as bad off as a kid can be."

"A what? What'd you say, Peg? You don't mean a youngster!"

Mrs. Grandoken bobbed her head, her face stoically expressionless. "An' bad off," she repeated querulously. "The young 'un's blind."

Before Lafe's mental vision rose Jinnie's lovely face, her parted lips and self-assured smile.

"But where'd she get it? It must belong to some 'un."

Mrs. Grandoken shook her head.

"I dunno. It's a boy. He was with a woman—a bad 'un, I gather. She beat 'im until the little feller ran away to find his own folks, he says—and—Jinnie brought 'im home here. She says she's goin' to keep 'im."

The speaker drew her brown skin into a network of wrinkles.

"Where'd she find 'im?" Lafe burst forth, "Of course he can't stay——"

Mrs. Grandoken checked the cobbler's words with a rough gesture.

"Hush a minute! She got 'im over near the plank walk on the hill—he was cryin' for 'is ma."

Lafe was plainly agitated. He felt a spasmodic clutch at his heart when he imagined the sorrow of a homeless, blind child, but thinking of Peg's struggle to make a little go a long way, he dashed his sympathy resolutely aside.

"Of course he can't stay—he can't!" he murmured. "It ain't possible for you to keep 'im here."

In his excitement Lafe bent forward and closed his hands over Peg's massive shoulder bones. Peggy coughed hoarsely and looked away.

"Who says the kid can't stay?" she muttered roughly. "Who said he can't?"

The words jumped off the woman's tongue in sullen defiance.

"But you got too much to do now, Peg. We've made you a lot of trouble, woman dear, an' you sure don't want to take another——"

Like a flash, Peg's features changed. She squinted sidewise as if a strong light suddenly hurt her sight.

"Who said I didn't?" she drawled. "Some husbands do make me mad, when they're tellin' me what I want, an' what I don't want. I hate the blind brat like I do the girl, but he's goin' to stay just the same."

A deep flush dyed Lafe's gray face. The intensity of his emotion was almost a pain. Life had ever vouchsafed Lafe Grandoken encouragement when the dawn was darkest. Now Peg's personal insult lined his clouds of fear with silver, and they sailed away in rapid succession as quickly as they had come; he saw them going like shadows under advancing sun rays.

"Peggy," he said, touching her gently, "you've the biggest heart in all the world, and you're the very best woman; you be, sure! If you let the poor little kid stay, I'll make more money, if God gives me strength."

Peggy pushed Lafe's hand from her arm.

"I 'spose if you do happen to get five cents more, you'll puff out with pride till you most bust.... Anyway, it won't take much more to buy grub for a kid with an appetite like a bird.... Come on! I'll wheel you to the kitchen so you can have a look at 'im."

Jinnie glanced around as the husband and wife entered the room. She pushed Happy Pete from her lap and got up.

"Lafe," she exclaimed, "this is Bobbie—he's come to live with us."

She drew the blind boy from his chair and went forward.

"Bobbie," she explained, "this is the cobbler. I told you about him in the park. See 'im with your fingers once, and you'll know he's the best man ever."

The small boy lifted two frail arms, his lips quivering in fright and homesickness. Some feeling created by God rose insistent within Lafe. It was a response from the heart of the Good Shepherd, who had always gathered into his fold the bruised ones of the world. Lafe drew the child to his lap.

"Poor little thing!" he murmured sadly.

With curling lips, his wife stood watching the pair.

"You're a bigger fool'n I thought you was, Lafe Grandoken," she said, turning away sharply. "I wouldn't make such a fuss over no one livin'. That's just what I wouldn't."

She threw the last remark over her shoulder as if it were something she spurned and wanted to be rid of.

Bobbie slipped from Lafe's arms and described a zigzag course across the kitchen floor toward the place where Mrs. Grandoken stood. His hands fluttered over Peg's dress, as high as they could reach.

"I like you awful well, Mrs. Peggy," he told her, "and I just love your kisses, too, Mrs. Peggy dear. They made my stars shine all over my head."

The cobbler's wife started guiltily, casting her eyes upon Lafe. He was silent, his patient face expressing melancholy sweetness. As far as the woman could determine, he had not heard the boy's words. Relieved, she allowed her eyes to rest upon Jinnie. The girl was looking directly at her. Then Jinnie slowly dropped one white lid over a bright, gleeful blue eye in a wicked little wink. This was more than Peggy could endure. She had kissed the little boy several times during the process of washing the tear-stained face and combing the tangled hair, but that any one should know it! Just then, Peggy secretly said to herself, "If uther one of them kids get any more kisses from me, it'll be when water runs uphill. I 'spose now I'll never hear the last of them smacks."

"Let go my skirt! Get away, kid," she ordered Bobbie.

The boy dropped his hands reluctantly. He had hoped for another kiss.

"Peggy," said Lafe, "can I hold him? He seems so sad."

Mrs. Grandoken, consciously grim, placed the boy in her husband's lap.

"You see," philosophized Jinnie, when she and the blind child were with the cobbler, "if a blind kid hasn't any place to live, the girl who finds 'im has to bring him home! Huh, Lafe?"

Then she whispered in his ear, "Couldn't Bobbie join the 'Happy in Spite'?"

"Sure he can, lass; sure he can," assented Lafe.

Jinnie whirled back to the little boy.

"Bobbie, would you like to come in a club that'll make you happy as long's you live?"

The bright blind eyes of the boy flashed from Jinnie to the man, and he got to his feet tremulously. In his little mind, out of which daylight was shut, Jinnie's words presaged great joy. The girl took his hand and led him to the cobbler.

"You'll have to explain the club to 'im, Lafe," she said.

"Yes, 'splain it to me, Lafe dearie," purred Bobbie.

"It's just a club," began Lafe, "only good to keep a body happy. Now, me—well, I'm happy in spite a-havin' no legs; Jinnie there, she's happy in spite a-havin' no folks. Her and me's happy in spite a everything."

Bobbie stood alongside Lafe's bench, one busy set of fingers picking rhythmically at the cobbler's coat, the other having sought and found his hand.

"I want to be in the club, cobbler," he whispered.

Mr. Grandoken stooped and kissed the quivering face.

"An' you'll be happy in spite a havin' no eyes?" he questioned.

The little boy, pressing his cheek against the man's arm, cooed in delight.

"And happy in spite of not finding your mother right yet?" interjected Jinnie.

"Yes, yes, 'cause I am happy. I got my beautiful Peggy, ain't I? And don't she make me a hull lot of fine soup, and ain't I got Lafe, Happy Pete."

"You got me, too, Bobbie," Jinnie reminded him gently.

Bobbie acquiesced by a quick bend of his head, and Lafe grasped his hand.

"Now you're a member of the 'Happy in Spite', Bob," said he smiling. "This club is what I call a growin' affair. Four members——"

62

"Everybody's in," burst forth Jinnie.

"Except Peggy," sighed Lafe. "Someday something'll bring her in, too."

CHAPTER XVI

JINNIE'S EAR GETS A TWEAK

Bobbie had been at the Grandoken home scarcely a week before Jinnie again got into difficulty. One morning, wide-awake, beside the blind boy, she happened to glance toward the door. There stood Peg, her face distorted by rage, staring at her with terrible eyes. Jinnie sat up in a twinkling.

"What is it, Peggy, dear?" she faltered. "What have I done now?"

Without reply, Peggy marched to the bed and took the girl by the ear. In this way she pulled her to the floor, walking her ahead of her to the kitchen.

"I don't know what I've done, Peggy," repeated Jinnie, meekly.

"I'll show you. You'll know, all right, miss! Now if you've eyes, squint down there!"

She was pointing to the floor, and as the room was rather dark, Jinnie at first could discern nothing. Then as her eyes became accustomed to the shadows, she saw——

"Oh, what is it, Peggy? Oh, my! Oh, my!"

Peggy gave her a rough little shake.

"I'll tell you what, Jinnie Grandoken, without any more ado. Well, they're cats, just plain everyday cats! Another batch of Miss Milly Ann's kits, if y' want to know. They can't stay in this house, miss, an' when I say a thing, I mean it! My word's law in this shanty!"

She was still holding the girl's ear, and suddenly gave it another tweak. Jinnie pulled this tender member from Peggy's fingers with a delighted little chuckle.

"Peggy darling, aren't they sweet? Oh, Peggy——"

"Ain't they sweet?" mimicked Peggy. "They're just sweet 'nough to get chucked out. Now, you get dressed, an' take 'em somewhere. D' you hear?"

Jinnie wheeled about for another tug of war. It was dreadful how she had to fight with Peggy to get her own way about things like this. First with Happy Pete, then with Bobbie, and now—to-day—with five small kittens, not one of them larger than the blind child's hand. She looked into

Mrs. Grandoken's face, which was still grim, but Jinnie decided not quite so grim as when the woman appeared at her bedroom door.

"I suppose you'll go in an' honey round Lafe in a minute, thinkin' he'll help you keep 'em," said Mrs. Grandoken. "But this time it won't do no good."

"Peggy!" blurted Jinnie.

"Shut your mouth! An' don't be Peggyin' me, or I'll swat you," vowed Peg.

The woman glared witheringly into a pair of beseeching blue eyes.

"Get into your clothes, kid," she ordered immediately, "then you—"

"Then I'll come back, dear," gurgled Jinnie, "and do just what you want me to." Then with subtle modification, she continued, "I mean, Peg, I'll do just what you want me to after I've talked about it a bit... Oh, please, let me give 'em one little kiss apiece."

Peggy flounced to the stove.

"Be a fool an' kiss 'em if you want to... I hate 'em."

In the coarse nightdress Peggy had made for her, Jinnie sat down beside Milly Ann. The yellow mother purred in delight. She'd brought them five new babies, and no idea entered her mother heart that she would have to part with even one.

Out came the kittens into the girl's lap, and one by one they were tenderly lifted to be kissed. Both Peggy and the kisser were silent while this loving operation was in process. Then Jinnie, still sitting, looked from Milly Ann to Peggy.

"I guess she's awful fond of her children, don't you, Peg?"

Peggy didn't answer.

"You see it's like this, Peg——"

"Didn't I tell you not to Peggy me?"

"Then it's like this, darling," drawled Jinnie, trying to be obedient.

"An' you needn't darlin' me nuther," snapped Peggy.

Jinnie thought a minute.

"Then it's like this, honey bunch," she smiled again.

Peg whirled around on her.

"Say, you kid——"

"Wait, dearie!" implored Jinnie. "Don't you know mother cats always love their kitties just like live mothers do their babies?"

Peggy rattled the stove lids outrageously. Hearing these words, she stopped abruptly. Who knows where her thoughts flew? Jinnie didn't, for sure, but she thought, by the sudden change of Mrs. Grandoken's expression, she could guess.

The woman looked from Milly Ann to the wriggling kittens in Jinnie's lap, then she stooped down and again brought to view Jinnie's little ear tucked away under the black curls.

"Get up out o' here an' dress; will you? I've said them cats've got to go, and go they will!"

Jinnie returned the kittens to their mother, and when she got back to her room, Bobbie was sitting up in bed rubbing his eyes.

64

"I couldn't find you, girl," he whimpered. "I felt the bed over and you was gone."

Jinnie bent over him.

"Peg took me out in the kitchen, dear... What do you think, Bobbie?"

Bobbie began to tremble.

"I got to go away from here ... eh?"

"Mercy, no!" laughed Jinnie. "Milly Ann's got a lot of new babies."

Bobbie gave a delighted squeal.

"Now I'll have something else to love, won't I?" he gurgled.

Jinnie hoped so! But she hadn't yet received Peg's consent to keep the family, so when the little boy was dressed and she had combed her hair and dressed herself, they went into the shop, where the cobbler met them with a smile.

"Peg's mad," Jinnie observed with a comprehensive glance at Mr. Grandoken.

"Quite so," replied Lafe, grinning over the bowl of his pipe. "She had frost on her face a inch thick when she discovered them cats. I thought she'd hop right out of the window."

"She says I must throw 'em away," ventured Jinnie.

"Cluck! Cluck!" struck Lafe's tongue against the roof of his mouth, and he smiled. Jinnie loved that cluck. It put her in mind of the Mottville mother hens scratching for their chickens.

"Hain't she ever said anything like that to you before, lass?" the cobbler suggested presently.

"She said it about me," piped in Bobbie.

"An' about Happy Pete, too," added Lafe.

"I bet I keep 'em," giggled Jinnie.

"I'll bet with you, kid," said the cobbler gravely.

"I want to see 'em!" Bobbie clamored with a squeak.

But he'd no more than made the statement before the door burst violently open and Peg stood before them. Her apron was gathered together in front, held by one gripping hand; something moved against her knees as if it were alive. In the other hand was Milly Ann, carried by the nape of her neck, hanging straight down at the woman's side, her long yellow tail dragging on the floor. The woman looked like an avenging angel.

"I've come to tell you folks something," she imparted in a very loud voice. "Here's this blasted ragtail, that's went an' had this batch of five cats. Now I'm goin' to warn y' all——"

Bobbie interrupted her with a little yelp.

"Let me love one, Peggy, dear," he begged.

"I'm goin' to warn you folks," went on Peg, without heeding the child's interjection, "that—if—you don't want their necks wrung, you'd better keep 'em out of my way."

Saying this, she dropped the mother cat with a soft thud, and without looking up, dumped the kittens on top of her, and stalked out of the room.

65

When Jinnie appeared five minutes later in the kitchen with a small kitten in her hand, Peg was stirring the mush for breakfast.

"You hate the kitties, eh, Peg?" asked Jinnie.

The two tense wrinkles at the corners of Mrs. Grandoken's mouth didn't relax by so much as a hair's line.

"Hate 'em!" she snapped, "I should say I do! I hate every one of them cats, and I hate you, too! An' if y' don't like it, y' can lump it. If the lumps is too big, smash 'em."

"I know you hate us, darling," Jinnie admitted, "but, Peg, I want to tell you this: it's ever so much easier to love folks than to hate 'em, and as long as the kitties're going to stay, I thought mebbe if you kissed 'em once—" Then she extended the kitten. "I brought you one to try on."

"Well, Lord-a-massy, the girl's crazy!" expostulated Peg. "Keep the cats if you're bound to, you kid, but get out of this kitchen or I'll kiss you both with the broom."

Jinnie disappeared, and Peggy heard a gleeful laugh as the girl scurried back to the shop.

CHAPTER XVII

JINNIE DISCOVERS HER KING'S THRONE

Two years and almost half of another had passed since Jinnie first came to live with Lafe and Peggy Grandoken. These two years had meant more to her than all the other fifteen in her life. Lafe, in his kindly, fatherly way, daily impressed upon her the need of her studying and no day passed without planting some knowledge in the eager young mind.

Her mornings were spent gathering shortwood, her afternoons in selling it, but the hours outside these money-earning duties were passed between her fiddle and her books. The cobbler often remarked that her mumbling over those difficult lessons at his side taught him more than he'd ever learned in school. Sometimes when they were having heart-to-heart talks, Jinnie confided to him her ambitions.

"I'd like to fiddle all my life, Lafe," she told him once. "I wonder if people ever made money fiddling; do they, Lafe?"

"I'm afraid not, honey," he answered, sadly.

"But you like it, eh, Lafe?"

"Sure!... Better'n anything."

One day in the early summer, when there was a touch of blue mist in the clear, warm air, Jinnie wandered into the wealthy section of the town, hoping thereby to establish a new customer or two.

Maudlin Bates had warned her not to enter his territory or to trespass upon his part of the marshland, and for that reason she had in the past but turned longing eyes to the hillside besprinkled with handsome homes.

But Lafe replied, when she told him this, "No section belongs to Maudlin alone, honey.... Just go where you like."

She now entered a large open gate into which an automobile had just disappeared, and walked toward the house.

She paused to admire the exterior of the mansion. On the front, the porches were furnished with rocking chairs and hammocks, but no person was in sight. She walked around to the back, but as she was about to knock, a voice arrested her action.

"Do you want to see somebody?"

She turned hastily. There before her was her King, the man she had met on that memorable night more than two years before. He doffed his cap smiling, recognizing her immediately, and Jinnie flushed to the roots of her hair, while the shortwood strap slipped slowly from her shoulders.

"Ah, you have something to sell?" he interrogated.

Jinnie's tongue clove to the roof of her mouth. She had never completely forgotten him, and his smile was a delightful memory. Now as he watched her quizzically, all her former admiration returned.

"Well, well," laughed the man, "if this isn't my little violin girl. It's a long time since I saw you last.... Do you love your music as much as ever?"

Her first glance at him brought the flushing consciousness that she was but a shortwood gatherer; the strap and its burden placed a great barrier between them. But his question about the fiddle, her fiddle, placed her again on equal footing with him. She permitted herself to smile.

"I play every day. My uncle loves it, but my aunt doesn't," she answered naïvely.

"And you're selling wood?"

"Yes, I must help a little."

She made the assertion proudly, offering no excuse for her chosen trade.

"And this is all for sale?" indicating the wood.

"Yes," said Jinnie, looking down upon it.

"I'll take it all," Theodore offered, putting his hand into his pocket. "How much do you want for it?"

The girl gave him a puzzled glance. "I don't just know, but I wish——I wish I could give it to you without any pay."

She moved a little closer and questioned eagerly:

"Won't you please take it?"

An amused expression crossed the man's handsome face.

"Of course not, my child," he exclaimed. "That wouldn't be business. I want to buy it.... How about a dollar?"

Jinnie gasped. A dollar, a whole dollar! She made but little more during an entire week; she had made less. A dollar would buy——Then a thought flashed across her mind.

"I couldn't take a dollar," she refused, "it's too much. It's only worth about twenty cents."

"But if I choose to give you a dollar?" pursued the man.

Again the purple black curls shook decidedly.

"I couldn't take more'n it's worth. My uncle wouldn't like me to. He says all we can expect in this world's our own and no more. Twenty cents is all."

Mr. King studied her face, thoughtfully.

"I've an idea, a good one. Now what do you say to furnishing me wood every morning, say at fifty cents a day. We use such a lot! You could bring a little more if you like or—or come twice."

Jinnie could scarcely believe she'd heard aright. Unshed tears dimmed her eyes.

"I wouldn't have to peddle to anyone else, then, would I?" she stammered.

"No! That's just what I meant."

Then the tears welled over the drooping lids and a feeling of gratitude surged through the girl's whole being. Fifty cents a day! It was such a lot of money—as much as Lafe made five days out of six.

Jinnie sent the man a fleeting glance, meeting his smiling eyes with pulsing blood.

"I'd love to do it," she whispered gratefully. "Then I'd have a lot of time to—to—fiddle."

Mr. King's hand slipped into his pocket.

"I'll pay you fifty cents for to-day's wood," he decided, "and fifty for what you're going to bring to-morrow. Is that satisfactory?"

As if in a dream, Jinnie tumbled out the contents of the shortwood strap. As she took the money from Mr. King's hand, his fingers touched hers; she thrilled to the tips of her curls. Then she ran hastily down the long road, only turning to glance back when she reached the gate. Mr. King stood just where she had left him, and was looking after her. He raised his cap, and Jinnie, with burning face, fled on again.

She wondered what Lafe would say about her unexpected good fortune. She would tell him first, before she saw Peggy. She imagined how the sweet smile would cross his lips, and how he would put his arm gently around her.

Lafe heard her open the side door and called,

"Come in, honey!... Come on in."

She entered after one hasty glance proved the cobbler was alone.

"You sold quick to-day, lass," said he, holding out his hand.

Jinnie had planned on the way home to make great rehearsing of Theodore King's kindness, but in another instant she broke forth:

"Lafe, Lafe! I've got something to tell you! Oh, a lovely something! I sold all the wood to one man, and I'm going to take him a load every day, and get fifty cents for it. Regular customer, Lafe!... Here's a dollar for Peg."

Lafe did just what Jinnie expected he would, slipped an arm about her waist.

"The good God be praised!" he ejaculated. "Stand here an' tell me all about it."

"It was Mr. King——"

"Theodore King?" asked Lafe. "Why, he's the richest man in town. He owns the iron works."

Jinnie nodded. "Yes! He's the one I played for in the train when I first came here. You remember my telling you, Lafe? And he wants wood every day from me. Isn't it fine?"

"'Tis so!" affirmed Lafe. "Jinnie, lass, them angels come in shapes of human bein's—mostly so. Now go tell Peggy. It'll take a load off'n her heart."

As Jinnie told her story to Mrs. Grandoken and handed her the money, the woman's lips twitched at the corners, but she only said, warningly:

"Don't get a swelled head over your doin's, lass, for a brat ain't responsible for her own smartness."

One morning, about a week afterward, Jinnie rapped at the back door of the King mansion.

"Is Mr. King in?" she asked timidly of the servant.

The girl stared hard at the flushed, pretty face.

"He's in, but you can leave the wood if you want to."

"No," refused Jinnie. "I want to see him."

The maid turned away, grumbling, and Jinnie backed from the door with bated breath.

Mr. King appeared immediately, seemingly embarrassed. He took both her hands.

"Why, my dear child!" he exclaimed. "I'd completely forgotten to leave the money for the wood, and you've been bringing it every day."

"Peggy made the dollar go a long ways—that and Lafe's money. We didn't need any till to-day.... So—so I asked for you."

"I'm glad you did," responded King, counting and giving her the money.

Then his glance fell upon the bulging shortwood strap.

"I'm afraid you carry too much at a time," he admonished, gravely. "You mustn't do that."

Jinnie dropped her eyes.

"I was talking to my uncle about it," she explained embarrassedly, "and he thought same's I, that you were paying too much for that little wood. I'm goin' to bring more after this."

"I'm satisfied, though, and I can't have you hurting yourself by being too strenuously honest.... I might—yes, I will! I'll send for you every day or every other——"

Jinnie's eyes lighted up with happiness.

"Oh, sir,——" she began entreatingly.

"Wait——" said Mr. King. "It's this way! If you brought it up here in one of my cars, it would save a lot of your time, and you wouldn't have to come every day."

"I could fiddle more," Jinnie blurted radiantly. She remembered how sympathetically he had listened to her through the blizzard. He liked the fiddle! She went a little nearer him. "I'm trying to make a tune different from any I've ever done, and I can't always play well after lugging shortwood all day.... I'd love to deliver it the way you said."

King stood gazing at her. How strangely beautiful she was! Something in the wind-browned face stirred his heart to its depths.

"Then that's settled," he said kindly. "You tell me where to have my man and what time, and to-morrow he'll meet you."

Jinnie thought a moment.

"I wonder if he knows where Paradise Road ends near the edge of the marsh."

"He could find it, of course."

"There's a path going into the marsh right at the end of the road. I'll meet him there to-morrow at twelve o'clock, and—and I'm so much obliged to you."

When Jinnie told Lafe of the new arrangement, she gurgled with joy.

"Lafe, now I'll make that tune."

"Yes, honey," murmured Lafe contentedly. "Now get your fiddle and practice; after that you c'n study a while out of that there grammar book."

CHAPTER XVIII

RED ROSES AND YELLOW

The days went on peacefully after the new arrangements for the shortwood. Every other day, at twelve o'clock, one of Theodore King's cars waited for Jinnie at the head of the path leading into the marsh.

When the weather was stormy, Bennett, the chauffeur, took the wood, telling Jinnie to run along home.

All this made it possible for Jinnie to study profitably during the warm months, and by the last of August she had mastered many difficult subjects. Lafe helped her when he could, but often shook his head despondently as she sat down beside him on the bench, asking his advice.

"The fact is, honey, I ain't got much brains," he said to her one afternoon. "If I hung by my neck till I could see through them figures, I'd be as dead as Moses."

One Thursday morning, as she climbed into the big car with her load, Bennett said,

"I ain't goin' to pay you this mornin'! The boss'll do it. Mr. King wants to see you."

Jinnie nodded, her heart pounding.

It was delightful to contemplate seeing him once more. She wondered where he had been all these days and if he had thought of her. Jinnie's pulses were galloping along like a race horse. She stood quietly until the master was called, and he came quickly without making her wait.

"I'm going to ask you to do me a favor," he said, coming forward, holding out his hand.

Now when Jinnie first heard that he wished to see her, she thought her heart could beat no faster, but his words made that small organ tattoo against her sides like the flutter of a bird's wing in fright. She could do something for him! Oh, what joy! What unutterable joy!

"We're going to have some friends here Sunday evening——"

The sudden upfling of Jinnie's head cut off his words.

What difference would his having friends make to her? Oh, yes, they wanted more wood. How gladly she would get it for him; search all day for the driest pieces if he needed them!

"I was wondering," proceeded Mr. King, "if you would come here with your violin and play for—for—us?"

Jinnie's knees relaxed and she staggered back against the wall.

"You musn't feel embarrassed about it," he hurried on. "I'd be very much indebted to you if you thought you could."

Tears were so perilously near Jinnie's lids that some of them rolled into her throat. To regain her self-possession enough to speak, she swallowed several times in rapid succession. Such a compliment she'd never been paid before. She brought her hands together appealingly, and Mr. King noticed that his request had heightened her color.

"I'd love to do it," she breathed.

"Of course I'll pay you for it," he said, not able to think of anything else,

"I couldn't take any money for fiddling," replied Jinnie. "But I'll come. Lafe says money can't be made that way."

She turned to go, but Mr. King detained her.

"Wait a minute," he insisted. "I want to tell you something! You've a great gift—a wonderful genius—and out of such genius much money is made.... I couldn't think of letting you come here unless you allowed me to remunerate you."

Jinnie listened attentively to all he said, but refusal was still in her steady gaze. Mr. King, seeing this, continued quickly:

"I want you very much, but on that one point I must have my way. I shall give you twenty-five dollars for playing three pieces."

Then Jinnie thought she was going to faint. Twenty-five dollars! It was a fortune—a huge fortune! But she couldn't take money for playing tunes that came from her heart—tunes that were a part of herself the same as her hands or feet. But before she could offer another argument, the man finished hurriedly:

71

"It's settled now. You're to come here Sunday night at eight. I'll send for you."

Lafe was sitting at the window as she ran through the shortcut along the tracks. Her curls were flying in the wind, her cheeks glowing with flaming color. Every day the cobbler loved her more, for in spite of the dark soil in which Jinnie thrived, she grew lovelier in spirit and face.

He waved his hand to her, and both of her arms answered his salute. When the door burst open, Lafe put down his hammer expectantly. Before he could speak, she was down upon her knees at his side, her curly head buried in his loving arms, and tears were raining down her face.

Lafe allowed her to cry a few moments. Then he said:

"Something's hurt my lassie's heart.... Somebody!... Was it Maudlin?"

Through the tears shone a radiant smile.

"I'm crying for joy, Lafe," she sobbed. "I'm going to play my fiddle at Mr. King's house and make twenty-five dollars for three tunes."

Lafe's jaws dropped apart incredulously.

"Twenty-five dollars for playin' your fiddle, child?"

Jinnie told all that had happened since leaving home.

Then Peggy had to be told, and when the amount of money was mentioned and Jinnie said:

"It'll all be yours, Peggy, when I get it,"

Mrs. Grandoken grunted:

"You didn't make your insides, lassie. It ain't to your credit you can fiddle, so don't get stuck up."

Jinnie laughed gaily and went to the kitchen, where for two hours, with Bobbie curled up in the chair holding Happy Pete, she brought from the strings of the instrument she loved, mournful tunes mingled with laughing songs, such as no one in Bellaire had ever heard.

Over and over, as Lafe listened, he wondered where and how such music could be born in the child—for Jinnie, to the lame cobbler, would always be a little, little girl.

Later Jinnie went to the store, and when Peggy had watched her cross the street, she sat down in front of her husband.

"Lafe," she said, "what's the kid goin' to wear to King's?... She can't go in them clothes she's got on."

Lafe looked up, startled.

"Sure 'nough; I never thought of that," he answered. "An' I don't believe she has uther."

It was the cobbler who spoke to Jinnie about it.

"I suppose you hain't thought what you're going to wear Sunday night?"

Jinnie whirled around upon him.

"Oh, Lafe!" she faltered, sitting down quickly.

"Peggy 'lowed you'd forgotten that part of it."

"I did, Lafe; I did! Oh, I don't know what to do!"

"I wisht I had somethin' for you, Jinnie dear," breathed Bobbie, touching her hand.

Jinnie's only response was to put her fingers on the child's head—her eyes still on the cobbler.

"What did Peggy say, Lafe?"

"Nothin', only you couldn't go in the clothes you got."

Jinnie changed her position that she might see to better advantage the plain little dress she was wearing.

"But I've got to go, Lafe; oh, I've got to!" she insisted. "Mr. King wants me.... Please, Lafe, please!"

"Call Peggy, Bobbie," said Lafe, in answer to Jinnie's impetuous speech.

Bobbie felt his way to the door, and Peggy came in answer to the child's call.

"I only thought of the twenty-five dollars and the fiddling, Peggy," said Jinnie as Mrs. Grandoken rolled her hands in her apron and sat down. "Did you say I couldn't go in these clothes?"

"I did; I sure did. You can't go in them clothes, an' what you're goin' to wear is more'n I can make out. I'll have to think.... Just let me alone for a little while."

It was after Jinnie had gone to bed with Bobbie that Peg spoke about it again to Lafe.

"I've only got one thing I could rig her a dress out of," she said. "I don't want to do it because I hate her so! If I hated her any worse, I'd bust!"

The cobbler raised his hand, making a gesture of denial.

"Peggy, dear, you don't hate the poor little lass."

"Yes, I do," said Peg. "I hate everybody in the world but you.... Everybody but you, Lafe."

"What'd you think might make a dress for 'er?" asked Grandoken presently.

Before answering, Peg brought her feet together and looked down at her toes. "There's them lace curtains ma give me when she died," she said. "Them that's wrapped up in paper on the shelf."

Lafe uttered a surprised ejaculation.

"I couldn't let you do that, Peg," he said, shaking his head. "Them's the last left over from your mother's stuff. Everything else's gone.... I couldn't let you, Peggy."

Mrs. Grandoken gave a shake of defiance.

"Whose curtains be they, Lafe?" she asked. "Be they mine or yourn?"

"Yourn, Peggy dear, and may God bless you!"

All through the night Jinnie had dreadful dreams. The thought of either not going to Mr. King's or that she might not have anything fit to wear filled the hours with nightmares and worryings. In the morning, after she crawled out of bed and was wearily dressing Bobbie, the little blind boy felt intuitively something was wrong with his friend.

"Is Jinnie sick?" he whispered, feeling her face. "My stars ain't shinin' much."

The girl kissed him.

"No, honey," she said, "Jinnie's only sad, not sick."

Together they went into the shop, where Peggy stood with the most gorgeous lacy stuff draped over her arms. Strewn here and there over the yards and yards of it were bright yellow and red roses. Nothing could have been more beautiful to the girl, as with widening eyes she gazed at it. Lafe's face was shining with happiness. Peggy didn't seem to notice the two as they entered, but she lifted the lace, displaying its length stolidly.

Jinnie bounded forward.

"What is it, Peg? What is it?"

Lafe beamed through his spectacles.

"A dress for you, girl dear. Peggy's givin' you the things she loves best. She's the only woman in the world, Jinnie."

Reverently Jinnie went to Mrs. Grandoken's side. She felt abjectly humble in the presence of this great sacrifice. She looked up into the glum face of the cobbler's wife and waited in breathless hesitation. Peg permitted her eyes to fall upon the girl.

"You needn't feel so glad nor look's if you was goin' to tumble over," she said. "It ain't no credit to anyone them curtains was on the shelf waitin' to be cut up in a dress for you to fiddle in. Go put the mush on that there stove!"

CHAPTER XIX

THE LITTLE FIDDLER

Jinnie's heart was skipping about like a silly little kitten as she sat watching Peg's stiff fingers making large stitches in the lace.

"Oh, Peg, isn't it lovely? Perfectly beautiful! Nobody ever had a dress like that!... My, Peggy! How your fingers fly!"

Peg's face was noncommittal to the point of blankness.

"Tain't no credit to me what my hands do, Miss Jinnie," she said querulously. "I didn't make 'em."

The girl's happiness was absolutely complete. The dress would be finished and Sunday evening——oh, Sunday evening! Then she walked restlessly to the window and studied the sky.

"I hope it doesn't rain to-morrow!... Oh, Peggy, don't you hope so too?" Mrs. Grandoken glowered at her.

"Kid," she said, "come away from that window. You been doin' nothin' but wishin' 'twon't rain all day. You'll wear out the patience of the Almighty; then he'll make it rain an' soak you through a-purpose."

"I don't know which I like best, Lafe," the girl remarked presently, turning to the cobbler, "the red roses or the yellow."

Bobbie came to Jinnie's side and fingered the lace.

"Tell me how the dress looks, dear," he whispered, tugging at her sleeve.

"Sure," agreed Jinnie. "Feel right here! Well, that's a beautiful red rose and here's a yellow one." She took his small finger and traced it over a yard of lace. "Feel that?"

"Yes," murmured Bobbie.

"Well, that's a green vine running up and down, and all around among the roses."

"Oh, my!" gasped Bobbie. "Red and yellow. That's how the sun looks when it's goin' down, ain't it? And green's like the grass, eh?"

"Just the same," replied Jinnie, laughing.

"It's a beauty," supplemented Lafe, glowing with tenderness. "There won't be a dress at that party that'll beat it."

Mrs. Grandoken shook out the voluminous folds of lace.

"Anybody'd think to hear you folks talk that you'd made these rag tags with your toe nails," she observed dryly. "The smacking of some folks' lips over sugar they don't earn makes me tired! Laws me!... Now I'll try it on you, Jinnie," she ended.

Jinnie turned around and around with slow precision as Mrs. Grandoken ascertained the correct hanging of the skirt. When the last stitches had been put in, and the dress lay in all its gorgeous splendor across the chair, Peg coughed awkwardly and spoke of shoes.

"You can't wear them cowhides with lace," said she.

"I might make a pair if I had a day and the stuff," suggested Lafe, looking around helplessly.

"Ain't time," replied Peg. And of course it was she who gave Jinnie some money taken from a small bag around her neck and ordered her to the shop for shoes.

"She ought to have a fiddle box," Lafe suggested.

"There ain't 'nough money in the house for that," replied Peg—"but I'll give her a piece of the curtains to wrap it up in."

"That'll look better'n a box," smiled Lafe. "I'm a happy cobbler, I am."

When Jinnie returned with a pair of low black slippers, no one noticed that they weren't quite what should have been worn with a lace frock. Contentment reigned supreme in the Grandoken home that day.

Sunday evening at seven Jinnie displayed herself to Lafe. The cobbler gave a contented nod.

"You and the dress're beautiful," he ruminated. "Wonderful!... Kiss me, Jinnie!"

She not only kissed Lafe, but Bobbie, Happy Pete, and Milly Ann, too, came in for their share. Peg looked so sour, so forbidding, that Jinnie only faltered,

"Much obliged, Peggy darling.... Oh, I'm so happy!" She stood directly in front of Mrs. Grandoken. "Aren't you, dear?" she besought.

"We're all glad, lass," put in the cobbler.

Jinnie's blue, blue eyes were seeking approbation from the gaunt, frowning woman.

"None of you've got the sense of my bedpost," snapped Peg, sniffing the air. "Get along. They're waitin' for you."

Jinnie arrived in great excitement at Theodore King's door. She stumbled up the stone steps of the mansion with the fiddle carefully wrapped under her arm.

"Is Mr. King here?" she asked of the maid, hesitatingly.

She stood very still, scarcely breathing, until they called the master of the house, and as Theodore's eyes fell upon the lace dress, with its red and yellow roses and green vines running the length of the slim young figure, he smoothed away a smile that forced itself to his lips.

Out of gratitude to Peggy, Jinnie felt she ought to speak of the frock, so with an admiring glance downward, she confided:

"Peggy made my dress out of her dead mother's curtains, and gave me this piece for my fiddle.... Wasn't it lovely of her?"

The pleading, soulful, violet eyes stirred Theodore King with a new sensation. He had passed unscathed through the fires of imploring, inviting glances and sweet, tempting lips, nor yet realized that some day this black-haired girl would call him to a reckoning.

"It's very pretty, very pretty," he affirmed hurriedly. "I'm glad you're here.... Just wait for a moment. I'll come back for you."

There was a fixed line between his handsome eyes as he faced his guests. Theodore couldn't analyze his feelings toward Jinnie, but he was determined none should make sport of her.

"I've prepared a great treat for you," he stated, smiling, "but I want to ask you to overlook anything that may seem incongruous, for the musician is very sensitive."

Then he went back for Jinnie, and she followed him into the large room. The gorgeous red and yellow roses in the limply hanging blouse lent a color to her sunburned skin.

"You may play anything you like," Theodore whispered.

"All right," nodded Jinnie.

She unwrapped the fiddle and tuned it with nimble fingers. Not until she placed the instrument under her chin did she raise her head. Her eyes went searchingly from face to face of the attentive assembly. It so happened that they fell upon a crown of golden hair above a pair of dark eyes she vividly remembered. The glance took her back to that night more than two years before—to the night when her father died.

Molly Merriweather was seated in queenly fashion in one of the large chairs, a questioning look stealing over her countenance. Jinnie smiled at her and began to play. It might have been the beautiful woman opposite that brought forth the wild hill story, told in marvelous harmonies. The rapt young face gave no sign of embarrassment, for Jinnie

76

was completely lost in her melodious task. Above the dimpled chin that hugged the brown fiddle, Theodore King could see the brooding genius of the girl, and longed to bring a passionate lovelight for himself into the glorious eyes. The intensity of the music established in him an unconquerable hope—a hope that could not die as long as life was in him, as long as life was in the little fiddler.

As Jinnie finished with dramatic brilliancy, great applause and showers of congratulations fell upon her ears. Theodore went to her quickly.

"Wonderful! Splendid, child!" he declared joyously. "You're a genius!"

His words increased her joy—his compelling dark eyes added to her desire to do her best.

She meditated one moment. Then thoroughly unconscious of herself, turned and spoke to the audience.

"I'll play about fairies ... the ones who live in the woods and hide away in the flowers and under the leaves."

Once more she began to play. She believed in fairies with all her heart and had no doubt but that everyone else did. Under the spell of her music and her loveliness, imaginary elves stole from the solitude of the summer night, to join their tiny hands and dance to the rhythm of her song.

As she lowered her violin and looked around, she saw astonishment on the faces of the strangers about her. A deathlike hush prevailed and Jinnie could hear the feverish blood as it struck at her temples. Into her eyes came an unfathomable expression, and Theodore King, attracted by their latent passion, went rapidly to her.

"It's exquisite!" he said vehemently. "Can't you see how much everyone likes it?"

"Do you?" queried Jinnie, looking up at him.

"I love it, child; I love it.... Will you play again, please?"

A flame of joy suffused her as again she turned to the open-eyed crowd.

"Once," she informed them, "a big lion was hurt in the forest by lightning.... This—is—how he died."

She slowly raised the instrument, and sounded a vibrant, resonant, minor tone, measured, full and magnificent. Each listener sank back with a sigh.

Jinnie knew the mysteries of the forest as well as a singer knows his song, and she had not presented ten notes to the imagination of Theodore's friends before they were carried away from the dainty room in which they sat—away into a dense woodland where, for a few minutes, she demonstrated the witching wonders of it. Then she slipped the bow between her teeth and struck the violin strings with the backs of her fingers. The vibrations of impetuous harmony swept softly through the lighted room. Louder and louder was heard the awful fury of approaching thunder, while twinkling string-touches flashed forth the lightning between the sonorous peals.

Jinnie never knew how the fiddle was capable of expressing the cautious tread of the terrified king of beasts in his isolated kingdom, but her listeners beheld him steal cautiously from the underbrush. They saw him crouch in abject terror at the foot of a wide-spreading, gigantic tree, lashing his tail in elemental rage. Then another scintillating flash of lightning, and the beast caught it full in the face. The slender hand of the little player was poised above the strings for a single vibrating moment, during which she stood in a listening attitude. Then, with the sweep of three slender fingers, the lion's scream cut the air like a two-edged sword.

Death came on rapidly in deep, resounding roars, and the misery of the cringing, suffering brute was unfolded—told in heart-rending intonations, until at last he gave up his breath in one terror-stricken cry.

Jinnie dropped her hands suddenly. "He's dead," she said tremulously. "Poor, poor lion!"

She turned tear-wet eyes to Theodore King.

"Shall I play anymore?" she asked, shyly.

The man shook his head, not permitting himself to speak.

"Miss Grandoken has given us a wonderful entertainment," said he to his friends; then turning to her, he held out his hand, "I want to thank you, Miss Grandoken."

Many people crowded around her, asking where and how she had learned such music.

Molly the Merry, the mystified expression still on her face, drew near.

Again Jinnie smiled at her, hoping the lovely lips would acknowledge their former acquaintanceship. But as another person, a man, stepped between her and the woman, Jinnie glanced up at him. He was very handsome, but involuntarily the girl shuddered. There was something in the curling of his lips that was cruel, and the whiteness of his teeth accentuated the impression. His eyes filled her with dread.

"Where did you learn that wonderful music?" he smiled.... "I mean the music itself."

"Out of my heart," she said simply. "I couldn't get it anywhere else."

"She's very delightful!" said the stranger, turning to Theodore. "I've forgotten her name?"

He was so near her that Jinnie shrank back, and the master of the house noted her embarrassment.

"Her name is Grandoken, Miss Grandoken.... Come," he said, holding out his hand to Jinnie, and as she placed her fingers in his, he led her away.

A large car was waiting at the front door, and he held her hand in his for a few seconds. The touch of her fingers thrilled him through and through. He noticed her head just reached his shoulder and a conscious desire to draw her to him for one blessed moment surged insistent within him. He dropped her hand suddenly.

78

"I wish now," he said, smiling, "I had sent for you to come here before. It was such a treat!"

Jinnie shrank away as he offered her a roll of bills. An unutterable shyness crept over her.

"I don't want it," she said, gulping hard. "I'd love to fiddle for you all day long."

"But you must take it," insisted King. "Now then, I want to know where you live. I'm coming to see your uncle very, very soon."

Lafe and his wife were waiting for the girl, and the cobbler noticed Peggy's eyes were misty as Jinnie gave her the money. Over and over she told them all about it.

"And he's coming to see you, Lafe," she cried with a tremulous laugh. "Mr. King says someday I'll be a great player. Will I, Lafe? Will I, Peggy?"

"You may," admitted Peggy, "but don't get a swelled head, 'cause you couldn't stop fiddlin' any more'n a bird could stop singin'.... Go to bed now, this minute."

And as Jinnie slept her happy sleep in Paradise Road, another woman was walking to and fro with a tall man under the trees at Theodore King's home.

"I thought I'd scream with laughter when she came in," said Molly the Merry. "If it hadn't been for Theo's warning, I'm sure most of us would.... Did you ever see such a ridiculous dress, Jordan?"

The man was quiet for a meditative moment. "I forgot about the dress when she began to play," he mused. "The sight of her face would drive all thoughts of incongruity out of a man's mind."

"Yes, she's very pretty," admitted Molly, reluctantly. "And Jordan, do you know there's something strangely familiar about her face?... I can't tell where I've seen her."

"Never mind. The important thing to me is I must have money. Can't keep up appearances on air."

"You know I'll always help you when I can, Jordan."

"Yes, I know it, and I'll not let you forget it either."

The woman gave him a puzzled look and the man caught her meaning.

"You're wondering why I don't open offices here, aren't you? Well, a person can't do two things at once, and I've been pretty busy tracing Virginia Singleton. And when I find her, you know very well I will return every penny I've borrowed."

And later, when Molly went to her room, she walked up and down thoughtfully, trying to bring to her mind the familiar violet eyes and the mass of purple black curls which were the crowning glory of Jinnie Grandoken.

CHAPTER XX

THE COBBLER'S SECRET

One Sunday morning, Jinnie sat with Lafe in the shop. In hours like these they thoroughly enjoyed themselves. The quietude of these precious Sabbath moments made the week, with its arduous tasks, bearable to the sensitive girl.

For several days past Jinnie had noticed Lafe had something on his mind, but she always allowed him to tell her everything in his own good time. Now she felt the time had come. His gray face, worn with suffering, was shining with a heavenly light as he read aloud from a little Bible in his hand. To-day he had chosen the story of Abraham and Sarah. When he came to the part where Abraham said:

"Lord, if now I have found favor in Thy sight, pass not away, I pray Thee, from Thy servant," he pronounced the last word with sobbing breath. One quick glance was enough for Jinnie's comprehension.

She leaned forward breathlessly.

"What is it, Lafe?... Something great?"

"Yes, something great, lassie, and in God's name most wonderful."

Before Jinnie's world of imagery passed all the good she had desired for Lafe. His softly spoken, "In God's name most wonderful," thrilled her from head to foot.

"And you've been keeping it from me, Lafe," she chided gently. "Please, please, tell me."

Lafe sat back in the wheel chair and closed his eyes. "Wait, child," he breathed hesitatingly. "Wait a minute!"

As Jinnie watched him, she tried to stifle the emotion tugging at her heart—to keep back the tears that welled into her eyes. Perhaps what he had to tell her would make her cry. Jinnie hoped not, for she disliked to do that. It was so childlike, so like Blind Bobbie, who always had either a beatific smile on his pale lips, or a mist shining in his rock-gray eyes.

At length Lafe sighed a long, deep-drawn sigh, and smiled.

"Jinnie," he began——

"Yes, Lafe."

"I've been wonderin' if you remember the story of the little feller God sent to Peg an' me—the one I told you would a been six years old."

"Yes, I remember, Lafe."

"An' how good Peggy was——"

"Oh, how good Peggy always is!" interjected Jinnie.

"Yes," breathed Lafe, dreamily. "May God bless my woman in all her trials!"

Jinnie hitched her chair nearer his and slipped her arm about his neck soothingly.

"She doesn't have trials you don't share, Lafe," she declared.

Lafe straightened up.

"Yes, Peg has many, lassie, I can't help 'er with, an' she'll have a many more. To get to tell you something, Jinnie, I asked Peg to take Bobbie out with 'er. We can't turn the little feller from the club room when he ain't out with Peg; can we, Jinnie?"

"Of course not," agreed Jinnie, nodding.

"So when Peg said she was goin' out," proceeded Lafe, gravely, "I says, thinkin' of the things I wanted to say to you, I said to Peggy, 'Take the little blind chap along with you, Peggy dear,' an' without a word she put the youngster into his clothes an' away they went."

Jinnie's curiosity was growing by the minute.

"And you're going to tell me now, Lafe?"

"An' now I'm goin' to tell you, Jinnie."

But he didn't tell her just then. Instead he sat looking at her with luminous eyes, and the expression in them—that heavenly expression—compelled Jinnie to kneel beside him, and for a little while they sat in silence.

"Dear child," Lafe murmured, dropping a tender hand on her shining head, "dear, dear girl!"

"It must be a joyful thing, Lafe, for your face shines as bright as Bobbie's stars."

"I'm blessed happy to-day!" he sighed, with twitching lips.

Jinnie took his hand in hers and smoothed it fondly.

"What is it, Lafe, dear?" she asked.

"Do you want to kneel while I tell you?" queried the cobbler.

"Yes, right here."

"Then look right at me, Jinnie lass!"

Jinnie was looking at him with her whole soul in her eyes.

"I'm looking at you, Lafe," she said.

"An' don't take your eyes from me; will you?"

"Sure not!"

It must be a great surprise for Lafe to act like this, thought the girl.

"Lassie," commenced Lafe, "I want you to be awful good to Peggy.... It's about her I'm goin' to speak."

Jinnie sank back on the tips of her toes.

"What about Peg? There isn't——"

"Dear Peggy," interrupted Lafe softly, his voice quick with tears, "dear, precious Peggy!" Then as he bent over Jinnie and Jinnie bent nearer him, Lafe placed his lips to her ear and whispered something.

She struggled to her feet, strange and unknown emotions rising in her eyes.

"Lafe!" she cried. "Lafe dear!"

"Yes," nodded the cobbler. "Yes, if you want to know the truth, the good God's goin' to send me an' Peg another little Jew baby."

Jinnie sat down in her chair quite dazed. Lafe's secret was much greater than she had expected! Much!

"Tell me about it," she pleaded.

81

Keen anxiety erased the cobbler's smiling expression.

"Poor Peggy!" he groaned again. "She can't see where the bread's comin' from to feed another mouth, but as I says, 'Peggy, you said the same thing when Jinnie came, an' the blind child, an' this little one's straight from God's own tender breast.'"

"That's so, Lafe," accorded Jinnie, "and, Oh, dearie, I'll work so hard, so awful hard to get in more wood, and tell me, tell me when, Lafe; when is he coming to us, the Jew baby?"

Lafe smiled at her eagerness.

"You feel the same way as I do, honey," he observed. "The very same way!... Why, girlie, when Peg first told me I thought I'd get up and fly!"

"I should think so, but—but—I want to know how soon, Lafe, dear."

"Oh, it's a long time, a whole lot of weeks!"

"I wish it was to-morrow," lamented Jinnie, disappointedly. "I wonder if Peg'll let me hug and kiss him."

"Sure," promised Lafe, and they lapsed into silence.

At length, Jinnie stole to the kitchen. She returned with her violin box and Milly Ann in her arms.

"Hold the kitty, darling," she said softly, placing the cat on his lap. "She'll be happy, too. Milly Ann loves us all, Milly Ann does."

Then she took out the fiddle and thrummed the strings.

"I'm going to play for you," she resumed, "while you think about Peggy and the—and—the baby."

The cobbler nodded his head, and wheeled himself a bit nearer the window, from where he could see the hill rise upward to the blue, making a skyline of exquisite beauty.

Jinnie began to play. What tones she drew from that small brown fiddle! The rapture depicted in her face was but a reflection of the cobbler's. And as he meditated and listened, Lafe felt that each tone of Jinnie's fiddle had a soul of its own—that the instrument was peopled with angel voices—voices that soothed him when he suffered beyond description—voices that now expressed in rhythmical harmony the peace within him. Jinnie was able to put an estimate on his moods, and knew just what comfort he needed most. Until that moment the cobbler's wife had seemed outside the charm of the beloved home circle. But to-day, ah, to-day!—Jinnie's bow raced over the strings like a mad thing. To-day Peggy Grandoken became in the girl's eyes a glorified woman, a woman set apart by God Himself to bring to the home a new baby.

Jinnie played and played and played, and Theodore in spirit-fancy stood beside her. Lafe thought and thought and thought, while Peggy walked through his day dreams like some radiant being.

"A baby——my baby, in the house," sang the cobbler's heart.

"A baby, our baby, in the house," poured from Jinnie's soul, and "Baby, little baby," sprang from the fiddle over and over, as golden flashes of the sun warms the earth. Truly was Lafe being revivified; truly was Jinnie! Theodore King! How infinitely close he seemed to her! How the memory of his smile cheered and strengthened her!

From the tip of the fiddle tucked under a rounded chin to the line of purple-black hair, the blood rushed in riotous confusion over the fiddler's lovely face. What was it in Lafe's story that had brought Theodore King so near?

Jinnie couldn't have told, but she was sure the fiddle knew. It was intoning to Lafe—to her—the language of the birds and the mystery of the flower blossoms, the invisible riddles of Heaven and earth, of all the concealed secrets beyond the blue of the sky; all the panorama of Nature strung out in a wild, sweet forest song. Jinnie had backed against the wall as she played, and when out of her soul came the twitter of the morning birds, the babbling of the brook on its way to the sea, the scream of the owl in a high woodland tree, Lafe turned to watch her, and from that moment until she dropped exhausted into a chair, he did not take his eyes from her.

"Jinnie!" he gasped, as he thrust forth his hand and took hers. "You've made me happier to-day'n I've been in many a week. Peg'll be all right.... Everybody'll be all right.... God bless us!"

Jinnie sat up with bright, inquiring eyes.

"Did you tell Peg I was to know about——"

"About our baby?" intervened Lafe tenderly.

He dwelt lovingly on those precious words.

"Yes, about your baby," repeated Jinnie.

"Yes, I told 'er, dear. I said you'd want to be happy too."

"I'm so glad," sighed Jinnie, reverently. "Look!... Peg's coming now!"

They both watched Mrs. Grandoken as she stolidly crossed the tracks, leading Bobbie by the hand.

And later Jinnie hovered over Peggy in the kitchen. The woman had taken on such a new dignity. She must be treated with the greatest and most extra care. If Jinnie had done what she craved, she'd have bounded to Peg and kissed her heartily. Of course that wouldn't do, but talk to her she must,

"Peggy," she said softly, tears lurking in her eyes.

Peg looked at her without moving an eyelash. Jinnie wished she would say something; her task would be so much easier.

"Peggy," she begged again.

"Huh?"

"Lafe told me, dear," and then she did something she hadn't done with Lafe; she began to cry, just why, Jinnie didn't know; Peg looked so sad, so distant, and so ill.

It was probably Jinnie's tears that softened Peg, for she put her hand on the girl's shoulders and stood silent. After the first flood of tears Jinnie ventured:

"I'm awful happy, Peggy dear, and I want you to know I'm going to work harder'n I even did for Blind Bobbie.... I will, Peg, I promise I will.... Kiss me, Oh, kiss me, dear!"

Peggy bent over and kissed the upturned, tearful face solemnly. Then she turned her back, beginning to work vigorously, and Jinnie returned to the shop with the kiss warm on her cheek.

CHAPTER XXI
THE COMING OF THE ANGELS

"You'd better make it a special prayer, Lafe," said Jinnie, a little pucker between her eyes. "Every day I'm more'n more afraid of Maudlin."

"I will, honey, an' just pop into Bates' cottage an' tell Maudlin's pa to run in the shop.... Go long, lass, nobody'll hurt you."

After leaving Lafe's message at the Bates' cottage, Jinnie stepped from the tracks to the marshes with a joyful heart. Of course nothing could harm her! Lafe's faith, mingled with her own, would save her from every evil in the world.

When Bates opened the shop door, the cobbler looked up gravely. He nodded his head to Jasper's, "Howdy do, Grandoken?"

"Sit down," said Lafe.

"Jinnie says you wanted me."

"Yes, a few minutes' chat; that's all!"

"Spit it out," said Bates.

Lafe put down his hammer with slow importance.

"It's this way, Jasper. Maudlin's——"

"What's Maudie done now?" demanded Bates, lighting his pipe.

"He's been botherin' my girl, that's what," responded Lafe.

"Jinnie?"

"Sure. She's all the girl I got.... Maudlin's got to stop it, Bates."

A cruel expression flitted over Jasper's face.

"I ain't nothin' to do with Maudlin's love affairs," said he. "Jinnie could do worse'n get him, I'm a guessin'! Maudie adds up pretty good, Maudie does!"

Lafe shook his head with a grim serenity that became the strained white face.

"His addin' up ain't nothin' to his credit, Jasper," he protested. "He's as crooked as a ram's horn an' you know it. If you don't, take my word for it! There ain't nothin' doin' for him far's Jinnie's concerned!... I sent for you to bargain with you." Jasper pricked up his ears. The word "bargain" always attracted him.

"Well?" he questioned.

"You keep your boy from my girl and I'll do all your family cobblin' for nothin' till Jinnie's a woman."

Bates leaned back in his chair and crossed his legs.

"It's a bargain, all right. Them kids of mine do wear out the soles of their shoes some. But, Lafe, I can't tag Maudlin around all day."

Lafe took up his hammer.

"Lick him if he won't mind you, Bates. He's got to let my girl be, and that's all there is to it."

Saying this, he started to work, giving the shortwood gatherer his dismissal. Bates left his chair thoughtfully.

"I'll talk to Maudie," said he, "but he's an onery kid; has been ever since his mother died. He don't git along with his stepma very well, and she's got such a lot of little kids of 'er own she ain't time to train no hulk of a boy like Maudlin."

Pausing a moment, he went on, "Maudlin's been madder'n hell because that duffer King's been haulin' Jinnie's wood. He says——"

"It ain't any of Maudlin's business who helps Jinnie," interrupted Lafe. "If you got any shoes needin' fixin', tote 'em over, Jasper."

Bates left the shop and Lafe fell to work vigorously.

Maudlin Bates stood at the path leading to the marshes. He was waiting for Jinnie to appear with her load of shortwood. To the young wood gatherer, a woman was created for man's special benefit, and a long time ago he had made up his mind that Jinnie should be his woman.

He was leaning against a tree when the girl came in sight, with her wood-strap on her shoulders. She paid no attention to him, and was about to turn into Paradise Road when the man stepped in front of her.

"Wait a minute, Jinnie," he wheedled.

Jinnie threw him a disdainful glance.

"I can't wait. I'm in a hurry," she replied, and she hoped the fellow would go on before the car arrived.

Young Bates' face was crossed by an obstinate expression.

"I'm goin' to find out," he said, gruffly, "why you're ridin' in rich folks' motor cars."

"Isn't anything to you," snapped Jinnie.

The wood gatherer came so close that he forced her back a step on the marsh path. Her disdainful eyes had drawn him to her, for, like all men, he could be drawn by the woman who scorned him, and mesmerized by the sheer repulse. By great effort, Jinnie had escaped from Maudlin's insults for many months, but he had never been quite so aggressive as this! Now she could see the dark blood in his passionate face mount even to the whites of his eyes, those eyes which coveted the youngness of her body, the vitality of her girl life, and all the good within her.

"Get out of my way!" she said sharply. "You let me alone. I've got a right to get my wood hauled if I can."

"Well, you don't do it anymore," said Maudlin. "If you're too lazy to carry your own wood, I'll help you myself.... You can't go no more to King's in his car."

Jinnie turned a pair of glinting blue eyes upon him.

"Who said I couldn't?" she demanded. "Uncle Lafe lets me."

"Your Uncle Lafe said you could marry me," said Maudlin in slow, drawling tones.

Jinnie's blood boiled up behind her ears. She was eyeing him in bewilderment. Maudlin's words made her more angry than she'd ever been in her life.

"You lie, you damn fool!" she cried, and then caught her breath in consternation. It was the first oath that had escaped her lips in many a long day, and she felt truly sorry for it. She would tell Lafe of the provocation that caused it and beg to be forgiven. She moved back a step as Maudlin pinched her.

"I don't lie," he growled. "You think because you can scrape on a fiddle you're better'n other folks. Pa an' me'll show you you ain't."

"You and your pa don't know everything," answered Jinnie, wrathfully.

"We know 'nough to see what King's doin' all right."

He made a dive at the girl and laid a rough hand on the shortwood strap.

"Here! Gimme that wood if you're too lazy to carry it."

Jinnie turned her eyes up the road. It was time Bennett came. The sound of his motor would be like sweet music in her ears. She jerked the strap away from the man and turned furiously upon him.

"Don't touch me again, Maudlin Bates.... I don't interfere with you. I'll—I'll——"

But Maudlin paid no heed to her insistence. He was dragging the strap from her shoulders.

Jinnie's face grew waxen white, but she held her own for a few minutes. Maudlin was big in proportion to her slenderness, and in another instant her shortwood lay on the ground, and she was standing panting before him.

"Now, then, just to show what kind of a feller I be," said he, "I'm goin' to kiss you."

Jinnie felt cold chills running up and down her back.

"It's time you was kissed," went on Maudlin, "and after to-day I'm goin' to be your man.... You can bet on that."

He was slowly forcing her backward along the narrow path that led into the marshes. Jinnie knew intuitively he wanted her to turn and run into the underbrush that he might have her alone in the great waste place.

Like a mad creature, she fought every step of the way, Maudlin's anger rising at each cry the girl emitted.

"I'll tell my uncle," she screamed, with sobbing breath.

"You won't want to tell 'im when I get done with you," muttered the man. "Why don't you run? You c'n run, can't you?"

Oh, if Bennett would only come! She was still near enough to Paradise Road for him to hear her calling.

Maudlin reached out his hand and caught the long curls between his dirty fingers.

"If you won't run," he said, "then, that for you!" and he gave a cruel twist to the shining hair, pulling Jinnie almost off her feet.

Then the ruffian turned, slowly dragging her foot by foot into the marshland. She opened her lips, and gave one long scream; then another and another before Maudlin pulled her to him and closed her mouth with a large hand, and Jinnie grew faint with fright and terror.

86

They were out of sight now of Paradise Road, still Jinnie struggled and struggled, gripping with both hands at Bates' fingers jerking at her curls.

Suddenly Lafe's solemn words surged through her mind. "He has given His angels charge over thee." Oh God! Dear God! What glorious, blessed words! Lafe's angels, her angels—Jinnie's heart throbbed with faith. Once Lafe had told her no one, no, not even Maudlin Bates, could keep her own from her! Her honor and her very life were in the tender hands of the cobbler's angels. Suddenly in fancy Jinnie saw the whole world about teeming with bright ecstatic beings, and multitudes of them were hurrying through the warm summer air to the Bellaire marshes. They were coming—coming to help her, to save her from a fate worse than death! Her mind reeled under the terrible pain Maudlin was inflicting upon her, and she closed her eyes in agony. With one mighty effort, she dragged her face from the brown, hard hand and screamed at the top of her lungs.

Theodore King swung his car around into Paradise Road with busy thoughts. He had decided to go himself that morning to bring the little fiddler back to his home with the shortwood. He had a plan for Jinnie.

Past the cobbler's shop sped the big motor, and as it drew up to the marshes, he heard a blood-curdling cry from the depths of the underbrush. In another instant he was out on the ground, dashing along the path. He saw Jinnie and Maudlin before either one of them knew he was near. He saw the fellow pulling the black curls, and saw a hand almost covering the fair young face.

Then Jinnie saw him, and sent him one swift, terrified, appealing glance.

In the smallest fraction of a second Maudlin was sprawling on the ground, and Theodore was soundly kicking him. Jinnie sank down on the damp moss and began to cry weakly. Her face was scratched from the man's fingers, her head aching from the strenuous pulling of her hair. Then she covered her eyes with her hands. God had sent an angel—she was saved! When Mr. King touched her gently, she sat up, wiping away little streams of blood running down her face and neck.

"Oh, you came," she sobbed, raising her head, "and oh, I needed you so!"

Theodore lifted her to her feet.

"I should say you did, you poor child! I should certainly think you did."

Then he turned to Maudlin Bates.

"What, in God's name, were you trying to do?"

Maudlin, raging with anger, scrambled from the ground.

"Get out o' here," he hissed, "an' mind your own business."

"When I keep a bully away from a nice little girl, I'm minding my business all right.... What was he trying to do, Jinnie?"

Maudlin walked backward until he was almost in the brush.

"I'm goin' to marry her," he said, surlily.

"He isn't," cried Jinnie. "Oh, don't believe him, Mr. King! He says Uncle Lafe said he can marry me, but he can't."

Once more Theodore turned on Maudlin, threateningly, his anger riding down his gentleness to Jinnie.

"Now get out of here," he exclaimed, "and don't ever let me hear of your even speaking to this child again."

The shortwood gatherer stood his ground until Theodore, with raised fist, was almost upon him.

"I said to get out!" thundered Mr. King.

With a baffled cry, Bates turned, rushed back into the marsh, and for several seconds they heard him beating down the brushwood as he ran.

Theodore tenderly drew the girl into Paradise Road.

"I wanted to see your uncle to-day," he explained, without waiting for the question which he read in Jinnie's eyes, "so I came over myself instead of sending Bennett.... There, child! Don't tremble so! Never mind the wood."

Jinnie hung back.

"I've got to sell it to you this afternoon," she murmured brokenly. "Peg's got to have the money."

"We've enough at home until to-morrow.... Wait until to-morrow."

Jinnie looked longingly at the wood.

"Somebody'll take it," she objected, "and it's awful hard to gather."

A grip of pain stabbed Theodore's heart. This slender, beautiful girl, rosy with health and genius, should gather wood no more for any one in the world.... To soothe her, he said:

"I'll come by and pick it up on my way back.... Come along."

He lifted her into the car, and they moved slowly through Paradise Road, and drew up before the cobbler's shop.

Lafe put down his hammer as they entered, and bade King take a chair. Jinnie sat weakly on the bench beside Mr. Grandoken. He took her hand, and the loving pressure brought forth a storm of outraged tears.

"'Twas Maudlin, Lafe," she wept.

Then her arms stole around the cobbler. "The angels sent Mr. King!... Lafe, Lafe, save me from Maudlin! He—he——"

Theodore King rose to his feet, his face paling. Lafe, smoothing Jinnie's head now buried in his breast, lifted misty eyes to the young man.

"My poor baby! My poor little girl!" he stammered. "She has much to stand, sir."

The other man took several nervous turns around the shop. Presently he paused near the cobbler and coughed in embarrassment.

"I'm interested in doing something for your niece, Mr. Grandoken," said he lamely.

On hearing this, Jinnie lifted her head, and Lafe bowed.

"Thank you, sir," said he.

"I don't approve of her going into the marshes alone to gather wood," continued Mr. King. "She's too young, too——"

"I don't uther, sir," interrupted Lafe sadly, "but we've got to live."

Not heeding the cobbler's explanation, Theodore proceeded deliberately.

"She plays too well on the violin not to have all the training that can be given her. Now let me be of some service until she is self-supporting."

Again Lafe repeated, "Thank you, sir, but I don't think Jinnie could accept money from any one."

"I don't see why not! It's quite customary when a young person is ambitious to receive——"

"Is it, sir?" ejaculated Lafe.

"Indeed yes, and I've been making inquiries, and I find there's a very good teacher on the hill who'll give her the rudiments.... After that, we'll see."

Jinnie was breathing very fast.

"Lessons cost lots of money," objected Lafe feebly, drawing the girl closer.

"I know that," interposed Mr. King, "but I want to pay for them. She ought to take one every day, the teacher says, commencing to-morrow."

Jinnie stood up. "I couldn't let you pay for 'em," she said quickly. "I——"

She sat down again at a motion from Theodore.

"Please don't object until I have finished," he smiled at her. "It's like this: If you study, you'll be able to earn a lot of money. Then you can return every dollar to me."

Suddenly it came to her mind to tell him she would have all the money she needed when she should be eighteen.

"I'll have——" she began, but Lafe, feeling what she was going to say, stopped her. It wasn't time to confide in any one about the danger hanging over her. He took the matter in his own hands with his usual melancholy dignity.

"Jinnie'll be glad to let you help her, sir, providin' you keep track of the money you spend," he agreed.

The girl could scarcely believe her ears. Suddenly her indignant sense of Maudlin's abuse faded away, leaving her encouraged and warm with ambition.

Theodore took one more stride around the little room.

"Now that's sensible, Mr. Grandoken," he said contentedly. "And before I go, I want you to promise me your niece won't go into the marshes even once more. I must have your word before I can be satisfied. As it is now, she earns three dollars a week bringing me wood. That I must add to the lesson money——"

Lafe's dissenting gesture broke off Mr. King's statement, but he resumed immediately.

"If you're sensitive on that point, I'll add it in with the other money. I think it wise to keep our arrangements to ourselves, though." He stopped, his face changing. "And I—I would like to make you more comfortable here."

Lafe shook his head.

"I couldn't take anything for me and Peggy," he announced decidedly, "but Jinnie'll give back all you let her have some day."

Then Theodore King went away reluctantly.

CHAPTER XXII

MOLLY'S DISCOVERY

Peggy had given Jinnie a violin box, and as the girl walked rapidly homeward, she gazed at it with pride, and began to plan how the woman's burdens could be lightened a little—how she could bring a smile now and then to the sullen face. This had been discussed between Lafe and herself many times, and they had rejoiced that in a few months, when Jinnie was eighteen, Mrs. Grandoken's worries would be lessened.

She reached the bottom of the hill just as a car dashed around the lower corner, a woman at the wheel. One glance at the occupant, and Jinnie recognized Molly Merriweather. The woman smiled sweetly and drove to the edge of the pavement.

"Good afternoon," she greeted Jinnie. "Won't you take a little ride with me? I'll drive you home afterwards."

Jinnie's heart bounded. As yet Molly had not discovered her identity, and the girl, in spite of Lafe's caution, wanted to know all that had passed in Mottville after she left. She wanted to hear about her dead father, of Matty, and the old home. She gave ready assent to Molly's invitation by climbing into the door opened for her.

"You don't have to go home right away, do you?" asked Miss Merriweather pleasantly.

"No, I suppose not," acceded Jinnie shyly.

She connected Molly the Merry with all that was good. She remembered the woman's kindly smiles so long ago in Mottville, and—that she was a friend of Theodore King. She was startled, however, after they had ridden in silence a while, when the woman pronounced his name.

"Have you seen Mr. King lately?"

Jinnie shook her head.

"I guess it's three days," she answered, low-voiced.

Three days! Molly racked her brain during the few seconds before she spoke again to bring to mind when Theodore had been absent from home out of business hours.

"He's a very nice man," she remarked disinterestedly.

Jinnie's gratitude burst forth in youthful impetuosity.

"He's more'n nice,—he's the best man in the world."

"Yes, he is," murmured Molly.

"Theo—I mean Mr. King," stammered Jinnie.

Molly turned so quickly to look at the girl's reddening face that the car almost described a circle.

"You call him by his first name, then?" she asked, with a sharp backward turn of the wheel.

"No," denied Jinnie, extremely confused. "Oh, no! Only—only——"

"Only what?"

"When I think of him, then I do. Theodore's such a pretty name, isn't it?"

Molly bit her lip. Here was the niece of a cobbler who dared to think familiarly of a man in high social position. She had tried to make herself believe Theo was simply philanthropic, but now the more closely she examined the beautiful face of the girl, the more she argued with herself, the greater grew her fear.

"What does he call you?" Molly spoke amiably, as if discussing these unimportant little matters for mere politeness' sake.

"Mostly Jinnie," was the prompt reply. "I'm just Jinnie to everyone who loves me."

She said this without thought of its import. Angrily Molly sent the motor spinning along at a higher rate. She was growing to hate the little person at her side.

"Where are your own people?" she demanded, when they were on the road leading to the country.

Jinnie glanced up. "Dead!" she answered.

"And the cobbler, Mr. Grandoken, is he your father's or mother's brother?"

Jinnie pondered a moment, undecided how to answer.

"Why, you see it's like this——"

Molly lessened the speed. Turning squarely around, she looked keenly at the scarlet, lovely face.

"Why are you blushing?" she queried.

Then like a flash she remembered. What a silly fool she had been! Jordan Morse would give his eyes almost to locate this girl.

"I remember now who you are," she said, taking a long breath. "You're Virginia Singleton."

Jinnie touched her arm appealingly.

"You won't tell anybody, will you, please? Please don't.... There's a reason why."

"Tell me the reason."

"I couldn't now, not now. But I have to live with Lafe Grandoken quite a long time yet."

"You ran away from your home?"

"Yes."

"Your father died the same night you came away."

"Yes, and—please, what happened after I left?"

91

"Oh, he was buried, and the house is empty."

Molly forebore to mention Jordan Morse, and Jinnie's tongue refused to utter the terrifying name.

Presently the girl, with tears in her eyes, said softly:

"And Matty, old Matty?"

"Who's Matty?" interjected Molly.

"The black woman who took care of me. She lived with me for ever so long."

Molly didn't reply for some time. Then:

"I think she died; at least I heard she did."

A cold shudder ran over Jinnie's body. Matty then had gone to join those who, when they were called, had no choice but to answer. She leaned against the soft cushions moodily. She was harking back to other days, and Molly permitted her to remain silent for some time.

"You must have people of your own you could live with," she resumed presently. "It's wrong for a girl with your money——"

Jinnie's lovely mouth set at the corners.

"I wouldn't leave Lafe and Peggy for anybody in the world, not if I had relations, but I haven't."

"I thought—I thought," began Molly, pretending to bring to mind something she'd forgotten. "You have an uncle," she burst forth.

Jinnie grew cold from head to foot. Her father's words, "He won't find in you much of an obstacle," came to her distinctly.

"Does your uncle know where you are?"

This question brought the girl to the present.

"No. I don't want him to know, either. Not till—not till I'm eighteen."

"Why?"

Molly's tone was so cold and unsympathetic Jinnie regretted she had accepted her invitation to ride. But she need not be afraid; Lafe would keep her safe from all harm. Had she not tried out his faith and the angels' care with Maudlin Bates? However, she felt she owed some explanation to the woman at her side.

"My uncle doesn't like me," she stammered, calming her fear. "And Lafe loves me, Lafe does."

"How do you know your uncle doesn't love you?"

Thinking of Lafe's often repeated caution not to divulge her father's disclosure of Morse's perfidy, Jinnie remained quiet.

The birds above their heads kept up a shrill chatter. On ordinary occasions Jinnie would have listened to mark down in her memory a few notes to draw from her fiddle, but at this moment she was too busy looking for a proper explanation. Glancing sidelong at the woman's face and noting the expression upon it, she grew cold and drew into the corner. She would not dare——

"I almost think it's my duty to write your uncle," said Molly deliberately.

Jinnie gasped. She straightened and put forth an impetuous hand.

"Please don't! I beg you not to. Someday, mebbe, someday——"

92

"In the meantime you're living with people who can't take care of you."

"Oh, but they do, and Mr. King's helping me," faltered Jinnie. "Why, he'd do anything for me he could. He loves my fiddle——"

"Does he love you?" asked Molly, her heart beating swiftly.

"I don't know, but he's very good to me."

Molly with one hand carefully brushed a dead leaf from her skirt.

"Do you love him?" she asked, forcing casuality into her tone.

Did she love Theodore King? The question was flung at Jinnie so suddenly that the truth burst from her lips.

"Oh, yes, I love him very, very much——"

The machine started forward with a tremendous jerk. Jinnie gave a frightened little cry, but the woman did not heed her. The motor sped along at a terrific rate, and there just ahead Jinnie spied a lean barn-cat, crossing the road. She screamed again in terror. Still Molly sped on, driving the car straight over the thin, gaunt animal. Jinnie's heart leapt into her mouth. All her great love for living things rose in stout appeal against this ruthless deed. She lifted her slight body and sprang up and out, striking the hard ground with a sickening thud. She sat up, shaking from head to foot. A short distance ahead Molly Merriweather was turning her machine. Jinnie crawled to the middle of the road, still dizzy from her fall. There, struggling before her, was the object for which she had jumped. The cat was writhing in distracted misery, and Jinnie picked him up in her arms. She was sitting on the ground when Molly, very pale, rolled back.

"You little fool! You silly little fool!" she exclaimed, leaping out. "You might have been killed doing such a thing."

"You ran over the kitty," wept Jinnie, bowing her head.

"And what if I did? It's only a cat. Throw it down and come with me immediately."

Jinnie wasn't used to such sentiments. She got to her feet, a queer, rebellious feeling buzzing through her brain.

"I'm going to walk home," she said brokenly, "and take the kitty with me."

Saying this, she took off her jacket and wrapped it about the cat. Molly glared at her furiously.

"You're the strangest little dunce I ever saw," she cried. "If you're determined to take the little beast, get in."

Molly was sorry afterward she had not let Jinnie have her way, for they had driven homeward but a little distance when she saw Theodore's car coming toward them. He himself was at the wheel, and waved good-naturedly. Molly reluctantly stopped her machine. The man looked in astonishment from the girl to the woman. He noticed Jinnie's white face and the long blue mark running from her forehead to her chin. Molly, too, wore an expression which changed her materially. He stepped to the ground and leaned over the edge of their car.

"Something happened?" he questioned, eyeing first one, then the other.

Molly looked down upon the girl, who was staring at Mr. King.

"I—I——" began Jinnie.

Molly made a short explanation.

"She jumped out of the car," she said. "I was just telling her she might have been killed."

"Jumped out of the car?" repeated Theodore, aghast.

"And we were going at a terrible rate," Molly went on.

Her voice was toned with accusation, and Jinnie saw a reprimanding expression spread over the man's face. She didn't want him to think ill of her, yet she was not sorry she had jumped. He was kind and good; he would pity the hurt thing throbbing against her breast.

"We—we—ran over a cat——" she said wretchedly.

"A barn-cat," cut in Molly.

"And he was awfully hurt," interpolated Jinnie. "I couldn't leave him in the road. I had to get him, didn't I?"

Theodore King made a movement of surprise.

"Did you notice it in the road?" he asked Miss Merriweather.

The woman was thoroughly angry, so angry she could not guard her tongue.

"Of course I saw him," she replied haughtily, "but I wouldn't stop for an old cat; I can tell you that much."

"Miss Grandoken looks ill," Theodore answered slowly, "and as I am going her way, I think she'd better come with me."

Molly was about to protest when two strong arms were thrust forth, and Jinnie with the cat was lifted out. Before the girl fully realized what had happened, she was sitting beside her friend, driving homeward. She could hear through her aching brain the chug-chug of Molly's motor following. It was not until they turned into Paradise Road that Mr. King spoke to her. Then he said gently:

"It was a dreadful risk you took, child."

"I didn't think about that," murmured Jinnie, closing her eyes.

"No, I suppose not. Your heart's too tender to let anything be abused.... Is the cat dead?"

Jinnie pulled aside her jacket.

"No, but he's breathing awful hard. It hurts him to try to live. I want to get home quick so Peggy can do something for him."

"I'll hurry, then," replied Mr. King, and when he saw Lafe's face in the window, he again addressed her:

"You'd better try to smile a little, Miss Jinnie, or your uncle'll be frightened."

Jinnie roused herself, but she was so weak when she tried to walk that Theodore picked her up in his arms and carried her into the shop.

94

CHAPTER XXIII

NOBODY'S CAT

Lafe uttered a quick little prayer as the door opened. His glance through the window had shown him Jinnie's pale face and her dark head drooping against Mr. King's shoulder. Theodore smiled as he entered, which instantly eased the fear in the cobbler's heart and he waited for the other man to speak.

"Jinnie had a fall," explained Mr. King, "so I drove her home."

He placed the girl in a chair. She was still holding the mangled cat in her arms.

"Is she much hurt?" questioned Lafe anxiously.

"No, Lafe, I'm not hurt a bit. Miss Merriweather took me for a little ride. I jumped out to get this kitty because she ran over 'im."

She displayed the quivering grey tiger cat.

"Jumped out of a fast-goin' car, honey!" chided Lafe. "That was some dangerous."

Jinnie's eyes were veiled with wonder.

"But I couldn't let him stay and get run over again, could I, Lafe?"

"No, darlin', of course you couldn't.... Are you pretty well broke up?"

Mr. King explained the accident as best he could, and after he departed Mrs. Grandoken came in with Bobbie clinging to her skirts. Then the story was repeated.

"Can't we do something for him, Peg?" pleaded Jinnie.

Peg knelt down and examined the animal as it lay on the floor. She would not have admitted for anything that she was disturbed because of Jinnie's fall. She only said:

"'Twasn't your fault, miss, that you ain't almost dead yourself.... I'll get a dish with some water.... You need it as much as the cat."

It was Bobbie who brought from Peggy a fierce ejaculation. He was standing in the middle of the floor with fluttering hands, a woebegone expression on his upturned face.

"My stars're goin' out," he whimpered. "I want to touch my Jinnie."

"She ain't hurt much, kid," said Peg, hoarsely. "Don't be shakin' like a leaf, Bobbie! You'd think the girl was dead."

Jinnie called the boy to her.

"I'm here, honey," she soothed him, "and I'm all right. I got a little whack on the ground, that's all.... There, don't cry, dearie."

Peg looked down on them frowningly.

"You're both of you little fools," she muttered. "Get out of my way till I go to the kitchen, or I'll kick you out."

When Mrs. Grandoken brought the water, they worked over the cat for a long time, and at length Peg carried the poor little mangled body to the kitchen, Bobbie following her.

Jinnie sat down beside the cobbler on the bench.

"There's something I don't know, Jinnie," he said.

Fully and freely she told him all—all that had happened that day. She explained Molly's recognition of her and the terrors of the afternoon's ride.

"She hates barn-cats," went on the girl, "and, Lafe, when the wheels gritted over him, I flew right out on the ground."

Lafe's arms tightened about her.

"You just couldn't help it," he murmured. "God bless my little girl!"

"Then Mr. King took me with him," concluded Jinnie.

Lafe had his own view of Molly the Merry, but he didn't tell the faint, white girl at his side that he thought the woman was jealous of her.

As Jinnie again recounted nervously the conversation about her Uncle Jordan, the cobbler said softly:

"It's all in the hands of the angels, pet! No harm'll come to you ever."

Jordan Morse answered Miss Merriweather's telephone call.

"I want to talk with you," said she peremptorily.

"I'll come right up," replied Morse.

She stood on the porch with her hands tightly locked together when Jordan dashed up the roadway. She walked slowly down the steps.

"What's up?" demanded Morse.

Molly glanced backward at the quiet home. Theodore's mother was taking her afternoon siesta, and no one else was about. She slipped her hand into Morse's arm and led him under the trees.

"Let's go to the summer house," she urged.

Once seated, Morse looked at her curiously.

"You're ill," he said, noting her distorted face.

"No, only furious.... I've made a discovery."

"Anything of value?"

"Yes, to you—and to me."

Morse bent a keen glance upon her.

"Well?" was all he said.

"I know where your niece, Virginia Singleton, is."

She said this deliberately, realizing the while the worth of her words.

Morse got to his feet unsteadily.

"I don't believe it," he returned.

"I knew you wouldn't, but I do just the same."

"Where?"

"In this town."

"No!"

"Yes."

Morse dropped back on the seat once more.

"For God's sake, don't play with me. Why don't you——"

"I'm going to! Keep still, can't you?"

"You're torturing me," muttered the man, mopping his brow.

"She's—she's Jinnie Grandoken—the girl who played at Theo's party."

"Good God!" and then through the silence came another muttered, "Great merciful God!"

Molly allowed him to regain his self-control.

"I told you that night, Jordan, I thought I remembered her," she then said. "To-day I found out it was she."

"Tell me all you know," ordered Morse, with darkening brow.

Molly openly admitted her jealousy of Jinnie. She had no shame because, long before, she had told her husband of her absorbing passion for Theodore King.

"I discovered it purely by accident," she went on, relating the story.

Morse chewed the end of his cigar.

"Now what're you going to do?" demanded Molly presently.

Jordan threw away his cigar and thrust his hands deep into his pockets, stretching out a pair of long legs. There he sat considering the tips of his boots in silence.

"I've got to think, and think quick," he broke out suddenly. "My God! I might have known she didn't belong in that cobbler's shop.... I'll go now.... Don't mention this to Theo."

As he was leaving, he said with curling lip:

"I guess now you know my prospects you won't be so stingy. I'll have to have money to carry this through."

"All right," said Molly.

When she was alone, Molly's anger decreased. She had an ally now worth having. She smiled delicately as she passed up the stairs to her room, and the smile was brought to her lips because she remembered having begged Jordan to help her in this matter several times before. Then he had had no incentive, but to-day——Ah, now he would give her a divorce quietly! The social world in which she hoped to move would know nothing of her youthful indiscretion.

That night Jinnie and Peg were bending anxiously over a basket near the kitchen stove. All that human hands and hearts could do had been done for the suffering barn-cat. He had given no sign of consciousness, his breath coming and going in long, deep gasps.

"He'll die, won't he, Peg?" asked Jinnie, sorrowfully.

"Yes, sure. An' it'll be better for the beast, too." Peg said this tempestuously.

"I'd like to have him live," replied Jinnie. "Milly Ann mightn't love him, but she got used to Happy Pete, didn't she?"

"This feller," assured Peggy, wagging her head, "won't get used to anything more on this earth."

"Poor kitty," mourned Jinnie.

She was thinking of the beautiful world, the trees and the flowers, and the wonderful songs of nature amidst which the dying animal had existed.

"I hope he'll go to some nice place," she observed sadly, walking away from Mrs. Grandoken.

Later, after cogitating deeply, Jinnie expressed herself to the cobbler.

"Lafe, Lafe dear," she said, "it's all true you told me, ain't it?... All about the angels and God?... The poor kitty's suffering awful. He's got the Christ too, hasn't he, Lafe?"

The man looked into the agonized young face.

"Yes, child," he replied reverently, "he's got the Christ too, same's you an' me. God's in everything. He loves 'em all."

That night the girl sat unusually long with paper and pencil. Just before going to bed she placed a paper on the cobbler's knee.

"I wrote that hurt kitty some poetry," she said shyly.

Lafe settled his spectacles on his nose, picked up the sheet, and read:

> "I'm nobody's cat and I've been here so long,
>   In this world of sorrow and pain,
> I've no father nor mother nor home in this place,
>   And must always stay out in the rain.
> "Hot dish water, stones at me have been thrown,
>   And one of my hind legs is lame;
> No wonder I run when I know the boys
>   Come to see if I'm tame.
> "I've a friend in the country, and he's nobody's dog,
>   And his burdens're heavy as mine,
> He told me one day the boys had once tied
>   A tin can to his tail with a line.
> "Now they talk in the churches of God and his Son,
>   Of Paradise, Heaven and Hell;
> Of a Savior who came on earth for mankind,
>   And for His children all should be well.
> "Now I'd like to know if God didn't make me,
>   And cause me to live and all that?
> I believe there's a place for nobody's child,
>   And also for nobody's cat."

Mr. Grandoken lifted misty eyes.

"It's fine," he said, "an' every word true!... Every single word."

The next morning Jinnie went to the basket behind the stove. The cat was dead,—dead, in the same position in which she had left him the night before, and close to his nose was the meat Peggy had tried to entice him to eat. She lifted the basket and carried it into the shop.

"Poor little feller," said Lafe. "I 'spose you'll have to bury him, lass."

Bobbie edged forward, and felt for Jinnie's fingers.

"Bury him on the hill, dearie, where you found me," he whispered. "It's lovely there, and he can see my stars."

"All right," replied Jinnie, dropping her hand on the boy's golden head.

That afternoon, just before the funeral, Jinnie stood quietly in front of the cobbler.

"Lafe," she said, looking at him appealingly, "the kitty's happy even if he is dead, isn't he?"

"Sure," replied Lafe. "His angels've got charge of him, all right."

"I was wondering something," ventured the girl, thoughtfully. "Couldn't we take him in the 'Happy in Spite'?... Eh, Lafe?"

Lake looked at her in surprise.

"I never thought of takin' anything dead in the club," said he dubiously.

"But he's happy, you said, Lafe?"

"He's happy enough, yes, sure!"

"Then let's take him in," repeated Jinnie eagerly.

"Let's take 'im in, cobbler," breathed Bobbie, pressing forward. "He wants to come in."

They lifted the cover of the basket, and there in quietude the barn-cat was sleeping his long last sleep.

Jinnie lifted one of the stiff little paws, and placed it in Lafe's fingers. The cobbler shook it tenderly.

"You're in the club, sir," said he in a thick, choked voice. Then Jinnie and Bobbie, carrying their precious dead comrade, started for the hill.

CHAPTER XXIV

"HE MIGHT EVEN MARRY HER"

"I don't see why you must have her out of the way entirely," hesitated Molly Merriweather, looking up into Jordan Morse's face. "Couldn't you send her to some girls' place?"

"Now you don't know anything about it, Molly," answered the man impatiently. "If she doesn't disappear absolutely, the cobbler and Theodore'll find her."

"That's so," said Molly, meditatively, "but it seems horrible——"

Morse interrupted her with a sarcastic laugh.

"That's what Theodore would think, and more, too, if he thought any one was going to harm a hair of the child's head."

Molly flamed red.

"To save her, he might even marry her," Morse went on relentlessly.

Molly gestured negatively.

"He wouldn't. He couldn't!" she cried stormily. She had never permitted herself to face such a catastrophe save when she was angry.

Jordan Morse contemplated his wife a short space of time.

"I can't understand your falling in love with a man who hasn't breathed a word of affection for you," he said tentatively.

Molly showed him an angry face.

"You're not a woman, so you can't judge," she replied.

"Thank God for that!" retorted Morse.

"We wouldn't have had any of this trouble," he continued, at length, "if you'd let me know about the boy. There's no excuse for you, absolutely none. You know very well I would have come back."

All the softness in the woman turned to hardness.

"How many times," she flamed, "must I tell you I was too angry to write or beg you to come, Jordan?... I've told you over and over."

"And with all you say, I can't understand it. Are you going to impart your precious past to Theodore?"

"No," replied Molly, setting her lips.

Presently Morse laughed provokingly.

"How you women do count your chickens before they're hatched! Where did you get the idea Theodore was going to ask you to marry him?"

"I'll make him," breathed Molly, with confidence.

"Well, go ahead," bantered Morse. "All I ask for releasing you is that you'll help me rid myself of my beautiful niece, Virginia, at the same time ridding yourself, my lady, and give me my boy when we find him."

His tones in the first part of the speech were mocking, but Molly noted when he said "boy" his voice softened. She looked at him wonderingly. What a strange mixture of good and evil he was! When he got up to leave, she was not sorry. She watched him stride away with a deep sigh of relief.

She was still sitting in the summer house when Theodore King swung his motor through the gate and drew up before the porch. He jumped out, wiped his face, saw Molly, and smiled.

"Well, it's cool here," he said, walking toward her.

"Yes," said Molly. "Come and sit down a minute."

Theodore looked doubtfully at the house.

"I really ought to do some writing, but I'll sit a while if you like. I passed Jordan on the way home."

Molly nodded, and Theodore quizzed her with laughing eyes.

"Isn't he coming pretty often?" he asked. "Jordan's got prospects, Molly! If his niece isn't found, you know, he'll have a fortune.... Better set your cap for him."

Molly blushed under his words, trying not to show her resentment. Was Theodore a perfect fool? Couldn't he see she desired no one but himself, and him alone?

"Jordan doesn't care for me that way," she observed with dignity, "and I don't care for him."

Theodore flicked an ash from his cigar.

100

"I think you're mistaken, Molly—I mean as far as he is concerned."

"I'm not! Of course, I'm not! Oh, Theodore, I've been wanting to ask you something for a long time. I do want to go back home for a day.... Would you take me?"

Theodore eyed her through wreaths of blue smoke.

"Well, I might," he hesitated, "but hadn't you better ask Jordan? I'm afraid he wouldn't like me——"

Molly got up so quickly that Theodore, surprised, got up too.

"I don't want Jordan, and I do want you," she said emphatically. "Of course if you don't care to go——"

"On the contrary," interrupted Theodore, good-naturedly, "I would really like it.... Yes, I'll go all right.... I have a reason for going."

Molly's whole demeanor changed. She gave a musical laugh. He could have but one reason, and she felt she knew that reason! What a handsome dear he was, and how she loved the whole bigness of him!

As she turned to walk away, Theodore fell in at her side, suiting his steps to hers.

"Mind you, Molly, any day you say but Saturday."

"Why not Saturday?" asked Molly, pouting. "I might want you then!"

Unsuspecting, Mr. King explained.

"The fact is, Saturday I've planned to go on the hill. You remember Grandoken's niece? I want to find out how she's progressing in her music."

If Theodore had been watching Molly's face, he would have noted how its expression changed darkly. But, humming a tune, he went into the house unconcernedly, and Molly recognized the rhythm as one Jinnie had played that night long ago with Peg Grandoken's lace curtains draped about her.

Jinnie's youth, her bright blue eyes, her wonderful talent, Molly hated, and hated cordially. Then she decided Theodore should go with her Saturday.

That evening when Jordan Morse came in, Molly told him she would help him in any scheme to get Jinnie away from Bellaire.

"You're beginning to understand he likes her pretty much, eh?" asked the man rudely.

Molly wouldn't admit this, but she replied simply:

"I don't want her around. That's all! As long as she's in Bellaire, the Kings'll always have her here with her fiddle."

"Some fiddle," monotoned Jordan.

"It's the violin that attracts Theodore," hesitated Molly.

"And her blue eyes," interrupted Jordan, smiling widely.

"Her talent, you mean," corrected Molly.

"And her curls," laughed Morse. "I swear if she wasn't a relation of mine I'd marry the kid myself. She's a beauty!... She's got you skinned to death."

"You needn't be insulting, Jordan," admonished Molly, flushing.

"It's the truth, though. That's where the rub comes. You can't wool me, Molly. If she were hideous, you wouldn't worry at all.... Why, I know seven or eight girls right here in Bellaire who'd give their eye teeth and wear store ones to get Theodore to look at 'em crosseyed.... Lord, what fools women are!"

Molly left him angrily, and Morse, shrugging his shoulders, strolled on through the trees. Not far from the house he met Theodore, and they wandered on together, smoking in silence. Morse suddenly developed an idea. Why shouldn't he sound King about Jinnie? Accordingly, he began with:

"That's a wonderful girl, Grandoken's niece."

This topic was one Theodore loved to speak of, to dream so, so he said impetuously:

"She is indeed. I only wish I could get her away from Paradise Road."

Morse turned curious eyes on his friend.

"Why?"

"Well, I don't think it's any place for an impressionable young girl like her."

"She's living with Jews, too, isn't she?"

"Yes, but good people," Theodore replied. "I want her to go away to school. I'd be willing to pay her expenses——"

Morse flung around upon him.

"Send her away to school? You?"

"Yes. Why not? Wouldn't it be a good piece of charity work? She's the most talented girl I ever saw."

"And the prettiest," Jordan cut in.

"By far the prettiest," answered King without hesitation.

His voice was full of feeling, and Jordan Morse needed no more to tell him plainly that Theodore loved Jinnie Grandoken. A sudden chill clutched at his heart. If King ever took Jinnie under his protection, his own plans would count for nothing. He went home that night disgusted with himself for having stayed away from his home country so long, angry that Molly had not told him about the baby, and more than angry with Theodore King.

CHAPTER XXV

WHEN THEODORE FORGOT

For the next few days Jordan Morse turned over in his mind numerous plans to remove Jinnie from Grandoken's home, but none seemed feasible. As long as Lafe knew his past and stood like a rock beside the girl, as long as Theodore King was interested in her, he himself was powerless to do anything. How to get both the cobbler and his niece out of the way was a problem which continually worried him.

He mentioned his anxiety to Molly, asking her if by any means she could help him.

"I did tell her I'd write to you," said Molly.

Morse's face fell.

"She's a stubborn little piece," he declared presently. "Theo's in love with her all right."

"You don't really mean that!" stammered Molly, her heart thumping.

"Perhaps not very seriously, but such deep interest as his must come from something more than just the girl's talent. He spoke about sending her away to school."

"He shan't," cried Molly, infuriated.

Morse's rehearsal of Theodore's suggestion was like goads in her soul.

"If she'd go," went on the man, "nothing you or I could do would stop him. The only way——"

Molly whirled upon him abruptly.

"I'll help you, Jordan, I will.... Anything, any way to keep him from her."

They were both startled and confused when Theodore came upon them suddenly with his swinging stride, but before Morse went home, he whispered to Molly:

"I've thought of something—tell you to-morrow."

That night Molly scarcely slept. The vision of a black-haired girl in the arms of Theodore King haunted her through her restless dreams, and the agony was so intense that before the dawn broke over the hill she made up her mind to help her husband, even to the point of putting Jinnie out of existence.

That morning Morse approached her with this command:

"You try to get Jinnie to go with you to Mottville. You wouldn't have to stay but a day or so. There your responsibilities would end.... I'll be there at the same time.... Will you do it, Molly?"

"Yes," said Molly, and her heart began to sing and her eyes to shine. Her manner to Jordan as he left was more cordial than since his return from Europe.

At noon time, when Theodore King saw her walking, sweetly cool, under the trees, he joined her. Molly had donned the dress he had complimented most, and as he approached her, she lifted a shy gaze to his.

"You couldn't take me to-morrow, you're sure?" she begged, her voice low, deep and appealingly resonant.

Theodore hesitated. Being naturally chivalrous and kindly, he disliked to refuse, but he had already sent a note to Jinnie to meet him at the master's Saturday, and it went against his inclination to break that appointment.

103

"I don't see how I can," he replied thoughtfully, "but choose any day next week, and we'll make a real picnic of it."

"I'm so disappointed," Molly murmured sadly. "I wanted to go Saturday. But of course——"

"I'll see if I can arrange it," he assured her. "Possibly I might go up to hear her play to-day.... I'll see.... Later I'll 'phone you."

Leaving the house, he headed his car toward the lower end of the town. He was glad of an excuse to go to Paradise Road. Lafe smiled through the window at him, and he entered the shop at the cobbler's cordial, "Come in!"

"I suppose you want Jinnie, eh?" asked Lafe.

"Yes. I'll detain her only a moment."

Bobbie got up from the floor where he was playing soldiers with tacks and nails.

"Boy'll call Jinnie," said he, moving forward.

The two men watched the slender blind child feel his way to the door.

"Bobbie loves to take a part in things," explained Lafe. "Poor little fellow!"

"Is he hopelessly blind?" asked Theodore.

"Yes, yes," and Lafe sighed. "I sent him once by Peg to ask a big eye specialist. He's a good little shaver, but his heart's awful weak. You wouldn't think he's almost eleven, would you?"

Theodore shook his head, shocked.

"It isn't possible!" he exclaimed.

"He ain't growed much since he come here over two years ago. Jinnie can carry him in one arm."

"Poor child!" said Theodore sympathetically.

Just then Jinnie came into the room shyly. Bobbie had excitedly whispered to her that "the beautiful big man with the nice hands" wanted her. She hesitated at the sight of Mr. King, but advanced as Lafe held out his hand to her.

Before Theodore could explain, she had told him:

"The master isn't giving me a lesson to-day, but he will to-morrow because you're coming."

With pride in her voice, she said it radiantly, the color mantling high in her cheeks. Molly's importunate insistence escaped Theodore's mind. When with Jinnie, ordinary matters generally did fade away.

"I'm very glad," he replied. "I hope you've progressed a lot."

"She has, sir, she sure has," Lafe put in. "You'll be surprised! How long since you've heard her play?"

"A long time," answered Theodore, and still forgetting Molly, he went on, "I wonder if you'd like to come to the house to-morrow to dinner and play for us. My mother was speaking about how much she'd enjoy it only a short time ago."

Jinnie's eyes sparkled.

"I should love to come," she answered gladly.

He rose to go, taking her hand.

"Then I'll send the car for you," he promised her.

He was sitting at his office desk when Molly the Merry once more came into his mind. An ejaculation escaped his lips, and he made a wry face. Then, in comparison, Jinnie, with all her sparkling youth, rose triumphant before him. He loved the child, for a child she still seemed to him. To tell her now of his affection might harm her work. He would wait! She was so young, so very young.

For a long time he sat thinking and dreaming of the future, and into the quiet of his office he brought, in brilliant vision, a radiant, raven-haired woman—his ideal—his Jinnie. Suddenly again he remembered his promise to Molly and slowly took down the telephone. Then deliberately he replaced it. It would be easier to explain the circumstances face to face with her, and no doubt entered his mind but that the woman would be satisfied and very glad that Jinnie was coming with her violin to play for them. Molly wouldn't mind postponing her trip for a few days.

Molly was reclining as usual in the hammock with a book in her hand when he ran up the steps.

"Molly," he began, going to her quickly, "I want to confess."

"Confess?" she repeated, sitting up.

"Yes, it's this way: When I went out this morning I felt sure I could arrange about to-morrow.... But what do you think?"

Miss Merriweather put down the book, stood up, her hand over her heart.

"I can't guess," she breathed.

"Well, I went to Grandoken's——"

"You could have sent a note," Molly cut in.

Theodore looked at her curiously.

"I could, but I didn't. I wanted Jinnie to understand——"

His voice vibrated deeply when he spoke that name, and the listener's love-laden ears caught the change immediately.

"Well?" she murmured in question.

"When I got there and saw her, I forgot about Saturday. Before I had a chance, she told me she wasn't going to the master's to-day. Then without another thought——"

"Well?" interviewed Molly with widening eyes.

"Pardon me, Molly," Theodore said tactlessly, "for forgetting you— you will, won't you? I asked her to play here to-morrow night."

Molly felt the structure of her whole world tumbling down about her ears. He had forgotten her for that girl, that jade in Paradise Road, the girl who stood between her and all her hopes. She took one step forward and forgot, her dignity, forgot everything but his stinging insult.

"How dared you?" she uttered hoarsely. Her voice grew thin as it raised to the point of a question.

"Dare!" echoed Theodore, his expression changing.

Molly went nearer him with angry, sparkling eyes.

"Yes, how dared you ask that girl to come here when I dislike her? You know how I hate her——"

Mr. King tossed his cigar into the grass, gravity settling on his countenance.

"I hadn't the slightest idea you disliked her," he said.

Molly eagerly advanced into the space between them.

"She is trying to gain some sort of influence over you, Theo, just the same as she got over that Jewish cobbler."

Theodore King gazed in amazement at the reddening, beautiful face. Surely he had not heard aright. Had she really made vile charges against the girl? To implicate Jinnie with a thought of conspiracy brought hot blood about his temples. He wouldn't stand that even from an old-time friend. Of course he liked Molly very much, yes, very much indeed, but this new antagonistic spirit in her——

"What's the matter with you, Molly?" he demanded abruptly. "You haven't any reason to speak of the child that way."

"The child!" sneered Molly. "Why, she's a little river rat—a bold, nasty——"

Theodore King raised his great shoulders, throwing back his closely cropped head. Then he sprang to refute the terrible aspersion against the girl he loved.

"Stop!" he commanded in a harsh voice, leaning over the panting woman. "And now I'll ask you how you dare?" he finished.

Molly answered him bravely, catching her breath in a sob.

"I dare because I'm a woman.... I dare because I know what she's doing. If she hadn't played her cards well, you'd never've paid any attention to her at all.... No one can make me believe you would have been interested in a—in a——"

The man literally whirled from the porch, bounded into the motor, turned the wheel, and shot rapidly away.

CHAPTER XXVI

MOLLY ASKS TO BE FORGIVEN

All the evening Molly waited in despair. She dared not appear at dinner and arose the next morning after a sleepless night. For two or three hours she hovered about the telephone, hoping for word from Theodore. He would certainly 'phone her. He would tell her he was sorry for the way he had left her, for the way he had spoken to her. Even his mother noticed her pale face and extreme nervousness.

"What is it, dear?" asked Mrs. King, solicitously.

"Nothing, nothing—much," answered Molly evasively.

Mrs. King hesitated before she ventured, "I thought I heard you and Theo talking excitedly last night. Molly, you musn't quarrel with him.... You know the wish of my heart.... I need you, child, and so does he."

Miss Merriweather knelt beside the gentle woman.

"He doesn't care for me, dear!" she whispered.

For an instant she was impelled to speak of Jinnie, but realizing what a tremendous influence Theodore had over his mother, she dared not. Like her handsome son, Mrs. King worshipped genius, and Molly reluctantly admitted to herself that the girl possessed it.

"He's young yet," sighed the mother, "and he's always so sweet to you, Molly. Someday he'll wake up.... There, there, dearie, don't cry!"

"I'm so unhappy," sobbed Molly.

Mrs. King smoothed the golden head tenderly.

"Why, child, he can't help but love you," she insisted. "He knows how much I depend on you.... I'd have had you with me long before if your father hadn't needed you.... Shall I speak to Theodore?"

"No, no——" gasped Molly, and she ran from the room.

Under the tall trees she paced for many minutes. How could she wait until dinner—until he came home? She felt her pride ebbing away as she watched the sun cross the sky. The minutes seemed hours long. Molly went swiftly into the house. First assuring herself no one was within hearing distance, she paused before the telephone, longing, yet scarcely daring to use it. Then she took off the receiver and called Theodore's number. His voice, deep, low and thrilling, answered her.

"It's I, Theo," she said faintly.... "Molly."

"Yes," he answered, but that was all.

He gave her no encouragement, no opening, but in desperation she uttered,

"Theodore, I'm sorry!... Oh, I'm so sorry!... Won't you forgive me?"

There was silence on the wire for an appreciable length of time.

"Theodore?" murmured Molly once more.

"Yes."

"I want you to forgive me.... I couldn't wait until you came home."

She heard a slight cough, then came the reply.

"I can't control your thoughts, Molly, but I dislike to have my friends illy spoken of."

"I know! I know it, Theodore! But please forgive me, won't you?"

"Very well," answered Theodore, and he clicked off the 'phone.

Molly dropped her face into her hands.

"He hung the receiver up in my ear," she muttered. "How cruel, how terrible of him!"

It was a wan, beautiful face that turned up to Theodore King when he came home to dinner. Too kindly by nature to hurt anyone, he smiled at

Molly. Then he stopped and held out his hand. The woman took it, saying earnestly:

"I'm sorry, Theo.... I'm very sorry. I think I'm a little cat, don't you?" and she laughed, the tension lifted from her by his cordiality.

There was a wholesomeness in her manner that made Theodore's heart glad.

"Of course not, Molly!... You couldn't be that!... And next week we will have a lovely day in the country."

Molly turned away sadly. She had hoped he would do as she wanted him to in spite of his appointment with Jinnie Grandoken.

That evening Jinnie wore a beautiful new dress when she started for the Kings. Of course she didn't know that Theodore had arranged with Peggy to purchase it, and when Mrs. Grandoken had told her to come along and buy the gown, Jinnie's eyes sparkled, but she shook her head.

"I'd rather you'd spend the money on Lafe and Bobbie," she said.

But Peggy replied, "No," and that's how it came that Jinnie stepped quite proudly from the motor car at the stone steps.

Molly Merriweather met her with a forced smile, and Jinnie felt strained until Theodore King's genial greeting dissipated the affront. After the dinner, through which she sat very much embarrassed, she played until, to the man watching her, it seemed as if the very roof would lift from the house and sail off into the Heavens.

When Jinnie was ready to go home, standing blushing under the bright light, she had never looked more lovely. Molly hoped Theo would send the girl alone in the car with Bennett, but as she saw him put on his hat, she said, with hesitancy:

"Mayn't I go along?"

She asked the question of Theodore, and realized instantly that he did not want her.

Jinnie came forward impetuously.

"Oh, do come, Miss Merriweather! It'll be so nice."

And Molly hated the girl more cordially than ever.

On arriving home Jinnie beamed out her happiness to the cobbler and his wife.

"And the fiddle, Peggy, they loved the fiddle," she told the woman.

"Did you make it, Jinnie?" asked Peggy gruffly.

"What, the fiddle?" demanded Jinnie.

Peggy nodded.

"No," faltered Jinnie in surprise.

"Then don't brag about it," warned Peggy. "If you'd a glued them boards together, it'd a been something, but as long as you didn't, it ain't no credit to you."

Lafe laughed, and Jinnie, too, uttered a low, rueful sound. How funny Peg was! And when Mrs. Grandoken had gone to prepare for the night, Lafe insisted that Jinnie tell him over and over all the happenings of the evening. For a long time afterwards she sat dreaming, reminiscing in sweet fancy every word and smile Theodore had given her.

CHAPTER XXVII

"HAVEN'T YOU ANY SOUL?"

Whenever Molly Merriweather was mentioned to Theodore King, that young man felt a twinge in his conscience. His mother had taken him gently to task. Out of respect for Molly's wishes she refrained from speaking of the girl's affection for him, but cautioned him to be careful not to offend her companion.

"She's very sensitive, you know, Theodore dear, and very good to me. I really don't know what I'd do without her."

"I was thoughtless!... I'll do better, mother mine," he smiled. "I'll go to her now and tell her so."

Theodore found Molly writing a letter in the library. He sank into an easy chair and yawned good-naturedly. The woman was still furious with him, so merely lifted her eyes at his entrance, and went on writing. Theodore was quiet for a few moments, then with a laugh went to the desk and took the pen forcibly from Molly's hand.

"Come and make up," he said.

"Have we anything to make up?" she asked languidly, keeping her eyes on the paper.

"Of course we have. You know very well, Molly, you're angry with me.... Now mother says——"

She caught his bantering tone, and resenting it, drew her fingers away haughtily.

"You learn good manners from your mother, it seems."

Her tone was insolent and angered him. Theodore returned quickly to his chair.

"No, I don't," he denied. "You know I don't! But before you asked me to go with you Saturday, I told you I had an appointment——"

"Yes, and you told me who it was with, too," Molly thrust back in his teeth.

"Exactly, because there's no reason why I shouldn't. I've taken an extreme interest in the little girl.... You offended me by talking against her."

Molly's temper was rising by the minute. She had armored herself with a statement, the truth of which she would force upon him.

"I'm not sure I said anything that wasn't true," she returned discourteously.

Theodore leaned back in his chair.

"Then you didn't mean it when you said you were sorry?" he demanded shortly.

"I wanted you to go with me, that's all."

"And you took that way to make me. Was that it?"

Molly picked up her pen and made a few marks with it.

109

"I'm not interested in Miss Grandoken," she replied.

"So I notice," retorted Theodore, provokingly.

She turned around upon him with angry, sparkling eyes.

"I think you've a lot of nerve to bring her into your home."

She hazarded this without thought of consequences.

"What do you mean?" he asked presently, searching her face with an analytical gaze.

Molly was wrought up to the point of invention, perhaps because she was madly jealous.

"Men generally keep that sort of a woman to themselves," she explained. "A home is usually sacred to the ordinary man."

Theodore was stung to silence. It was a bitter fling, and his thoughts worked rapidly. It took a long moment for his tall figure to get up from the chair.

"Just what do you mean?" he demanded, thrusting his hands into his pockets.

"I don't believe I need tell you anymore," she answered.

Theodore stood in the middle of the room as if turned to stone.

"I'm dense, I guess," he admitted huskily.

Angered beyond reason or self-control, Molly pushed the letter away impatiently and stood up.

"Well, if you're so terribly dense, then listen. No man is ever interested in a girl like that unless she is something more to him than a mere——" She broke off, because a dark red flush was spreading in hot waves over the man's face. But bravely she proceeded, "Of course you wouldn't insult your family and your friends by marrying her. Then what conclusion do you want them to draw?"

Theodore looked at her as if she'd suddenly lost her senses. She had cast an aspersion upon the best little soul in God's created world.

"Well, of all the villainous insinuations I ever heard!" he thundered harshly. "My God, woman! Haven't you any soul ... any decency about you?"

The question leaped out of a throat tense with uncontrollable rage. It was couched in language never used to her before, and caused the woman to stagger back. She was about to demand an apology, when Theodore flung out of the room and banged the door behind him.

Molly sat down quickly. Humiliating, angry tears flowed down her cheeks and she made no effort to restrain them. What cared she that Theodore had repudiated her accusation? She felt she had discovered the truth, and nothing more need be said about it.

After growing a little calmer, she saw that she'd made another mistake by enraging Theodore. He had not taken her insults against the girl as she had expected.

Half an hour later she called his office and was informed he was out.

Theodore left Molly more angry than he'd ever been in his life. Instead of making him think less of Jinnie, Molly's aspersions drew him more tenderly toward the girl. As he strode through the road under the trees, his heart burned to see her. He looked at his watch—it was four o'clock. Jinnie had had her lesson in the morning, so he could not call for her at the master's. Just then he saw her walking quickly along the street, and she lifted shy, glad eyes as he spoke her name. By this time his temper had cooled, yet there lingered in his heart the stabbing hurt brought there by Molly's slurs. He felt as if in some way he owed an apology to Jinnie; as if he must make up for harm done her by a vile, gossiping tongue.

He fell into step beside her and gently took the violin box from her hand.

"And how is my little friend to-day?" he asked.

His voice, unusually musical, made Jinnie spontaneously draw a little nearer him.

"I'm very well," she returned, demurely, "and I've learned some very lovely things. I went up twice to-day—sometimes the master makes me come back in the afternoon."

It eased his offended dignity to see her so happy, so vividly lovely. He had gone to Molly with the intention of asking her to go with him some day soon to Mottville. He thought of this now with a grim setting of his teeth; but looking at Jinnie, an idea more to his liking came in its place. He would take her somewhere for a day. She needed just such a day to make her color a little brighter, although as he glanced at her again, he had to admit she was rosy enough. Nevertheless a great desire came over him to ask her; so when they had almost reached the cobbler's shop, he said:

"How would a nice holiday suit you?"

Jinnie looked up into his face, startled.

"What do you mean by a holiday? Not to take lessons?"

Theodore caught her thought, and laughed.

"Oh, no, not that! But I was thinking if you would go with me into the country——"

"For a whole day?" gasped Jinnie, stopping point blank.

"Yes, for a whole day," replied Theodore, smiling.

"Oh, I couldn't go. I couldn't."

"Why?... Don't you want to?"

Of course she wanted to go. Jinnie felt that if she knew she was going with him, she'd fly to the sky and back again.

"Yes," she murmured. "I'd like to go, but I couldn't—for lots of reasons!... Lafe wouldn't let me for one, and then Bobbie needs me awfully."

They started on, and Jinnie could see Lafe's window, but not the cobbler himself.

"But I'd bring you back at dusk," Theodore assured her, "and you'd be happy——"

"Happy! Happy!" she breathed, with melting eyes. "I'd be more'n happy, but I can't go."

Theodore raised his hat quickly and left her without another word.

CHAPTER XXVIII

JINNIE DECIDES AGAINST THEODORE

Now for a few days Theodore King had had in mind a plan which, as he contemplated it, gave him great delight. He had decided to send Jinnie Grandoken away to school, to a school where she would learn the many things he considered necessary.

So one morning at Jinnie's lesson hour he appeared at the cobbler's shop and was received by Lafe with his usual grave smile.

"Jinnie's at the master's," said Mr. Grandoken, excusing the girl's absence.

"Yes, I know. The fact is, I wanted to talk with you and Mrs. Grandoken."

Lafe looked at him critically.

"Bobsie," said he to the blind boy, "call Peggy, will you?"

When the woman and child came in hand in hand, Peggy bowed awkwardly to Mr. King. Somehow, when this young man appeared with his aristocratic manner and his genial, friendly advances, she was always embarrassed.

Theodore cleared his throat.

"For some time," he began, "I've had in mind a little plan for Miss Jinnie, and I do hope you'll concur with me in it."

He glanced from the cobbler to his wife, and Lafe replied,

"You've been too kind already, Mr. King——"

"It isn't a question of kindness, my dear Mr. Grandoken. As I've told you before, I'm very much interested in your niece."

Bobbie slipped from Mrs. Grandoken and went close to the speaker.

"She's my Jinnie," breathed the boy with a saintly smile.

Theodore laughed.

"Yes, I know that, my lad, but you want her to be happy, don't you?"

"She is happy," interjected Lafe, trembling.

"You might tell us your plan," broke in Peg sourly, who always desired to get the worst over quickly.

"Well, it is to send her away to school for a few years."

Bobbie gave a little cry and staggered to Peg, holding out his hands. She picked him up, with bitterness depicted in her face. But when she looked at her husband she was shocked, for he was leaning against the wall, breathing deeply.

"I knew the thought of letting her go would affect you, Mr. Grandoken," soothed Theodore. "That's why I came alone. Jinnie's so tender-hearted I feared the sight of your first grief might cause her to refuse."

"Does she know you was goin' to ask us this?" demanded Peg suspiciously.

Mr. King shook his head.

"Of course not! If she had, she and I would have asked it together."

"God bless 'er!" murmured Lafe. "You see it's like this, sir: Peg and me don't want to stand in her light."

"I won't let my Jinnie go," sighed Bobbie. "I haven't any stars when she's gone."

"The poor child's devoted to her," excused Lafe. "That's what makes him act so about it."

Theodore's sympathy forced him to his feet.

"So I see," said he. "Come here, young man! I want to talk to you a minute."

Reluctantly Bobbie left Mrs. Grandoken, and Theodore, sitting again, took him on his knee.

"Now, Bobbie, look at me."

Bobbie turned up a wry, tearful face.

"I've got my eyes on you, sir," he wriggled.

"That's right! Don't you want your Jinnie to learn a lot of things and be a fine young lady?"

"She is a fine young lady now," mumbled Bobbie stubbornly, "and she's awful pretty."

"True," acquiesced Theodore, much amused, "but she must study a lot more."

"Lafe could learn her things," argued Bobbie, sitting up very straight. "Lafe knows everything."

Mr. King smiled and glanced at the cobbler, but Lafe's face was so drawn and white that Theodore looked away again. He couldn't make it seem right that he should bring about such sorrow as this, yet the thought of Jinnie and what he wanted her to be proved a greater argument with him than the grief of her family.

"I've told you, sir," Lafe repeated, "and I say again, my wife and me don't want to stand in our girl's light. She'll decide when she comes home."

Theodore got up, placing Bobbie on his feet beside him.

"I hope she'll think favorably of my idea, then," said he, "and to-morrow I'll see her and make some final arrangements."

After he had gone, Peggy and Lafe sat for a long time without a word.

"Go to the kitchen, Bobbie," said Mrs. Grandoken presently, "and give Happy Pete a bit of meat."

The boy paused in his stumbling way to the kitchen.

"I don't want my Jinnie to go away," he mumbled.

When the door closed on the blind child, Peggy shook her shoulders disdainfully.

"She'll go, of course," she sneered.

"An' we can't blame 'er if she does, Peg," answered Lafe sadly. "She's young yet, an' such a chance ain't comin' every day."

The woman got heavily to her feet.

113

"I hate 'er, but the house's dead when she ain't in it," and she went rapidly into the other room.

Jinnie came into the shop wearily, but one look at the cobbler brought her to a standstill. She didn't wait to take off her hat before going directly to him.

"Lafe—Lafe dear, you're sick. Why, honey dear——"

"I ain't very well, Jinnie darlin'. Would you mind askin' Peggy to come in a minute?"

Mrs. Grandoken looked up as the girl came in.

"Lafe wants you, Peg. He's sick, isn't he? What happened to him, Peggy?"

Bobbie uttered a whining cry.

"Jinnie," he called, "Jinnie, come here!"

Peg pushed the girl back into the little hall.

"You shut up, Bobbie," she ordered, "and sit there! Jinnie'll come back in a minute."

Then the speaker shoved the girl ahead of her into the shop and stood with her arms folded, austerely silent.

"I want to know what's the matter," insisted Jinnie.

"You tell 'er, Peg. I just couldn't," whispered Lafe.

Mrs. Grandoken drew a deep breath and ground her teeth.

"You've got to go away, kid," she began tersely, dropping into a chair.

Jinnie blanched in fright.

"My uncle!" she exclaimed, growing weak-kneed.

"No such thing," snapped Peg. "You're goin' to a fine school an' learn how to be a elegant young lady."

"Who said so?" flashed Jinnie.

"Mr. King," cut in Lafe.

Then Jinnie understood, and she laughed hysterically. For one blessed single moment her woman's heart told her that Theodore would not be so eager for her welfare if he didn't love her.

"Was that what made your tears, Lafe?"

Her eyes glistened as she uttered the question.

Lafe nodded.

"And what made Bobbie cry so loud?"

"Yes."

"Was Mr. King here?"

"Sure," said Peg.

"And he said I was to go away to school, eh?"

"Yes," repeated Peg, "an' of course you'll go."

Jinnie went forward and placed a slender hand on Lafe's shoulder. Then she faced Mrs. Grandoken.

"Didn't you both know me well enough to tell him I wouldn't go for anything in the world?"

If a bomb had been placed under Mrs. Grandoken's chair, she wouldn't have jumped up any more quickly, and she flung out of the door before Jinnie could stop her. Then the girl wound her arms about the cobbler's neck.

"I wouldn't leave you, dear, not for any school on earth," she whispered. "Now I'm going to tell Mr. King so."

Jinnie sped along Paradise Road and into the nearest drug store. It took her a few minutes to find Theodore's number, and when she took off the receiver, she had not the remotest idea how to word her refusal. She only remembered Lafe's sad face and Bobbie's sharp, agonizing calling of her name.

"I want to speak to Mr. King," she said in answer to a strange voice at the other end of the wire.

Her voice was so low that a sharp reply came back.

"Who'd you want?"

"Theodore King."

She waited a minute and then another voice, a voice she knew and loved, said,

"This is Mr. King!"

"I'm Jinnie Grandoken," Theodore heard. "I wanted to tell you I wouldn't go away from home ever; no, never! I wouldn't; I couldn't!"

"Don't you want to study?" Mr. King asked eagerly.

Jinnie shook her head as if she were face to face with him.

"I'm studying all the time," she said brokenly, "and I can't go away now. If they couldn't spare me one day, they couldn't all the time."

"Then I suppose that settles it," was the reluctant reply. "I hoped you'd be pleased, but never mind! I'll see you very soon."

"I told him!" said Jinnie, facing the cobbler. "Now, Lafe, don't ever think I'm going away, because I'm not. I've got some plans of my own for us all when I'm eighteen. Till then I stay right here."

At dinner Peg cut off a very large piece of meat and flung it on Jinnie's plate.

"I suppose you're plumin' yourself because you didn't go to school; but you needn't, 'cause nothin' could drag you from this shop, an' there's my word for it." Then she glanced at Lafe, and ended, "If 'er leg was nailed to your bench, she wouldn't be any tighter here. Now eat, all of you, an' keep your mouths shut."

CHAPTER XXIX

PEG'S VISIT

One morning Bobbie sat down gravely some distance from Lafe, took up one of Milly Ann's kittens, and fell into troubled thought. After permitting him to be silent a few moments, the cobbler remarked,

"Anything on your mind, comrade?"

"Yes," said Bobbie, sighing.

"Can't you tell a feller what it is?"

Bobbie pushed the kitten from his lap. He crept to the cobbler's side slowly. Then, as he leaned his golden head against his friend, Lafe's arm fell about him.

"Tell me, laddie," insisted Mr. Grandoken.

"My stars're all gone out," faltered the boy sadly.

"What made 'em go out, Bob?... Can you tell?"

"Yes," blubbered Bobbie. "I guess Jinnie's sick, that's what's the matter."

"Sick?" asked Lafe, in a startled voice. "Who said so?... Did she?"

Bobbie shook his head.

"No, but I know!... She cried last night, and other nights too."

Lafe considered a moment.

"I'm glad you told me, Bob," he said, knocking the ashes from his pipe.

Jinnie left the master's home with lagging footsteps. The idea of going away to school had not appealed to her, but never in all her life had she been so tempted to do anything as to go with Theodore for one blessed day in the country—but a whole day from home could not be thought of.

The cobbler saw her crossing the tracks, and after the daily salute, she came on with bent head. He watched her closely during the evening meal and gave Bobbie credit for discovering the truth. After Peg had wheeled him back to the shop and he was alone with Jinnie, Lafe called her to him.

"Bring the stool," said he, "an' sit here."

Languidly she sank down, resting against him. She was very tired besides being very unhappy. Lafe placed two fingers under her chin, lifting her face to his. Her eyes were full of tears, and she no longer tried to conceal her suffering. The cobbler remained quiet while she cried softly. At last:

"It's Maudlin Bates, ain't it, darlin'?" he asked.

"No, Lafe."

"Can't you tell your friend what 'tis?"

"I guess I'm crying because I'm foolish, dear," she replied.

"No, that's not true, Jinnie. I feel as bad seeing you cry's if 'twas Peggy."

This was a compliment, and Jinnie tried to sit up bravely, but a friendly hand held her close.

"Just begin, an' the rest'll come easy," Lafe insisted.

Jinnie's tongue refused to talk, and of a sudden she grew ashamed and dropped her scarlet face.

"I don't believe I can tell it, Lafe dear," she got out.

"Something about a man?"

Jinnie nodded.

"Then I got to know! Tell me!" he directed.

116

His insistence drew forth a tearful confession.

"Before Mr. King spoke about the school, he asked me to go a day in the country with my fiddle, and I couldn't."

After the telling, she caught her breath and hid her face.

"Why?" Lafe demanded. "Why couldn't you?"

Jinnie raised startled eyes to the cobbler's for the better part of a minute. What did he mean? Was it possible——

"I thought you wouldn't let me——"

"You didn't ask me, did you, Jinnie?"

"No, because—because——"

"Because why?" Lafe intended to get at the root of the matter.

"Too long from the shop! Bobbie needs me," replied Jinnie.

"I don't think so, child.... The kid'd be all right with me and Peg."

"Lafe?" cried Jinnie, standing up and throwing her arms around him.

"You ought to a told me when he spoke of it, Jinnie. I could a fixed it."

The cobbler smiled, and then laughed.

Once more on the stool in front of him, Jinnie said:

"I'm afraid Mr. King was a little offended."

"It would a done you a lot of good to get out in the fields——" chided Lafe.

"And the woods, Lafe. I'd taken my fiddle. He asked me to."

"Sure," replied Lafe.... "Call Peggy."

Mrs. Grandoken, looking from one to the other, noticed Lafe's gravity and signs of Jinnie's tears.

"What's the matter?" she inquired.

Lafe told her quietly, and finished with his hand on Jinnie's head.

"Our little helper ought to have some fun, Peggy."

Jinnie glanced up. What would Peggy think? But for a few minutes Peg didn't tell them. Then she said:

"She ought a went, I think, Lafe."

Jinnie got up so quickly that Happy Pete and Milly Ann stirred in their sleep.

"Oh, Peg, I do want to—but how can I, now I've said I wouldn't?... How can I?"

"You can't," decided Peg gruffly, and Jinnie dropped down once more at Lafe's feet.

"I guess you'll have to forget about it, child, an' be 'Happy in Spite'," said Lafe, with a sigh.

The next day Peggy took Lafe into her confidence.

"I think it could be did," she ended, looking at her husband.

"Mebbe," said Mr. Grandoken thoughtfully.

"I'll do it," snapped Peg, "but I hate 'er, an' you can bang me if that ain't a fact, but—but I'll go, I said."

About ten o'clock Peggy dressed and went out.

Theodore King was in his office, trying to keep his mind on a line of

117

figures. Of late work palled on him. He sighed and leaned back thoughtfully, striking and touching a match to his cigar. Memories of blue-eyed Jinnie enveloped him in a mental maze. She stood radiant and beckoning, her exquisite face smiling into his at every turn.

He realized now how much he desired Jinnie Grandoken—and were she with him at that moment, life could offer him nothing half so sweet.

"I want her always," he said grimly, aloud to himself.

A boy's head appeared at the door.

"Woman to see you, sir," said he.

"Who?"

"Mrs. Grandoken."

"Show her in," and Theodore stood up.

Peggy came in embarrassedly. She had a mission to perform which she very much disliked.

"Good morning, Mrs. Grandoken," said Theodore, holding out his hand.

"Good morning, sir," said Peg, flushing darkly.

Her tongue clove to the roof of her mouth. How could she state her errand to this dignified, handsome young man? He was looking at her questioningly; but that wasn't all—he was smiling encouragingly also.

"Won't you sit down?" said he.

Peggy coughed, smoothed her mouth with her hand, pulled the thin shawl more closely about her shoulders, and took the indicated seat. Taking no time to reflect on the best way to present her case, she blurted out,

"Lafe didn't know till last night about your askin' Jinnie to go for a holiday?"

"Oh!"

The man was at a loss to say more than that one word in question.

"No," replied Peggy, "and she's been cryin'——"

"Crying?" ejaculated Theodore. "Crying, you say?"

"Yes," nodded Peggy.

"What'd she cry for?" asked Theodore. "She positively refused to go with me."

"I know it, but she thought me an' Lafe wouldn't let 'er."

Theodore moved uneasily about the office.

"And would you?" he asked presently.

"Sure," responded Peggy, nodding vigorously. "Sure! Jinnie's been workin' awful hard for years, an' Lafe'd like you to take 'er. But you musn't tell 'er I come here."

Saying this, Peggy rose to her feet. She had finished what she had come to say and was ready to go. Theodore King laughingly thanked her and shook her heartily by the hand. Then he escorted her to the door, and she returned to Lafe a little less grim.

It was nearly noon when Jinnie left the master's music room, carrying her fiddle box. Her teacher noticed she played with less spirit than usual, but had refrained from mentioning it.

118

She was coming down the steps when King's car dashed up to the door. Her meetings with him were always unexpected and found her quite unprepared for the shock to her emotions.

"I've come to take you home, Jinnie," said Theodore, jumping out.

Jinnie's throat filled, and silently she allowed him to help her to the seat. They were in the flat of the town before he turned to her.

"I haven't given up my plan to take you away for a day," he said gently.

Jinnie gulped with joy. He was going to ask her again! Lafe and Peg had said she could go. She waited for him to proceed, which he did more gravely.

"When I make up my mind to do a thing, I generally do it. Now which day shall it be, Jinnie?"

"I guess I'll have to let you tell," whispered Jinnie, which whisper Theo caught despite the noise of the chugging motor.

"Then, to-morrow," he decided, driving up to the cobbler's shop. "I'll come for you at nine o'clock.... Look at me, Jinnie."

Slowly she dragged a pair of unfathomable blue eyes to his.

"We're going to be happy for one whole beautiful day, Jinnie," said he hoarsely.

He helped her out, and neither one spoke again. The motor started away, and the girl rushed into the shop.

Lafe had just said to Peggy, "There they be! He's been after 'er!"

"Lafe, Lafe dear," Jinnie gurgled. "I'm going with 'im to-morrow. All day with the birds and flowers! Oh, Peggy dear, I'm so happy!"

Mrs. Grandoken glared at her.

"Ugh! 'S if it matters to me whether you're happy or not!"

Jinnie stooped and smothered Bobbie with caresses. With his arms tightly about her neck, he purred contentedly,

"My stars're all shinin' bright, Jinnie."

"Kiss me, both of you kids!" was all Lafe said.

CHAPTER XXX

WHAT THE FIDDLE TOLD THEODORE

Jinnie looked very sweet when she bade farewell to Peg and Lafe the next morning. Mr. King's car was at the door, and the cobbler watched him as he stepped from it with a monosyllabic greeting to the girl and helped her to the seat next to his. Peggy, too, was craning her neck for a better view.

"They're thick as thieves," she said, with a dubious shake of her head.

"I guess he likes 'er," chuckled Lafe. "To make a long story short, wife, a sight like that does my eyes good!"

Mrs. Grandoken shrugged her shoulders, growled deep in her throat, and opined they were all fools.

"An' quit doin' yourself proud, Lafe!" she grumbled. "You're grinnin' like a Cheshire cat. 'Tain't nothin' to your credit she's goin' to have the time of her life."

"No, 'tain't to my credit, Peggy," retorted the cobbler, "but 'tis to yours, wife."

By the time Lafe finished this statement, Mr. King and Jinnie Grandoken were bowling along a white road toward a hill bounding the west side of the lake.

"See that basket down here?" said the man after a long silence.

"Yes."

"That's our picnic dinner! I brought everything I thought a little girl with a sweet tooth might like."

Jinnie had forgotten about food. Her mind had dwelt only upon the fact she was going to be with him all day, one of those long, beautiful days taken from Heaven's cycle for dear friends. The country, too, stretched in majestic splendor miles ahead of them, trees rimming the road on each side and making a thick woodland as far as one could see.

"I'm glad I brought my fiddle," Jinnie remarked presently.

"I am, too," said Theodore.

The place he chose for their outing was far back from the highway, and leaving the car at one side of the road, they threaded their way together to it. The sky above was very blue, the lake quietly reflecting its sapphire shades. Off in the distance the high hills gazed down upon the smaller ones, guarding them in quietude.

Theodore spread one of the auto robes on the ground, and shyly Jinnie accepted his invitation to be seated.

"Oh, it's lovely," she said in soft monotone, glancing at the lake.

"Yes," replied Theodore dreamily.

His eyes were upon the placid water, his thoughts upon the girl at his side. Jinnie was thinking of him, too, and there they both sat, with passionate longing in their young hearts, watching nature's great life go silently by.

"Play for me," Theodore said at length, without taking his eyes from the water. "Stand by that big tree so I can look at you."

Flushed, palpitating, and beautiful, Jinnie took the position he directed. She had come to play for him, to mimic the natural world for his pleasure.

"Shall I play about the fairies?" she asked bashfully.

"Yes," assented King.

As on that night in his home when first she came into his life in full sway, the man now imagined he saw creeping from under the flower petals

120

and from behind the tall trees, the tiny inhabitants of Jinnie's fairyland. Then he turned his eyes toward her, and as he watched the lithe young figure, the pensive face lost and rapt in the lullaby, Theodore came to the greatest decision of his life. He couldn't live without Jinnie Grandoken! No matter if she was the niece of a cobbler, no matter who her antecedents were—she was born into the world for him, and all that was delicate and womanly in her called out to the manhood in him; and all that was strong, masterful, and aggressive in him clamored to protect and shield her, and in that fleeting moment the brilliant young bachelor suddenly lost his hold on bachelordom, as a boy loses his hold on a kite. There are times in every human life when such a decision as Theodore then made seemed the beginning of everything. It was as if the past had wrapped him around like the grey shell of a cocoon.

A loose lock of hair fell coquettishly from the girl's dark head low upon the fiddle, and Theodore loved and wanted to kiss it, and when the instrument dropped from under the dimpled chin, he held out his hand.

"Come here, Jinnie," he said softly. "Come sit beside me."

She came directly, as she always did when he asked anything of her. He drew her down close to his side, and for a long time they remained quiet. Jinnie was facing the acme of joy. The day had only begun, and she was with the object of her dreams. Just as when she had lived in the hills the fiddle had held the center of her soul, so now Theodore King occupied that sacred place. The morning light rose in her eyes, the blue fire transforming her face.

Theodore turned, saw, and realized at that moment. He discovered in her what he had long desired. She loved him! All the old longing, all the strength and passion within him broke loose at the nearness of her. Suddenly he stretched out his arms and drew her still nearer. Jinnie felt every muscle of his strongly fibered body grow tense at her touch. She tried to draw away from his encircling arms, but the rise and fall of her bosom, girlishly curved—the small-girl shyness that caused her to endeavor to unloose his strong hands, only goaded him to press her closer.

"Don't leave me, my dearest, my sweet," he breathed, kissing her lids and hair. "I love you! I love you!"

She gasped once, twice, and her head fell upon his breast, and for a moment she lay wrapped in her youthful modesty as in a mantle.

"Kiss me, Jinnie," Theodore murmured entreatingly.

She buried her head closer against him.

"Kiss me," he insisted, drawing her face upward. His lips fell upon hers, and Jinnie's eyes closed under the magic of her first kiss.

The master-passion of the man brought to sudden life corresponding emotions in the girl—emotions that hurt and frightened her. She put her hand to his face, and touched it. He drew back, looking into her eyes.

"Don't," she breathed. "Don't kiss me any more like—like that."

"But you love me, my girlie, sweet?" he murmured, his lips roving over her face in dear freedom. "You do!... You do!"

121

Jinnie's arms went about him, but her tongue refused to speak.

"Kiss me again!" Theodore insisted.

Oh, how she wanted to kiss him once more! How she gloried in the strong arms, and the handsome face strung tense with his love for her! Then their lips met in the wonders of a second kiss. Jinnie had thought the first one could never be equaled, but as she lay limply in his arms, his lips upon hers, she lost count of everything.

It might have been the weird effect of the shadows, or the deep, sudden silence about them that drew the girl slowly from his arms.

"I want my fiddle," she whispered. "Let me go!"

Faint were the inflections of the words; insistent the drawing back of the dear warm body.

Theodore permitted her to get up, and with staggering step she took her position at the tree trunk.

Then he sank down, hot blood coursing through his veins. Long ago he had realized in Jinnie and the fiddle essentials—essentials to his future and his happiness, and to-day her kisses and divine, womanly yielding had only strengthened that realization. Nothing now was of any importance to him save this vibrant, temperamental girl. There was something so delightfully young—so pricelessly dear in the way she had surrendered herself to him. The outside world faded from his memory as Jinnie closed her eyes, and with a very white face began to play. For that day she had finished with the song of the fairies, the babbling of the brook, and the nodding rhythm of the flowers in the summer's breeze. All that she considered now was Theodore and his kisses. The bow came down over a string with one long, vibrating, passionate call. It expressed the awakening of the girl's soul—awakened by the touch of a man's turbulent lips—Jinnie's God-given man. Her fiddle knew it—felt it—expressed it!

With that first seductive kiss the soul-stirring melody was full born within her, as a world is called into the firmament by one spoken word of God. And as she played, Theodore moved silently toward her, for the fiddle was flashing out the fervor of the kisses she had given him.

He was close at her feet before he spoke, and simultaneously the white lids opened in one blue, blue glance.

"Jinnie!" breathed Theodore, getting up and holding out his arms. "Come to me! Come to me, my love! I can't live another moment without you."

The bow and fiddle remained unnoticed for the next half hour, while the two, the new woman and the new man, were but conscious of one another, nothing else.

At length Theodore spoke.

"Jinnie, look up and say, 'Theodore, I love you'."

It was hard at first, because her mind had never reached the point of speaking aloud her passionate love for him, but Theodore heard the halting words, and droned them over to himself, as a music lover delights in his favorite strains.

"And you love me well enough to marry me some day?" he murmured.

Marry him! This, too, was a new thought. Jinnie's heart fluttered like a bird in her breast. To be with him always? To have him for her own? Of course, he was hers, and she was his! Then into her mind came the thought of Lafe, Peggy, and Bobbie, and the arms around him relaxed.

"I love you better'n anybody in the world," she told him, pathetically, "but I can't ever leave the cobbler.... They need me there."

"They can't keep you," he cried passionately. "I want you myself."

His vehemence subdued her utterly. She glanced into his face. In his flashing eyes, Jinnie read a power inimitable and unsurpassed.

"I couldn't ever leave 'em," she repeated, quivering, "but couldn't they live——"

"We'd take the little blind boy," promised Theodore.

Jinnie remained pensive. To bring the shine in her eyes once more, he said:

"Wouldn't you like Bobbie to live with us?"

"Yes, of course; but I couldn't leave Lafe and Peg in Paradise Road."

Theodore surrounded the entreating, uplifted face with two strong hands.

"I know that. We'll take care of them all——"

Still Jinnie held back her full surrender.

"Can I take Happy Pete, too? And the cats? There's an awful lot of 'em.... Milly Ann does have so many kitties," she ended naïvely.

Theodore laughed delightedly.

"Dearest little heart! Of course we'll take them all, every one you love!"

"Will you tell Lafe about—about us?" Jinnie asked shyly, "I—I——" but she had no more time to finish.

"I'll tell him to-morrow, Jinnie!" exclaimed Theodore. "Are you happy, dearest?"

"So happy," she sighed, with loving assurance.

The rest of the day they were like two frolicking children, eating their luncheon under the tall trees. When the shadows fell, they left their trysting place, and with their arms about each other, went slowly back to the automobile.

CHAPTER XXXI

WHAT THEODORE TOLD HIS FRIEND

"He's been gone all day," mourned Molly miserably to Jordan Morse. They had finished dinner; Molly had put Mrs. King to bed, and the two were seated in chairs on the lawn. Every minute that passed and found

123

Theodore still away was like an eternity to the woman. She had always hated the office hours which took him from the house, hated the business friends who dropped in now and then and changed the conversation from the delicate personal things she always managed to dwell upon.

During the years she had been companion to Mrs. King, Theo's dinner and luncheon hours were ones of joy to her. Now this day had passed without him.

"He'll show up before long," Morse said presently. "What a lot of worry you have over that man!... Now if you had a problem on your hands like mine——"

The soft chug of a motor cut off his ejaculation.

"He's coming, now," he said, getting up.

Molly responded coldly to Theodore's friendly salute from the car.

As Mr. King walked quickly toward them, Morse called laughingly, "We had just decided you'd been kidnapped."

"Nothing like that," answered Theodore, "I've been in the country.... Sit down, Jordan; no use standing up!" And Theodore seated himself on the grass.

"It's been a fine day," he went on boyishly, scarcely knowing what to say.

"Lovely," agreed Molly, and Jordan supplemented this by asking: "Have a—pleasant ride?"

"Yes, delightful! One doesn't realize how murky the city is until he goes in the country for a day."

After a time, during which he looked up through the enfolding green of the trees, he proceeded calmly,

"I took Miss Grandoken on a picnic."

Morse's sudden glance at Molly warned her to control herself.

"She's an odd child," continued Theodore, "but, then, all geniuses are. I don't know when I've so thoroughly enjoyed myself."

Morse's "That's good," was closely followed by Molly's curt question, "Where'd you go?"

"Just up the lake a ways. We took some picnic stuff——"

"And her fiddle, I suppose?" cut in Molly sarcastically.

"Of course. Jinnie's not Jinnie without her fiddle."

"She does play well," admitted Jordan.

"More than well," interpolated Theodore. "She plays divinely."

Then again they fell into an oppressive silence.

Molly was so curious to know the events of the day she could scarcely control her impatience.

Suddenly Mr. King announced:

"I'm going to marry Jinnie Grandoken."

Molly and Morse slowly got to their feet. They stood looking down upon the young millionaire with jaws apart and startled eyes.

"Well, you needn't look as if I were about to commit some crime," he said, quizzing them with laughing eyes. "I suppose a chap can get married if he wants to; can't he?"

"It's ridiculous," blurted Miss Merriweather.

A drawn, helpless expression had crept into her eyes, making her appear like an old woman.

Theodore got to his feet.

"What's ridiculous?" he demanded, immediately on the defensive. "My wanting to be happy?"

"Not that quite," replied the woman, "but surely you can't——"

"I can and I will!" exclaimed Theodore decidedly. "I couldn't be happy without her, and mother——"

"It'll kill 'er," warned Molly significantly.

"Not at all," denied Theodore. "My mother's a woman of sense! When she knows her big boy's madly in love with the sweetest girl in the world, she'll take it as a matter of course."

Miss Merriweather turned toward the house.

"I think I'll go," she said in strained tones.

She had almost reached the veranda when Theodore called her.

"Molly!" he shouted.

"Yes?"

"Don't tell mother. I want to surprise her."

"Very well," and the woman went on again, trembling from the blow which had struck her in the face.

The two men, lolling under the trees, said but little more, and with burning heart and unsettled mind, Jordan Morse went back to his apartment.

He had scarcely settled himself before his telephone tinkled. Taking down the receiver, he said,

"Well?"

A faint voice answered him.

"It's Molly, Jordan!... Listen! I'm down at the foot of the hill. Do come here! I'm nearly frantic.... Yes, I'll wait."

Very soon Molly saw Jordan crossing the street, and she went to meet him.

"Let's walk," she said fretfully. "I can't breathe."

"If you feel like I do," replied Morse moodily, "I pity you."

He led her to a small park where they sat down upon one of the wooden benches.

"I'm shocked beyond expression," said Molly wearily.

"So am I," replied Morse. Then picking up the thread of thought which had troubled him all the evening, he went on, "I need my boy! Every night I'm haunted by dreams. I'd give up my plans about Jinnie if I had him...."

"Well, I never!" ejaculated Molly.

"The trouble with you is you haven't any heart," went on Jordan. "How you put your mind on anything but finding that child I don't know. But I notice you manage to keep close on Theo's heels every minute."

"I love him," admitted Molly.

"Don't you love your son, your poor little lost son?"

"Of course, Jordan! Don't be stupid!... Of course I do, but I don't know where he is."

"And you're making very little effort to find him, that's evident. You've seen him, and I haven't, yet I'd give half my life to get my hands on him." He paused, drew a long breath, and proceeded, "I'll warn you of this much, Molly. When I do find him—and find him I will—you won't get a chance to even see him."

"Oh, Jordan!" gasped Molly.

"That's right," he insisted, with an ugly shrug. "I tell you, Molly, I've always been impressed with the idea mothers cared more for their children than fathers, but I'm over that now since knowing you."

"Oh, Jordan!" repeated Molly faintly once more.

Not heeding her appealing voice, he rushed on, "I'd be willing to strangle half the world for money to hire detectives to search for him. But as I've said before, I'd let Jinnie alone if I had him—and work for him with my two hands—if I had to dig graves."

Molly turned her startled eyes upon the excited man. She had never known the depths of his nature.

"You make me tired," he proceeded with sarcasm. "What in hell do you think Theodore could see in you when a girl like Jinnie cares for him?"

"Why, Jordan Morse!" stammered the woman. "How dare you talk to me like that?"

"Because it's true," replied Jordan hotly. "You're like a lot of women—if a man looks sidewise at you, you think he's bowled over with your charms. Good Heavens! It's sickening!"

"I didn't ask you here to talk like this," said Molly.

"What if you didn't?" snapped Jordan. "You can talk now if you want to! I'm going home in five minutes, and I want some money before I go, too."

"I'll give you some to-morrow. Now what're you going to do about Theodore?"

"Well, he won't marry Jinnie," replied Morse slowly.

"How can you help it?"

"That's what I'm going to figure out. If I can get her away from Grandoken's, she won't get back, I can tell you that. But that damn cobbler and Theo'll make such a devilish row——"

"You needn't be profane," chided Molly.

"A woman like you's enough to make any man swear.... Now listen to me. The very fact that Jinnie ran away from home shows me that Tom Singleton told her I put 'im in a mad house! Jinnie, of course, told Grandoken. I've got to get that cobbler—and—you've got to help me get Jinnie——"

"Haven't I done all I could?" gasped Molly. "I can't go down there and take her by the nape of the neck, can I?"

"No, but I will! Now let's go! I want to do some pretty tall thinking before morning. Once let those two people be married and I'm lost."

"So am I," muttered Molly, swaying at his vehement words.

126

They threaded their way back to the hill, and Morse left Molly at her gate. As she walked slowly up the road, she could see the light in Theodore's window, and his shadow thrown on the curtain.

CHAPTER XXXII

JORDAN MORSE'S PLAN

The next morning Jordan Morse rose after a sleepless night, his face drawn in long, deep-set lines. The hours had been spent in futile planning. To save himself from the dire consequences of his misdeeds, to procure the money which would come to Jinnie when she was eighteen years old, was the one idea that dinned constantly at his brain. She and the cobbler would have to be put out of the way, and this must be done before Theodore announced publicly his intention of marrying the girl. Jordan had no wish to break his friendship with Theodore, so he could do nothing openly. If it were a mere case of filching what little he could from Jinnie's estate before she became of age, it would be an easy matter, but the girl must disappear. How? Where? There was finality in one of his decisions that moment. He must get possession of her that very day. Theodore would let no grass grow under his feet. He would marry her offhand, and educate her afterwards.

Jordan wondered vaguely if the Jewish cobbler had an enemy among the shortwood gatherers. If so, and the man could be found, it would bring his own salvation.

With this desire uppermost in his mind, Jordan wended his way to the lower part of the town, passed into Paradise Road, and paused a second in front of Lafe Grandoken's shop to read the sign:

"Lafe Grandoken: Cobbler of Folks' and Children's Shoes and Boots."

His lips curled at the crude printing, and he went on past the remaining shanties to the entrance to the marsh. At the path where Jinnie had so many times brought forth her load of wood, he paused again and glanced about. As far north as he could see, the marsh stretched out in misty greenness. The place seemed to be without a human being, until Jordan suddenly heard the crackling of branches, and there appeared before him a young man with deep-set, evil eyes, and large, pouting mouth. Upon his shoulders was a shortwood strap.

At the sight of Mr. Morse, the wood gatherer hesitated, made a sort of obeisance, and proceeded to move on. Jordan stopped him with a motion of his hand.

"In a hurry?" he asked good-naturedly.

"Got to sell my wood," growled the man.

Morse appraised him with an analytical glance.

"What's your name?" he demanded.

"Maudlin Bates. What's yours?"

"Jordan Morse.... Just wait a minute. I want to talk to you."

Down came the shortwood strap on the ground. Maudlin scented something interesting.

"I got to sell my wood," he repeated, surly-toned. However, he nodded his head when Jordan explained that it might be to his advantage to tarry a while.

"I'll pay you for your time," agreed Morse eagerly.

Side by side they seated themselves on a fallen tree. The young wood gatherer looked wicked enough to do anything that might be requested of him.

"Are you married?" asked Morse.

Maudlin's face darkened.

"No," he grunted moodily.

"Ha! In love? I see!" laughed the other.

Maudlin turned sheepish eyes on his interrogator; then looked down, flushed, and finished:

"I'd a been married all right if it hadn't been for a damn bloke along Paradise Road," he explained.

"Yes? Tell me about it."

"Oh, what's the use! Everybody's stickin' their noses in my business, and it ain't nothin' to do with 'em uther."

"I might help you," suggested Jordan, seemingly interested.

"Ain't anybody c'n help me," sulked Maudlin. "Got the richest man in town 'gainst me, and money's what makes the mare go."

The words "richest man" startled Morse, but he only said, "That's so! But tell me just the same."

"Aw, it's only a wench I wanted! A mutt by the name of King butted in on me."

Jordan Morse mentally congratulated himself that he had struck the right nail on the head the very first whack.

To gain possession of Jinnie's money meant finding his boy, and that was the dearest wish of his heart.

"You might tell me about it," he reiterated slowly. "I ought to be able to help you."

"Naw, you can't!" scoffed Maudlin. "My pa and me's tried for a long time, but there ain't nothin' doin' with Jinnie. She's a sure devil, Jinnie is."

Jordan's blood tingled in anticipation.

"Is that the girl's name?" he queried.

"Yes, she's a niece of a cobbler up the track yonder, and as pretty a little minx as walks Paradise Road. If I had 'er I'd fix her. I'd beat her till she minded me, I c'n tell y' that!"

"I believe beating's the way to subdue most women," said Morse, lighting a cigarette. But as he said this, a slight smile passed over his face. He thought of Molly Merriweather in connection with the man's logic.

"It's the way pa done to my stepmother," observed Maudlin presently. "She was a onery woman as ever you see, but pa one day just licked her, and then licked 'er every day till now she don't dast but mind 'im.... I'd do that with Jinnie if I had 'er."

Morse watched rings of smoke curl upward in the summer air, breaking among the branches of the trees.

"Why don't you steal 'er?" he demanded at length.

Bates' lower jaw fell down, showing discolored teeth. He stared at his inquisitor in consternation. Then he dropped back into his former slovenly attitude.

"I never thought o' that," said he.

"I'll help you," offered Morse, carelessly, brushing ashes from his coat lapel.

Maudlin turned his eyes slowly from their straight ahead position until they came directly upon the handsome face of the other man. Then the two looked long and steadily at each other.

"What're you drivin' at?" blurted Bates.

"Only that I'm also interested in getting Jinnie away from Grandoken. The fact is I hate King, and I think it's a good way to get even with him."

He refrained, however, from mentioning he was Jinnie's relative.

"D'you have me in mind when you come here?" questioned Bates.

"No! But I felt sure there'd be some young buck round here who'd fallen in love with the girl before this. And I found you without asking——"

"I'd make her beg me to marry her after I'd had 'er a week or two," interrupted Maudlin, with dilating pupils. "How could we steal 'er?"

"Just steal 'er, I said," replied Morse.

"And I said, 'How?'"

Morse waited a minute until Bates repeated once more, "How, mister?" then he asked:

"Can you run a motor car?"

"No, but my pa can."

"My God! You musn't mention this to any one, not even your father. I'll run the car myself. You go to the cobbler and by some excuse get the girl in the car—after that I'll see to her."

Bates narrowed his eyes.

"No, you won't see to nothin'," he growled surlily. "I don't take a step till I know I get 'er. I'll marry 'er all right, but she's got to want to marry me first."

"I don't care what you do with 'er," replied Morse morosely. "Marry 'er or not, just get her, that's all!"

"The cobbler's got a vixen of a wife," complained Maudlin at length.

"Persuade her to go somewhere, can't you?" snapped Morse.

"Yes, that's easy," drawled Maudlin, wobbling his head.

For a long time they sat talking and planning, until at length Morse put his hand in his pocket and handed the other man some money. Maudlin tucked it away with a grin.

"Easy cash, eh? What'd you say the dame's name was?"

"Merriweather—Molly Merriweather. She's companion to Mr. King's mother."

"Jinnie fiddles all the afternoon.... Mebbe she won't go."

"Yes, she will. Tell her Miss Merriweather wants her to arrange a surprise for Theodore King. Tell 'er Miss Merriweather wants her to play."

Bates laughed evilly.

"That'll fix the huzzy. Anything about that damn fiddle'll fetch 'er every time! When I get 'er I'll bust it up for kindlin' wood."

"Then it's settled," said Morse, rising. "You go this afternoon at three o'clock to Grandoken's, tell Jinnie what I told you to, get the cobbler into an argument, and I'll do the rest."

"You'll be sure to be there?"

"Of course! What'd you think I am? Keep your mouth shut! Be sure of that."

"Three o'clock, then," said Maudlin, getting up. "So long!" and lifting his wood, he went on his way rejoicing.

CHAPTER XXXIII

THE MURDER

At half past one that afternoon a messenger appeared at Grandoken's with a letter for Jinnie.

Peggy called the girl to the shop.

"Boy's got something for you," she declared. "It's a letter, I guess."

Jinnie held out her hand with thumping pulses, took the extended pencil, and signed her name to a blank page. Then the boy held out the missive. Of course it was from Theodore, thought Jinnie. She had scarcely slept the night before, fitfully dreaming of him. Throwing a shy smile at Peg, she went into her bedroom and shut the door. With a long, ecstatic breath, she set herself to the delightful task of slowly perusing the beloved epistle.

"My darling," Jinnie read, and she kissed those two words, each one separately. Then she whispered them again, "My darling," and read on:

"I'm coming this afternoon at three to see your uncle, and I thought you might like me to talk with him alone. It will be a simple matter for you to take the little blind boy and go away for an hour or so, but be sure and

130

return at four. By that time I'll have our arrangements all made, but I won't go until I see you.

"I send all my love to you, my sweetheart.

"Your own,

"THEODORE."

Jinnie kissed the words "my sweetheart" too, and then joyfully slipped the letter inside her dress. She daren't speak of his coming, for how could she conceal her happiness from Lafe?

At two o'clock, she said to Peggy:

"May I take Bobbie for a little walk, dear?"

The blind child heard the request and scrambled up.

"Can I go, Peggy?" he pleaded.

Peg glared at the girl.

"I thought you always fiddled in the afternoon," she queried.

"I do generally," acquiesced Jinnie, "but—to-day——"

"Well, go 'long," said Peg, not very graciously. "I'm goin' over to Miss Bates' a while. Maudlin come by just now, an' said would I come over.... Get back early!"

Jinnie dressed Bobbie with trembling fingers. The boy noticed she could scarcely button his jacket.

"What's the matter, Jinnie dear?" he whispered.

Jinnie was just slipping on his cap as he spoke. She bent and kissed him passionately.

"Nothing, honey, only Jinnie's happy, very happy."

"I'm so glad," sighed Bobbie, with a smiling wag. "I'm happy too. Let's go on the hill, and take Petey."

"It'd be lovely, dear," replied the girl.

A few minutes later, with the little dog at their heels, they were wending their way up the board walk to the hill.

Mr. Grandoken, alone in his shop, worked with contented vigor. The days, those beautiful summer days, were bringing untold joy to him. Peggy seemed in brighter spirits, and Jinnie's radiant face made Lafe rejoice. Little Bobbie's stars were always shining nowadays, so what more could the dear man want? As he sat tip-tapping, he took himself in fancy to that day ahead when Heaven would unfold another blessing for Peg—for him. He put down his hammer and glanced out of the window, and suddenly Maudlin Bates loomed up, with all his hulking swagger obliterating the shoemaker's mental bliss.

Lafe nodded as Maudlin stepped into the shop. There was an unusually aggressive expression upon the young wood gatherer's face, and Mr. Grandoken refrained from asking him to sit down. Instead he questioned:

"Brought some cobblin'?"

"No," said Bates. "Wanted to talk to you; that's all."

"Hurry up, then, 'cause I'm busy."

"Where's Jinnie?" queried Maudlin.

Swift anger changed the cobbler's face.

131

"What's that to you?" he demanded. "And you needn't be drippin' tobacco juice around my shop."

"Won't hurt it, I guess," answered Maudlin insolently, sitting down heavily.

With every passing minute, Lafe was growing more and more enraged.

"Yap me your business and get out," he ordered, picking up his hammer.

He settled his eyes on the sodden face before him, and for a minute or two each plumbed the strength of the other.

"I'm goin' to marry Jinnie," announced Maudlin, drawing his large feet together and clasping his fingers over his knees.

The cobbler deliberately placed the hammer beside him once more and leaned back against the wall.

"Who said so?" he asked.

"I do," defied Maudlin, swaggering.

"Is that what you come to say to me?"

"Yep."

"Well, now you're done with your braggin', get out, an' get out quick."

But Maudlin didn't move.

"I said to scoot," said Lafe presently, in suppressed tones. He was magnificent in his ferocity.

"I heard you!" observed Maudlin, still sitting, though a little cowed in his former egotistical spirit.

Lafe picked up the hammer and pounded frantically on the sole of a shoe.

"I'm goin' to have money," muttered Maudlin when the cobbler paused for a few nails.

As Lafe proceeded with his work silently, Maudlin said:

"I'll marry Jinnie and take the empty shack next to pa's. I got money, I said."

Lafe's lips were moving rapidly, but the other could not hear what he was saying. The fact was, the cobbler was asking for strength and self-control.

"Where's Jinnie?" demanded Maudlin again.

"She ain't here," said Lafe, "an' I want you to get out before she comes."

He said this more gently, because his muttered prayers had somewhat assuaged his rage.

Just then a motor car dashed into the little lane at the side of the house, and Maudlin knew that Morse had arrived.

"I'll go when I see Jinnie," he insisted, sinking deeper into his chair, "I want to tell 'er somethin' about a party."

"Ain't no show o' your seein' 'er to-day," replied Lafe. "I bargained with your pa about you lettin' my girl alone, and that's all there is to it."

"Pa's cobblin' ain't nothin' to do with me," observed Maudlin darkly. "I'll wait for 'er!"

At that minute Theodore King's car drew up in front of the shop, and he stepped out. Maudlin caught a glimpse of him and set his teeth sharply. He'd have it out with this man, too. They might as well all understand what his intentions were. He wondered if Morse, from his point of vantage, had seen Mr. King arrive.

When Theodore swung into the shop, he paused at the sight of Bates and frowned. He brought to mind the chastening he had given the fellow, and how Jinnie had suffered through his brutality.

Lafe smiled cordially at the young man and asked him to be seated.

"Jinnie's out," stated the cobbler.

"I know it!" responded Theodore, taking a chair. "I've come to have a talk with you." Then looking from Mr. Grandoken to Maudlin, he queried, "Will you soon be disengaged?"

Lafe nodded.

"I hope so," he said disinterestedly.

Lafe always disciplined himself after a siege with his temper.

"He won't be alone till I get through with 'im," grunted Maudlin, with an ugly expression. "I been tellin' 'im I'm goin' to marry Jinnie."

Lafe straightened with a throat sound that boded no good for the speaker, and Theodore got swiftly to his feet.

"Don't repeat what you've just said," the latter gritted between his teeth, whirling on Maudlin.

Bates shot out of his chair at this command.

"My tongue's my own," he roared, "and Jinnie'll be glad to marry me before——"

Theodore's big fist swept out, striking the man full in the face, and Maudlin dropped like an ox hit with an axe, but he was on his feet in another minute. His rapidly swelling face was blanched with rage.

"Damn you, twicet and three times damn you——"

Lafe made an ejaculation, and neither one of the three men noticed that the door to the little hall at the back had opened a trifle.

Jordan Morse was peering in upon the enraged trio. He saw the man he'd hired to help him take the first knock down and get up swiftly. He saw Theodore King make another dive at the wood gatherer. The cobbler was in direct range of Jordan's vision, and he slipped his hand into his pocket, from which he took a revolver. Two quick, short cracks, and the pistol came flying through the room and landed near the cobbler's bench. Then the kitchen door slammed suddenly. Theodore staggered forward and sank slowly to the floor, while Maudlin fell headlong without a cry.

As in a maze Lafe heard a motor leap away like a mad thing. Through the window he could see Theodore's car where the young man had left it. He made a desperate effort to rise, but sank back with a shuddering groan. He forced his eyes to Bates, who was close to the shop door, then dragged them backward to Mr. King, whose head was almost under his bench. Each had received a bullet, and both lay breathing unconsciously. The cobbler stooped over and placed his hand under Theodore's head to straighten it a little. For a full minute nothing was heard but the loud rattling in Maudlin's throat and the steady, laborious breath of the man at his feet.

Sudden tears diffused the cobbler's eyes, and he leaned over and tenderly touched the damp forehead of Jinnie's friend.

"He's given His angels charge over thee, boy," he murmured, just as Jinnie, leading Bobbie by the hand, walked in.

The girl took one impetuous step forward and noted Lafe's white, agonized face. Then she caught a glimpse of the stricken men on the floor. Her tongue refused its office, and dropping the blind child's fingers, she came quickly forward.

"Call help! Hurry! Get a doctor!" gasped Lafe, and Jinnie, without saying a word, rushed out.

Afterward she could not measure with accuracy the events of that afternoon. Peggy came home and put the terrified Bobbie in bed, telling him curtly to stay there until she allowed him to get up. Several doctors rushed in and examined both Theodore and Maudlin. Not one word had escaped Jinnie's pale lips until the wounded men were removed from the shop. Then she sank at the cobbler's feet.

"Will he die?" she whispered, in awe-stricken tones.

"Maudlin's dyin'," replied the cobbler, with bowed head, "an' Mr. King's awful bad off, the doctor says."

Jinnie went to Lafe's side and put her arm about his neck, and as if it had never been, their joy was blotted out by the hand of a bloody tragedy.

CHAPTER XXXIV
THE COBBLER'S ARREST

Tearing away from Paradise Road, Jordan Morse drove madly up the hill. No one had seen him come; no one had seen him go. He must get in touch with Molly immediately. In his nervous state he had to confide in some one.

Molly had settled Mrs. King in an easy chair and was on the lawn, pacing restlessly to and fro, when Jordan swiftly drove his machine through the gate and up to the veranda. Catching one hasty glimpse of his haggard face, the woman knew something extraordinary had happened.

"I've put my foot in it, all right," he ejaculated, jumping to the soft grass. "My God! I don't know what I have done!"

Molly's face blanched.

"Tell me quickly," she implored.

Jordan repeated his conversation with Maudlin Bates, stating how his plans had suddenly matured on hearing the wood gatherer denounce King and Grandoken.

Then he proceeded a little more calmly.

"It seems I hadn't been at the side door of Grandoken's shack a minute before Theodore drove up."

Molly's hands came together.

"Theodore?" she repeated breathlessly.

"Yes, and the Bates man was with Grandoken. I heard loud talking, stole into the little hall, and found the back part of the house empty. Jinnie wasn't there; at least I didn't see her. Bates had already inveigled Mrs. Grandoken away. I opened the door into the cobbler's shop just as Theo was striking Bates in the face. I waited a minute, and as Theo struck out again, I fired——"

"Fired!" gasped Molly.

"Yes, at Grandoken. I wanted to kill him——"

"But Theo—you might have hit Theodore, Jordan."

"But I didn't, I tell you! I'm sure I didn't. If I hit any one, 'twas Bates or the cobbler.... Get back near the veranda for fear Theodore 'phones."

No sooner had the words left his lips than a bell sounded from the house. Molly ran up the steps. As she took down the receiver, she dropped it, but picked it up again.

"Halloa," she called faintly.

"Is this Theodore King's home?" shouted a voice.

"Yes."

"Mr. King's had an accident. He's in the hospital. Break the news carefully to his mother, please."

Dazedly, Molly slipped the receiver back to its hook. She stumbled to the porch and down the steps, her face ashen with anguish.

"You shot Theo, Jordan," she cried hysterically.

"Shut your head," growled Morse, glancing furtively about. "Don't talk so loud.... Now then, listen! There'll be hell to pay for this. But Bates won't peach, and I'm sure I clipped the cobbler's wings. Keep quiet till you hear from me."

He sprang again into the machine and was gone before the woman could gather her wits together.

She turned and went slowly up the steps. It was her duty to break the news to Theodore's mother—she who knew so much, but dared to tell so little! How to open the conversation with the gentle sufferer she knew not.

Mrs. King smiled a greeting as she entered, but at the sight of Molly's face, her book dropped to the floor.

"What is it?" she stammered.

Molly knelt down beside her.

"Probably very little," she said hastily. "Don't get excited—please—but—but——"

"It's Theodore!" gasped the mother, intuitively.

"He's hurt a little, just a little, and they've taken him to the hospital."

Mrs. King tried to rise, but dropped back weakly.

"He's badly hurt or he'd come home."

"I'll find out," offered Molly eagerly. Then as an afterthought, "I'll go if you'll promise me to stay very quiet until I get back."

"I promise," said Mrs. King, sobbing, "but go quickly! I simply can't be still when I'm uncertain."

In another house of lesser proportions, a girl was huddled in a chair, gazing at Lafe Grandoken.

"An' they told you over the telephone he was dyin'?" he demanded, looking at Jinnie.

"Yes," gulped Jinnie, "and Maudlin's dead. The hospital people say Mr. King can't live." The last words were stammered and scarcely audible. "Lafe, who shot him?"

"I dunno," said Lafe.

"Didn't you see who had the gun?" persisted the girl, wiping her eyes.

"Mr. King didn't have it; nuther did Maudlin. It came from over there, an' I heard a car drive away right after."

Jinnie shook her head hopelessly. It was all so mysterious that her heart was gripped with fright. A short time before, an officer had been there cross-questioning Lafe suspiciously. Then he had gone away with the pistol in his pocket. She stared out of the window, fear-shadowed. In a twinkling her whole love world had tumbled about her ears, and she listened as the cobbler told her once more the story of the hour she'd been away with Bobbie.

"There're two men coming here right now," she said suddenly, getting up. "Lafe, there's Burns, the cop on this beat."

"They're wantin' to find out more, I presume," replied Lafe wearily.

As the men entered the shop, Jinnie backed away and stood with rigid muscles. She was dizzily frightened at the sight of the gruff officers, who had not even saluted Lafe.

The foremost man was a stranger to them both.

"Are you Lafe Grandoken?" he demanded, looking at the cobbler.

"Yes," affirmed Lafe.

The man flourished a paper with staid importance.

"I'm the sheriff of this county, an' I've a warrant for your arrest for murderin' Maudlin Bates," he sing-songed.

Jinnie sprang forward.

"Lafe didn't shoot 'im," she cried desperately.

The man eyed her critically.

"Did you do it, kid?" he asked, smiling.

"No, I wasn't here!" answered Jinnie, short-breathed.

"Then how'd you know he didn't do it?"

For a moment Jinnie was nonplussed. Then she came valiantly to her friend's aid.

"I know he didn't. Of course he didn't, you wicked, wicked men! Don't you dare touch 'im, don't you dare!"

"Well, he's got to go with me," affirmed the man in ugly, sneering tones. "Whistle for the patrol, Burns, and we'll wheel the Jew in!"

Jinnie heard, as in a hideous dream, the shrill, trilling whistle; heard the galloping of horses and saw a long black wagon draw up to the steps.

When the two sullen men laid violent hold of the wheelchair, Jinnie's terrified fingers reached toward the cobbler, and the sheriff gave her hand a sharp blow. Lafe uttered an inarticulate cry, and at that moment Jinnie forgot "Happy in Spite," forgot Lafe's angels and the glory of them, and sprang like a tiger at the man who had struck her. She flung one arm about his neck and fought him with tooth and nails. So surprised was Policeman Burns that he stood with staring eyes, making no move to rescue his mate from the tigerish girl.

"Damn you! Damn you!" screamed Jinnie. "I'll kill you before you take 'im."

Lafe cried out again, calling her name gently, imploringly, and tenderly. When his senses returned, Burns grasped Jinnie in his arms and held her firmly. There she stood panting, trying to break away from the policeman's detaining fingers. She looked half crazed in the dimming late afternoon light.

"Merciful God, but you're a tartar, miss!" said the sheriff ruefully. "Well, if she ain't clawed the blood clean through my skin!"

"She comes of bad stock," exclaimed Burns. "You can't expect any more of Jews. Go on; I'll hold 'er till you and Mike get the chair out."

Hearing this, Jinnie began to sob hysterically and make more desperate efforts to free herself. The viselike fingers pressed deeper into her tender flesh.

"Here, huzzy, you needn't be tryin' none of your muck on me," said Burns. "Keep still or I'll break your arm."

Jinnie sickened with pain, and her eyes sought Lafe's. If he'd been in his coffin, he couldn't have been whiter.

"Jinnie," he chided brokenly, "you've forgot what I told you, ain't you, lass?"

Through the suffering, tender mind flashed the words he'd taught her.

"There aren't any angels, Lafe," she sobbed. "There aren't any."

Then, as another man entered the shop, she cried: "Don't take 'im, oh, please don't take 'im, not now, not just yet, not till Peggy gets back."

Turning around in his chair, Lafe looked up at the men.

"Could—I—say—good-bye—to my—wife?" he asked brokenly.

"Where is she?" demanded the officer.

"Gone to the store," answered Lafe. "She'll be here in a minute."

"Let 'er come to the jail," snapped the angry sheriff. "She'll have plenty of time to say good-bye there."

At that they tugged the chair through the narrow door. Then two boards were found upon which to roll it into the patrol.

Inside the shop Jinnie was quiet now, save for the convulsions that rent her body. She looked up at the man holding her.

"Let me go," she implored. "I'll be good, awful good."

Perhaps it was the pleading blue eyes that made the officer release her arms. Jinnie sprang to the door, and as Lafe saw her, he smiled, oh such a smile! The girl ran madly to him.

"Lafe! Lafe!" she screamed. "Lafe dear!"

Lafe bent, touched the shining black curls, and a glorified expression spread over his face.

"He's given His angels charge over you, lass," he murmured, "an' it's a fact you're not to forget."

Then they rolled him up the planks and into the wagon. With clouded eyes Jinnie watched the black patrol bowl along toward the bridge, and as it halted a moment on Paradise Road to allow an engine to pass, the cobbler leaned far out of his wheel chair and waved a thin white hand at her. Then like a deer she ran ahead until she came within speaking distance of him. The engine passed with a shrieking whistle, and the horses received a sharp crack and galloped off. Jinnie flung out her arms.

"Lafe!" she screamed. "I'll stay with Peg till you come."

He heard the words, waved once more, and the wagon disappeared over the bridge.

For full ten minutes after Lafe was taken away, Jinnie sat in the shop like one turned to stone. The thing that roused her was the side door opening and shutting. She got up quickly and went into the little hall, closing the shop door behind her. Mrs. Grandoken, with bundles in her hands, was entering the kitchen. Jinnie staggered after her.

"Peggy," murmured Jinnie, throwing her arms about the stooped shoulders. "You'll be good——"

It was as if she had said it to Bobbie, tenderly, low-pitched, and imploring. Peg seemed so miserable and thin.

"What's the matter with you, kid?" growled Mrs. Grandoken.

"The town folks," groaned Jinnie, "the town folks've made a mistake, an awful mistake."

Mrs. Grandoken turned sunken eyes upon the speaker.

"What mistake've they made?"

Jinnie's throat hurt so she couldn't say any more.

"What mistake?" asked Peg again.

"They think Lafe shot——"

Peggy wheeled on the hesitating speaker. Shoving her to one side, she stalked through the door. Jinnie flew after her.

"Peggy, Peg, he'll come back!"

Mrs. Grandoken opened the shop door and the empty room with overturned chairs and scattered tools told its silent, eloquent tale.

"Honey," whispered Jinnie. "Honey dear——"

"God's Jesus," muttered Peg, with roving eyes, "God's Jesus, save my man!"

Then she slid to the floor, and when she once more opened her eyes, Jinnie was throwing water in her face.

CHAPTER XXXV

ALONE IN THE SHOP

Later in the day Jordan Morse and Molly Merriweather met at the hospital. They looked into each other's eyes, not daring to mention the terrible consternation that possessed them.

"Have you heard anything?" murmured Molly, glancing about before speaking.

Jordan nodded his head.

"It's awful," he said. "Bates is dead—if you say a word, I'm lost."

"Depend on me," Molly assured him. "Oh, how dreadful it all is! Theodore must get well," she continued in agitation.

"Well, he won't!" snarled Morse. Then he went on passionately. "Molly, I swear I didn't intend to shoot him. I was mad clear through and aimed at the cobbler."

"Hush!" warned Molly. "Some one's coming."

A young doctor approached them with gravity.

"Mr. King?" murmured Molly.

"Is slowly failing. The bullet found a vital spot——"

"And the other man—Bates? Is it true he's dead?" interjected Morse eagerly.

"Yes, he died shortly after the tragedy. It's all a mystery, but I think they've arrested the guilty man."

Both listeners stared at the speaker as if he'd told them the world had come to an end. It was Morse who managed to mutter:

"What man?"

"Haven't you heard? They've arrested Lafe Grandoken. The shooting occurred in his cobbling shop, and the gun was found as proof of his crime. Of course, like all Jews, he's trying to invent a story in his own favor.... He's undoubtedly the criminal."

Not until they were in the street did Jordan express himself to Molly.

"What heavenly luck! So they've arrested Grandoken. If Theodore lives——"

Molly clutched his arm.

"Oh, he must! He must! Jordan! I shall die myself if he doesn't."

Jordan Morse turned sharply upon her.

"Don't throw a fit right here. You're not the only one suffering. My atmosphere is cleared a little with Grandoken's arrest, though."

"But you've still to reckon with Jinnie," ventured Molly.

"Easy now," returned the man. "I'll get her before Theodore is well."

"Take me home," pleaded Molly wearily. "Such a day as this is enough to ruin all the good looks a woman ever had."

Disgustedly, Jordan flung open the motor door.

139

"Well, my God, you've got about as much brains and heart as a chipmunk. Climb in!"

Later, as the two separated, Morse said, with low-pitched voice:

"Now, then, I'm going to plan to get Jinnie. Might's well be hung for a sheep's a lamb——I'm just as well satisfied that Bates is dead. After I secure Jinnie—then for my boy. God! I can scarcely wait until I have him."

Miss Merriweather went into the house in utter exhaustion, nor did she pause to take off her hat before telling Theodore's mother the little she could to encourage her.

If Molly was suffering over the crime which had sent the man she loved to the hospital, Jinnie was going through thrice that agony for the same man. He had almost met his death in coming to tell Lafe of their love, and had been struck down in his mission by an unknown hand. Jinnie knew it was an unknown hand, because just as sure as she lived, so sure was she that Lafe had not committed the crime. The cobbler had explained it all to her, and she believed him. Peggy was dreadfully ill! After her fainting spell, the girl put Mrs. Grandoken to bed, and then went to comfort Bobbie. She found him huddled on his pillow, clasping Happy Pete in his arms. The small face was streaked with tears and half buried from sight.

"Bobbie," called Jinnie softly.

The yellow head came up with a jerk, the flashing grey eyes begging in mute helplessness an explanation for these unusual happenings.

"I'm here, Jinnie. What's the matter with everybody?"

Jinnie lay down beside him.

"Peggy's sick," she said, not daring to say more.

"Where's Lafe?"

An impulsive arm went across the child's body.

"He's gone away for a little while, dear, just for a few days!"

Something in her tones made Bobbie writhe. With the acuteness of one with his affliction, his ears had caught the commotion in the shop.

"But he can't walk, Jinnie. Did he walk?" he demanded.

"No."

"How'd he go, in a motor car?"

"No," repeated the girl.

"Some one took him, then?" demanded Bobbie.

"Yes."

"In a wagon?"

By this time she could feel the tip-tap of his anguished heart against hers.

"Yes," she admitted, but that was all. She felt that to tell the truth then would be fatal to the throbbing young life in her arms.

"Bobbie," she whispered, cuddling him. "Lafe's coming home soon. Be a good boy and lie still and rest. Jinnie'll come back in a few minutes."

She crawled off the bed, and went to the shop door. By main force she had to drag her unwilling feet over the threshold. She stood for two tense minutes scanning the room with pathetic keenness. Then she walked forward and stood beside the bench. It seemed to be sentiently alive with the magnetism of the man who had lately occupied it. Jinnie sat on it, a cry bursting from her white lips. She wanted to be with him, but she had promised to take care of Peggy, and she would rather die than betray that trust. Her eyes fell upon two dark spots upon the floor, one near the door and one almost under her feet. She shuddered as she realized it was blood. Then she went to the kitchen for water and washed it away. This done, she gathered up Lafe's tools, reverently kissing each one as she laid it in the box under the bench. How lonely the shop looked in the gathering gloom! To dissipate the lengthening shadows in the corners, she lighted the lamp. The flickering flame brought back keenly the hours she had spent with Lafe—hours in which she had learned so much. The whole horror that had fallen on the household rushed over her being like a tidal wave over a city. Misery of the most exquisite kind was tearing her heart in pieces, stabbing her throat with long, forklike pains. Tense throat muscles caught and clung together, choking back her breath until she lay down, full length, upon the cobbler's bench.

In poignant grief she thought of the expression of Lafe's face when he had been wheeled from the room. His voice came back through the faint light.

"He has given His angels charge over thee, lassie."

But how could she believe in the angels, with Lafe in prison and Theodore dying? She got up, spent and worn with weeping, and went in to Peggy, sitting for a few minutes beside the agonized woman, but she could not say one word to make that agony less. In losing the two strong friends, she had lost her faith too. Peg's face was turned to the wall, and as she didn't answer when the girl laid her hand on her shoulder, Jinnie tiptoed out. In her own room she lay for seemingly century-long hours with Bobbie pressed tightly to her breast.

CHAPTER XXXVI

JINNIE EXPLAINS THE DEATH CHAIR TO BOBBIE

Seven days had dragged their seemingly slow length from seconds to minutes, from minutes to hours, from hours to days. In the cobbler's shop Jinnie and Bobbie waited in breathless anxiety for Peg's return. She had gone to the district attorney for permission to visit her husband in his cell. Nearly three hours had passed since her departure, and few other thoughts were in the mind of the girl save the passionate wish for news of her two beloved friends. She was standing by the window looking out upon the tracks, and as a heavy train steamed past she counted the cars with melancholy rhythm. There came to her mind the day she had found Bobbie on the hill, and all the sweet moments since when the cobbler had been with them. She choked back a sob that made a little noise in her tightened throat.

Bobbie stumbled his unseeing way to her and shoved a small, cold hand into hers.

"Jinnie's sad," he murmured. "Bobbie's stars're blinkin' out."

Mrs. Grandoken and Jinnie had come to an understanding that Bobbie should not know of the cobbler's trouble, so the strong fingers closed over the little ones, but the girl did not speak. At length she caught a glimpse of Peg, who, with bent head, was stumbling across the tracks. Peggy had failed in her mission! Jinnie knew it because the woman did not look up as she came within sight of the house.

As Mrs. Grandoken entered slowly, Jinnie turned to her.

"You didn't see him?" she said in a tone half exclamation, half question.

"No," responded Peg, wearily, sitting down. "I waited 'most two hours for the lawyer, an' when he come, I begged harder'n anything, but it didn't do no good. He says I can't see my man for a long time. I guess they're tryin' to make him confess he killed Maudlin."

Jinnie's hand clutched frantically at the other's arm. Both women had forgotten the presence of the blind child.

"He wouldn't do that," cried Jinnie, panic-stricken. "A man can't own up to doing a thing he didn't do."

"Course not," whispered Bobbie, in an awed whisper, and the girl sat down, drawing him to her lap. She could no longer guard her tongue nor hide her feelings. She took the afternoon paper from Mrs. Grandoken's hand.

"Read about it aloud," implored the woman.

"It says," began Jinnie, "Mr. King's dying."

The paper fluttered from her hand, and she sat like a small graven image. To see those words so cruelly set in black and white, staring at her with frightful truth, harrowed the very soul of her. A sobbing outburst from Bobbie mingled with the soft chug, chug of the engine outside on the track. Happy Pete, too, felt the tragedy in the air. He wriggled nearer his young mistress and rested his pointed nose on one of her knees, while his twinkling yellow eyes demanded, in their eloquent way, to know the cause of his loved ones' sorrow.

Peggy broke a painful pause.

"Everybody in town says Lafe done it," she groaned, "an'——" she caught her breath. "Oh, God! it seems I can't stand it much longer!"

Jinnie got up, putting the limp boy in her chair. She was making a masterful effort to be brave, to restrain the rush of emotion demanding utterance. Some beating thing in her side ached as if it were about to burst. But she stood still until Peg spoke again.

142

"It's all bad business, Jinnie! an' I can't see no help comin' from anywhere."

If Peg's head hadn't fallen suddenly into her hands, perhaps Jinnie wouldn't have collapsed just then. As it was, her knees gave way, and she fell forward beside the cobbler's wife. Bobbie, in his helpless way, knelt too.

Since Lafe's arrest the girl had not prayed, nor could she recall the promises Lafe had taught her were made for the troubled in spirit. Could she now say anything to make Peg's suffering less, even if she did not believe it all herself?

"Peg," she pleaded, "don't shiver so!.... Hold up your head.... I want to tell you something."

Peggy made a negative gesture.

"It ain't to be bore, Jinnie," she moaned hoarsely.

"Lafe ain't no chance. They'll put him in the chair."

Such awful words! The import was pressed deeper into two young hearts by Peg's wild weeping.

Jinnie staggered to her feet. Blind Bobbie broke into a prolonged wail.

"Lafe ain't never done nothin' bad in all his life," went on the woman, from the shelter of her hands. "He's the best man in the world. He's worked an' worked for everybody, an' most times never got no pay. An' now——"

"Don't say it again, Peggy!" Jinnie's voice rang out. "Don't think such things. They couldn't put Lafe in a wicked death chair—they couldn't."

Bobbie's upraised eyes were trying to pierce through their veil of darkness to seek the speaker's meaning.

"What chair, Jinnie?" he quivered. "What kind of a chair're they goin' to put my beautiful Lafe in?"

Jinnie's mind went back to the teachings of the cobbler, and the slow, sweet, painful smile intermingled with her agony. Again and again the memory of the words, "He hath given his angels charge over thee," swelled her heart to the breaking point. She wanted to believe, to feel again that ecstatic faith which had suffused her as Maudlin Bates pulled her curls in the marsh, when she had called unto the Infinite and Theodore had answered.

Peg needed Lafe's angels at that moment. They all needed the comfort of the cobbler's faith.

"Peg," she began, "your man'd tell you something sweet if he could see you now."

Peg ceased writhing, but didn't lift her face. Jinnie knew she was listening, and continued:

"Haven't you heard him many a time, when there wasn't any wood in the house or any bread to eat, tell you about—about——"

Down dropped the woman's hands, and she lifted a woebegone face to her young questioner.

"Yes, I've heard him, Jinnie," she quavered, "but I ain't never believed it!"

143

"But you can, Peggy! You can, sure! Lots of times Lafe'd say, 'Now, Jinnie, watch God and me!' And I watched, and sure right on the minute came the money." She paused a moment, ruminating. "That money we got the day he went away came because he prayed for it."

The girl was reverently earnest.

"Lafe's got a chance, all right," she pursued, keeping Peg's eye. "More'n a chance, if—if—if——Oh, Peggy, we've got to pray!"

"I don't know how," said Peg, in stifled tones.

Jinnie's face lighted with a mental argument Lafe had thrown at her in her moments of distrust. She was deep in despondency, but something had to be done.

"Peg, you don't need to know anything about it. I didn't when I came here. Lafe says——"

"What'd Lafe say?" cut in Peggy.

"That you must just tell God about it——" Jinnie lifted a white, lovely face. "He's everywhere—not away off," she proceeded. "Talk to Him just like you would to Lafe or me."

Mrs. Grandoken sunk lower in her chair.

"I wisht I'd learnt when Lafe was here. Now I dunno how."

"But will you try?" Jinnie pleaded after a little.

"You know 'em better'n I do, Jinnie," Peg muttered, dejectedly. "You ask if it'll do any good."

Jinnie cleared her throat, coughed, and murmured:

"Close your eyes, Bobbie."

Bobbie shut his lids with a gulping sob, and so did Peg.

Then Jinnie began in a low, constrained voice:

"God and your angels hovering about Lafe, please send him back to the shop. Get him out of jail, and don't let anybody hurt him. Amen."

"Don't let any chair hurt my beautiful cobbler," wailed Bobbie, in a new paroxysm of grief. "Gimme Lafe an' my stars."

In another instant Peggy staggered out of the room, leaving the blind boy and Jinnie alone.

As the door closed, Bobbie's voice rose in louder appeal. Happy Pete touched him tenderly with a cold, wet nose, crawling into his arms with a little whine.

Jinnie looked at her two charges hopelessly. She knew not how to comfort them, nor could she frame words that would still the agony of the child. Yet she lifted Bobbie and Happy Pete and sat down with them on her lap.

"Don't cry, honey," she stammered. "There! There! Jinnie'll rock you."

Her face was ashen with anxiety, and perspiration stood in large drops upon her brow. Mechanically she drew her sleeve across her face.

"I'm going to ask you to be awful good, Bobbie," she pleaded presently. "Lafe's being arrested is hard on Peg—and she's sick."

Bobbie burst in on her words.

144

"But they'll sit my cobbler in a wicked chair, and kill him, Jinnie. Peggy said they would."

"You remember, Bobbie," soothed the girl, "what Lafe said about God's angels, don't you?"

The yellow head bent forward in assent.

"And how they're stronger'n a whole bunch of men?"

"Yes," breathed Bobbie; "but the chair—the men've got that, an' mebbe the angels'll be busy when they're puttin' the cobbler in it."

This idea made him shriek out louder than before: "They'll kill Lafe! Oh, Jinnie, they will!"

"They can't!" denied Jinnie, rigidly. "They can't! Listen, Bobbie."

The wan, unsmiling blind face brought the girl's lips hard upon it.

"I want to know all about the death chair," he whimpered stubbornly.

"Bobbie," she breathed, "will you believe me if I tell you about it?"

"Yes," promised Bobbie, snuggling nearer.

"Hang on to Pete, and I will tell you," said Jinnie.

"I'm hangin' to 'im," sighed Bobbie, touching Pete's shaggy forelock. "Tell me about the chair."

Jinnie was searching her brain for an argument to satisfy him. She wouldn't have lied for her own welfare—but for Bobbie—she could feel the weak, small heart palpitating against her arm.

"Well, in the first place," she began deliberately, "Peg doesn't know everything about murders. Why, Bobbie, they don't do anything at all to men like Lafe. Why, a cobbler, dear, a cobbler could kill everybody in the whole world if he liked."

Bobbie's breath was sent out in one long exclamation of wonder.

"A cobbler," went on Jinnie impressively, "could steal loaves of bread right under a great judge's nose and he couldn't do anything to him."

Jinnie had made a daring speech, such a splendid one; she wanted to believe it herself.

"Tell me more," chirped Bobbie. "What about the death chair, Jinnie?"

She had nursed the hope that the boy would be satisfied with what she had already told him, but she proceeded in triumphant tones:

"Oh, you mean the chair Peg was speaking about, huh? Sure I know all about that…. There isn't anything I don't know about it…. I know more'n all the judges and preachers put together."

A small, trustful smile appeared at the corners of Bobbie's mouth.

"I know you do, Jinnie," he agreed. "Tell it to me."

Jinnie pressed her lips on his hair.

"And if I tell you, kiddie, you'll not cry any more or worry Peggy?"

"I'll be awful good, and not cry once," promised the boy, settling himself expectantly.

"Now, then, listen hard!"

Accordingly, after a dramatic pause, to give stress to her next statement, she continued:

145

"There isn't a death chair in the whole world can kill a cobbler."

Bobbie braced himself against her and sat up. His blind eyes were roving over her with an expression of disbelief. Jinnie knew he was doubting her veracity, so she hurried on.

"Of course they got an electric chair that'll kill other kinds of men," she explained volubly, "but if you'll believe me, Bobbie, no cobbler could ever sit in it."

Bobbie dropped back again. There was a ring of truth in Jinnie's words, and he began to believe her.

"And another thing, Bobbie, there's something in the Bible better'n what I've told you. You believe the Bible, don't you?"

"Lafe's Bible?" asked Bobbie, scarcely audible.

"Sure! There isn't but one."

"Yes, Jinnie, I believe that," said the boy.

"Well," and Jinnie glanced up at the ceiling, "there's just about a hundred pages in that book tells how once some men tried to put a cobbler in one of those chairs, and the lightning jumped out and set 'em all on fire——"

Bobbie straightened up so quickly that Happy Pete fell to the floor.

"Yes, yes, Jinnie dear," he breathed. "Go on!"

Jinnie hesitated. She didn't want to fabricate further.

"It's just so awful I hate to tell you," she objected.

"I'd be happier if you would," whispered Bobbie.

"Then I will! The fire, jumping out, didn't hurt the cobbler one wee bit, but it burned the wicked men——" Jinnie paused, gathered a deep breath, and brought to mind Lafe's droning voice when he had used the same words, "Burned 'em root and branch," declared she.

Bobbie's face shone with happiness.

"Is that all?" he begged.

"Isn't it enough?" asked Jinnie, with tender chiding.

"Aren't there nothin' in it about Lafe?"

"Oh, sure!" Again she was at loss for ideas, but somehow words of their own volition seemed to spring from her lips. "Sure there is! There's another hundred pages in that blessed book that says good men like Lafe won't ever go into one of those chairs, never, never.... The Lord God Almighty ordered all those death chairs to be chopped up for kindling wood," she ended triumphantly.

"Shortwood?" broke out Bobbie.

Unheeding the interruption, Jinnie pursued: "They just left a chair for wicked men, that's all."

Bobbie slipped to the floor and raised his hands.

"Jinnie, pretty Jinnie. I'm goin' to believe every word you've said, every word, and my stars're all shinin' so bright they're just like them in the sky."

Jinnie kissed the eager little face and left the child sitting on the floor, crooning contentedly to Happy Pete.

"Lafe told me once," Jinnie whispered to herself on the way to the kitchen, "when a lie does a lot of good, it's better than the truth if telling facts hurts some one."

She joined Peggy, sighing, "I'm an awful liar, all right, but Bobbie's happy."

CHAPTER XXXVII

WHAT THE THUNDER STORM BROUGHT

In the past few weeks Jinnie Grandoken had been driven blindly into unknown places, forced to face conditions which but a short time before would have seemed unbearable. However, there was much with which Jinnie could occupy her time. Blind Bobbie was not well. He was mourning for the cobbler with all his boyish young soul, and every day Peggy grew more taciturn and ill. The funds left by Theodore were nearly gone, and Jinnie had given up her lessons. She was using the remaining money for their meagre necessities.

So slowly did the days drag by that the girl had grown to believe that the authorities would never bring Lafe to trial, exonerate him, and send him home. Then, too, Theodore was still in the hospital, and she thought of him ever with a sense of terrific loss. But the daily papers brought her news of him, and now printed that his splendid constitution might pull him through. It never occurred to her that her loved one would believe Lafe had shot him and Maudlin Bates. Theodore was too wise, too kindly, for such suspicions.

For a while after receiving permission from the county attorney, she visited Lafe every day. Peggy had seen him only once, being too miserable to stand the strain of going to the jail. But Mrs. Grandoken never neglected sending by the girl some little remembrance to her husband. Perhaps it was only a written message, but mostly a favorite dish of food or an article of his wearing apparel.

One afternoon Bobbie sat by the window with his small, pale face pressed close to the pane. Outside a great storm was raging, and from one end of Paradise Road to the other, rivulets of water rushed down to the lake. Several times that day, when the boy had addressed Mrs. Grandoken, she had answered him even more gruffly than of yore. He knew by her voice she was ill, and his palpitating heart was wrung so agonizingly that he was constantly in tears. Now he was waiting for Jinnie, and the sound of the buffeting rain and the booming roar of heavy thunder thrilled him

147

dismally. To hear Jinnie's footsteps at that moment would be the panacea for all his grief.

Peg came into the shop, and Bobbie turned slightly.

"Jinnie's stayin' awful long at the jail to-day," said the woman fretfully. "Do you hear her comin', Bobbie?"

"No," said Bobbie, "I've been stretchin' my ears almost to the hill to hear her. If she doesn't come soon, I'll die—my stars've been gone a long time."

"I wish she'd come," sighed Mrs. Grandoken.

"Bend over here, Peg," entreated Bobbie, "I want to touch your eyes!"

Without comment the woman leaned over, and the boy's fingers wavered over her wrinkled countenance.

"You're awful sick, dearie," he grieved, pressing against her. "Can Blind Bobbie do anything?"

Peg dropped her arm around him.

"I'm afraid," she whispered. "I wish Lafe and Jinnie was here."

One long shiver shook Bobbie's slender body. That Peg could ever be afraid was a new idea to him. It terrified him even to contemplate it. He began to sob wistfully, but in another instant raised his head.

"She's comin'," he cried sharply. "I hear 'er. I got two stars, mebbe three."

When Jinnie opened the door, the water was dripping from her clothes, and her hair hung in long, wet curls to her waist. One look into Peg's twisted, pain-ridden face, and she understood.

"I'm glad you're here," said the woman, with a gesture of helplessness. And Bobbie echoed, with fluttering hands, "I'm glad, too, Jinnie. Me and Peg was so 'fraid."

The girl spoke softly to Bobbie, and drew Peggy into the bedroom. There, with her arm thrown across Mrs. Grandoken's shoulder, she gave all the assurance and comfort of which she was capable.

Long after midnight, the rain still came down in thrashing torrents, and through the pieces of broken tin on the roof the wind shrilled dismally.

There was a solemn hush in the back bedroom where Peggy lay staring at the ceiling. In front of the shadowy lamp was a bit of cardboard to protect the sick woman's eyes from the light. At Peggy's side sat Jinnie, and in her arms lay a small bundle. Jinnie had gained much knowledge in the last few hours. She had discovered the mystery of all existence. She had seen Peg go down into that wonderful valley of life and bring back Lafe's little boy baby, and the girl's eyes held an expression of impenetrable things. She moved her position slightly so as to study Mrs. Grandoken's face.

Suddenly Peg's eyes lowered.

"Jinnie, gimme a drink, will you?"

Placing the child on the bed, the girl got up instantly. She went to the kitchen and returned with a glass of milk. It had scarcely touched the woman's lips before she raised her hand and pushed it away.

148

"I mustn't drink that," she whispered feebly.

"I got it specially for you, Peggy dear," insisted Jinnie.... "Drink it," she wheedled, "please."

Then Jinnie sat down again, listening as the elements kept up their continuous rioting, and after a while they lulled her to rest. Suddenly her head dropped softly on the bundle in her arms, and the three—Peggy, Jinnie and the tiny Jewish baby—slept.

Jinnie's name, spoken in low tones, roused her quickly. She raised her head, a sharp pain twisting her neck. Peggy was looking at her, with misery in her face.

"I feel awful sick, Jinnie," she moaned. "Can't you say somethin' t'me, somethin' to make me feel better?"

Something to make her feel better! The words touched the listener deeply. Oh, how she wanted to help! To alleviate Peg's suffering was her one desire. If it had been Bobbie, or even Lafe, Jinnie would have known exactly what to say; but Peggy, proud, stoical Peggy!

"Let me put the baby with you where it's warm, Peg," she said, gently. "I'm going to talk to you a minute.... There, now, you're all safe, little mister, near your mammy's heart."

Then she knelt down by the bed and took the woman's hot fingers in hers.

"Peggy," she began softly, "things look awful bad just now, but Lafe told me once, when they looked that way, it was time for some one to come along and help. I'll tell you about it, Peg! Eh?"

"Who c'n come?" demanded Mrs. Grandoken, irritably. "Mr. King can't, an' we hain't no other friends who'll come to a cobbler's shop."

The question in her voice gave Jinnie the chance she was looking for.

"Yes, there is," she insisted. "Now listen, while I say something; will you?"

"Sure," said Peg, squeezing Jinnie's fingers.

Then Jinnie started to repeat a few verses Lafe had taught her. She couldn't tell exactly where they were in the Bible, but the promise in them had always made her own burdens lighter, and since seeing Lafe daily, she had partially come back to her former trust.

"'The Lord is my Shepherd,'" she droned sleepily. Then on and on until she came to, "'Yea, though I walk through the valley of the shadow of death,'" and Peg broke into a sob.

"'I will fear no evil,'" soothed Jinnie, amid the roaring of the wind and the crackling of the thunder over the hill.

"'For thou art with me,'" she finished brokenly. "He's the one I was talking about, Peggy. He'll help us all if we can believe and be——"

Then she quickly ended, "Happy in Spite."

Peg continued to sob. One arm was across her baby boy protectingly, and the other hand Jinnie held in hers.

"Somehow things seem easier, Peggy, when you hold your head up

149

high, and believe everything'll come all right…. Lafe said so; that's why he started the club."

"I wisht I could think that way. I'm near dead," groaned the woman.

Jinnie smoothed the soft, grey-streaked hair.

"Wouldn't you like to come into the club, dear?" she faltered, scarcely daring to put the question. "Then you'll be happy with us all—with Lafe and Bobbie and—and——"

Jinnie wanted to say another name, but doubted its wisdom—and then abruptly it came; "and Jinnie," she finished.

Peggy almost sat up in bed.

"Darlin'," she quivered. "Darlin' girl, I've been cussed mean to Lafe an' you. I've told you many a time with my own mouth I hated you, but God knows, an' Lafe knows, I loved you the minute I set eyes on you." She dropped back on the pillow and continued, "If you'll take me in your club, an' learn me how to believe, I'll try; I swear I will."

For a long time Jinnie sat crooning over and over the verses she'd learned from Lafe, and bye-and-bye she heard Peg breathing regularly and knew she slept. Then she settled herself in the chair, and sweet, mysterious dreams came to her through the storm.

CHAPTER XXXVIII

THE STORY OF A BIRD

Lafe Grandoken, in his wheel chair, sat under the barred prison window, an open Bible on his knees. Slowly the shadows were falling about him, and to the man every shade had an entity of its own. First there trooped before him all the old memories of the many yesterdays—of Peg— his little dead lad—and Jinnie. And lastly, ghostlike, came the shattered hopes of to-morrow, and with these he groaned and shivered.

Jinnie stole in and looked long upon her friend through the iron-latticed door. The smile that played with the dimples in her cheeks and the dancing shadows in the violet eyes indicated her happiness. Lafe looked older and thinner than ever before, and her heart sang when she thought of the news she had to tell him. She longed to pronounce his name, to take away the far-away expression that seemed to hold him in deep meditation. During her tramp to the jail she'd concocted a fairy story to bring a smile to the cobbler's lips. So at length:

"Lafe," she whispered.

Mr. Grandoken's head came up quickly, and he turned the chair and wheeled toward her. There was the same question in his eyes that had been there for so many days, and Jinnie smiled broadly.

"Lafe," she began mysteriously, "a great big bird flew right into the house last night. He flopped in to get out of the storm!"

"A bird?" repeated Lafe, startled.

"Yes, and everybody says it's awful good luck."

Lafe's expression grew tragic, and Jinnie hurried on with her tale.

"I'll bet you can't guess what kind of a bird 'twas, Lafe."

Lafe shook his head. "I can't lessen 'twas a robin," said he.

Jinnie giggled.

"My, no! He was a heap bigger'n a robin. Guess again!"

Such chatter from Jinnie was unusual, especially of late, but Lafe bore it patiently.

"I can't," he sighed, shaking his head.

Jinnie clapped her hands.

"I knew you couldn't! Well, Lafe, it was a—a——"

"Yes?" queried Lafe wearily, during her hesitation. "Well, Jinnie?"

"It was a great, big, beautiful white stork, Lafe, and he brought you a new Jew baby. What'd you think of that?"

"Jinnie, girl, lass, you ain't tellin' me——"

"Yes, dear, he's there, as big as life and twice as natural, Peg says.... Of course," she rambled on, "the stork went away, but the Jew baby—to make a long story short, he's with——"

"His ma, eh, dear?" interjected Lafe. "How's Peg, honey?"

"Oh, she's fine," replied Jinnie, "and I've a lot to tell you, dearest."

"Begin," commanded Lafe, with wide, bright eyes.

Jinnie commenced by telling how lovely the baby was. Of course she didn't rehearse Peg's suffering. It wouldn't do any good.

"And the baby looks like you, Lafe," she observed.

"Does he really?" gasped Lafe, trying to smile.

"He's got your Jew look 'round his nose," added Jinnie gravely. "You wanted him to look like you, didn't you, Lafe?"

"Sure, Jinnie. And now about Peggy? Tell me about Peggy."

"Peggy's with us, Lafe——" Jinnie stopped and drew a long breath. "What'd you think? Oh—guess!"

"I couldn't! Tell me, Jinnie! Don't keep me waitin' for good things."

"Peggy's in the 'Happy in Spite', and I'm learning her all the verses you taught me."

Then Lafe's head dropped on his hands and tears trickled through his fingers.

"I wish I could see her," he groaned deeply.

"When she gets well, you can," promised Jinnie, "and mebbe the baby."

Lafe's head was raised quickly and his eyes sparkled.

"I'd love to see 'em both," was all he could stammer.

The girl thrust her fingers through the bars to him, and they stood thus, regarding each other in all confidence and faith, until Jinnie dropped his hand.

"Mr. King's getting well," she said softly.

"I'm glad, very glad. He don't think I done it, does he, Jinnie?"

"No, and when I see him I'll tell him you didn't."

And as if that settled it, she turned to go; then hesitating, she smiled upon him.

"Give me four nice kisses, Lafe. I'll take one to Peg, Bobbie, and the baby, and keep one for myself." Then after their lips had met through the bars in resounding smacks, Jinnie gasped, "We can't forget Milly Ann and Happy Pete. Two more, honey!"

"God bless you, Jinnie lass," murmured Lafe, trying to hide his emotion, and then he wheeled quickly back into the falling afternoon light under the window.

Jinnie's energetic mind was busy with a scheme. She wasn't sure it would meet with Peg's approval, but when she arrived home, she sat down beside Mrs. Grandoken.

"Now, Peggy," she began emphatically, "I want you to pay attention to what I'm saying to you."

"I will," said Peggy.

"Lafe wants to see the baby!"

"Now?" asked Mrs. Grandoken, surprised.

"Well, he didn't say just now, but his eyes asked it, and, Peg, I was wondering if I couldn't take the little kid up to the jail."

Peggy shook her head.

"They wouldn't let you in with 'im," she objected.

Jinnie thought a long time. Presently she laughed a little, chuckling laugh.

"I know how to get him in there!"

"How?" asked Peggy, incredulously.

"Why, everybody knows I've been a shortwood girl. I'll roll him up in a bundle——"

Peg's hand sought the little body under the covers protectingly.

"Oh, I won't hurt him, Peg," assured Jinnie. "We'll wrap him up the first fine day! You can do it yourself, dear."

One week later Jinnie went slowly up the incline that led to the prison. On her back was a shortwood strap filled with brush and small twigs.

"I want to see Lafe Grandoken," she said.

To surprise Lafe she crept softly along the corridor until she halted at his cell door. She could see him plainly, and the troubled lines were almost erased from between his brows. She was glad of that, for she wanted him to smile, to be "Happy in Spite."

She called his name and he turned, wheeling toward her.

"I hoped you'd be comin'," he said, smiling gravely. Then noting the shortwood, he exclaimed, "Have you had to go to work again, lass?"

152

"Just for to-day," and Jinnie displayed her white teeth in a broad smile. "I've brought you something, Lafe, and I wrapped it up in shortwood."

The girl carefully slipped the strap from her shoulders and sat down beside it on the floor. Watching eagerly, Lafe peered between the bars, for surely his Peggy had sent him some token of her love. The girl paused and looked up.

"Shut your eyes tight, Lafe," she commanded playfully.

Lafe closed his eyes, wrinkling down his lids. Then Jinnie lifted the baby and uncovered the small face. The little chap opened his eyes and yawned as the girl held him close to the bars.

"Now, Lafe, quick! Look! Ha! It's a Jew!"

The cobbler's eyes flew open, and he was staring squarely into a small, rosy, open-eyed baby face. For a moment he thought he was dreaming—dreaming a dream he had dreamed every night since the thunder storm. He caught at his chin to stay the chattering of his teeth.

"It ain't him, Jinnie, my Jew baby?" he murmured brokenly.

"Yes, 'tis," and she laughed. "It's your own little feller. I brought him to get a kiss from his daddy. Kiss him! Kiss him smack on the mouth, Lafe."

And Lafe kissed his baby—kissed him once, twice, and three times, gulping hard after each caress. He would never have enough of those sweet kisses, never, never! And as his lips descended reverently upon the smooth, rose-colored skin, Mr. Grandoken laughed, and Jinnie laughed, and the baby, too, wrinkled up his nose.

"Lafe," Jinnie said tenderly, drawing the baby away, "I knew you wanted to see him; didn't you?"

Lafe nodded. "An' I'll never be able to thank you for this, Jinnie.... Let me kiss him once more.... Oh, ain't he beautiful?"

Just before the girl wrapped the boy again in the shortwood, she suggested,

"Lafe, what's against taking him into the 'Happy in Spite'? He's happier'n any kid in the whole world, having you for a daddy and Peg for his mother."

Jinnie thrust the baby's plump hand through the bars, and Lafe, with tears in his eyes, shook it tenderly, then kissed it.

"Lafe Grandoken, Jr," he whispered, "you're now a member of the 'Happy in Spite' Club."

And then Jinnie took the baby back to Peggy.

CHAPTER XXXIX
JINNIE'S VISIT TO THEODORE

So suddenly had the two strong, friendly forces been swept from Jinnie's daily life that as yet she had not the power to think with precision. Lafe she had had every day for almost three years, and Theodore King—oh, how she loved him! Rumors were afloat that no power could save Lafe—her dear, brave cobbler.

Day by day the girl's faith increased, and of late she had uttered silent prayers that she might be allowed to see Theodore.

One morning she was in the kitchen rocking little Lafe when Peggy called her.

"There's some one to see you," said she.

Jinnie gave the mother her baby and went to the shop door. A man in a white suit smiled down upon her.

"I'm from the hospital," said he. "Mr. King would like to see you this morning."

Jinnie's heart seemed to climb into her throat.

"Mr. Theodore King?" she murmured.

"Yes," said the young man. "I've got a car here. Will you come?"

"Of course! Wait till I get my hat."

Once at their destination, they tiptoed into Theodore's room noiselessly, and as Jinnie stood over the bed, looking down upon him, she suffered keenly, he looked so deathlike; but she resolutely controlled her feelings. When Theodore glanced at her, she forced herself to smile, and the sight of the lovely girl refreshed the sick man, giving him a new impetus to recover.

He smiled back, endeavoring not to show his weakness.

"You see I'm getting well," he whispered.

Jinnie nodded. She wasn't sure whether he was or not. How her heart ached to do something for him!

One of his long, thin hands lay over the coverlet, and Jinnie wanted to kiss it. Tears were standing thick on her lashes.

The doctor stood beside her, consulting his watch.

"If you wish to speak, Mr. King," he said kindly, "you must do so quickly, for the young lady can stay but two minutes more. That's all!"

The doctor turned his back upon them, watch in hand.

"Kiss me, dear!" murmured Theodore.

Oblivious of the doctor's presence, Jinnie stooped and kissed him twice, taking the thin hand he extended.

"I sent for you because I feared you'd go to work at the wood again."

Jinnie would reassure him on this point even by an untruth, for she might be driven, for the sake of Peggy and the children, to go back into that hated occupation.

"I promise I won't," she said.

"Are you still taking lessons?"

Jinnie shook her head.

"I couldn't when you were sick. I just couldn't."

"But you must; you must go to-morrow. I have something here for you," he said, reaching under the pillow with his free hand.

Jinnie drew back abashed.

"You're too sick to think of us," she murmured.

Theodore raised her hand to his lips.

"No! No, darling, I think of you always—every day and shall even when I'm dead. You must take this money. Do you love me, dearest, very much?"

He smiled again as she stooped impetuously to kiss him, and with her face very close to his, she whispered,

"Lafe didn't do it, darling!"

"I know it," replied Theodore, closing his eyes.

Then the doctor turned and sent her away.

When she sank back in the automobile, Jinnie opened her hand with the roll of bills in it, and all the way home, she repeated, "He has given His angels charge over thee." She was hoping and praying for Theodore King.

Two days later, coming down the hill, she met Miss Merriweather on horseback. The young woman stopped her and asked her to accompany her home. Jennie hesitated. She still had memories of the cat sent to its death in Molly's fit of anger and the woman's chilling reception of her at the King dinner. Nevertheless she turned and walked slowly beside the horse. When they reached the porch of Mr. King's home, a groom came and led the animal away. Jinnie laid down her fiddle, taking the chair indicated by Molly. It had been Jordan Morse's idea that she should endeavor to again talk with the girl, but the woman scarcely knew how to begin. Jinnie looked so very lovely, so confiding, so infinitely sweet. Molly leaned over and said:

"Wasn't it queer how suddenly I remembered who you were? That night at the party your name refused to come to my mind. I've wanted to tell you several times how sorry I was about your accident!"

"I recognized you the minute I saw you," said Jinnie, smiling, relieved a little by Molly's apology.

"You've a good memory," answered Molly. "Now I want to tell you something, and I hope you'll be guided by my judgment."

Jinnie looked straight at her without a sign of acquiescence.

"What is it?" she asked presently.

"You must leave Grandoken's!"

Jinnie started to speak, but Molly's next words closed her lips.

"Please don't get nervous! Listen to me! You're a very young and very pretty girl and there—there is some one interested in you."

Jinnie pricked up her ears. Some one interested in her! Of course she knew who it was. Theodore! But she wouldn't leave Peggy even for him, and the thought that he would not ask this of her brought her exquisite joy.

"Is it Mr. King who's interested in me?" she asked, timidly.

Molly's eyes narrowed into small slits.

"No, it isn't Mr. King who's interested in you!" she replied a trifle mockingly. "Mr. King's too sick to be interested in anybody."

Jinnie couldn't refrain from saying, "He looked awful ill when I saw him at the hospital."

Molly stared at her blankly. She grew dizzy and very angry. This girl always made her rage within herself.

"You've seen him since—since——"

A maddened expression leapt into Molly's eyes.

"I drive there every day, but they won't let me see him," she said, reddening.

"Mr. King sent for me," Jinnie replied, resolutely.

And as the girl admitted this, with deepening flushes, Molly looked away. When she had first spoken of Jinnie's future to Jordan Morse, she had pleaded with him to be kind to her, but now she could surround that white throat and strangle the breath from it without compunction.

"Will you tell me what he said to you?" she queried, trying to hide her anger.

Jinnie looked down, and locked her fingers together.

"I can't tell," she said at length, moving in discomfort.

She wanted to go—to get away from the woman who looked at her so analytically, so resentfully. She got up nervously and picked up her fiddle.

"Don't go," urged Molly, starting forward.

Then she laughed a little and went on, "I suppose I did feel a bit jealous at first because we—Mr. King and I—have been friends so many years. But now we won't think any more about it. I do want you to go from that terrible Paradise Road. It's no place for a girl in your position."

"You've told me that before," retorted Jinnie, with clouded eyes. "My position isn't anything. I haven't any other home, and I'm a sort of a helper to Peggy."

A helper to Peggy! Doubtless if Lafe had heard that he would have smiled. Truly she was a wonderful little helper, but she was more than that, much more—helper, friend, and protector all in one.

"Another thing," added Jinnie quickly, "I love 'em all."

"You've your own home in Mottville," the woman suggested. "You ought to be there."

Jinnie sank back into the chair.

"Oh, I couldn't ever go there!" she cut in swiftly. "But I can't tell you why."

"Don't you want me to help you?"

Jinnie shook her head doubtfully.

"It wouldn't help any, taking away from Peggy. I'd rather you'd do something for Lafe. Help him get out of prison. Will you?"

"I'm not interested in him," said Molly. "But I am in you——"

"Why?" blurted Jinnie.

Molly colored.

156

"One can't explain an interest like mine. But I'd go back to Mottville with you, and help you with your——"

Jinnie shook her head violently.

"I wouldn't go there for anything in the world," she interjected.

"I can't understand why not!"

"Well, first I couldn't, and I won't.... Then Peggy needs me in Paradise Road, and there's the baby and Bobbie."

"Who's Bobbie?"

"Our little kid," replied Jinnie, smiling sweetly.

She did not think it necessary to explain that she had found Bobbie in the woods. He was as much one of them as Lafe's baby or herself. Neither did she speak of the boy's pitiful condition.

In spite of Jinnie's absolute refusal, Molly went on:

"But you don't understand. You've got your own life to think of!"

Jinnie burst in with what she thought was a clinching triumph.

"I take lessons on my fiddle every day. Some time I hope——"

Molly's eyes gleamed again.

"How can you afford to take lessons?"

The questioner read the truth in the burning blush that swept the girl's dark hair line, and her little white teeth came together.

"Mr. Grandoken is not your uncle," she snapped.

"He's more'n my uncle; he's a father to me, and when he comes home——"

"He's not coming home. Murderers don't get off so easily."

Jinnie got up and again picked her fiddle from the floor.

"He isn't a murderer!" she stammered, with filling eyes. "Lafe wouldn't kill anything.... I've been with him almost three years and I know. Why, he wouldn't let Peg or me swat flies."

Miss Merriweather saw her mistake. She realized then as never before that nothing could take from the girl her belief in the cobbler.

"Sit down," she urged. "Don't go yet."

"I don't want to sit down," said Jinnie, very much offended. "I'm going! I'm sorry you think Lafe——"

Molly rose too. Impetuously she held out her hand.

"I really shouldn't have spoken that way, because I don't know a thing about it."

Jinnie relented a little, but not enough to sit down. She was too deeply hurt to accept Molly's hospitality further.

"And we musn't quarrel, child," decided the woman. "Now won't you reconsider my proposition? I should love to do something for you."

Resolutely the dark curls shook in refusal.

"I'm going to stay with Peggy till Lafe gets out, and then when I'm eighteen I'm going to school. I've been studying a lot since I left Mottville.... Why sometimes——" she resumed eagerly, "when we haven't had enough to eat, Lafe's made me buy a book to study out of, and I promised him I'd stay with his family till he came back. And——" she

157

walked to the edge of the porch, turning suddenly, "and he's coming back, all right," she ended, going down the stairs.

Molly watched the slim young figure swing out to the road. The girl didn't look around, and the woman waited until she had disappeared through the gate.

"He'll not get out, and you, you little upstart," she gritted, "you'll not stay in Paradise Road, either."

CHAPTER XL

AN APPEAL TO JINNIE'S HEART

One afternoon she was on her way home from her lesson when she heard a voice call, "Miss Grandoken!" She glanced up swiftly, recognizing the speaker immediately. He had been present that first night she had played for Theodore's guests, and she remembered vividly her intuitive dislike of him; but because he was a friend of Theodore's she went forward eagerly. The man drove his car to the side of the pavement and bowed.

"Would you care to be of service to Mr. King?" he asked, smiling.

Jinnie noticed his dazzling teeth and scarlet lips.

"Oh, yes, indeed! I wish I might."

"Then come with me," replied the man. "Will you?"

Without fear she entered the open car door and sat down, placing her violin on the seat beside her. She sank back with a sigh. The time had come she had so longed for; she was going to do something for Theodore. She was glad now she had consented to take two lessons that day, or she would have missed this blessed opportunity to show her gratitude to her dear one, in acts, as well as words. The car turned and sped up the hill.

If Jinnie wondered where the man was taking her, she did not allude to it. They were driving in the same direction she took every day to visit the master, and the very familiarity of it turned aside any question that arose in her mind. As he helped her from the machine, she looked up at the sombre building in front of them. In passing it daily she had often wondered what it was and if any one lived within its vast stone walls. One hasty glance, as she was being ushered in, showed paint pails, brushes, and long ropes fastened from the roof to broad planks below.

"Miss Merriweather will be here very soon," the man explained good-naturedly. "She wants you to go with her to the hospital."

Jinnie's mind flew to that one time she had visited Theodore's sick bed. She would be glad to see Molly the Merry.

She had forgiven all the woman's cruelty.

158

The long flights of stairs they mounted were dark and uncarpeted. Their footsteps made a hollow sound through the wide corridors, and there was no other sign of human life about the place. But still Jinnie followed the man in front of her, up and up, until she had counted five floors. Then he took a key from his pocket and put it in the lock, turning it with a click.

Jinnie waited until, stepping inside, he turned and smilingly bade her enter. There was so little natural suspicion in the girl's heart that she never questioned the propriety, much less the safety, of coming into a strange place with an unknown man. Her dear one was ill. She was anxious to see him again, to help him if possible. She felt a little shy at the thought of seeing Miss Merriweather once more. The man led her to an inner room and suavely waved to a chair, asking her to be seated. Casting anxious eyes about the place, she obeyed.

"I'm going after Miss Merriweather now, if you'll wait a few moments," explained the stranger. "She wasn't ready and asked me to bring you first. I think she's preparing a surprise for Mr. King."

Jinnie's tender little heart warmed toward Molly the Merry. Just then she had untold gratitude for the woman who was allowing her to take Theodore something with her own hands. Oh, what joy!

She smiled back at the speaker as he moved toward the door. Then he left her, asking her politely to make herself at home until he returned.

Jinnie waited and waited until she thought she couldn't possibly wait any longer. Peg would be worried, terribly worried, and little Bobbie wouldn't eat his supper without her. But because of Miss Merriweather's kindness and her own great desire to see her sweetheart, she must stay until the last moment. She grew tired, stiff with sitting, and the little clock on the mantel told her she'd been there over two hours. She got up and went to the window. The building stood high on a large wooded bluff overlooking a deep gorge. The landscape before her interested her exceedingly, and took her in fancy to the wilderness of Mottville. The busy birds fluttered to and fro, twittering sleepily to each other, and for a short time the watcher forgot her anxiety in the majesty of the scene.

Miles of hills and miles and miles of water stretched northward as far as her eyes could discern anything. The same water passed and repassed the old farmhouse, and for some time Jinnie tried to locate some familiar spot, off where the sky dipped to the lake. It wasn't until she noticed the hands of the clock pointed to half past six that she became terribly nervous.

She wanted to go to the hospital and get back to Peg. Mrs. Grandoken couldn't leave the baby with Blind Bobbie, and there was supper to buy. Once more she paced the rooms, then back to the window. She shivered for some unknown reason, and a sharp consciousness of evil suddenly grew out of the lengthening hours. With the gathering dusk the hills and gorge had fallen into voiceless silence, and because her nerves tingled with vague fear, Jinnie drew the curtains to shut out the yawning dark, and lighted a lamp on the table.

The room was arranged simply with a small divan, at the head of which was a pillow. Jinnie sat down and leaned back. Her face held a look of serious attention. She wondered if anything had happened to Molly the Merry. Then abruptly she decided to go downstairs. If they weren't coming, she'd have to go home. She went to the door and, turning the knob, pulled hard. The door was locked, and the key was gone! Her discovery seemed to unmake her life in a twinkling. She was like one stricken with death—pale, cold and shivering. She did not know what she was going to do, but she must act—she must do something! A round of inspection showed her she could not open one of the doors. The windows, too, had several nails driven into their tops and along the sides, and the doors were securely fastened with keys. She went back to the window, raised the curtains, and looked out into the gloom. There was not another light to be seen.

The clock on the mantel had struck nine, and Jinnie had grown so horrified she dared not sit down. Many a time she went to the door and pressed her ear to it, but no sound came through the deep silence.

It was after eleven when she dropped on the divan and drew the coverlet over her. The next she knew, daylight was streaming in upon her face.

CHAPTER XLI

JINNIE'S PLEA

Jinnie sprang up, unable at first to remember where she was. Then it all came to her. She was locked away from the world in a big house overlooking the gorge. However, the morning brought a clear sun, dissipating some of her fear—filling her with greater hope.

The dreadful dreams during the night had been but dreams of fear and pain—of eternal separation from her loved ones. Such dreams, such fears, were foolish! No one could take her away from Peggy. She wouldn't go! Ah, the man would return very soon with Molly the Merry.

The clock struck eight. What would Blind Bobbie think—and Peggy? The woman might decide she had left her forever; but no, no, Peg couldn't think that!

Childlike, she was hungry. If some one had intentionally imprisoned her, they must have left her something to eat. Investigation brought forth some cold meat, a bottle of milk, and some bread. Jinnie ate all she could swallow. Then for an hour and a half she paced up and down, wishing something would happen, some one would come. Anything would be better than such deadly uncertainty.

Perhaps it was the overwhelming stillness of the building, possibly a natural alertness indicative of her fear, that allowed Jinnie to catch the echoes of footsteps at the farther end of the corridor. But before she got to the door, a key grated in the lock, and the man who had brought her there was standing beside her. Their eyes met in a clinging, challenging glance— the blue of the one clashing with the sinister grey, as steel strikes fire from steel. An insolent smile broke over his face and he asked nonchalantly:

"Did you find the food?"

Jinnie did not answer. She stood contemplating his face. How she hated his smile, his white teeth, and his easy, suave manner. Their glances battled again for a moment across the distance.

"Why did you bring me here?" she demanded abruptly.

He spread his feet outward and hummed, toying the while with a smooth white chin.

"Sit down," said he, with assumed politeness.

Jinnie stared at him with contemptuous dread in her eyes.

"I don't want to; I want to know why I'm here."

"Can't you guess?" asked the stranger with an easy shrug.

"No," said Jinnie. "Why?"

"And you can't guess who I am?"

"No," repeated Jinnie once more, passionately, "and I want to know why I'm here."

He came toward her, piercing her face with a pair of compelling, mesmeric eyes that made her stagger back to the wall. Then he advanced a step nearer, covering the space Jinnie had yielded.

"I'm Jordan Morse," he then said, clipping his words off shortly.

If a gun had burst in Jinnie's face, she could have been no more alarmed. She was frozen to silence, and every former fear her father had given life to almost three years before, beset her once more, only with many times the amount of vigor. Nevertheless, she gave back look for look, challenge for challenge, while her fingers locked and interlocked. Her uncle, who had sent her father to his grave, the man who wanted her money, who desired her own death!

Then her eyes slowly took on a tragic expression. She knew then she was destined to encounter the tragedy of Morse's terrific vengeance, and no longer wondered why her father had succumbed to his force. He stood looking at her, his gaze taking in the young form avidiously.

"You're the most beautiful girl in the world," he averred presently.

Jinnie's blue eyes narrowed angrily. However, in spite of her rage, she was terribly frightened. An instinct of self-preservation told her to put on a bold, aggressive front.

"Give me that key and let me go," she insisted, with an upward toss of her head.

She walked to the door and shook it vigorously. Morse followed her and brought her brutally back to the center of the room.

"Not so fast," he grated. "Don't ever do that again! I've been hunting you for almost three years.... Sit down, I said."

"I won't!" cried Jinnie, recklessly. "I won't! You can't keep me here. My friends'll find me."

The man hazarded a laugh.

"What friends?" he queried.

Jinnie thought quickly. What friends? She had no friends just then, and because she knew she was dependent upon him for her very life, she listened in despair as he threw a truth at her.

"The only friends you have're out of business! Lafe Grandoken will be electrocuted for murder——"

The hateful thing he had just said and the insistence in it maddened her. She covered her face with her hands and uttered a low cry.

"And Theodore King is in the hospital," went on Morse, mercilessly. "It'll do no good for you to remember him."

She was too normally alive not to express the loving heart outraged within her.

"I shall love him as long as I live," she shivered between her fingers.

"Hell of a lot of good it'll do you," grunted the man coarsely.

Keen anxiety empowered her to raise an anguished face.

"You want my money——" she hesitated. "Well, you can have it.... You want it, don't you?"

Her girlish helplessness made Morse feel that he was without heart or dignity, but he thought of his little boy and of how this girl was keeping from him the means to institute a search for the child, and his desire for vengeance kindled to glowing fires of hate. He remembered that, steadily of late, he had grown to detest the whole child-world because of his own sorrow, and nodded acquiescence, supplementing the nod with a harsh:

"And, by God, I'm going to have it, too!"

"Then let me go back to Lafe's shop. I'll give you every cent I have.... I won't even ask for a dollar."

It took some time for Morse to digest this idea; then he slowly shook his head.

"You wouldn't be allowed to give me what would be mine——"

"If I die," breathed Jinnie, shocked. She had read his thought and blurted it forth.

"Yes, if you die. But I haven't any desire to kill you.... I have another way."

"What way? Oh, tell me!"

"Not now," drawled Morse. "Later perhaps."

The man contemplated the tips of his boots a minute. Then he looked at her, the meditative expression still in his eyes.

"To save your friends," he said at length, "you've got to do what I want you to."

"You mean—to save Lafe?" gasped Jinnie, eagerly.

Morse gave a negative gesture.

"No, not him. The cobbler's got to go. He knows too much about me."

Jinnie thought of Lafe, who loved and helped everybody within helping distance, of his wonderful faith and patience, of the day they had arrested him, and his last words.

She could not plan for herself nor think of her danger, only of the cobbler, her friend,——the man who had taken her, a little forlorn fugitive, when she had possessed no home of her own—he who had taught her about the angels and the tenderness of Jesus. From her uncle's last statement she had received an impression that he knew who had fired those shots. He could have Lafe released if he would. She would beg for the cobbler's life, beg as she had never begged before.

"Please, please, listen," she implored, throwing out her hands. "You must! You must! Lafe's always been so good. Won't you let him live?... I'll tell him about your wanting the money.... You shall have it! I'll make any promise for him you want me to, and he'll keep it.... He didn't kill Maudlin Bates, and I believe you know who did."

Morse lowered his lids until his eyes looked like grey slits across his face.

"Supposing I do," he taunted. "As I've said, Grandoken knows too much about me. He won't be the first one I've put out of my way."

He said this emphatically; he would teach her he was not to be thwarted; that when he desired anything, Heaven and earth, figuratively speaking, would have to move. He frowned darkly at her as Jinnie cut in swiftly:

"You killed my father. He told me you did."

Morse flicked an ash from a cigar he had lighted, and his eyes grew hard, like rocks in a cold, gray dawn.

"So you know all my little indiscretions, eh?" he gritted. "Then don't you see I can't give you—your liberty?"

Liberty! What did he mean by taking her liberty away? She asked him with beating heart.

"Just this, my dear child," he advanced mockingly. "There are places where people're taken care of and—the world thinks them dead. In fact, your father had a taste of what I can do. Only he happened to——"

"Did you put him somewhere?"

"Yes."

"Where?"

"Same kind of a place I'm going to put you——" He hesitated a moment and ended, "A mad house!"

"Did you let him come home to me?"

"Not I. Damn the careless keepers! He skipped out one day, and I didn't know until he'd a good start of me. I followed as soon as possible, but you were gone. Now—now—then, to find such a place for you!"

Jinnie's imagination called up the loathsome thing he mentioned and terrified her to numbness. At that moment she understood what her father had written in that sealed letter to Lafe Grandoken.

But she couldn't allow her mind to dwell upon his threat against herself.

"What'd you mean when you said I could save my friends?"

"You're fond of Mrs. Grandoken, aren't you?"

Jinnie nodded, trying to swallow a lump in her throat.

"And—and there's a—a—blind child too—who could be hurt easily."

Jinnie's living world reeled before her eyes. During this speech she had lost every vestige of color. She sprang toward him and her fingers went blue-white from the force of her grip on his arm.

"Oh, you couldn't, you wouldn't hurt poor little Bobbie?" she cried hysterically. "He can't see and he's sick, terribly ill all the time. I'll do anything you say—anything to help 'em."

Then she fell to the floor, groveling at his feet.

"Get up! You needn't cry; things'll be easy enough for you if you do exactly as I tell you. The first order I give you is to stay here quietly until I come again."

As he spoke, he lifted her up, and she stood swaying pitiably.

"Can't I let Peg know where I am?" she entreated when she could speak. "Please! Please!"

"I should think not," scoffed Morse. Then, after a moment's consideration, he went on, "You might write her a note, if you say what I dictate. I'll have it mailed from another town. I don't want any one to know you're still in Bellaire."

"Could I send her a little money, too?" she asked.

"Yes," replied Morse.

"Then tell me what to write, and I will."

After he had gone and Jinnie was once more alone, she sat at the window, her eyes roving over the landscape. Her gaze wandered in melancholy sadness to the shadowy summit of the distant hills, in which the wild things of nature lived in freedom, as she herself had lived with Lafe Grandoken in Paradise Road, long before her uncle's menacing shadow had crossed her life. Then her eyes lowered to the rock-rimmed gorge, majestic in its eternal solitude. She was on the brink of some terrible disaster. She knew enough of her uncle's character to realize that. She spent the entire day without even looking at her beloved fiddle, and after the night closed in, she lay down, thoroughly exhausted.

Peggy took a letter from the postman's hand mechanically, but when she saw the well-known writing, she trembled so she nearly dropped the missive from her fingers. She went into the shop, where Bobbie lay face downward on the floor. At her entrance, he lifted a white face.

"Has Jinnie come yet?" he asked faintly.

"No," said Peg, studying the postmark of the letter. Then she opened it. A five-dollar bill fell into her lap, and she thrust it into her bosom with a sigh.

"PEGGY DARLING," she read with misty eyes.

"I've had to go away for a little while. Don't worry. Here's some money. Use it and I'll send more. Kiss Bobbie for me and tell him Jinnie'll come back soon. And the baby, oh, Peggy, hug him until he can't be hugged any more. Don't tell Lafe I'm away.

164

"With all my love,
        "JINNIE."

Peggy put down the letter.

"Bobbie!" she said.

The boy looked up. "I ain't got any stars, Peggy," he wailed tragically. "I want Jinnie and Lafe."

"I've got a letter from Jinnie here," announced Peggy.

The boy got to his feet instantly.

"When she's comin' back?"

"She don't say, but she sends a lot of kisses and love to you. She had to go away for a few days.... Now don't snivel!... Come here an' I'll give you the kisses she sent."

He nestled contentedly in Peggy's arms.

"Let me feel the letter," came a faltering whisper presently.

Bobbie ran his fingers over the paper, trying with sensitive finger tips to follow the ink traces.

"Can I keep it a little while?" he begged.... "Please, Peggy!"

"Sure," said Peg, putting him down, and when the baby cried, Mrs. Grandoken left the blind child hugging Happy Pete, with Jinnie's letter flattened across his chest between him and the dog.

CHAPTER XLII
BOBBIE TAKES A TRIP

Jinnie had been gone two weeks. Nearly every day the postman brought a letter from the girl to Peggy, and after reading it several times to herself, she gave it to Blind Bobbie. Mrs. Grandoken had discovered this was the way to keep him quiet.

One afternoon the boy sat on the front steps of the cobbler's shop, sunning himself.

"You can hear Jinnie better when she comes," said Peg, as an excuse to coax him out of doors. "Now sit there till I get back from the market."

Bobbie had Happy Pete in his arms when he heard strange footsteps walking down the short flight of steps. He lifted his head as he heard a voice speak his name.

"Bobbie," it said softly. "Are you Bobbie?"

"Yes," replied the boy tremblingly.

The soft voice spoke again. "Do you want to see Jinnie?"

Bobbie clutched Happy Pete with one arm and struggled up, holding out a set of slender fingers that shook like small reeds in a storm.

165

"Yes, I want to see 'er," he breathed. "Do you know where she is?"

"If you'll come along with me, I'll take you to her. Bring the dog if you like."

"I want to see her to-day," stated Bobbie.

Jordan Morse took Bobbie's hand in his.

"Come on then, and don't make a noise," cautioned the man. "Put down the dog; he'll follow you."

Once in Paradise Road, he stooped and lifted the slight boyish figure and walked quickly away. Beyond the turn in the road stood his car. He placed Bobbie and the dog on the seat beside him, and in another moment they were speeding toward the hill.

At that moment Jinnie was brooding over her violin. Her fiddle was her only comfort in the lonely hours. The plaintive tones she drew from it were the only sounds she heard, save the rushing water in the gorge and the thrashing of the trees when the wind blew. The minutes hung long on her hands, and the hours seemed to mock her as they dragged along in interminable sequence. With her face toward the window, she passed several hours composing a piece which had been in embryo in her heart for a long time. The solitude, the grandeur of the scenery, the wonderful lake with its curves and turns, sometimes made her forget the tragic future that lay before her.

She was just finishing with lingering, tender notes when Jordan Morse came quickly through the corridor.

Bobbie stiffened in his arms suddenly.

"I hear Jinnie's fiddle," he gasped. "I'm goin' to my Jinnie."

When the key turned in the lock, the girl came to the door. At first she didn't notice the blind child, but her name, unsteadily called, brought her eyes to the little figure. Happy Pete recognized her with a wild yelp, wriggled himself past the other two, and whiningly crouched at her feet. Jinnie had them both in her arms before Morse turned the key again in the lock.

"Bobbie and Happy Pete!" she cried. Then she got up and flashed tearful eyes upon Morse.

"What did you bring them for? Did you tell Peg?"

"No, I didn't tell Peg and—and I brought him——" he paused and beckoned her with an upward toss of his chin.

Jinnie followed him agitatedly.

"I brought him," went on Morse, "because I don't just like your manner. I brought him as a lever to move you with, miss."

Then he left hurriedly, something unknown within him stirring with life. He decided afterward it was the sight of the blind child's golden head pressed against Jinnie's breast that had so upset him.

As he drove away, he crushed a desire to return again, to take them both, boy and girl, back to the cobbler's shop. But he must not allow his better emotions to attack him in this matter. He had known for a long time Jinnie could be wielded through her affection for the lad. He thought of his own child somewhere in the world and what it meant to him to possess

Jinnie's money, and set his teeth. He would bring the girl to his terms through her love for the slender blind boy.

That day Jinnie wrote a letter to Peg, telling her that Bobbie was with her, and Happy Pete, too.

The stolid woman had quite given way under the mysterious disappearance of the boy. When she returned home, she searched every lane leading to the marshes until dusk. In fact, she stumbled far into the great waste place, calling his name over and over. He was the last link that held her to the days when Lafe had been in the shop, and Peg would have given much if her conscience would cease lashing her so relentlessly. It eased her anxiety a little when a new resolution was born in her stubborn heart. If they all came back to the shop, she'd make up to them in some way for her ugly conduct. With this resolve, she went home to her own baby, sorrowful, dejected and lonely.

All the evening while Peg was mourning for them, Jinnie sat cuddling Bobbie, until the night put its dark hood on the ravine and closed it in a heavy gloom. Happy Pete, with wagging tail, leaned against the knees of the girl, and there the three of them remained in silence until Bobbie, lifting his face, said quiveringly:

"Peggy almost died when you went away, Jinnie."

Jinnie felt her throat throb.

"Tell me about it," she said hoarsely.

"There ain't much to tell," replied the child, sighing, "only Peggy was lonely. She only had me and the baby, and I didn't have any stars and the baby's got no teeth."

"And the baby? Is he well, dear?" questioned Jinnie.

"Oh, fine!" the boy assured her. "He's growed such a lot. I felt his face this morning, and oh, my, Jinnie, his cheeks puff out like this!"

Bobbie gathered in a long breath, and puffed out his own thin, drawn cheeks.

"Just like that!" he gasped, letting out the air.

"And Lafe?" ventured Jinnie.

"Lafe's awful bad off, I guess. Bates' little boy told me he was going to die——"

"No, Bobbie, no, he isn't!" Jinnie's voice was sharp in protestation.

"Yes, he is!" insisted Bobbie. "Bates' boy told me so! He said Lafe wouldn't ever come back to the shop, 'cause everybody says he killed Maudlin."

As the words left his lips, he began to sob. "I want my cobbler," he screamed loudly, "and I want my beautiful stars!"

"Bobbie, Bobbie, you'll be sick if you scream that way. There, there, honey!" Jinnie hushed him gently.

"I want to be 'Happy in Spite'," the boy went on. But his words brought before the pale girl that old, old memory of the cobbler who had invented the club for just such purposes as this. How could she be 'Happy in Spite' when Bobbie suffered; when Peg and baby Lafe needed her; happy when Lafe faced an ignominious death for a crime he had not committed;

167

happy when her beloved was perhaps still very ill in the hospital? She got up and began to walk to and fro. Suddenly she paused in her even march across the room. Unless she steadied her fluttering, stinging nerves, she'd never be able to still the wretched boy. There's an old saying that when one tries to help others, winged aid will come to the helper. And so it was with Jinnie. She had only again taken Bobbie close when there came to her Lafe's old, old words: "He hath given his angels charge over thee."

"Bobbie," she said softly, "I'm going to play for you."

As Jinnie straightened his limp little body out on the divan, she noticed how very thin he had become, how his heart throbbed continually, how the agonized lines drew and pursed the sensitive, delicate mouth.

Then she played and played and played, and ever in her heart to the rhythm of her music were the words, "His angels shall have charge over thee." Suddenly there came to her a great belief that out of her faith and Lafe's faith would come Bobbie's good, and Peg's good, and especially the good of the man shut up in the little cell. When the boy grew sleepy, Jinnie made him ready for bed.

"I'll lie down with you, Bobbie," she whispered, "and Happy Pete can sleep on the foot of the bed."

And as the pair of sad little souls slept, Lafe's angels kept guard over them.

CHAPTER XLIII

THEODORE SENDS FOR MOLLY

Theodore King was rallying rapidly in the hospital. All danger of blood poison had passed, and though he was still very weak, his surgeon had ceased to worry, and the public at large sat back with a sigh, satisfied that the wealthiest and most promising young citizen in the county had escaped death at the hand of an assassin.

One morning a telephone message summoned Molly Merriweather to the hospital. In extreme agitation she dressed quickly, telling Mrs. King she would return very soon. Never had she been so hilariously happy. Jinnie Grandoken had disappeared, as if she had been sunk in the sea. Molly now held the whip hand over her husband; she could force him to divorce her quietly. It was true of them both now their principal enemies were out of the way. Theo was getting well, and would come home in a few days.

While she had thought him dying, nothing save Jordan's tales of the girl's experiences in the gorge house had been able to rouse her to more than momentary interest.

With glowing cheeks she followed the hospital attendant through a long corridor to Theodore's room. She entered softly and for a moment stood gazing at him admiringly. How very handsome he was, even with the hospital pallor! When the sick man became cognizant of Molly's presence, he turned and smiled a greeting. He indicated a chair, and she sank into it.

"You sent for me, Theodore?" she reminded him softly, bending forward.

"Yes."

He was silent so long, evidently making up his mind to something, that Molly got up and smoothed out his pillow. Theodore turned to her after she had reseated herself.

"Molly," he began, "do you know where Jinnie Grandoken is?"

Molly's eyelids narrowed. So he was still thinking of the girl!

"No," she said deliberately.

"It seems strange," went on King somberly. "I've tried every way I know how to discover her whereabouts, and can't. I sent to the Grandoken's for her, but she was gone."

"You still care for her then?" queried Molly dully.

"Yes. I know you dislike the poor child, but I thought if you knew that I—well, I really love her, you might help me, Molly."

It was a bitter harvest to reap after all these weeks of waiting—his telling her he loved another woman—and as his voice rang with devotion for Jinnie Grandoken, Molly restrained herself with difficulty. She dared not lose her temper, as she had several times before under like conditions. With her hands folded gracefully in her lap, she replied:

"If I could help you, Theo, I would; but if Mrs. Grandoken doesn't know where her own niece is, how should I know?"

"You're so clever," sighed Theodore, "I imagined you might be able to discover something where a woman like Mrs. Grandoken would fail. She's got a young child, I hear."

"What do you suggest?" inquired Molly presently.

"I want to find out quickly where she's gone," the sick man said bluntly.

"You want to see her?" demanded Molly.

Theodore nodded.

"Yes, I'd get well sooner if I could," and he sighed again. Then his ivory skin grew scarlet even to his temples, but the blood rushed away, leaving him deathly white. Molly went to him quickly and leaned over the bed. She wanted—oh, how she wanted to feel his arms about her! But he only touched her cold hand lightly.

"Help me, Molly," he breathed.

Molly choked back an explanation. She would glory in doing anything for him—anything within her power; but nothing, nothing for Jinnie Grandoken. Suddenly an idea took possession of her. She would make him doubt Jinnie's love for him, even if she lied to him.

"Of course I knew you cared for her," she said slowly.

"Yes, I made that clear, I think," said Theo, "and she cares for me. I told you I asked her to marry me."

He laid stress on the latter half of his statement because of a certain emphasis in Molly's.

"I don't like to hurt you—while you're ill," she ventured.

Theodore thrust forth his hand eagerly.

"Come closer," he pleaded. "You know something; you can tell me. Please do, Molly."

"I don't know much, mind you, Theo——"

"Take hold of my hand, Molly!... Please don't keep me in such suspense."

She drew her chair closer to the bed, her heart throbbing first with desire, then with anger, and laid her white fingers in his.

"Tell me," insisted Mr. King.

"There was a boy——"

"You mean the little blind boy?"

"No, no," denied Molly, paling. The very mention of such an affliction hurt her sadly. "No," she said again, "I mean a friend of the boy who was shot; you remember him?"

"Oh, I remember Maudlin Bates; certainly I do; but I don't think I heard of any other."

Molly hadn't either; she had shot at random and the shot told.

Theodore sat up in bed with whitening face.

"Molly," he stammered, "Molly, has any one hurt her? Has——"

Molly shook her head disgustedly.

"Don't be foolish, Theo," she chided. "No one would want to hurt a grown girl like her."

"Then what about the man?"

"I think she went away with him."

"Where to?"

"I'm not sure——"

Theodore sank back. Molly's fingers slipped from his, and for a moment he covered his face with his hands, soundless sobs shaking his weak body. The woman knew by his appearance that he believed her absolutely.

"It'll kill me!" he got out at last.

Molly slipped an arm under his head. She had never seen him in such a state.

"Theo, don't! Don't!" she implored. "Please don't shake so, and I'll tell you all I know."

"Very well!... I'm listening."

The words were scarcely audible, but Molly knew and hugged the thought that his belief in Jinnie Grandoken had been shaken.

"Did you hear that Jinnie was in Binghamton?"

"Yes," murmured Theodore.

The woman released her hold on Theodore, and said:

170

"The man was over there with her."

Theodore turned his face quickly away and groaned.

"That's enough," he said. "Don't tell me any more."

They were quiet for a long time—very quiet.

Then Molly, with still enlarging plans, burst out:

"What if I should bring her back to you, Theo?"

He flashed dark-circled eyes toward her.

"Could you?" he asked drearily.

"I think so, perhaps. Suppose you write her a little note, and then——"

"Ring the bell for writing material quickly."

He had all his old-time eagerness. He was partly sitting up, and Molly placed another pillow under his head.

Theodore wrote steadily for some moments. Then he addressed an envelope to "Jinnie Grandoken," placed the letter in it, and fastened down the flap.

"You won't mind?" he asked wearily, handing it to Molly and sinking back.

Molly took the letter, and with a few more words, went out. Once at home in her bedroom, she sat down, breathing deeply. With a hearty good will she could have torn the letter into shreds, but instead she ripped open the envelope and read it.

After she had finished, she let the paper flutter from her hand and sat thinking for a long time. Then, sighing, she got up and tucked the letter inside her dress.

CHAPTER XLIV

MOLLY GIVES AN ORDER TO JINNIE

A motor car dashed to the side of the street, and Jordan Morse helped Molly to the pavement. She stood for a moment looking at the gorge building contemplatively.

"And she's been here all the while?" she remarked.

"Yes, and a devil of a time I've had to keep her, too. If there'd been any one in the whole place, I believe she'd have made them hear; though since the boy came she's behaved better." Morse's face became positively brutal under recollections. "I've made her mind through him," he terminated.

Jinnie had put Bobbie into bed and kissed him, and soon the child was breathing evenly. She knew Jordan Morse would come that night, so

171

she closed the door between the two rooms and walked nervously up and down. Bobbie was always ill for hours after Morse had made his daily calls. She hoped the man would allow the child to remain in bed. When the key grated in the lock, she was standing in the middle of the room, her eyes fastened on the door. Every time he came, she had hopes that he might relent, if but a little.

Morse entered, followed by Molly the Merry. Jinnie took a step forward when she saw the woman. Molly paused and inspected sharply the slim young figure, her mind comprehending all its loveliness. Then woman to woman they measured each other, as only women can. Jinnie advanced impulsively.

"You've come to take me home!" she breathed.

Molly shook her head.

"I've come to talk to you," she retorted hoarsely.

Never had she seen so beautiful a girl! The martyrdom Jinnie had endured had only enhanced her attractiveness.

"Sit down," said Molly peevishly.

Jinnie made a negative gesture.

"I'm tired of sitting.... Oh, you will do something for me, something for poor little Bobbie?"

Morse moved to the door between the two rooms, but Jinnie rushed in front of him.

"He's asleep," she said beseechingly. "Don't wake him up! He's had a dreadful spell with his heart to-day."

Morse turned inquiring eyes upon Molly.

"You wanted to see him, didn't you?" he asked.

Molly flung out a hand pettishly.

"Let him sleep," she replied. "I don't want to be bored with fits and tears."

Jinnie sank into a chair.

"He ought to have a doctor," she sighed, as if she were speaking to herself. Then turning to Molly, she bent an entreating look upon her.

"Please do something for him. Get a doctor, oh, do! He's so little and so sick."

"I'm not a bit interested in him," replied Molly with a shrug.

Jinnie's nerves had borne all they could. She trembled unceasingly. The girlish spirit had been broken by Morse's continual persecution.

"He's so little," she petitioned again, "and he can't live long."

As Molly had said, she was not interested in the sleeping child. The only time she cared to hear him mentioned was when Jordan told her of Jinnie's anguish over his treatment of the child. She had delighted in his vividly described scene of how he had forced the girl to do his will through her love for the little fellow. Now she, too, would wreak her vengeance on Jinnie through the same source.

"I've come to tell you something about Theodore King," she remarked slowly, watching the girl avidly the while.

Jinnie sat up quickly. If her dear one had sent her a message, then he must know where she was.

"Then tell it," was all she said.

Molly put her hand into a leather hand bag and drew forth a letter.

"It isn't for you," she stated, with glinting eyes. "I've known for a long time you thought he cared for you——"

"He does," interjected Jinnie emphatically.

"I think not. Here's a letter he wrote to me. It will dispel any idea you may have about his affection for you."

"I don't wish to read your letter," said Jinnie proudly.

"Read it!" ordered Morse frowning, and because she feared him, Jinnie took the letter nervously. The woman's words had shattered her last hope. For a moment the well-known handwriting whirled; then the words came clearly before her vision:

"MY DARLING," she read.

"Won't you come to me when you get this? My heart aches to have you once more in my arms. I shall expect you very soon. With all my love,
     "THEODORE"

It was not strange that she crushed the paper between her fingers.

"You needn't destroy my letter," Molly said mockingly, thrusting forth her hand. "Give it to me."

She took it from Jinnie's shaking hand and, smoothing it out, replaced it in her pocket book.

"I wouldn't have come but for your own good," she said, looking up. "Mr. Morse told me you had an idea that Mr. King loved you, and I want you to write him a letter——"

"Write who a letter?" asked Jinnie dully.

"Theodore."

"Why?"

"Because I tell you to," snapped Molly.

Then taking another letter from her bag, she held it out.

"You're to copy this and give it to Mr. Morse to-morrow."

Jinnie took the letter and read it slowly. She struggled to her feet.

"I'll not write it," she said hoarsely.

"I think you will," said Morse, rising.

Jinnie stared at him until he reached the closed door behind which Bobbie slept.

"Don't! Don't!" she shuddered. "I'll write, I'll do anything if you won't hurt Bobbie." Raising her eyes to Morse, she said in subdued tones, "I'll try to give it to you to-morrow."

Never had her heart ached as it did then. The perils she was passing through and had passed through were naught to the present misery. She realized then her hope had been in Theodore's rescuing her.

A certain new dignity, however, grew upon her at that moment. She stood up, looking very tall, very slight, to the man and woman watching her.

"I wish you'd both go," she said wearily. "I'd rather be alone with Bobbie."

Molly smiled and went out with Jordan Morse.

"She gave in all right," remarked Molly, when they were riding down the hill. "I knew she would."

Morse shrugged his shoulders.

"Of course. She worships Grandoken's youngster.... I was wondering there once how you felt when you knew she was reading her own letter."

Molly's face grew dark with passionate rebellion.

"He'll write me one of my own before the year is out," said she.

"I'm not so sure!" responded Morse thoughtfully.

For a long time after the closing of the door, Jinnie sat huddled in the chair. Nothing else in all the world could have hurt her as she had been hurt that night, and it wasn't until very late that she crept in beside the blind boy, and after four or five hours, dropped asleep.

CHAPTER XLV

WRITING A LETTER TO THEODORE

The first thing Jinnie saw the next morning was the rough draft of the letter Molly had ordered her to copy. To send it to Theodore was asking more of her than she could bear. She turned and looked at Bobbie. He was still sleeping his troubled, short-breathed sleep. She had shielded him with her life, with her liberty. Now he demanded, in that helpless, babyish, blind way of his, that she repudiate her love.

In the loneliness of the gorge house she had become used to the idea of never again seeing Theodore, but to allow him to think the false thing in that letter was dreadful. She picked it up and glanced it over once more, then dropped it as if the paper had scorched her fingers. She'd die rather than send it, and she would tell her uncle so when he came that morning.

She was very quiet, more than usually so, when she gave the blind boy his breakfast.

"Bobbie," she said, "you know I'd do anything for you in this whole world, don't you? I mean—I mean anything I could?"

Mystified, the boy bobbed his curly head.

"Sure I do, Jinnie, and I'd do anything for you too, honey."

She kissed him passionately, as her eyes sought the letter once more. It lay on the floor, the words gleaming up at her in sinister mockery. She tore her eyes from it, shaking in dread. Would she have the courage to stand against Jordan Morse in this one thing? She had given in to him at every point, but this time she intended to stand firmly upon the rock of her love. Once more she picked up the letter and put it away.

Two hours later, with loathing and disgust depicted in her white face, she saw Mr. Morse enter, and her blazing blue eyes stabbed the man's anger to the point of desiring to do her harm. For a moment he contemplated her in silence. He was going to have trouble with her that day. What a fool Molly was! It was she who insisted upon that bally letter. What did he care about Theodore King? Still his wife had him completely within her power, and he was really afraid of her now and then when she flew into rages about his niece and Theodore. He mopped his brow nervously.

A few days more and it would be ended. Inside of one week he would be free from every element which threatened him, free to commence the search for his child. He strode across the room to Jinnie.

"Come on with me," he ordered under his breath.

Jinnie obediently followed him into the inner room. Morse slammed the door with his foot.

"Where's the letter?" he growled between his teeth.

Jinnie went to the table, got the original draft and handed it over.

"Here it is," she said slowly.

He glanced over the paper.

"Why, this is the one we left here yesterday, isn't it?"

"Yes!"

"Where is the one you wrote? I don't want this."

A glint of understanding flashed upon him.

"Where is the other?" he demanded once more.

"I haven't written it and I don't intend to."

For one single instant Morse's mind swept over the sacrifices she had made. She had done every single thing he had told her, not for her sake but for others. He shuddered when he thought of the trouble he would have had with her had not the blind boy been within his power also.

"Get the paper and write it now," he said ominously.

"I will not!"

She meant the words, a righteous indignation flaming her face, making her eyes shine no longer blue, but opal color. Morse wondered dully if she could and would stand out against what he would be forced to do.

"I see," he began shiftily. "I have to teach you a lesson every time I come here, eh?"

"This time you won't," she flashed at him.

"This time I will," he taunted.

"I'd rather be dead," she faltered. "I'd rather be dead than write it."

175

"Perhaps! But would you rather have——" he made a backward jerk of his thumb toward the other room—"him dead?"

Jinnie's eyes misted in agony, but Theodore was still near her in spirit, and she remembered the dear hours they had spent together and how much she loved him. A sudden swift passion shook her as his kisses lived warm again upon her face. That letter she would not write. But as she made this decision for the hundredth time that day, Morse's words recurred to her. Would she rather have Bobbie dead? Yes, if she were dead too. But life was so hard to part with! She was so strong. How many times she had prayed of late to die! But every morning found her woefully and more miserably alive than the one before.

"I understand you'd rather, then," drawled Morse.

Jinnie shook her head.

"I don't know what I'd rather have, only I can't write the letter." She made one rapid step toward him—"I know," she went on feverishly, "I won't ever see Theodore again——"

Morse's emphatic nod broke off her words, but she went on courageously. "I don't expect to, but I love him. Can't you see that?"

"Quite evident," replied the man.

"Why hurt me more than necessary then?" she demanded.

"This is part of Miss Merri——"

"She loves him too?" cried Jinnie, staggering back.

"Yes, and he—well, you saw his letter yesterday."

"Yes, I saw it," breathed Jinnie with swift coming breath.

"Miss Merriweather thinks Theodore might still feel his obligations to you unless you——"

"Does she know he asked me to marry him?" In spite of her agony, she thrilled in memory.

"Yes, and he told me, too. But Miss Merriweather intends to marry him herself, and all she wants is to wipe thoughts of you from his mind."

A powerful argument swept from her lips.

"It wouldn't make any difference to him about me if he loved her."

"You're an analytical young miss," said Morse with one of his disagreeable smiles.

"You've taught me to be," she retorted, blazing. "Now listen! You asked me if I'd rather have Bobbie die than write the letter, didn't you?"

He nodded.

"Then I say 'yes'." She caught her breath. "We'll both die."

"Well, by God, you're a cool one! Theodore's more lucky than I thought. So that's the way you love him?"

She grew more inexplicable with each passing day.

"Poor Theodore!" murmured Morse, to break the tense silence.

"I thought it all out this morning," explained Jinnie. "Bobbie's awfully ill, terribly. He can't live long anyway, and I——" A terrific sob shook her as a raging gale rends a slender flower.

Jinnie controlled her weeping that the blind child in the other room might not hear. Never had Jordan been so sorely tempted to do a good

176

deed. Good deeds were not habitual to him, but at that moment a desire possessed him to take her in his arms, to soothe her, to restore her to Peggy and give her back to Theodore. But the murder scene in the cobbler's shop came back with strong renewed vigor. He had gone too far, and he must have money. Molly held him in her power, and as he thought of her tightly set lips, the danger signal she had tossed at him more times than once, he crushed dead his better feeling.

"Your plan won't work," he said slowly. "Write the letter—I am in a hurry."

"I will not," she refused him once more.

Morse walked to the door, and she allowed him to open it. Then with clenched hands she tottered after him. He was going to kill Bobbie and herself. Somehow within her tortured being she was glad. Morse waited and looked back, asking her a question silently.

She made no response, however, but cast her eyes upon the blind boy sitting dejectedly upon the floor, one arm around Happy Pete.

"Jinnie," said Bobbie, rolling his eyes, "I was afraid you were goin' to stay in there all day."

"Come here, boy," ordered Morse. "Get up and come here."

Bobbie turned his delicate, serious face in the direction of the voice.

"I don't want to," he gulped, shaking his head. "I don't like you, Mister Black Man. I can't get up anyway, my heart hurts too much!"

Still the girl stood with the vision of Theodore King before her.

"I won't write it, I won't," she droned to herself insistently.

Morse sprang forward and grasped the child.

"Get up," he hissed.

Bobbie scrambled up because he was made to. He uttered a frightened, terrified cry.

Then, "Jinnie!" he gasped.

Jinnie saw Morse shake the slender little body and drop into a chair, dragging the child forward. Bobbie could no longer speak. The dazed girl knew the little heart was beating in its very worst terror. She couldn't bear the sight and closed her eyes for an instant. When she opened them, Morse's hand was raised above the boy's golden head, but she caught it in hers before it descended.

"I'll do it," she managed to whisper. "Look! Look! You've killed him."

In another moment she had Bobbie in her arms, his face pressed against her breast.

"Get out of here!" she said, deathly white, to Morse. "I'll do it, come back to-morrow."

And Morse was glad to escape.

After Jinnie brought Bobbie to his senses and he lay like a crumpled leaf on the divan, she took up the hated letter. She sat down to read it once more.

It was short, concise, and to the point.

177

"MR. KING:

"I made a mistake in ever thinking I cared for you. I have some one else now I love better, and expect to be very happy with him.

"JINNIE GRANDOKEN"

The next morning when Morse came jauntily in, she handed him the copy of it without a word. He only said to her:

"You'd have saved yourself a lot of trouble if you'd done this in the first place. You won't bother me long now. Mr. King is home and almost well." Then he smiled, showing his white, even teeth. "He'll be glad to receive this letter."

"Get out," Jinnie gritted. "Get out before I—I kill you!"

Two days later Molly Merriweather was in the seventh heaven of bliss. As Morse had said, Theodore was home, looking more like himself. With her heart in her mouth, the woman entered his sitting room with Jinnie's letter. Jordan had had it mailed to King from Binghamton.

"I've brought you a letter, Theodore," smiled Molly nervously.

He extended his hand, and upon recognizing the handwriting, turned deadly white.

"I'd like to be alone," said he without looking up.

When he sent for her a little while later, and she sat opposite him, he said:

"I'd rather not speak of—of—Miss Grandoken again. Will you give me a drink, Molly?" And the woman noted the hurt look in his eyes.

CHAPTER XLVI

"BUST 'EM OUT"

"Jinnie, ain't we ever goin' back to Peggy?" Bobbie asked one day, his eyes rolling upward. His small face was seamed with questioning anxiety.

The girl drew him to her lap.

How many times Jinnie had asked that question of herself! How she longed for Paradise Road, with its row of shacks, Peggy and the baby! Bobby knew how she felt by the way she squeezed his hand.

"Ain't we?" he asked again.

"Some time," answered Jinnie limply.

"Did the black man say we could go, Jinnie?" the boy demanded.

Jinnie patted his head comfortingly.

"I hope he'll take us home soon," she remarked, trying to put full assurance into her tones.

Bobbie zigzagged back to the divan, drew himself upon it, and Jinnie knew by his abstracted manner that he was turning the matter over in his busy little brain.

Two hours later, when Jordan Morse came in, the child was still sitting in the same position, and the man beckoned the girl into the other room.

"Grandoken's trial is to start this afternoon within an hour," he informed her. "You'll be here to-day and to-morrow. You see the court won't be long in proving the cobbler's guilt."

If he had expected her to cry, he was mistaken. She was past crying, seemingly having shed all of her tears.

"He didn't do it," she averred stubbornly. "I know he didn't."

In justice to Lafe, she always reiterated this.

Morse gave a sinister laugh.

"What you know or don't know won't matter," he responded, and looking at the angry, beautiful face, he ejaculated, "Thank God for that!"

Jinnie turned her back, but he requested her sharply to look at him.

"Have you told the boy where I'm going to take you?" he demanded, when she was eyeing him disdainfully.

"No."

"I never knew a woman before who could hold her tongue," he commented in sarcasm.

Jinnie didn't heed the compliment.

"When he asks you questions, what do you tell him?"

"That you will come for us soon."

"I will, all right."

Jinnie went nearer him.

"Where are you going to take him?"

Morse shrugged his shoulders.

"You'll know in time," said he.

How ominous his words were, and how his eyes narrowed as he looked at her! She was thoroughly afraid of that tone in his voice. Her own fate she was sure of, but Bobbie—desperation filled her soul. She would beg Morse to let him go back to Peggy.

Lifting clasped hands, she walked very close to him.

"You're going to have all my money," she said with emphasis. "I've done everything I can, and I'll make Bobbie promise not to say a word to any one if you'll take him to Mrs. Grandoken."

Morse shook his head.

"Too dangerous," he replied, and he went out without a glance at the blind boy on the divan.

Once more alone with Bobbie, Jinnie sat down to think. How could she rescue him from this awful position? How get him back to Peggy? Somehow she felt that if she could be sure the little boy was safe, she could go away to the place Morse had described with at least a little relief. That

179

day Lafe's accusers were to try him before a jury——. She had almost lost hope for the cobbler—he was lame, had no friends, and was a Jew, one of the hated race. She knew how the people of Bellaire despised the Jews. For Peggy she didn't worry so much. Jordan Morse had given his solemn promise that, if Lafe died in the electric chair—and she died to the world—he would be of financial assistance to Peggy.

She sat studying Bobbie attentively. The child's face was pathetically white and she could see the quick palpitation of his heart under his jacket.

"I heard what the black man said, Jinnie," Bobbie blurted presently, sinking in a little heap. "I mean when he had you in the other room a little while ago. You was beggin' him to help me; wasn't you, Jinnie?"

Jinnie went to him quickly and gathered him into her arms.

"Bobbie," she implored, "you must never let him know, never, never, that you heard him talking. He might hurt you worse than he has."

Bobbie flashed his eyes questioningly in evident terror.

"What'd he hurt me more for? I ain't done nothin' to him."

"I guess because he's bad, dear," said Jinnie sadly.

"Then if he's bad, why do you stay here?" He clung to her tremulously. "Take me away, Jinnie!"

"I can't!" lamented Jinnie. "I've told you, Bobbie, the door's locked."

She could lovingly deceive him no longer.

How the little body trembled! How the fluttering hands sought her aid in vain!

"My stars're all gone, Jinnie," sobbed Bobbie. "My beautiful stars! I can't see any of 'em if I try. I'm awful 'fraid, honey dear. It's so dark."

Jinnie tightened her arms about him, racking her brain for soothing words.

"But Lafe's God is above the dark, Bobbie," she whispered reverently. "We've got to believe it, dearie! God is back up there ... just up there."

She took his slender forefinger and pointed upward.

"How does God look, Jinnie? Just how does he look?"

"I've never seen him," admitted the girl, "but I think, Bobbie, I think he looks like Lafe. I know he smiles like him anyway."

"I'm glad," sighed the boy. "Then He'll help us, won't He? Lafe would if he could. If you say He will, He will, Jinnie!"

Five tense minutes passed in silence. Then: "Sure we couldn't get out of the window, dearie?" asked Bobbie.

"They're locked, too," answered the girl, low-toned.

"I'd bust 'em out," volunteered the boy, with sudden enthusiasm.

"But there's a deep gorge in front of every one, honey," replied Jinnie sadly.

Yet Bobbie's words—"bust 'em out"—took hold of her grippingly, and the thought of leaving that unbearable place was like a tonic to the frantic girl. She crossed the room rapidly and examined the window panes. But even if she could break them, as Bobbie suggested, the water below would receive their bodies, and death would follow. If it were a street, she might manage. Yet the sight of the flowing water, the dark depths between the ragged rocks, did not send Bobbie's words, "bust 'em out," from her mind. If they fell together, the boy would never be tortured any more. To-morrow Jordan Morse would be in the courtroom all day. To-morrow—— God, dear God! She seemed to hear Lafe's monotone, "There's always to-morrow, Jinnie."

She was called upon to think, to act alone in a tragic way. Of course she would be killed if she jumped into the deep gorge with the child and Happy Pete. She tried to think, to plan, but after the manner of all believing sufferers, could only pray.

Bobbie need fear no evil! "Angels have been given charge over him, and Bobbie shall not want," Jinnie whispered, her mind spinning around like a child's top. A sudden faith boomed at the portals of her soul. What was the use of asking help for Bobbie if she didn't have faith in an answer?

To-day would bring forth a plan for to-morrow. To-morrow Bobbie would be saved from Jordan Morse. To-morrow would end his terror in the gorge house. To-morrow—she would be eighteen years old!

"Bobbie," she entreated, going to the child swiftly, "Bobbie, do you remember any prayers Lafe taught you?"

The child bobbed his head.

"Sure," he concurred. "'Now I lay me' and 'Our Father which art in Heaven.'... I know them, Jinnie."

"Then sit upon the divan again and say them over and over, and pray for Lafe, and that you'll get out of here and be happy. You mustn't tell Mr. Morse if he comes, but I'm going to try to get you out of the window."

As she stood in the gathering gloom and peered into the water below, Jinnie could hear the child lisping his small petitions.

At that moment a new faith came for herself. Lafe's angels would save her, too, from Jordan Morse's revenge.

At ten-thirty the next morning Morse came. With trepidation Jinnie heard him open the door. He was extremely nervous and stayed only a few moments.

"I've got to be in court at eleven," he explained, "and I'll come for you both about ten this evening. Be ready, you and the boy, and remember what I told you!"

When they were alone once more, she sat down beside the blind child and placed her arm around him.

"Bobbie, will you do exactly what I tell you?"

"Sure," responded Bobbie, cheerfully. "Are we goin' home?"

Without answering him, Jinnie said:

"Then take Happy Pete and don't move until I get back. Just pray and pray and pray! That's all."

Happy Pete snuggled his head under Bobbie's arm and they both sat very still. The boy scarcely dared to breathe, he was so anxious to please his Jinnie.

The farthest window in the inner room door seemed to be the best one to attack. If Morse surprised her, it would be easier to cover up her work. With a frantic prayer on her lips, she took off her shoe and gave the pane of glass one large, resounding blow. It cracked in two, splinters not only flying into the room, but tumbling into the gorge below. Then she hastily hammered away every particle of glass from the frame, and, shoving her shoulders through, looked out and down. The very air seemed filled with angels. They could and would save her and Bobbie even in the water—even if they were within the suction of the falls there, some distance below and beyond. Then her eyes swept over the side of the building, and she discovered a stone ledge wide enough for a human being to crawl along. Would she dare try it with her loved ones? She distinctly remembered seeing a painter's paraphernalia in the front, and they might be there still! The more she thought, the greater grew her hope, and with this growing hope came a larger faith. At least she'd find what was at the end of the building away off there to the east.

To-day, yes, now!... She couldn't wait, for her uncle was coming to-night. It must be now, this minute. She went back to Bobbie.

"I'm going to try it, darling," she told him, kissing his cheek. "Sit right here until I get back. Hang to Petey. He might follow me."

Then cautiously she dragged her body through the hole in the window, and began to crawl along the stone ledge. The roar of the water on the rocks below made her dizzy. But over and over did she cry into God's ever listening ear:

"He has given—he has given his angels—angels charge over thee."

Jinnie reached the corner of the building, and looked out over the city. The ledge extended around the other side of the building, and she turned the corner and went slowly onward. At the south end she stopped still, glancing about.

Only one thing of any value was in the range of her vision. The two long ropes she had seen long before were still hanging from the roof and fastened securely to a large plank almost on the ground. It brought to Jinnie's mind what Lafe had told her,—of Jimmie Malligan who had been killed, and of how he himself had lost his legs.

Could she, by means of the rope, save the three precious things back in that awful room—Bobbie, Happy Pete, and her fiddle?

To be once more under God's sun with the blue above gave her new strength. Then she turned and crawled slowly back.

At the corner she grew faint-hearted. It must have been the gorge below that made her breath come in catching sobs. But on and on she went until through the window she could see Bobbie with Happy Pete asleep in his arms. The child was still muttering over his little prayers, his blind eyes rolling in bewildered anxiety.

Jinnie was very white when she sat down beside him. Putting her face close to his, she brushed his cheek lovingly.

"Bobbie," she said, touching his hair with her lips, "how much do you love Jinnie?"

"More'n all the world," replied Bobbie without hesitation.

"Then if you love me that much, you'll do just what I tell you."

"Yes," Bobbie assured her under his breath.

Jinnie took a towel—she couldn't find a rope—and strapped the violin to Bobbie's back.

"I've got to take my fiddle with me, dearie," she explained, "and I can't carry it because I've got you. You can't carry it because you've got to hold Happy Pete.... Now, then, come on!"

Jinnie drew the reluctant, trembling child to his feet and permitted him to feel around the window-sash; she also held him tightly while he measured the stone ledge with his fingers.

"I'm awful 'fraid," he moaned, drooping.

Jinnie feared he was going to have another fainting spell. To ward it off, she said firmly:

"Bobbie, you want to see Lafe, don't you?"

"S'awful much," groaned Bobbie.

"Then don't hold your breath." She saw him stagger, and grasping him, cried out "Breathe, Bobbie, breathe! We're going to Peggy."

Bobbie began to breathe naturally, and a beatific smile touched the corners of his lips.

"I got so many stars to-day, Jinnie," he quavered, "one slipped right down my throat."

"But you mustn't be scared again, Bobbie! If we stay, the black man'll come back and shake you again and take us to some place that'll make us both sick. You just keep on praying, and I will, too.... Now, then, I'm going out, and when I say, 'Ready,' you crawl after me."

"What's that noise?" shivered Bobbie, clutching Happy Pete.

"It's water," answered Jinnie, "water in the gorge."

Bobbie's teeth chattered. "Do we have to jump in it?"

"No, I'm going to take you down a rope."

With that she crawled through the hole, and when once on the stone ledge, she put her hand in on the boy's head.

"Lift up your leg and hang tight to Petey," she shuddered, and the blind boy did as he was bidden, and Jinnie pulled him, with the dog and fiddle, through the opening. She put him on his knees in front of her with her arms tightly about him.

"Jinnie, Jinnie!" moaned Bobbie. "My heart's jumpin' out of my mouth!"

Jinnie pressed her teeth together with all her might and main, shivering so in terror that she almost lost the strength of her arms.

"Don't think about your heart," she implored, "and don't shake so! Just think that you're going to Lafe and Peg."

Then they began their long, perilous journey to the corner of the building. It must have taken twenty minutes. Jinnie had no means by which to mark the time. She only knew how difficult it was to keep the blind child moving, with the water below bellowing its stormy way down the rock-hill to the lake. Happy Pete gave a weird little cry now and then. But on and on they went, and at the corner Jinnie spoke:

"Bobbie, we've got to turn here. Let your body go just as I shove it."

Limp was no word for Bobbie's body. He was dreadfully tired. His heart thumped under Jinnie's arms like a battering-ram.

"Bobbie, don't breathe that way, don't!" she entreated.

"I can't help it, honey! my side hurts," he whispered. "But I'll go where you take me, Jinnie dear."

The girl turned him carefully around the sharp ledge corner, and they went on again. Her arms seemed almost paralyzed, but they clung to the child ahead, and the child ahead clung to the little dog, who hung very straight and inert in front of his body.

When they reached the south corner, Jinnie explained their next move to Bobbie in this way:

"Now listen," she told him. "You get on my back with your legs under my arms, hang to me like dear life, and keep Happy Pete between us. Don't hurt him if you can help it."

They were within touch of one of the dangling ropes and far below Jinnie saw the swaying plank to which it was fastened. Once on that board, she could get to the ground.

Then she continued: "Now while I lean over, you get on my back."

As she guided his slender hands, she felt them cold within her own, but in obedience to her command, Bobbie put his legs about her, one arm around her neck, and with the other held Happy Pete.

"We won't fall, will we, Jinnie?" quavered the boy.

"No," said Jinnie, helping to settle him on her back.

Then she crawled closer to the rope, took up her skirt and placed it about the rough hemp. She was afraid to use her bare hands. The rope might cut and burn them so dreadfully that she'd have to let go. With a wild inward prayer, she swung off into the air, with the boy, the dog and the fiddle on her back, and began her downward slide. She counted the windows as they passed, one, two, three, and then four. Only a little distance more before she would be upon firm ground. As her feet touched the plank, she glanced into the street and in that awful moment saw Jordan Morse crossing the corner diagonally, within but a few yards of where she stood, terrified.

CHAPTER XLVII

BOBBIE'S STARS RENEW THEIR SHINING

Jinnie stood rooted to the spot, the burden on her back bearing heavily upon her. She scarcely dared breathe, but kept her startled eyes upon the advancing man. Her uncle was walking with his head down. As he approached the building, a terrible shiver passed over the blind boy.

"The black man's comin'!" he shuddered. "I hear——"

"Hush!" whispered Jinnie, and Bobbie dropped his head and remained quiet.

The girl's heart was thumping almost as fast as his.

In the oppressive silence she heard Bobbie's faint whisper: "Our—our Father who art in Heaven," and her own lips murmured: "He has given his angels charge over thee."

Without raising his eyes, Jordan Morse sprang to the steps and entered the door.

Jinnie turned her head and almost mechanically watched him disappear. Then she took one long, sobbing breath.

"Bobbie, Bobbie," she panted, "get down quick!"

The boy slid to the plank, dropping Happy Pete.

Jinnie grasped the child's cold hand in hers, and they ran rapidly to a thick clump of trees. Once out of sight of the building, she picked up the little dog and sank down, clutching Bobbie close to her heart.

The beginning of the second day of Lafe's trial brought a large crowd to the courthouse. All the evidence thus far given had been against him, but he sat in his wheelchair, looking quietly from under his shaggy brows, and never once, with all that was said against him, did the sweet, benevolent expression change to anger. The cobbler had put his life into higher hands than those in the courtroom, and he feared not.

After the morning session, Jordan Morse left the room with a satisfied smile. He walked rapidly to the streetcar and took a seat, with a thoughtful expression on his countenance. Lafe would be convicted, and he would get rid of the girl now shut away from the world in the gorge building. Then, with the money that would be his, he'd find his child,—the little boy who was his own and for whom he so longed. He often looked at Molly and wondered how she could smile so radiantly when she knew she had lost her child,—her own flesh and blood,—her own little son.

Even after he left the car and was approaching the gorge, he worried about the two in the house. It was because his mind was bent on important plans that he did not see Jinnie swinging in the sunshine between heaven and earth. He climbed the stairs, framing a sentence for the girl's benefit. As he unlocked the door, the silence of the room bore down upon him like an evil thing. He went hurriedly into the second room, only to find it also empty. For the moment he did not notice the shattered glass on the floor, and his heart sank within him, but the breeze that drifted to his face brought his eyes to the broken window. With an oath, he jumped to it and looked out. Far below, the water tumbled as of yore over the rocks. He strained horrified eyes for a glimpse of a human body. The girl and boy must have dropped together into the deep abyss, preferring death to uncertainty. They were gone—gone over the ragged rocks, where their bodies would be lost in some of the fathomless juts a mile beyond. He would never be bothered with Jinnie again. Then he turned from the window. His most terrifying obstacle was out of his way. The blind child did not concern him. He was but a feather in the wind,—the little fellow who always shrank from him.

As if leaving a tomb, he went softly from the room and turned the key in the lock with a sigh. Jinnie had relieved him of an awful responsibility. At least fate had taken from his hands a detestable task, at which he had many a time recoiled. So far all of his enemies, with the exception of Theodore King, had one by one been taken away, and he swung himself out of the building with a great burden lifted from his shoulders.

As he passed, Jinnie was still drawing long breaths under the thick bushes, Bobbie's face against her breast, and it was not until she was sure Morse had gone that she ventured to speak.

"We're going to Lafe and Peg, Bobbie," she said. "Can you walk a long way?"

"Yes," gurgled Bobbie, color flaming his face. "My legs'll go faster'n anything."

And "faster'n anything" those thin little legs did go. The boy trotted along beside his friend, down the hill to the flats. Jinnie chose a back street leading to the lower end of the town.

"I'd better carry you a while, dearie," she offered presently, noting with what difficulty he breathed. "You take the fiddle!" And without remonstrance from the boy she lifted him in her arms.

From the tracks Lafe's small house had the appearance of being unoccupied. Jinnie went in, walking from the shop to the kitchen, where she called "Peggy!" two or three times. Then the thought of the cobbler's trial rushed over her. Peggy and the baby were at court with Lafe, of course.

Knowing she must face her uncle in the courtroom, she went to Lafe's black box and drew forth the sealed letter her father had sent to Grandoken. This she hid in her dress, and taking Bobbie and the fiddle, she went out and closed the door.

Another long walk brought them to the courthouse, which stood in solemn stone silence, with one side to the dark, iron-barred jail. Jinnie shivered when she thought of the weary months Lafe had sat within his gloomy cell.

She entered the building, holding Bobbie's hand. Every seat in the room was filled, and a man was making a speech, using the names of Maudlin Bates and Lafe Grandoken.

Then she looked about once more, craning her neck to catch sight of those ahead. Her eyes fell first upon Lafe, God bless him! There he sat, her cobbler, in the same old wheelchair, wearing that look of benign patience so familiar to her. Only a little distance from him sat Peggy, the baby sleeping on her knees. Molly the Merry was seated next to Jordan Morse, whose large white hand nervously clutched the back of the woman's chair.

Several stern-looking men at a table had numerous papers over which they were bending. Then Jinnie's gaze found Jasper Bates. She could see, by the look upon his face, that he was suffering. She felt sorry, sorry

186

for any one who was in trouble, who had lost a son in such a manner as Jasper had. Then she awoke to the import of the lawyer's words.

"Before you, Gentlemen of the Jury," he was saying, "is a murderer, a Jew, Lafe Grandoken. You know very well the reputation of the people on Paradise Road. The good book says 'a life for a life.' This Jew shot and killed his neighbor——"

Jinnie lost his next words. She was looking at Lafe, and saw his dear face grow white with stabbing anguish. The girl's throat filled with sobs, and she suddenly remembered something Theodore had once said to her.

"If you want anything, child, just play for it."

And she wanted the life of her cobbler, the man who had taken her, with such generosity, into his heart and meagre home. She slipped the fiddle from the case and stooped and whispered in Bobbie's ear:

"Grab the back of my dress, dearie, and don't let go!"

She moved into the aisle, making ready to start on her life mission. She lifted the bow, and with a long sweep, drew an intense minor note from the strings. A sea of faces swung in her direction. Jinnie forgot every one but the cobbler—she was playing for his life—improvising on the fiddle strings a wild, pleading, imploring melody. On and on she went, with Blind Bobbie, in trembling confusion, clinging to her skirts, and Happy Pete with sagging head at their heels. At the first sound of the fiddle Lafe tried to rise, and did rise. He stood for a moment on his shaking legs, and there, to the amazement of the gaping crowd of his townsfolk, he swayed to and fro, watching and listening as the wonderful music filled and thrilled through the room.

A heavenly light shone on the wrinkled face.

Jordan Morse got to his feet, chalk white. Molly the Merry was looking at Jinnie as if she saw a ghost.

The onlookers saw Lafe's unsteady steps as he tottered toward the lovely girl and blind child. When he was within touching distance, she put the instrument and bow under one arm and took Lafe's hand in hers. Her voice rang out like the tone of a bell.

"I've come for you, Lafe. I've come to take you back."

Then Molly's eyes dropped from Jinnie to the boy, and a cry broke from her. Before her was the child for whom, in spite of the evidence of her smiling lips, she had truly mourned. The wan, blind face was turned upward, the golden hair lying in damp curls on the lovely head. Spontaneously the woman reached forward and took the little hand in hers. All the mother within her leaped up, like a brilliant flash of lightning.

"My baby!" was all she said; and Bobbie, white, trembling and palpitating, cried in a weird, high voice:

"I've found my mother!"

Then Jordan Morse understood. The hot blood was tearing to his ear drums. The blind boy he had persecuted and tortured, the boy he had made suffer, was his own son. That wonderful quality in the man, the fatherhood within him, rose in surging insistence. Instant remorse attacked him, as an oak is attacked by fierce winter storms. He saw the boy's angelic face grow the color of death; saw Molly the Merry gather him up. Then a stab of jealousy cut his heart like a knife. He bent over with set jaws.

"Give him to me," he cried. "He's mine!"

Molly surrendered the child with reluctance, but terror and fright were depicted upon Bobbie's face.

"Jinnie! Lafe! Peggy!" he screamed. "He'll hurt me! The black man's goin' to kill me! Jinnie, pretty Jinnie——"

The passionate voice grew faint and ceased. Then the loving little heart burst in the boyish bosom, and Bobbie's angels bore away his young soul to another world where blindness is not,—where his uplifted being would understand that the stars he'd loved,—the stars he'd gathered in his small, unseeing head,—were but a reflection of those in God's firmament. With one final quiver he straightened out in his father's arms and was silent. All his loves and sorrows were in the eternal yesterdays, and to-day had delivered him into the charge of Lafe's angels.

Jinnie was crying hysterically, and her father's dying curse upon her uncle leapt into her mind. She was clinging to the cobbler, and both had moved to Peg, where the woman sat as if turned to stone.

Not a person in the courtroom stirred. In consternation the jury sat in their chairs like graven images, taking in the freshly wrought tragedy with tense expressions. The judge, too, leaned forward in his chair, watching.

Jordan Morse faced the room, with its silent, observant crowd, pressing to his breast the dead body of his child. Then he turned to Lafe, white, twitching, and suffering.

"I shot Maudlin Bates," he said, haltingly; then turning to the jury he continued: "The cobbler's an innocent man——"

A menacing groan fell from a hundred lips at his words.

He deliberately took from his hip pocket a revolver, lifted the weapon and finished:

"I'm—I'm sorry, Jinnie, I'm——"

Then came the sharp, short bark of the gun, and the bullet found a path to his brain. He staggered, frantically clutching the slender body of Bobbie closer—and toppled over.

CHAPTER XLVIII

FOR BOBBIE'S SAKE

Lafe's homecoming was one of solemn rejoicing. The only shadow hanging over the happy family was the absence of Blind Bobbie, who now lay by the side of his dead father.

After the first greetings, Lafe took his boy baby and pressed him gratefully to his heart.

"He's beautiful, Peggy dear, ain't he?" he implored, drinking in with affectionate, fatherly eyes the rosy little face. "Wife darlin', make a long story short an' tell me he's beautiful."

Mrs. Grandoken eyed her husband sternly.

"Lafe," she admonished, "you're as full of brag as a egg is of meat, and salt won't save you. All your life you've boasted till I thought the world'd come to an end, an' I ain't never said a word against it. Now you can't teach me none of your bad habits, because I won't learn 'em, so don't try." She paused, her lips lifting a little at the corners, and went on: "But I'm tellin' you with my own lips there ain't a beautifuller baby in this county'n this little feller, nor one half so beautiful! So there's my mind, sir."

"'Tis so, dear," murmured the cobbler, rejoicing.

About five o'clock in the afternoon, while Peggy was uptown replenishing the slender larder and Lafe and Jinnie were alone with the baby, there came a timid knock.

Jinnie went to the door and there stood Molly Merriweather. The woman's face was white and drawn, her eyes darkly circled underneath.

One glance at her and Jinnie lost her own color.

"I want to speak with you just a moment," the woman said beseechingly. "May I come in?"

Without answering, Jinnie backed into the room, which action Molly took as a signal to enter.

She inclined her head haughtily to the cobbler.

"Would you mind if I spoke to Miss Grandoken alone?"

Lafe looked to Jinnie for acquiescence.

"If Jinnie'll help me to the kitchen," he replied, "you can talk here. I'm a little unsteady on my feet yet, miss!"

It took some time for the tottering legs to bear him away, but the strong, confident girl helped him most patiently.

"You might just slip me the baby, Jinnie," said Lafe, after he was seated in the kitchen. "I could be lookin' at 'im while you're talkin'. You ain't mindin' the woman, honey lass, be you?"

"No, dear," answered Jinnie.

This done, the girl returned to Molly, who stood at the window staring out upon the tracks. She turned quickly, and Jinnie noticed her eyes were full of tears.

"I suppose you won't refuse to tell me something of my—my little boy?" she pleaded.

Tears welled over Jinnie's lids too. Bobbie's presence and adoration were still fresh in her mind.

"He's dead," she mourned. "My little Bobbie! Poor little hurt Bobbie!"

Molly made a passionate gesture with her gloved hands.

"Don't, please don't say those things! I'm so miserable I can't think of him. I only wanted to know how you got him."

189

"I just found him," stated Jinnie. Then, because Molly looked so white, she forgot the anguish the woman had caused her, and rehearsed the story of Bobbie's life from the time she had discovered him on the hill.

"I guess he was always unhappy till he came to us."

"And I helped to hurt him," cried Molly, shivering.

"But you didn't know he was yours," soothed Jinnie.

The woman shook her head.

"No, of course I didn't know," she replied, and then went on rapidly: "I was so young when I married your uncle, I didn't know anything. When I lost my baby, I knew no way to search for him."

"Won't you sit down?" Jinnie had forgotten that they were both standing. "Sit in that little rocker; it's Bobbie's," she finished.

Molly looked at the little chair and turned away.

"Lafe bought it for him," Jinnie explained eagerly. "He was too sick with his heart to get around much like other boys."

Miss Merriweather wrung her hands.

"Don't tell me any more," she begged piteously. "He's dead and nothing can help him now. I've—something else to say to you." Jinnie wiped her eyes.

"Mr. King is quite well now, and——"

"Oh, I'm glad!" cried Jinnie. "Does he—he ever speak of me?"

Molly shook her head mutely.

"I don't want him to see you!" she cried, her eyes growing hard and bright.

"Why?" Jinnie said the one word in bewilderment.

"He doesn't know yet what Jordan and I did to you, nor about— about—Bobbie. I don't want him to, either, just yet. I fear if he does, he won't care for me."

Jinnie's eyes drew down at the corners.

"Of course he wouldn't if he knew," she said, with tightly gripped fingers.

Molly paid no heed to this, but went on rapidly:

"Well, first, you don't love him as I do——"

"I love him very much," interjected Jinnie, "and he used to love me."

The woman's lips drew linelike over her teeth.

"But you see he doesn't any longer," she got out, "and if you go away——"

"Go away?" gasped Jinnie.

"Yes, from Bellaire. You won't stay here, now that you're rich." She threw a contemptuous glance about the shop. Jinnie caught the inflection of the cutting voice and noted the expression in the dark eyes.

"I'll stay wherever Lafe and Peggy are," she said stubbornly.

"Perhaps, but that doesn't say you're going to live in this street all your life.... I want you to go back to Mottville."

Jinnie still looked a cold, silent refusal.

Molly grew even whiter than before, but remembering Jinnie's kindly heart, she turned her tactics.

"I'm very miserable," she wept, "and I love Theodore better than any one in the world."

"So do I," sighed Jinnie, bowing her head.

"But he doesn't love you, child, and he does love me."

Jinnie's eyes fixed their gaze steadily on the other woman.

"Then why're you afraid for him to see me?" she demanded.

Molly got to her feet. She saw her flimsily constructed love world shattered by the girl before her. She knew Theodore still loved her, and that if he knew all her own wickedness, his devotion would increase a hundredfold. He must not see Jinnie! Jinnie must not see him! Rapidly she reviewed the quarrels she and Theodore had had, remembered how punctiliously he always carried out his honorable intentions, and then—Molly went very near the girl, staring at her with terror in her eyes.

"Jinnie," she said softly, "pretty Jinnie!"

Those words were Bobbie's last earthly appeal to her, and Jinnie's face blanched in recollection.

"Didn't you love my baby?" Molly hurried on.

A memory of fluttering fingers traveling over her face left Jinnie's heart cold. Next to Lafe and Theodore she had loved Bobbie best.

"I loved him, oh, very much indeed!" she whispered.

"And he often told you he loved—his—his—mother?"

"Yes."

Molly was slowly drawing the girl's hands into hers.

"He'd want me to be happy, Jinnie dear. Oh, please let me have the only little happiness left me!"

Jinnie drew away, almost hypnotized.

"I can't be a—a good woman unless I have Theodore," Molly moaned. "You're very young——"

Her eyes sought the girl's, who was struggling to her feet.

"For Bobbie's sake, Jinnie, for—for——"

Jinnie brought to mind the blind boy, his winsome ways, his desire for his beautiful mother, her own love for Theodore, and turning away, said with a groan:

"I want Theodore to be happy, and I want you to be happy, too, for—for Bobbie's sake. I—I promise not to see him, but I'll always believe he loves me—that—that——"

"You're a good girl," interrupted Molly with a sigh of relief.

Jinnie went to the door.

"Go now," she said, with proudly lifted head, "and I hope I'll never see you again as long as I live."

Then Molly went away, and for a long time the girl stood, with her back to the door, weeping out the sorrow of a torn young soul. She had promised to give up Theodore completely. She had lost her love, her friend, her sweetheart. Once more she had surrendered to Bobbie Grandoken the best she had to give.

Later, when the cobbler and his wife were crooning over their little son, Jinnie, with breaking heart, decided she would leave Bellaire at once, as Molly had asked her. She must never think of Theodore again. She'd renounced him, firmly believing he still loved her; she'd promised to depart without seeing him, but surely, oh, a little farewell note, with the assurances of her gratitude, would not be breaking that promise.

So, until Peggy carried the baby away to bed, the girl composed a letter to Theodore, pathetic in its terseness. She also wrote to Molly, telling her she had decided to go back to Mottville immediately.

When she had finished the letters, she took her usual place on the stool at the cobbler's feet.

"Lafe," she ventured, wearily, "some time I'm going to tell you everything that's happened since I last saw you, but not to-night!"

"Whenever you're ready, honey," acquiesced Lafe.

"And I've been thinking of something else, dear. I want to go to Mottville."

Lafe's face paled.

"I don't see how Peg an' me'll live without you, Jinnie."

Jinnie touched the hand smoothing her curls.

"I couldn't live without you either, Lafe, and I won't try——"

The cobbler bent and kissed her.

"I won't try, dear," she repeated. "You must all live with me, although I'll go first to arrange things a little. We'll never worry about money any more, dearest."

"And Mr. King," Lafe faltered, quite disturbed, "what about him?"

"I shan't ever see him again," Jinnie stated sadly. "I've just written him, and he'll understand."

Lafe knew by the finality of her tones that she did not care to discuss Theodore that night.

CHAPTER XLIX
BACK HOME

Late the next afternoon Jinnie left the train at Mottville station, her fiddle box in one hand, and a suitcase in the other. She stood a moment watching the train as it disappeared. It had carried her from the man she loved, brought her away from Bellaire, the city of her hopes. One bitter fact reared itself above all others. The world of which Theodore King had been the integral part was dead to her. What was she to do without him, without Bobbie to pet and love? But a feeling of thanksgiving pervaded her when she remembered she still had Lafe's smile, the baby to croon over, and dear, stoical Peggy. They would live with her in the old home. It was preferable to staying in Bellaire, where her heart would be tortured daily. Rather the brooding hills, the singing pines, and all the wildness of nature, which was akin to the struggle within her, and perhaps in the future she might gather up the broken threads of her life.

She shook as if attacked with ague as she came within sight of the gaunt farmhouse, and the broken windows and hanging doors gave her a sense of everlasting decay.

Below her in the valley lay the blue lake, a shining spread of water, quiet and silent, here and there upon it the shadow of a floating, fluffy cloud. She listened to the nagging chatter of the squirrels, mingled with the fluttering of the forest birds high above her head. As she stood on the hill, the only human being in all the wilderness about, in fancy she seemed to be at the very top of the world.

She heard the old familiar voices of the mourning pines, and remembered their soothing magic, and a stinging reproach swept over her at the thought of her forgetfulness of them. They had been friends when no other friends were near. Along with the flood of memories came Matty's ghastly ghost stories and her past belief that her mother's spirit hovered near her.

She went through the lane leading to the house and paused under the trees. Presently she placed her violin box and suitcase on the grass and lay down beside them. In the eaves of the house a dove cooed his late afternoon love to his mate, and Jinnie, because she was very young and very much in love, brought Theodore before her with that lingering retrospection that takes possession in such sensuous moments. She could feel again the hot tremor of his hands as they clung to hers, and she bent her head in shame at the acute, electrifying sensations. He belonged to another woman; he no longer belonged to her. She must conquer her love for him, and at that moment every desire to study, every thought of work seemed insipid and useless. The whole majestic beauty of the scene, her sudden coming into a great deal of money, did not add to her happiness. She would gladly give it all up to be again with her loves of yesterday. But that could not be! The future lay in a hard, straight line before her. She was striving against a ceaseless, resisting force,—the force of her whole passionate nature.

With their usual reluctance, the things of night at length crept forth. Jinnie felt some of them as they touched her hands, her face, and moved on. One of the countless birds fluttered low, as if frightened at the advancing dark, brushed her cheek, then winged on and up and was lost in the tree above her. Somewhere deep in the gloom shrouding the little graveyard came the ghostly flutter of an owl.

Jinnie was flat on her back, and how long she lay thus she could never afterward remember, but it was until the stars appeared and the moon formed queer fantastic pictures, like frost upon a window pane. In solemn review passed the days,—from that awful night when she had left her father dead upon the floor in the house nearby to the present moment.

She glanced at the windows. They looked back at her like square, darkening eyes.

She wondered dully how that wee star away off there could blink so peacefully in its nightly course when just below it beat a heart that hurt like hers. She closed her eyes, and when she opened them again, long black fingers were drawing dark pictures across the sky. A drop of rain fell upon her face, but still she did not move. Then, like rows of soldiers, the low clouds drew slowly together, and the stars softly wept themselves out.

Suddenly, from the other side of the lake, the thunder rolled up, and with the distant boom came the thought of Lafe's infinite faith, and the memory fell upon Jinnie like a benediction from God's dark sky.

She arose from the grass, took the fiddle box and bag, and walked to the porch. She went in through the broken door. It was dark, too dark to see much, and from the leather case she took a box of matches and a candle. Memories crowded down upon her thick and fast. In the kitchen, which was bare, she could mark the place where Matty used to sit and where her own chair had been.

The long stairs that led from the basement to the upper floor yawned black in the gloom. Candle and fiddle in hand, Jinnie mounted them and halted before the unopened door. Somehow it seemed as if she would find before the grate the long, thin body of her dead father, and she distinctly remembered the spindle fire-flames falling in golden yellow licks upon his face. In her imagination she could again see the flake-like ashes, thrown out from the smoldering fire, rise grey to the ceiling, then descend silently over him like a pale shroud.

After this hesitation, she slowly turned the handle of the door and walked in. The only things remaining in the room were a broken table and chair. She placed the violin on the floor and the candle on the table. Then with a shudder Jinnie drew from her blouse an unopened letter, studying it long in the flickering light. It had been written in this very room three years before, and within its sealed pages lay the whole secret which now none but the dead knew.

It took no effort on her part to bring back to her memory Jordan Morse's handsome face and his rock-grey eyes, eyes like Bobbie's. He and Bobbie had gone away together. She touched the corner of the envelope to the candle, watching it roll over in a brown curl as it burned.

"He's happy now," she murmured. "He's got his baby and Lafe's angels."

Then she gathered up the handful of ashes, opened the window, and threw them out. The hands of the night wind snatched them as they fell and carried them swiftly away through the rain.

On her way to the attic stairs, she stood a minute before the window, awe-stricken. From the north the great storm was advancing, and from among the hills rolled the distant roar of thunder. It brought to her mind the night when Peggy had gone into the life-valley and brought back Lafe's baby; and she remembered, too, with a sob, Blind Bobbie, and how she

194

missed him. Ah, it was a lonely, haunted little spirit that crept up the dark narrow stairs to the garret!

Only that the room seemed lower and more stuffy, it, too, was much the same as she had left it. She brushed aside some silvery cobwebs, raised the window, and sat down on a dilapidated trunk. On the floor at her feet, almost covered with dust, was the old fairy book about the famous kings. She picked it up mechanically. On the first page was the man in the red suit, with the overhanging nose and fat body,—he whom she at one time believed to be related to Theodore.

Again she was overwhelmed with her misery. Theodore belonged to another woman, and Jinnie, alone with her past and an uncertain future, sat staring dry-eyed into the stormy night.

CHAPTER L
"GOD MADE YOU MINE"

"I haven't seen any papers for three days, Molly. What's become of them all?"

Theodore and Molly were sitting in the waning sunshine, the many-colored autumn leaves drifting silently past them to form a varied carpet over the grass.

All fear had now left the woman. She had Jinnie's promise not to see Theodore, and he had apparently forgotten there ever was such a girl in the world.

"I'd really like to see the papers," repeated Theodore. "Dear me, how glad I am to be so well!"

"We're all glad," whispered Molly, with bright eyes.

She had kept the papers from him purposely, playfully pretending she would rather give him an account of the court proceedings. When she described how another man had confessed to the shooting, Theodore felt a glad thrill that the cobbler was exonerated. Later Molly decided she would tell him about Morse, but never that she had married him. It was she who suggested, after a time of silence:

"Theodore, don't you think a little trip would do us all good? Your mother's been so worried over you——"

"Where would we go?" he asked, without interest.

"Anywhere to get away from Bellaire for a season."

"We might consider it," he replied reluctantly. Then he fell to thinking of a blue-eyed girl, of the letter,—that puzzling letter she had sent him. When he could bear his thoughts no longer, he got up and walked away under the trees, and Molly allowed him to go. She watched him strolling slowly, and was happy. He had been so sweet, so kindly, almost thrilling to her of late. She would make him love her. It would be but a matter of a few weeks if she could get him away from Bellaire. Just at that moment Mrs. King's bell rang, and she went into the house. When she came back, Theodore was sitting on the veranda reading a letter, with another one unopened on his knee. The sight of his white face brought an exclamation from her lips.

"Theodore!" she cried.

He reminded her she was standing by saying:

"Sit down!"

This she was glad to do, for her knees trembled. Her eyes caught the handwriting on the unopened letter, resting like a white menace on Theodore's lap. She saw her own name upon it, but dared not, nor had she the strength, to ask for it.

At length, with a long breath, Theodore looked at her steadily.

"This letter is for you," he said, picking up her own. "Open it and then—give it to me."

Never had she heard such tones in his voice, nor had she ever been so thoroughly frightened. Mechanically she took the letter, tore open the flap, and read the contents:

"DEAR MISS MERRIWEATHER:

"After you left the shop, I decided to do as you wanted me to. I shall go back to Mottville, and afterwards Peggy and Lafe will come to me. I'll keep my promise and won't see Theodore. I hope you will make him happy.
JINNIE GRANDOKEN"

Molly crushed the paper between her fingers.

"Don't do that," commanded Theodore sharply. "Give it to me."

"It's mine," murmured Molly, lacking breath to speak aloud.

"Give it to me!" thundered Theodore.

And because she dared not disobey, she slowly extended the letter.

With deliberation the man spread out the crumpled page and read it through slowly. Then once more he took up his own letter and perused it.

"DEAR MR. KING:

"I'm going back to my home in the hills to-morrow. I'm so glad you're better. I thank you for all you've done for Lafe and Peggy, and hope you'll always be happy. For what you did for me I can't thank you enough, but as soon as I get my money, I'll send back all you've advanced for my lessons and other things. I'm praying all the time for you.
"JINNIE GRANDOKEN SINGLETON."

Sudden tears almost blotted the signature from Theodore's vision.

On the spur of the moment he picked up both letters and thrust them into his pocket.

196

"Come upstairs with me," he ordered the woman staring at him with frozen features.

Molly followed him as in a dream, preceding him when he stepped aside to allow her to enter the little sitting-room, where of late she had passed so many pleasant hours. Then as he closed the door, he whirled upon her.

"Now I want the meaning of those letters. Have you seen Miss Grandoken?"

"Yes!" She could say no more.

"When?"

"Yesterday."

"There's something I don't know. Ah! That's why you kept the papers from me." Quickly he turned to the bell.

"Theodore!" gasped Molly. "Wait! Wait! Don't—don't ring! I'll tell you; I will!"

He pressed the bell button savagely.

"I wouldn't believe you under oath," he muttered.

"I want all this week's papers, and I want 'em quick!" he snapped at the servant. "Every one! Last night's too!"

He walked to the window, but turned again as a knock came upon the door.

"I can't find the papers, sir," excused the maid.

"Wait!" Theodore closed the door, exclaiming in white heat, "Molly, where are those papers?"

"In my room," replied Molly sulkily.

Mr. King gave the order, and again they were behind closed doors. Molly made a sorry picture of shame when Theodore looked at her.

"I'll get to the bottom of this if it kills me," he said wearily.

"Theo, Theo, don't read the papers!" she gasped. Then she fell forward at his feet. "I love you, dear; I love you."

"You've lost your mind, Molly," he said harshly. "You're mad, completely mad."

"No, I'm not. Listen, Theodore, I'm here at your feet, miserable, unhappy; I want to be forgiven——"

"Then tell me what you did to Jinnie Grandoken."

"I can't! I can't!"

When another knock sounded on the door, Theodore opened it and took the papers through the smallest imaginable crack. Molly crawled to a chair and leaned her head upon the seat. Without a word, Theodore sat down and began to turn the pages of the papers nervously. As he read both accounts of Lafe's trial, bitter ejaculations fell from his lips. The story of Bobbie's dramatic death and Morse's suicide brought forth a groan. When he placed the papers slowly beside him on the floor, Molly raised her face, white and torn with grief.

"Now you know it all, forgive me!"

"Never, while I live!" he cried. "What ungodly wretchedness you've made that child suffer! And you were married all the time to Morse, and the mother of that poor little boy!"

"Yes," sobbed Molly.

Then a sudden thought took possession of him.

"You and Morse made Jinnie write me that first letter."

Molly nodded.

"May God forgive you both!" he stammered, and whirled out of the room.

An hour later, with new strength and purpose, Theodore threw a few clothes into a suitcase, ordered the fastest motor in the garage, and was standing on the porch when Molly came swiftly to him.

"Theodore," she said, with twitching face, "if you go away now, you won't find me here when you get back."

He glanced her over with curling lip.

"As you please," he returned indifferently. "You've done enough damage as it is. If you've any heart, stay here with the only person in the world who has any faith in you."

Vacantly the woman watched the motor glide away over the smooth white road, and then limply slid to the floor in a dead faint.

All the distance from Bellaire to Mottville Theodore was tortured with doubt. He brought to mind Jinnie's girlish embarrassment when they had been together; the fluttering white lids as his kisses brought a blue flash from the speaking love-lit eyes. She had loved him then; did she now? Of course she must love him! She had brought to him the freshness of spring—the love of the mating birds among the blossoms—the passionate desire of a heaven-wrought soul for its own, to whom could be entrusted all that was his dearest and best. He would follow her and win her,—yea, win the woman God had made for him and him alone, and into his eyes leapt the expression of the conquering male, the force God had created within him to reach for the woman sublime and cherish her.

When the car entered Mottville, rain was falling and the wind was mourning ceaselessly.

By inquiry, Theodore found the road to the Singleton farm, and again, as he impatiently sank back in the motor, he mentally vowed, with the vow of a strong man, that the girl should listen to him. He never realized, until they were climbing the rain-soaked hill, how starved was the very soul of him.

The road was running with water, but they ploughed on, until through the trees the farmhouse loomed up darkly. Bennett stopped the car at the gate and Theodore jumped out. A light twinkling in the upper part of the house told him she was there. Harmonious echoes were sounding and resounding in his ears. They were notes from Jinnie's fiddle, and for a moment, as they sobbed out through the attic window, he leaned back against the wet fence, feeling almost faint. The wild, sweet, unearthly melody surged over him with memories of the past.

Then he passed under the thrashing pines, mounted the broken steps, and entered the house.

It took but a minute to find the stairs by which to reach her, and there he stood in the gloom of the attic door, watching the swaying young figure and noting the whole pitiful dejection of her. In the single little light her eyes were as blue as the wing of a royal bird, and oh, what suffering she must have gone through! Then Jinnie ceased playing, and, as if drawn by a presence she knew not of, she turned her eyes slowly toward the door, and when she saw him, she fell, huddled with her violin on the garret floor, staring upward with frightened eyes.

"If you're there," she panted, "if—if—speak to me!"

He bounded forward and gathered her up, and the light of an adoring love shone full upon him.

"My sweet, my sweet, my beautiful, my little wonder-woman!" he breathed. "Did you think I could live without you?"

She was leaning, half fainting, against his breast, like a wind-blown flower.

"I've come for you," he said hoarsely. "Dearest, sweetest Jinnie!"

She pressed backward, loyalty for another woman rising within her.

"But Molly, Molly the Merry——" she breathed.

Theodore shook his head.

"I only know I love you, sweetheart, that I've come for you," and as his lips met hers, Jinnie clung to him, a very sweet young thing, and between those warm, passionate kisses she heard him murmur:

"God made you mine, littlest love!"

And so they went forth from the lonely farmhouse, with none but the cobbler's angels watching over them.